BINARY

BINARY

STEPHANIE SAULTER

®EVOLUTION BOOK 2

Jo Fletcher
BOOKS

First published in Great Britain in 2014 by

Jo Fletcher Books
an imprint of Quercus
55 Baker Street
7th Floor, South Block
London
W1U 8EW

A CIP catalogue record for this book is available
from the British Library

ISBN 978 1 78087 892 8 (TPB)
ISBN 978 1 78087 894 2 (EBOOK)

10 9 8 7 6 5 4 3 2 1

Typeset by Ellipsis Digital Limited, Glasgow
Printed and bound in Great Britain by Clays Ltd, St Ives plc

For Anna and Alison,
who wanted more

FESTIVAL

1

We are a split and splintered species. Every pivot-point of need and creed proves the ease with which we fracture; every heartfelt reunion warns against its own necessity. The lines of our division are as many and varied as the sins of our ancestors and the accidents of history; as varied as the lines on the palm of Mikal Varsi's hand, double-thumbed and huge at the end of a three-foot-long arm, as he raises it and takes the oath.

His eyes, split-lidded like a lizard's, blink slowly as he listens to the solemn proclamation of the clerk, stumbling over her words a little as she gazes up and up to his face, wondering as she does so if her tiny part in this moment will be remembered; and wondering also, fleetingly and with guilt, whether posterity will smile upon the memory, or revile her for it. Then he opens his mouth, an ordinary mouth, a mouth she has already learned is no less quick with smiles than with wit, and in a gentle, nasal voice repeats after her just as he should, and she thinks, *Well that wasn't so bad.*

She turns to set aside the edicts he has sworn to uphold, and he turns aside to the woman who stands behind him, a woman whose height and hands and eyes are steadfastly normal and who would, moreover, tell you that her heart is too; though there are still many who think this unlikely, for she has given both it and her name to a gem, a man designed for service and built for labour.

He bends now and the long arm wraps around her body, and the thumbs on either side of that well-lined palm squeeze her shoulder as she tips her head back to smile up at him and receive his kiss. There is applause from his fellow councillors and hearty laughter all round the chamber, but the clerk thinks she sees a hint of her own secret worry flit across more than a few faces.

And then he steps off the platform, eight towering feet of genetically modified humanity moving to take its place for the first time among the elect of the city; and they part for him like a sea, and like the sea close behind him once again.

Aryel Morningstar watched until Mikal had settled into his seat at the horseshoe-shaped council table from which London had been governed since the dawn of what had then been called the twenty-first century. The era had since been relegated, with distaste and a considerable suggestion of blame, to the third decade BS – Before Syndrome, the last generation to precede catastrophe. She often mused on how little had changed since then, and how much.

When the formal welcomes concluded without incident and they moved on to the tedium of minutes and motions she flicked her tablet to standby and stepped out of the column's shadow, enjoying the mid-morning warmth that radiated off the ancient stone of the cathedral. She was high up, standing on the circular balcony that ringed the dome, a place normally inaccessible to all but the few ecclesiastical staff who remained. Had any other gem, or norm for that matter, reached it unchallenged, the consternation and embarrassment of the custodians would have been intense.

That the rules did not apply to her – anywhere really, but especially not here – was a fact acknowledged at so base and basic a level that formal confirmation was neither necessary nor expected. Her gaze slipped idly past the discreetly placed and probably derelict security vidcam, grateful for this stolen moment of sunlit quiet. The low hum of the streets drifted up to her, but her view was fixed on the river, old Father Thames rolling slow, slate-grey and imperturbable. Her eyes, eagle-sharp and attuned to movement, caught the ripple and a flash of green as a pair of gillungs broke the surface, got their bearings and submerged again.

Visitors probably, in town for the Festival.

She had much to do herself, and could expect it all to take far longer than was strictly speaking necessary, given the added responsibilities of profile. But Mikal's ascension to the city council was a milestone that deserved to be marked, a victory that would have been unthinkable not that many years before and a validation which still bathed the residents of the Squats in a slightly stunned satisfaction. She had worked as hard for it as any of them, and with the added complication of fending off suggestions that the candidate should instead have been her. She knew better, as did Mikal himself.

'It's not that I want to be in the spotlight,' he'd said. 'But it can't only be you, all of the time. We need to really test how things are for the rest of us, and we need someone who can be a bellwether. Now I tick all their boxes for outsize, ugly, scary-looking gem, and they know I came up under the gemtechs. But the point is, they *do* know me. My abilities aren't mysterious, they know I was a factory model. They know my cognition and mannerisms fall within the standard range, they know I've got experience running a community, they know I'm married. To a *norm* cop.'

'I know they know. And they haven't been kind about it so far. Do you and Sharon really want to put yourselves through that again? Because you'd be perfect, Mik, but what it would do to you . . .'

'What it would do to us it's already done. And we're still standing.'

So it had been decided, and the campaign proved as bruising as she had predicted. Scrupulously proper public discourse had been leavened with whispered, withering, back-alley nastiness. The vitriol levelled at Sharon Varsi was muted and reduced this time, but no less vicious. She had rolled her eyes, set her jaw and stood up to it with a fortitude that made Aryel's eyes prickle.

It was Eli Walker, carefully monitoring the tides of opinion on the streams, who first observed that he thought the naysayers had overreached, tipped the balance of acceptability and triggered instead a groundswell of opprobrium. It was a phenomenon they'd seen before. He looked keenly at her as he said it, as though expecting her to declare herself unsurprised.

She was indeed less so than the others, but they were still all astonished when he won.

Now she considered the impact of those few minutes in the council chamber on the people they represented, and thought about what it must mean to Mikal himself, only a few years emancipated; and to Sharon. It was nearby, no more than a couple of minutes' flight across the river and downstream, and she could have been there to share the moment with them. But then she would have been unable to prevent the inevitable shift of focus from Mikal to herself.

So she had stayed away, allowing Mik to shine without the competition of her own strange and omnipresent spotlight. If there had been any subtleties of reaction in the chamber she'd missed them; but her presence would have skewed the responses anyway. So much that happened now had become so difficult for her to see.

Eli had been there. She would ask him later what he thought.

She slipped the tablet into its squeeze-pocket on her thigh and grabbed hold of the stone balustrade, stepping into a chink in its richly carved surface and levering herself up. Her other foot found the top of the rail, and she balanced easily there for a moment.

Sunlight glinted off bright bronze-coloured feathers as the first shouts came up from below. She spread her wings and leaned forward, falling into the wind, and angled to follow the gillungs up the river.

Further downstream, another woman also watched and pondered the significance of the morning's events. She too had been less surprised than many, although she had both amused and startled herself with the surge of reflexive envy she'd felt that the first gem to attain such status had been the product of a competitor. Such distinctions hardly mattered any more. More important was the impact on her own intentions, and she considered the matter carefully. On the face of it Mikal Varsi, né Recombin, should have little bearing on her plans, but she'd been wrong about such things before.

She rose from her desk, an elegantly sculptural piece made of wood engineered to grow in precisely the flowing, convoluted shapes that would render it both beautiful and functional, and walked over to the gently curving window that formed the back wall of her office. Her view was vast, towers of steel and turrets of stone and glass pinnacles stretching away in every direction. She caught a glimpse of the river between them, and a glint off the dome of the cathedral.

Like everyone else in the city, she scanned the skies.

She had seen many changes in her life, a life longer than most would guess. But there was something in this latest shift, in the election of Mikal Varsi and the insouciance of the gillungs and above all the flight of Aryel Morningstar, that felt indelible; less like a period to be weathered than one which heralded the beginning of an age.

Her compatriots in the once monolithic gemtech world gener-ally still decried it as a disgrace, or prophesied its derailment, or continued merely to wallow in a bewildered depression. She had worked hard to curb her own resentment and rethink the situa-tion in terms of opportunity. She knew that a large part of what drove her on, what kept her focused and sharp, was the anger and excitement and bitterness she felt every time the winged woman soared over the city.

Aryel Morningstar could not – should not – exist. All the manipu-lations of the human genome, even the most radical, had resulted only in variations on the basic mammalian body type – four limbs not six, except in those few dreadful cases where mistake or acci-dent had replicated an existing pair to painful and useless effect. All the careful, clever splicing of the DNA of other species had been subtle, incorporating new attributes into extant body parts: hyperspectral eyesight, oxygen exchange in an aquatic environ-ment, organ regeneration. Crafting wings greater than any bird had ever borne to spring from human shoulders, in a delicate, complicated double ball joint that existed nowhere in nature, was simply not possible.

Yet it had been done, and in the doing, proved so many other certainties false.

A soft chime sounded, directionless, and roused her from her brooding.

'Yes?'

The voice that responded was diffident, the undertone of apology for the interruption plain to hear.

'The latest status report's just come in, ma'am. From the new project? You said you wanted to know right away.'

'Post it to my private stream. Immediately.'

'Yes, Ms Klist. It's been done.'

She was already back at the desk, activating the holoscreen. After a beat that was just a second too long to signify close attention, as an afterthought, she said, 'Thank you.'

The unseen assistant knew better than to reply.

AWAKENING

It is a noise that comes back to her even now, in moments of fear or confusion, or sometimes in the instant of waking. She is never certain, then, if it is the lingering echo of a dream, or the grip of unguarded memory, or the memory perhaps of a dream dreamt long ago and never entirely shaken. It is a sound like the sea, a regular, implacable surge before the hissing retreat through shingle, incessant and foreboding. With that rushing, metronomic threat comes a waft of cold, the chill of bare skin dusted by a light draught that smells of nothing; an empty, antiseptic cleanness.

At some distance she cannot measure, over the steady bellows sound of the surf, a baby begins to wail.

There is light, finally, and the surprise of not having noticed its absence; but it is no more than a dull murk of blurred shapes that refuse definition. It adds little to her understanding. She wishes for something – warmth perhaps, or comfort – and another shadow flails feebly in the dimness before her. She thinks later that it might be her own hand. It slides out of her vision and she feels it subside onto the thinly cushioned surface upon which she lies.

She cannot tell whether the failure of illumination is due to a weakness in the light itself, or that it falls upon eyes that cannot yet see.

2

Eli was stopped twice on his way out of the venerable, bulbous city council building; once by a blushing sociology student with colour-streaked hair stammering out her admiration, and again by a newstream vidcam crew looking for a learned sound-bite on the latest entry to the city's political pantheon. When they realised he was accompanied by Sharon Varsi, trailing a little behind as she finished listening to messages on her earset, they abandoned him practically in mid-sentence. He shrugged, cocked an eyebrow and a grin at her over their shoulders, and escaped outside.

The riverwalk was buzzing with activity. He leaned against the guardrail, watching a group of gillungs and norms on a nearby pier as they signalled to a small tender that was helping to position an airwalk circuit. The inflated corridor began as a platform at the end of the pier, before it sloped gently away to become the entrance to a tunnel that projected out into the channel. He could see the buoys that marked its progress as it curved away upriver.

Some crucial decision made, the tender stood off as the water-breathing gems slipped into the river, submerging to swim out to an anchor point while their norm compatriots paralleled their progress from inside the airwalk. He quickly lost sight of the gillungs' shimmering lime-green hair in the bright sunshine glinting off the water's surface, and turned around to look for Sharon.

She emerged from behind the curved glass of the building and hurried over to him. 'Sorry about that.'

'Fine by me. Were they all right?'

'Oh yeah. Sweet as one of Bal's plum pies. Everyone's being just lovely, now.' She sighed and shook her head, leaning on the rail beside him. 'That's not fair of me, really. UrbanNews are always pretty okay.'

'Unlike some of the others.'

'Mmm.' She was distracted, staring out at the airwalk. 'I thought this would've been ready by now.'

'It's bigger than I expected.'

'Mik told me they want to showcase more than just the technology – they've expanded the original design so as you move further beneath the surface there's room for them to demonstrate all the different kinds of things they're starting to do, beyond just farming and fishing and foraging. He says the gillungs want it to be an immersive experience. Pun very much intended, of course.'

Eli laughed. Mikal's fondness for wordplay, already well known to his friends, had proved a surprising hit in the campaign. 'How is he today? Really?'

'Really? He's fine. You know Mik. Taking it in stride. There's nothing they can throw at him in terms of council business that he won't be able to handle, not after five years running the Squats. As for the rest of it—' She shrugged. 'He only really gets pissed off when they come after me. Everything else washes right off him. He's had to put up with worse than a few Reversionists being nasty to us on the streams.'

Eli nodded, although privately he thought that they remained more than a few; and suspected that Sharon thought so too. Outright opposition to the desegregation of gems had largely faded away, drowned out by horror and remorse in the wake of the fundamentalist violence that first brought both her and Mikal to public notice. Archive vids of the no-nonsense police sergeant and the giant gem, desperately trying to help survivors and impose order in the chaotic aftermath of the worst such attack, were re-posted with new rounds of heated commentary every time their union was criticised, or doubts raised about the wisdom of the new world order. The memory of those events kept even the more extreme Reversionists permanently in defensive mode.

And yet their numbers appeared to shrink only slowly, if at all. It seemed to Eli that in an era of such turbulence, their call for a return to traditional values and ways of life had found a resonance unrelated to logic.

He and Sharon strolled along the riverwalk, sidestepping other last-minute preparations as they headed towards the station. She glanced back as they passed workers making adjustments to a holo display, a shape-shifting cluster of light sculptures that swirled out Festival factoids, the images and text married to sound that insinu-ated itself softly into the earsets of those walking by. They caught a fragment of the list of events that formed part of the evening's launch as the field radius was widened.

'I'm still not sure what I think about this.'

'The holo?'

'No, the whole thing. A Festival of the Future. It sounds sort of . . . presumptuous.'

Eli chuckled. 'Tempting fate, maybe?'

'Maybe. It's just, you know. We may have come a long way in the last three or four years but it's not like we're in some state of perfect harmony and can go skipping off into the sunset. Things are tough still. I should know.' She shook her head. 'I don't know what it is we're supposed to be celebrating, exactly.'

'Possibility, I think. And the idea that events are being driven by a sense of vision, that it isn't all just random.' They clattered down the stairs into the ancient Underground station. 'There was a fashion for a while in something similar, a couple or three centuries back. They called them world's fairs, sort of international trade bazaars, where all the countries got together to show off how sophisticated and forward thinking they were.'

Sharon snorted.

'Yeah, well. They didn't know then where it was all heading. But the point is they were consciously trying to focus on the future. To anticipate what was to come, instead of just reflecting on what had already happened. They may have got it wrong but I can understand the motivation. The government feels like they need to do something to push us into a next phase.'

'Think it'll work?'

'Who knows?' They paused at a junction, where a pair of corridors diverged towards their differing destinations. 'What does Mikal think about it?'

'That it's an exercise in anticipatory self-congratulation.'

They fell out laughing, but there was an edgy sense of truth to the remark that followed Eli onto the train and all the way home.

Home was a small flat in the Squats, the gem enclave on the east London riverbank that had been first a refuge for escapees, and then for those who had gained their freedom on a rising tide of public opinion. After the international edicts outlawing retrieval and indenture, the derelict buildings had become a haven for thousands of gems suddenly released into communities unprepared, ill-equipped and often unwilling to handle the influx. They had banded together under the leadership of the still unrevealed Aryel Morningstar, been marshalled and managed by a phalanx of lieutenants with Mikal at their head, and built themselves a sanctuary.

A few norms had joined them since, including the eminent anthropologist Dr Eli Walker. He remembered the early mutterings that attended the genesis of the colony, about the creation of ghettoes and concentration of need, and his own surprise and unspoken glee when the gems turned their talents and training towards the repair of long-abandoned housing and the care of those of their number modified out of any hope of self-sufficiency. The gemtech claims of social inadequacy and limited potential had been effectively silenced.

With legal normalisation had come economic opportunity, and something of a vogue in gem culture and enterprise. The spectacle of Aryel, sweeping in and out on the wing to the gasps of visitors and the casual indifference of residents, added to the growing sense of an appealing exoticism. The shabby, insular neighbourhood Eli had moved into was rapidly becoming chic.

But integration brought its own challenges, he thought, not all of which could have been anticipated. He glanced into the ground-floor lounge as he went past, noting the increasing concentration of the disabled and malformed. Time was when their able-bodied and attractive neighbours would have been in there too, keeping them company. Now they were all out working, or simply elsewhere.

An alert chimed softly in his earset as he pushed back the door to his tiny balcony, letting out a wave of stale, sticky air. Aryel's tone. She must have picked up his message. He felt a quick little rush of pleasure, followed instantly by a spike of annoyance at himself. Over the years of their friendship he had never been able to pin down quite why it was that doing her even the smallest of favours made him feel so elevated. He had concluded only that it was a phenomenon widely shared, though rarely remarked upon.

Her response was typically succinct, grateful and gently suggestive.

I watched on tablet, but no comparison to the view from the room. Your impressions much appreciated. Similarly with this: and she'd inserted a link to an item on the Festival's opening programme. *Worth checking out I should think.*

Eli already knew he was going to go to whatever it was, even as he tapped up the link. The new information washed onto the screen, and he felt his eyebrows shoot up. It would have been worth checking out even if Aryel had not requested it.

Aryel herself was on the south bank of the river, close to where the airwalk Eli had observed outside City Hall terminated, this time at a staircase that dropped from the top of the embankment down to the foreshore. The tide was still coming in and the entry platform rose and extended smoothly, tread by tread, as gillungs swirled gracefully around it and made adjustments. She leaned against the rail, gazing down at them and politely ignoring the stares and whispers from her own level, the pointing fingers and surreptitious tablet flashes that accompanied her whenever she left the Squats.

One of the gillungs pulled herself onto an unsubmerged stair, glanced up and saw Aryel. She grinned and raised a hand. Sunlight glinted off the translucent webbing between her fingers.

'Hey! You going to stay up there and watch, or come down and get wet?'

Aryel laughed, both amused by the suggestion and grateful for the woman's easy informality. 'You know that's not my territory. I'd be about as useful as a cork.'

Other gillung heads popped up, and there were more calls and splashed greetings. Aryel waved back as the woman who had spoken to her ran up the remaining steps to the top. Water dripped from the tight cuffs of her bodysuit, trickling onto broad, webbed feet. Aryel leaned over the safety barrier and into a damp embrace.

'Graca, it's so good to see you. D'you know where the rest of my lot have got to? I'm going straight into messages.'

'There's a concert hall here? Gwen wanted to see it. Hear it too, no doubt. You know what she's like, probably made them switch their 'sets off.'

'How's Rhys?'

A shadow crossed the other woman's face. 'He's okay. Says he's okay, anyway.'

'You're not convinced.'

'Not completely, no.'

'I better go find them.'

Aryel left the quayside and headed into the cavernous interior, built long ago for another Festival and after a tumultuous history, returned to its original use. The attention went with her, murmurs rippling ahead and trailing behind like some strange existential wake. She had long since decided that the best course was generally to act as though it wasn't there; to treat people as if they behaved better than they did, and hope that with time and familiarity the pretence would become truth.

It was a careful and often, she thought, a hypocritical balance. She knew very well that the norm fascination with her – adulation even – was beyond the control, and usually even the awareness, of most of them. She also knew that she used it, gently and subtly, to keep herself and her people safe, to maintain their steady progress away from serfdom, and to counteract the very difficulties that celebrity created. It was a potent tool, and one that she should not, for purely practical reasons, wish to lose.

Now, for instance, it took no more than a smile and a quiet few words to detail a security guard to help her swiftly negotiate the maze of corridors and locked doorways that led to the hall. Far from resenting the task, the man's dazed look said he could not *believe* he would be able to boast to his friends that evening that he had acted as escort to Aryel Morningstar.

Still, he seemed honour-bound to protest that their errand was likely to be fruitless.

'It's, umm, it's locked, you can see,' as he pressed fingers to an identipad. 'There's no access to the hall for the general public just now, and no rehearsals or anything . . . I'm afraid your party must have gone somewhere else . . .'

She nodded and smiled and said, 'Let's just check.'

And sure enough, as he swung the heavy old door back, voices washed up at them from the direction of the stage. The man's jaw dropped. Aryel sighed and walked past him.

Lights had been switched on, illuminating only the front few rows. The elevated rear of the room, where they had entered, remained in dense shadow, as did much of the stage down below. Three figures could dimly be seen against the black of the backdrop; two heads glowed a deep wine red, like embers in the darkness.

Someone was singing, a clear, pure tone that rolled up the banks of seats and sent a shiver of pleasure up the guard's spine. It stopped abruptly and an excited female voice said, 'Just listen to it! The way the sound changes, it's so . . . so *round*, and *full* . . .'

'You do sound lovely, Gwen,' said another voice: older, benevolent, amused. It came from the figure without any gemsign glow, and changed abruptly as he became aware of movement in the shadows above. 'Who's there?'

'It's Aryel,' said the other two in unison. The third voice belonged to a younger male, who added, 'We're busted.'

'You are indeed,' she said. She was already halfway down the sloping chamber when the guard found the controls, and lights came up in the entire room.

They picked out the two glow-haired gems, who both looked to

18

be in their early twenties: a willowy, weary-looking youth, and a girl whose slender, athletic form and expressive face positively radiated well-being. It was the contrast between lassitude and fizzing energy, the guard realised as he hurried after Aryel, that was their least similar feature; otherwise the resemblance was remarkable. They were lean and long-limbed, and shared the same fine-boned, full-lipped features, along with flawless nut-brown skin and eyes so dark a blue they could almost be black.

Their companion was a white-haired man, norm to all appearances, who looked to be enjoying a hearty old age. He paced to the front of the stage, hands clasped behind his back, and twinkled at Aryel as he boomed, 'And why is that? This is the people's hall, after all. We are here only to appreciate our inheritance.'

'Appreciation is confined to specific times or with appropriate escorts, as you know very well,' Aryel shot back, but there was no hiding the answering smile in her voice. The girl jumped down from the stage, a distance and depth few norms could have managed safely, and skipped up to meet her. She threw her arms around the winged woman.

'Don't be cross, Ari. I just wanted to hear how it sounded.'

Aryel hugged her back, up on tiptoe in a vain attempt to match her height, wings billowing for balance. 'I'm not. I can't speak for this gentleman, though.'

The guard was standing behind them, mouth still hanging open in astonishment. 'I . . . but . . . how did you get in?'

The other two had descended the stage by the more sedate route of the steps, and now came up to meet them. The younger man raised his hand sheepishly. 'That was me. Sorry. Wasn't my idea,' shooting a glance at his fellow trespassers. 'I did lock everything behind us though. And we haven't touched anything.'

'Except the lights,' said Gwen helpfully.

'Except the lights.'

The guard looked from the beautiful girl to her brother – was he a brother? He thought gems didn't have siblings, not really – to the old man, now enveloping Aryel in another embrace.

'But the locks,' he said helplessly. 'And . . . and there's alarms and stuff.'

'Alarms?' said the young man, with an air of polite disbelief. 'Did we set off alarms? Sorry about that. Really. Didn't look like they were on.'

'Yes they were. I mean, no you didn't. I mean I don't think so. I'd have got a call.' He tapped his earset, wondering how to handle the situation. They had obviously bypassed the security systems somehow, but no harm appeared to have been done and Aryel Morningstar clearly knew all about them. She shook her head ruefully.

'Rhys has a way with comms systems, Gwen has a way with Rhys, and Reginald here,' she cast a fond look over her shoulder at the old man, 'has a way of indulging them. First trip to London, you see.'

'Really?' said the guard. His head was reeling. The names of Gwen and Rhys rang only the most distant of bells, but he recognised the reference to Reginald right away. It was a name he could connect with the trio's appearance, and begin to make some sense of it all.

The old man was dressed in the highly unfashionable, slightly shabby clothing characteristic of a Remnant. The two young people's attire was not quite so outmoded, but neither was it of recent vintage. The full dimensions of the tale he could tell at the pub that night dawned on him.

It would not be improved if he had to add that he had concluded the encounter by rousting Aryel Morningstar's foster family.

*

Later that afternoon, Aryel left Reginald, Rhys and Gwen resting in her own cavernous flat and tapped on another door in a quiet first-floor corridor. It slid back to reveal a man with glowing flame-coloured hair, and an air of subdued tension that receded when he saw her.

'Hey, Callan. Glad I caught you.' He smiled a little and stood back so she could step inside. 'Everything all right?'

'Fine. Just hanging out with him a bit, making sure he eats something.' He gestured towards the small open kitchen, where the debris of a meal was in the midst of being tidied away. 'I've got to go in a minute, though. Got some extra work on this evening.'

'Festival?'

'Yeah. Translating for some of the newstreams.'

'Will you be free to come to the show after?'

The flame-haired man shrugged. 'Should be. If I feel like it.'

Aryel looked at him keenly. Although he was young, well shy of thirty, he gave an impression of greater age. It was perhaps that subtle quality in his demeanour, a slightly hunted watchfulness; or maybe just the faint traces of scarring on his handsome face, the shadow of some old injury which had been expertly repaired, but not quite completely erased.

'Please come,' she said quietly. 'Lyriam's only just got back, he hasn't even made it home yet, but he messaged me to say how much he misses us. He's hoping as many as can make it will be there. I think he's got some new music up his sleeve.'

'Really?' He brightened a little. 'I'll try.'

'I'll be looking for you.'

She turned, finally, to the other occupant of the room.

'Hello, Herran. Are you well?'

The diminutive gem to whom she spoke had not looked around, or otherwise appeared to register her arrival or the conversation with Callan. He sat with his back to the door, before a bank of auxiliary screens that showed a dizzying array of stream feeds and code; most of it incomprehensible to Aryel. He rocked for a moment, as if processing the greeting, and then turned to look at her.

His curly hair glowed the same orange-red as Callan's. It was their only similarity. Herran had wide grey eyes and a face largely devoid of expression. Its most marked feature was a scar that ran between his nose and upper lip, old and pale but clearly mended with little care for the result.

'Aryel.' He nodded, lisping softly. She approached, holding out her hands. Herran touched them briefly, and she settled onto a stool.

'Good today,' he said. He had already turned back to the screens, and the input tablet on its stand before him, but she knew him well enough to sense that his attention was more broadly focused. This, along with the brief, ritualised response to her question, told her he was still listening to her as well.

'You keeping an eye on the Festival?'

'Yes.' He rocked a little. 'Fun. Lots to see.'

'I'm glad. There'll be lots going on this whole month. Funny thing happened there today though.'

Herran did not respond. The opening was too abstract, too lacking in specificity for him to engage with. Aryel knew this, but Callan had said they should keep lobbing innuendo at him occasionally, just in case.

'The thing that happened,' Aryel went on, 'was that Rhys opened some doors that had locks and alarms on them, only he said the alarm circuits weren't active when he went through. But they were *supposed* to be active, and when I went the same way a little later all of them *were* active. Like someone turned them off just for him, and then turned them back on again.'

Herran's rocking nod had become a little more emphatic. Though his expression did not change Aryel thought she detected a spark of something in the pale eyes.

'Easier for Rhys. No alarms. Quick quick.'

She sighed. 'Yes, it was easier and quicker. Did you turn them off for him, Herran?'

'Yes. Quick quick. Easy.'

She dropped her head into her hands and shook it wearily, a gesture of affectionate exasperation that she knew would have no effect on Herran whatsoever. Behind her there was a snort of suppressed laughter from Callan. She took a moment to tamp down her own amusement and told herself sternly that it wasn't funny. Herran could cause untold trouble.

When she looked up he was looking back at her, blankly innocent. She could suddenly have wept just as easily as laughed.

'How did you know he was there? Did he message you?'

'Yes. Festival first, Squats later, concert tonight. Meet tomorrow.' He kept his eyes on her, unblinking, as his fingers flew across the tablet. 'Found on cams.' The image on one of the auxiliaries shifted, becoming a chequerboard of vidcam feeds from the Festival Hall and riverfront. Aryel recognised the route she had walked earlier that day.

'Keeping an eye on the Festival. Lots to see. Saw Rhys, and Gwen, and Reginald.'

'Ah.'

'Going to singing place. Gwen likes to sing.' He was positively beaming now, or at least as close to it as he could get. 'I helped.'

'Yes. Yes you did help Rhys, Herran. But you know you're really not supposed to do things like that.'

'Wouldn't do for anyone else.' He did not sound affronted, just matter-of-fact. 'Only Rhys and Callan and Mikal and Sharon and Bal and Gaela and Franko and Aster and Eli and you.'

'Oh. Well, *that's* all right then.'

'Only you had man. With hands.' Aryel raised an eyebrow. 'Did himself.'

In the kitchen Callan had mostly been managing to turn his chortles into a reasonably convincing cough. Now he failed utterly. Aryel fought back a giggle of her own and focused on parsing what Herran actually meant.

'I had man with hands? I . . . oh, I see. The security guard with the fingerprint ident who opened the doors. Yes, I did have him to help me.'

'Didn't need me.'

'Well, not today. But I do need you a lot of the time, Herran. We all do. And it's okay if you keep an eye on the Festival . . . as long as nobody can tell you're doing it—'

He did look injured now.

She hurried on, '—but don't turn off any more alarms or change anything else there, okay? Not even for us.'

'Breaking rules.'

'Yes, that's breaking the rules. And we shouldn't break the rules very much. And when we do we need to have a very, very, very good reason.'

3

Eli waited until the room was almost full, with crowds still massed in the aisles, before slipping in as inconspicuously as possible. He was recognisable enough, especially in this crowd, for a few heads to turn, but no one spoke to him as he found a seat near the back, and he did not think he had been spotted by any of the organising staff. He had no wish to be hailed from the stage by whatever functionary was conducting the Festival's formal launch, as could very easily happen if they knew he was there.

There was no risk of such notice from the evening's keynote speaker, but he nevertheless felt an almost juvenile aversion to her discovering that he was in attendance. The terms on which they had last met had not been friendly. Mikal was down in front, amongst the other city officials, and it amused him to imagine the reaction that facing the giant gem would likely evoke; though doubtless she had been steeling herself since the election to keep her feelings well hidden.

Still, this last-minute trailing of a major announcement was a curious development, one which had attracted a flurry of comment from the business newstreams. He could understand Aryel's desire for a first-person report.

He had glimpsed her as he made his way inside the massive building, fluttering to earth near the stage that had been erected on the riverwalk's great park. Greeting Lyriam no doubt, and satisfying herself that all was in readiness for those attending the festivities at his invitation. Disability, either physical or psychological, was virtually unknown among norms but still distressingly common among gems. The older ones in particular had been designed, reared and trained at a time when such matters barely rated consideration. Even though they had all since been raised to legal equality with norms, ensuring that crippled, disfigured or dysfunctional gems got the assistance they needed still took a fair bit of coordination and cajoling.

The people here, he thought as he looked around him, were probably about equally divided between those who had fought early and with diligence for those freedoms and support, and others who had clambered aboard the bandwagon but in truth would have slept no less well had the bad old days of gemtech domination never ended. They would not wish for a return to it, not now that their consciences had been pricked, but there was a malleability about them that the woman he had come to hear would understand well how to manipulate.

Not unlike Aryel.

The thought felt immediately both unworthy – vile, even – and intriguing. Eli picked at it as the programme got under way. Aryel too knew how to play people, how to express a perspective and inspire a response. He wondered if the only real difference between the two women was that he happened to share the winged gem's sense of values.

He quickly decided – some deeply sceptical part of his mind whispered it might be *too* quickly – that it was more than that. Aryel's approach was subtle. She used neither brutality nor blackmail; her weapon was an almost preternatural ability to persuade, a manner that was somehow both emotive and calmly rational.

What she thought you should do became, after a few moments' conversation, the only logical thing *to* do. That intellectual clarity and ability to communicate had won him to her corner. It was how she had hauled her people out of their post-emancipation limbo and into the light.

That and her beauty, and the magic of her wings.

He emerged from his reverie in time to applaud the last of a parade of dignitaries. There were a few seconds of bustle before the lights tightened down again to illuminate only the stage. The Festival director reappeared on it, staring owl-like into the gloom of the audience, and gathered up his full pomp to announce that as they were no doubt aware, the chief executive of the Bel'Natur conglomerate would be the final speaker. What was less well known, he told them, was that Bel'Natur had been early and generous supporters of the Festival, helping to fund much of the launch and the month-long programme of events. He was sure they would all give a very warm welcome to a woman many had heard of but few – unlike himself of course – had been privileged to meet: Zavcka Klist.

As he took to the stage to make his introduction, in the instant after the lights went down, the door through which Eli had entered was pushed open once again. There was a rustle as some latecomer slipped quickly in.

When they did not immediately walk past him on the way to one of the few empty seats, he glanced around. He was astonished to recognise the distinctive profile of Aryel Morningstar against the soft blue glow of exit lights, stepping back against the wall, wings tucked in tight. A murmur started as those on either side of the aisle realised who stood there and he saw her raise a finger sharply to her lips. The murmur died away and she folded her arms, standing still as a stone.

*

Zavcka Klist stood in the spotlight, gazing out into the darkened auditorium while perfunctory applause died away. She carried no tablet, and ignored the lectern onto which a prepared speech might have been projected. She seemed, Eli thought, to be letting them all take a good long look, the better to emphasise whatever point she had come here to make.

She had changed little in the years since they had last met face to face. Slightly taller than the norm average, blonde and dark-eyed, she was possessed of a harsh, aristocratic beauty. She had the gift of elegance, of wearing expensive clothes well and looking glamorous with little embellishment. She had favoured scarlet lipstick then, he remembered, but no longer; her mouth was now a softer shade, and the lines of her stylish summer suit less stridently autocratic.

But she was still Zavcka Klist.

She still wasted little time on pleasantries.

'Our involvement with the Festival of the Future has struck many as anachronistic,' she began. 'You may well wonder how a company that was on the brink of collapse not so very long ago, part of an industry whose day many consider done, can imagine itself to have much of a future. You all know I'm not exaggerating when I tell you that the last few years have been, to say the least, challenging.'

There were a few titters of nervous laughter that degenerated hastily into scattered coughs.

'The financial challenges have been obvious and serious, but I am happy to report that they have largely been overcome. Bel'Natur remains a leader in agricultural gemtech and as a result we are once again approaching the levels of turnover and profitability that we enjoyed before the abolition of commercialised human gemtech.'

The silence rippled out. It was as though a stone had been

dropped into the massed memories of a century's shame; a deep, still pool of guilt and recrimination around which, by mutual and unspoken agreement, most norms preferred to tiptoe as silently as possible. Zavcka stared straight into the audience as she spoke, eyes travelling slowly along the seated ranks of gems and norms, a mingling made possible only by the abolition of which she spoke. Eli, who already knew what a bravura performance she was capable of, nevertheless found himself holding his breath.

'That was, of course, a watershed for the company, as indeed it has been for all of society. You will not be surprised to learn, ladies and gentlemen, gems and norms, that the cultural challenges it presented to us at Bel'Natur were beyond anything we'd ever dealt with. I'm not going to insult your intelligence by pretending that we had no difficulty facing up to the facts of our history, learning the lessons from it and instituting the changes, both in our business practices and in our attitudes, to ensure that such a cavalier and unthinking application of technology could never occur within our company again. I am certainly not going to insult your sense of justice by suggesting that no wrongs were done.'

A loud murmur, with more than a hint, Eli thought, of the kind of self-righteousness beloved of those who preferred not to consider their own complicity. People shifted and muttered to each other. He kept his eyes on the back of Mikal's head, shoulders and half a torso higher than anyone else's, and noted that he had not moved a muscle.

Zavcka stepped back a couple of paces, hands up in capitulation. 'Let me say this, loud and clear, so no one can be in any doubt where Bel'Natur stands on this today: wrongs *were* done, and we did them, along with the rest of the industry. And while we could justifiably add that a medical crisis and lax regulation and social apathy were contributing factors, that doesn't actually let us off the hook. It has been a difficult thing to come to terms with, collectively and individually. I might not have been the chief executive during that time, but as you know I've been in this business for many years and I, like all of us, should have known better.'

Eli felt an almost overwhelming disorientation. He remembered his first conversation with Zavcka Klist, just days before she took over the top job at what had once been the world's most prestigious gemtech. There had been no humility then, and precious little contrition. He could not square that recollection with the apparent sincerity on display before him. He shook himself and glanced back at Aryel. Her arms were still folded across her chest, a counterpoint to the high bulge of her wings, and he could almost see the frown she bent towards Zavcka.

He shifted his own attention back to the woman in the spotlight.

'So we deal with the past,' Zavcka said, and she seemed to be looking directly at Mikal before turning away to pace the stage. 'We admit our mistakes, we try to help the people we hurt, and we move on. And moving on is what I mainly want to talk about this evening, ladies and gentlemen. Moving on is why we're all here. In our case that involved a lesson from the past, and what we think it means for the future.

'As we examined the series of events that led us to where we are now, we noted the parallels between the way breakthroughs in genetic engineering were applied without due consideration for the consequences, and the way advances in information technology had been adopted with reckless speed a century and a half ago. Now we know where the latter led us – to the Syndrome, and a crisis that demanded we develop modification techniques just to survive. But what became apparent is that although society used gemtech to solve the problems created by infotech, we nevertheless abandoned infotech. Progress came to a crashing halt once the Syndrome was identified. Our technical capacity is almost exactly the same as it was at year zero. That is neither necessary nor desirable.'

She raised her hands again, this time a gesture of inclusion and uplift. The room murmured again, this time an expectant little ripple. They were hanging on her every word. Eli could not entirely conquer a reluctant sense of admiration.

'We believe that the next great advances in science and technology, the next wave of improvement in the way we live our lives, will come from picking up where we left off with infotech. So what I came here to tell you today is that, far from being consigned to the dustbin of history, the Bel'Natur Corporation is changing course. We are launching a major, long-term research and development programme into computing and information technologies. We now know how to do it safely, and as we travel down this new road we will be integrating what we've learned from human gemtech – both the scientific breakthroughs and the ethical imperatives. Over the next ten years we are going to be investing over a billion credits, creating thousands of new jobs, and bringing to market dozens of new products. We are going to be combining our unparalleled expertise in neural architecture with new concepts in software and hardware. We are going to launch the next phase of infotech.'

The midsummer sun was still high enough above the horizon to cast a golden glow over the gathering crowds on the riverwalk an hour later. Eli let himself be carried along in the flow of people heading towards the park, until he could step aside into a little nook where two ancient chestnut trees sheltered an empty bench. He sank down onto it and tried to think.

Zavcka had wrapped her speech up quickly. The grandee who had introduced her bounced back onstage, grinning widely, and invited questions. Eli wondered if Aryel would stay and challenge or slip away as unobtrusively as she had arrived, but she did neither. Instead she had waited until the lights came up, waited until they touched the wall where she stood and Zavcka Klist's eyes had focused on her and widened, before she sidestepped quickly to the door and out. By then people were on their feet all over the room and salvos were being fired at the stage.

They ranged predictably from anxious enquiries about safety, to what sorts of products she thought might emerge, to quantifying the economic impact. She had gone straight to Mikal's raised hand, though, despite knowing that he must be about to ask her to explain precisely what she meant by *integrating human gemtech*.

Work had already begun, she said, in the pre-Syndrome era, on direct interfaces. But they did not understand enough then about how the brain was structured and how it worked; progress was slow, patchy, and ultimately abandoned.

'We have the answers to those questions now,' she said. 'And while we can regret the manner in which much of that knowledge was gained, I don't think it honours anybody to simply not use it. On the contrary, it seems to me that we have an obligation to turn it into something worthwhile. Much of the original research focused on disability, for example, and working in difficult environments like space. Or underwater. If we can use what we already know to link *this*,' she pointed to her own head, 'directly to *this*,' and she took a tablet out of the Festival director's hand and held it up with the same restrained theatricality, 'then there are so *many* problems we can solve.'

She handed the tablet back, her attention still on Mikal. 'We're not talking about new gemtech. But I understand the concerns behind your question, Councillor, and I respect them. It's a question that should be asked.'

A few seconds of silence then, the audience bemusedly

contemplating the unexpected courtesy she was showing to Mikal. Eli could imagine the split-lidded blink with which he filled it, something he thought his friend sometimes did on purpose when he wished to be disconcerting.

'There are *many* questions that should be asked,' Mikal had replied evenly. 'And answered. I look forward to it.'

Eli knew her well enough to recognise the flash of anger in Zavcka Klist's eyes as she registered the rebuke. A few people seemed to realise that they had missed something, but it sailed too far over the heads of most. Mikal sat back, giving up the floor and watching her weather the torrent.

Now Eli kept an eye on the passing crowd until the giant loomed into view. He raised a hand. Mikal waved back and changed course, navigating to the edge of the flow of people so that Eli could fall into step beside him.

'Well,' he said, channelling well-worn irony, '*that* was interesting.'

Mikal laughed, a gusty tone with an edge of bitterness to it. 'Which part? The rebirth of infotech, the recycling of gemtech, or Zavcka Klist being my new best mate?'

'That last one is the killer. Did she speak to you again? I slipped out when it looked like there was going to be mingling. No love lost between us, as you know.'

'I think she would have been nice even to you. She came straight up to me, handshake, congratulations, the whole thing. Said she didn't think it would have been helpful to get into a technical discussion about neurochemistry from the stage but she didn't want me to think she was being evasive, they intend to be completely open, blah blah blah.'

'Subject to commercial constraints, of course.'

'Of course. Though she did make a point of saying they want to set up a protocol with the regulators to ensure that the protection of intellectual property doesn't undermine transparency. Quite how you manage that I don't know, but she'd be very happy for me to help work it out.'

'Blimey. Do you believe her?'

'Do I believe that she wants me on her private stream, or popping by the office? That she mortifies herself nightly over what Bel'Natur did? Over what *she* allowed to happen to Gabriel, and Callan, and goodness knows how many others? No, no and no. She doesn't look nearly shredded enough.'

The big man sighed and ran a hand through his hair. It was medium length and a nondescript lightish brown. The modifications he bore were more than sufficient gemsign; his designers had correctly judged that topping them off with a jewel-coloured, phosphorescent mane would have been redundant. His double thumbs left twin furrows on either side of his head.

'But is she now genuinely trying to chart a new course? She might be, Eli. She knows they can't go back to the old days. Innovate or die, as they used to say at Recombin. Infotech *has* been stagnant for a long time. We *are* all Syndrome-safe now, gems and norms, even the Remnants. Bel'Natur might be up to exactly what she says they're up to.'

'You sound like a politician, Mik.'

'Go wash your mouth out. With soap.'

UPBRINGING

She grows up in a city.

They live high above the sweat and dirt and horror that haunts most of it, in the heart of the old, proud seat of empire. She is accustomed to looking out of tall windows at soaring spires and swirling domes, their fairground gaiety at odds with the blocky, bland pragmatism of the modern buildings below. She gazes at the bright temples and palaces for hours sometimes, intensely, as if she could couple her concentration to their sleeping grandeur and bring a lost world to life; and in her mind's eye she does see the pennants and pageants that they once hosted, the great romances and golden ages and armies marching home in triumph. All her life she will love architecture that curves and sweeps and does more than merely contain.

Her father rarely looks out of the windows. His enchantment is reserved only for her, and she sometimes wishes she could interest him elsewhere, become less the laser-sharp focus of all his days. But she is his light and his life, he tells her, his greatest achievement and the only one which will matter in the end. Outside is only grief and despair and the slow degradation of all else he has treasured. He seems not to share her ability to unhear the moans of the afflicted and wails of the bereaved, to unsee the smoke that rises from a thousand thousand cremations. He worries endlessly about the emptiness of the world in which she will one day have to make her way, about how she will cope and whether she can be happy. To be the only precious child of a rich and powerful man guarantees little in this latter, desolate age.

She knows that he is among those battling against the plague, and that though they may have the answer now to the disease's vicious question, victory is still far from certain. They have lost so much ground. So few remain to fight. He is one of the rare ones able to protect his own, and he has bequeathed the armour of immunity to her.

It is not his only gift.

4

The park was already very full. Eli and Mikal headed for the bandstand. Heads turned as they went past, but the looks and half-overheard comments all seemed friendly enough as they skirted the families and couples spreading bioweave blankets and unpacking picnics. Children chased each other between the little encampments, shrieking with delight.

As usual the majority of the kids appeared to be norms, although this could be deceptive. It was not uncommon for naturally conceived gem children – at any rate those healthy enough to run and play – to bear no obvious gemsign. And it had only been a few years since gems were free to have their contraceptive implants removed and to find out, with trepidation and much heartache, whether their engineered genomes would allow conception, whether the resulting foetuses would be viable, and at what cost.

Eli stole a sideways glance at Mikal, caught him watching a gaggle of noisy five- and six-year-olds clambering over a climbing frame. His expression was hard to read; there was curiosity there, and longing, and loss. Eli looked away, not quickly enough. The giant spotted the motion and sighed.

'Since you're politely not asking, yes, we're still trying, and no, no luck yet.'

Eli let it sit for a moment, then said quietly, 'You could always go in vitro.'

'I know. Still no guarantee just mixing things up in a Petri dish would work, though. Unless we had them engineer us a solution.'

'That's what I meant.'

Mikal was silent for a while. The shouts and laughter of the children were well behind them when he said, 'Sharon is up for that, but I'm not sure I am. I really want kids, but it'd mean authorising human gemtech. On *myself*, my own offspring. I'm struggling with that. And if we did go ahead, what instructions would I give? We'd have to decide whether to opt for minimum interference, just enough for a healthy baby, or have them carve out all the weirdness in my genotype so our kids could have regular hands and eyes and inside leg measurements.' He turned his hands palm up, the four thumbs mirroring each other across their broad, creased surfaces, and looked at them for a moment as though they were found things whose provenance was uncertain. He dropped them back to swing at the level of Eli's midriff.

'What's the right thing to do there, Eli? What should I wish for my children?'

The question hung between them. Eli had known it must be part of what Mikal and Sharon were trying to reconcile, along with many thousands of gems worldwide. Relatively few of them, though, were in mixed couples, and he hesitated before asking the obvious question.

'What does Sharon think about that part?'

'As close to a normal random recombination as possible would be her choice. She says she doesn't want our kids to only look like her.' There was a note in his voice that brought a sudden lump to Eli's throat.

He waited until he was sure he could trust himself. 'For whatever it's worth, I agree with her, Mik. There's nothing wrong with the way you look . . .'

'Thanks, mate, but seriously.'

'I *am* being serious. The norm population was so homogenised by Syndrome-safety gemtech that even small variations in appearance look big to us. I know, I know,' holding up his hands, '... *small* is not a word that applies to you, but my point is, those reactions will fade over time. They really will. And in the meantime, if you undo all the things in your genetype that make you *you*, what does *that* say to your kids?'

'There is also that. So. I'm struggling.'

They reached a gate set into the fence that separated the backstage area and were waved through, to the envious looks of clusters of fans gathered outside. All norms, Eli noticed. Lyriam's music was hugely popular among his own people as well, but the concept of celebrity was one to which gems appeared mostly immune.

Inside, they made their way to a clump of marquees that had sprung up like angular, oversize white mushrooms, and wandered amongst them until Mikal, peering over a biocanvas slope, said, 'There she is,' and led them around the corner.

Aryel stood in a little courtyard formed by four of the white tents, talking to a young man with jet-black hair and long, elegant, seven-fingered hands. Reginald was with her, along with two ruby-haired youths who Eli recognised from their stream profiles as Rhys and Gwen. Even from a distance the girl radiated a sort of effervescent enthusiasm; he could see it in the way she leaned into the conversation and the expressive gestures of her hands as she described something. Rhys hung back, diffident and, Eli thought, a little tired-looking.

'It is our conquering hero, returned from the East,' trumpeted Mikal, and they all turned round. The black-haired man came forward laughing, and his seven fingers and Mikal's double thumbs met in what must have been one of the world's most complicated handclasps, before the giant pulled him into a hug. Eli busied himself shaking hands with Reginald and being introduced to the others.

'At last!' laughed Gwen. 'I was beginning to think you weren't really real.' Rhys shot her an unreadable look and said quietly, 'It's good to finally meet you, Dr Walker.'

Up close his initial impressions were confirmed: the young woman had a vivacity that was infectious. It was hard not to smile in her presence, not to become interested in turn in the myriad little details of preparation going on around them that had caught her attention. Her brother was clearly the introvert of the pair, less talkative and easy, but, Eli discovered as they chatted, just as keenly observant.

He was struck too by Reginald's paternal affection for them; a sense of proud guardianship that might once have also been there for Aryel. But she had flown so far now that theirs had become a friendship between equals. And though much of her early life among the Remnants remained mysterious, Eli knew she had been older when she came to them.

The three visitors appeared to have already become fast friends with Lyriam, who emerged, staggering a little for comic effect, from Mikal's embrace. Weary though he must have been after almost a year on tour, he was as energetic and focused as ever.

'Too busy to be tired,' he said when Eli commented on this. 'And you can't let yourself be distracted before a performance anyway. I've learned that. I might fall over for a few days after tonight, but then there are things to sort out. And I want to work on some new stuff . . . I heard the most amazing musicians in Australia . . .'

'D'you mean the aborigems?' asked Gwen. 'I listened to those links you posted, it's wonderful, sort of . . .' and she tipped her head back and let out a long, trilling series of notes, sweet and haunting.

Lyriam said, 'Yes, *exactly*, and then they do these chords,' and he sang a low, spine-tingling ululation, his fingers keeping time along an imaginary instrument, while the hairs on the back of Eli's neck stood up and he stared from one to the other. Reginald laughed at his expression.

'They've been doing that all evening. Whole new conversational form. Your mate Callan,' nodding to Aryel, 'should write a paper.'

They stood around chatting for a few more minutes, until Eli felt Aryel's eyes on him, and caught the tiny sideways inclination of her head.

They stepped away from the others. He glanced over his shoulder as they moved out of earshot.

'You'd think they've known each other all their lives. But where's Lyriam's other half?'

'We saw Bethany earlier, she's somewhere about. Seems there might be a little bit of tension there at the moment.'

'Really?' He was so astounded that Aryel laughed.

'I don't suppose they're immune. It's been a hard trip and, you know,' she shrugged, 'things are changing. They're growing up.'

'I guess. Still. Have to hope the socialstreams don't get hold of that.'

She did not respond, which for Aryel, Eli later thought, was significant. They wandered away from the pre-performance buzz of the tents to a quiet corner where she could perch gratefully on a tree stump, the gnarled tombstone of some ancient coppice. Eli was reminded of how much energy it took for her to fly, and how little time she would have had today to rest and eat. She must be exhausted.

She looked up at him, a sharp sky-blue gaze full of the lively intelligence that had first attracted him. There was no weariness in it.

'So. Our old friend Zavcka. What did you think?'

Straight to the point. He picked through his impressions, organising them.

'I don't think it can be a bluff, not announcing it in that way. She must really be making a play for infotech. From what I know of that industry – which isn't much – it's dominated by just a few big legacy players who've been churning out pretty much the same stuff for almost a hundred and fifty years. It's ripe for innovation. That part makes sense.'

She was looking at him oddly, and he realised too late that he had simply delivered his opinion without first describing the event. *Oh well. So much for waiting to see if she'd tell me herself.*

He was never able to dissemble with her anyway.

'I saw you there, Aryel, I know you heard for yourself what she had to say. What did *you* think?'

'Did you? Ah. Well as far as infotech is concerned, I agree with you. I'm less convinced by her assurances around gemtech.'

'I'm still trying to wrap my head around that. It's not like she could say anything different, not these days . . .'

'I know.'

' . . . But she went out of her way to say quite a *lot*. More than it seems she needed to.' He told her about Zavcka Klist's exchanges with Mikal after she had left. 'If she's acting she's got a lot better at it.'

'So you think she's a reformed character?'

'I wouldn't go that far.' He thought. 'What do we know about her from last time? That she's pragmatic and intelligent. And devious. This is a strategy.'

'Again, I agree. She's sharp enough to know there's no way back to the days of indenture, but it's clear she hasn't lost interest in us either. She wouldn't be courting Mik like that without a reason. And there's something else as well.'

She fell silent, as if thinking the something else over, until Eli said, 'She doesn't seem quite as unshakeable as she used to. Your being there rattled her, I think, though only for a moment.'

Aryel nodded, still musing. 'It was meant to. I'm not going to sit politely back and wait to see what she's up to this time.' She shook herself, wings rustling, and flicked a glance at Eli. 'They changed the schedule at the last minute this morning, some flunkey from the Bel'Natur press office replaced by Zavcka herself, so I knew it had to be important. But Mik was going to be there representing the city, and I thought you'd be interested given your history with her, and I knew I could rely on you both to tell me all about it. So there was really no need for me to go. And then, barely a couple of hours ago, she sent a message.'

'To you? She asked you to come?' It hadn't looked like it.

'Goodness no, and I probably wouldn't have gone if she had. It wasn't about her announcement, not on the face of it anyway. She sent it to Herran.'

'*Herran?*'

'Herran.' She paused, frowning into the distance again. 'It was from her personally, very polite and respectful. Said Bel'Natur was working on a new project that they thought would suit someone of his particular skills. Hastened to add that it wasn't gemtech and they particularly wanted to speak to him about working with them in a senior capacity, that they were sure he would find it a good fit and very rewarding. All of her contact details attached.'

'What the— Have they *met* Herran?'

'Not recently. But don't forget, they made him. There were cues buried in the message, command phrases she must have hoped he would still respond to. The Herran they knew was far more bid-dable than he is now.'

Again that bitter shake of the head. 'You should have seen him when he first came to us, Eli. His autism may make him seem a bit like an automaton, but he really *was* one then. He'd been trained to it, they'd worked out the most efficient way to get him to under-stand and obey orders, and it was the only way he knew how to be. Inputs and outputs. But he'd got out before the Declaration – at the time he couldn't even tell us how – and found his way to the Squats. So we knew there had to be more to him than *they* knew. They'll since have come to the same conclusion, but she probably didn't realise he'd immediately forward her message to me. With an addendum.'

'Which was?'

'*Aryel fix.*'

Eli shook with laughter. He could imagine the carefully crafted rhetoric Zavcka would have employed, and how annoyed she would be to have it both covered and dismissed by one of Herran's unvar-nished utterances.

'Good for him. So you decided to start the fixing by letting her know that whatever she's up to, she's going to have to deal with you.'

'Exactly.'

'And do you know what she *is* up to, Aryel? What does she want with Herran?'

'I'm not sure, but it must be connected. She was being fairly disingenuous when she said that infotech was a new direction for Bel'Natur.' She gazed thoughtfully back in the direction of the tents, where the ruby heads of her foster siblings twinkled next to the white mane of Reginald and the tower that was Mikal.

'That expertise she was talking about wasn't just bluster. They did lead the industry in neural engineering. What she didn't mention was why they focused on it so much. They were trying to design gems who could be plugged in. Literally. A bioprocessor. They didn't succeed, not in the way they intended, and the collateral damage was horrendous. But they were making progress. They'd got further than they realised. And I'm wondering if they do know, now.'

'You mean Herran . . . ?'

'Herran came out of the bioprocessor programme. The cleft palate he was born with was the result of them trying to engineer a physical neuroconnection point, but he doesn't need one. He can read – and write – raw code. He still has to do it through a tablet, but he can interface at the binary level.'

With showtime fast approaching, Lyriam had excused himself. Aryel was still deep in conversation with Eli over in a far corner as Mikal led the way to the hospitality tent, talking to Reginald about the gillung coastal technology and how it had been adapted for the Thames. Rhys, listening idly as he and Gwen strolled behind them, and enjoying the relative quiet of several conversations reduced finally to one, was struck suddenly by the unlikelihood of this. He glanced over at his sister. Her eyes flicked across everything around them as sharply as ever, but her expression had turned thoughtful, almost brooding.

She felt his gaze and returned it. He grunted a wordless question. She shrugged it away with a raised eyebrow and quirked lip, shifted her gaze to the ground in front of them. He waited a moment, then tried again.

'Guh.' *Gwennie.*

'Ah?' Clipped off, preoccupied. *What?*

'Ah.' *Tell me.*

'Nuh. D'no.' *Nothing. Don't know.*

'Suh. D'la?' *Something. Don't like?*

She looked up and around at that, at the evening deepening over the tents and the murmur of the crowd on the far side of the fence.

'Lu'loh.' *Like lots.*

'Ah?' *Then?*

He touched her arm, lightly but with a touch of anxiety. 'Ki?' *Are you feeling okay?*

'Of course I'm okay.' At the suggestion of this particular worry, she fell fast out of the truncated emotiveness of twin-speak. 'I'm not the one who has a problem, remember?'

'Oh, please rub it in.'

'Sorry, I didn't mean to. I just wish people would stop thinking that if I go quiet there must be something wrong with me.'

'Gwennie, as a rule that's the only time you ever *do* go quiet.'

She scowled at him, but did not argue the point. 'I was just taking it all in, imagining what it must be like to be part of something like this. To make music on this scale.' They stepped inside the bustling cavern of the tent. Rhys shot her an appraising look and shuffled sideways into an empty spot near the entrance, letting Mikal and Reginald plough on ahead. Gwen gazed after their receding backs, and turned to him with another twitch of lips and brow.

'I know this isn't the main reason we're here, but isn't it okay for me to get excited about it anyway? It's what I love, Rhys, it's what I want to do. And the reality of it is so much more . . .' Her hands shaped something enormous. 'And he's lovely, isn't he?'

'Who?'

'Lyriam, you nit.'

Rhys blinked at her. 'He's all right.'

'I thought he seemed really . . . generous.'

'For what?' Rhys' voice was dry. 'Babysitting us when Ari had to fly off, or complimenting your singing?'

'Oh, you *pillock*.'

She stared at him in dismay. It took no more than a mortified second for him to realise that he had actually hurt her feelings, confirmed when she punched him hard on the arm.

'Ow! Gwennie, stop. Since when can't you take a joke?' He rubbed his arm. 'I think he's really nice, I just didn't expect him not to be.'

'Neither did I. That's not what— Oh.'

Her eyes had picked out something in the crowd over his shoulder and Rhys turned around. An eddy in the swirl of people revealed a young woman, talking with who could only be more of Lyriam's guests. She broke off as she saw them. Her lips tightened for a moment, before she said something to the gems she was with and headed over. She had shiny blonde hair with no gem glow.

'Hi there.' Her voice as she arrived was so bright and brittle that Rhys felt his own face twitch in surprise. He stilled it. 'You two all right? Need anything? It was Rhys, wasn't it, and – and Gwyn?'

'Gwen,' said Gwen. 'We're fine, thank you, Bethany. Everything's wonderful.' There was a guarded, almost formal politeness in his sister's response that sank into Rhys' consciousness and briskly started to link up with all the other minor peculiarities of the past few hours.

'Where's that guy of mine? Has he left you all alone?' She laughed, too loudly.

'He went to get ready for the performance,' Gwen said quietly. She would have picked up the same cues he had from Bethany's tone and body language, and Rhys could hear her being careful, modulating her voice for calm. 'Da is here,' she nodded towards the bar, 'with Mikal. You know him too, don't you?'

'What?' Bethany jerked a look in the direction Gwen had

47

indicated. 'Yes of course.' She sounded more distracted than annoyed now. 'I know him very well. I should say hello.' She moved as though to go to the bar, then hesitated. 'I, ah . . . I'd better check on Lyriam first, though. See if he needs any help. I'll, umm,' edging towards the door now, 'I'll catch up with all of you later, yeah? Have fun. See you after the show.'

'See you,' said Rhys as she ducked out. He turned to Gwen, and let his eyebrows rise as high as they wanted. His sister was gazing at the empty spot where Bethany had just been standing.

'Does she seem,' said Gwen, 'a little stressed to you?'

'Oh, just a *bit*.'

'I wonder why. I mean she ought to be used to all this.'

Rhys opened his mouth to reply, then closed it again, shaking his head. Gwen had already turned away, making eye contact with the gems Bethany had abandoned and drifting over to introduce herself.

He knew this sister who was not a sister better than anyone else on earth; he knew that she was quite capable of simply switching off her normally razor-sharp perception when it might reveal to her things she did not particularly wish to know. It was a talent he would have liked to share. He had learned to read when best to shake her out of wilful ignorance, and when to leave her alone. She would come to her own understanding of the situation soon enough. Or not. In the meantime he had plenty to worry about.

5

The first of several opening acts were already halfway through their set when Eli flopped onto a curving grass bank with a good view of the stage. It formed a gentle rampart near the edge of the park, close to a hardtop path that had no doubt made it an easier destination for the less mobile gems, or those who for other reasons found the negotiation of a route through the packed crowd too great a challenge. There was a smattering of mobility chairs and walking aids below him, scattered among spectators with obvious abnormalities. Most passers-by gave them a wide berth and averted their eyes.

Still, it was reassuring to see how many others *had* congregated here, relaxed in the company of the less able. Although he had passed other gems along the way – few of whom could have been distinguished from norms were it not for their carefully coiffed hair – the highest concentration of glowing heads surrounded him.

Two of them belonged to Rhys and Gwen, and many had turned to look as they made their way across from the backstage gate. Some of the attention was no doubt due to Mikal, forging a path in front, or the curious figure of Reginald, with his fountain of white hair and shabby Remnant clothing. But much of it, Eli thought, was down to the strikingly similar beauty of the two young people who walked between them, and the unusually dark shade of their radiant hair. Reginald had emerged as the closest to an explanation of her own background that Aryel Morningstar was prepared to give, and his visits had made him familiar to both the streams and the Squats; but his other foster children had been no more than rumour, or at best stream-friends with a few of the city dwellers.

Now the old man folded easily down to the grass beside him, and dismissed Eli's concern for his comfort with a booming laugh.

'Lived outdoors all my life,' he said. 'And in the wet Welsh mountains at that. This is luxury, my friend.'

Eli suspected that this was true, although he knew that Remnant colonies like the one in the Beacons were no longer the isolated, frequently destitute groups of refugees many had been in the early days of the Syndrome. They might still live apart, but their ancestors had come in from the cold long enough to have the gene surgery that ensured their offspring would be Syndrome-safe, and they had tablets and access to the streams. It was they, self-sufficient and living close to the land, who had harboured runaways during the dark days of human gemtech, and who now mentored the new settlers of coast and countryside.

It was a paradoxical relationship: descendants of the doubters who had initially rejected modification found themselves in the end to have more in common with gems than with their homogenised, complacent norm cousins. And they were used to living on the margins. Eli wondered how much even he knew about what was really going on out there.

'Still haven't figured it out, have they?'

He started out of his reverie, surprised to hear his own thoughts virtually spoken out loud.

'Sorry?'

Reginald waved an arm to take in the massed audience sprawled over every square yard of park.

'Them. After all that work you did, after Newhope Tower, and finding out about little Gabriel and his parents. Both sets. You'd think people would have understood the lesson.'

Though the memory of Newhope Tower was seared into the very fibre of his being, Eli suspected that whatever lesson Reginald was referring to might have eluded him as well.

'Integration is a slow process,' he said carefully, against the retro wailing of a six-string guitar. 'We always knew that some would embrace it more easily than others.'

Reginald turned and looked at him. The old man had a penetrating gaze that Eli already knew could be disconcerting. Now he had the uncomfortable feeling that he was missing something important.

'Integration isn't going to be a problem, but not for the reasons people like to think. I'll tell you something, Eli, all those norms who still worry about mixing with gems, they've missed the point.'

So, he felt, had he – at least whatever point it was that Reginald was trying to make. Mikal, sitting near enough to have overheard, nodded thoughtfully and Eli felt even more lost. He was choosing his words to try again when there came a huge whoosh of displaced air at his back, a massive, unmistakable fluttering, and they looked around to see Aryel settling on top of the bank behind them. She must have circled in from the side, staying low and counting on the glare of the setting sun behind her and the crowd's focus on the stage to arrive relatively unnoticed. Now she dropped down onto the turf, wings half spread both for balance and to achieve what was, for her, the complicated geometry of sitting on the ground. She flashed them a quick smile, reaching up with both hands to smooth back her chocolate-dark hair and retighten the clasp that kept it firmly away from her face. Her wings shifted and rustled with the movement.

The lump that was so often there rose in Eli's throat, again. The pleasure he took in simply watching her seemed never to diminish. Her eyes, that astonishing midsummer blue in a delicate, pale bronze face, swept the gathering immediately around them and then further afield, checking, quartering. He could almost see her relax as she concluded that all was in order.

'What've I missed?'

'Four songs and accompanying criticism,' floated back from Rhys, propped up on his elbows just below them on the slope. 'They were flat, apparently.'

'They *were* flat.' Gwen, serene beside him, arms wrapped around her legs and chin on knees as she gazed at the stage. 'Not *terribly* flat. But a bit.'

'And poorly arranged, you said?'

'Nothing wrong with the arrangement as such, they just weren't really up to it.'

Practised chuckles from Aryel and Reginald, while Rhys arched back so they could see him roll his eyes in mock disbelief. Gwen calmly ignored them all. Rhys stopped in mid-motion, his face comically upside down for a moment, as two newcomers loomed into view behind Aryel. Sharon and Callan, Eli saw, trudging up the steep side of the bank, navigating no doubt by the twin silhouettes of Aryel and Mikal. Rhys rolled over onto his knees, Gwen swivelled gracefully, and once again onstream acquaintances finally met in person.

They settled down as the next act took to the stage, Sharon tucking herself into the crook of her husband's arm and Callan, after an awkward moment, allowing Aryel to pull him firmly down to sit in the little cluster over which she presided.

'I was worried you weren't coming after all,' she said softly, so that he had to lean in to hear her over the music. 'I'm glad you're here, Callan. You need to come back into the world, love.'

He pursed his lips, eyes far away on the singer, or perhaps something else. A breeze ruffled his hair, and in the deepening gloom the glow from it flickered across his face like firelight, picking out the tiny lines and hollows of damage.

'Do I?' he said finally. 'I'm not sure. When I'm out I'm glad to be. Mostly. But it's not always easy any more, Aryel. I'm never sure it's worth the effort.'

'It will be. Trust me. Just give it a chance.'

He nodded uncertainly and his gaze moved inward, grazing as hers had over the people around and below them, lingering a little on the darker glow of Rhys' head, poised in a listening stillness.

There were two more performances to sit through before the main event: a spoken-word troupe known for their choral a cappella accompaniment to poetry both ancient and modern, and a classical quartet riding high on the current fad for instrumental music. The reason for its popularity was the young man that the thousands packed into the park, and many more watching on live streams, were waiting to see.

The quartet departed and light sculptures morphed and swirled in front of the stage, camouflaging the set change and giving an impression of a deeper darkness behind. They died down slowly, like a fountain being turned gradually off, leaving the eye blinking at a pool of black in which a tight beam appeared, borne on a single sustained note. The note rippled into a phrase, then a melody, and the beam widened with it to illuminate at first only fretwork and flashing hands. Then the other instruments came in and the light broadened and strengthened, until Lyriam sat in a golden circle in the centre of the stage, guitharp on his lap, head bent over the instrument as he built the song.

It was the one that had made him famous, the first track on a playlist that had gone viral instantly, achieving streaming numbers not seen since the halcyon days before the Syndrome. He had written it quickly, in an outpouring of horror and fury and grief, and the world had taken it to heart in an act of collective catharsis. Even now, years later, it had lost none of its power to move; and Lyriam had built a career on it, composing complex pieces for a difficult instrument, writing music only he could play.

The tale had become legend: how a gem youth picking his way through a world newly liberalised and still chaotic, lurching from one momentary, menial job to another, had been sent packing with nothing but the old wooden guitharp rescued from a crumbling warehouse, instead of the meagre credits he'd been promised; how he had kept hold of it through thick and thin, teaching himself to play during sleepless nights on the streets and discovering chords and tones no ten-fingered musician could have managed; how a precarious life of busking had been transformed, first by the norm girl who fell in love with his music and with him, and then by the searing elegy he had played for the dead after the terror of Newhope Tower.

The guitharp raged and wept through it now, and Eli could again see the blood that had washed the Squats, splashed up against the closed lids of his eyes. He blinked hard and glanced over at Aryel, and at Callan, and Sharon and Mikal with their arms twined around each other, and felt the weight of memory. And then, just as the loss and the sorrow became unbearable, the song shifted, lifting almost imperceptibly from anguish into something lighter, weary but resolute, a whisper of survival, and redemption.

The applause was rapturous.

Eli shook himself and brushed at his eyes, saw the motion repeated all around him. Below them he could see people on their feet all over the park. Reginald, sitting bolt upright, murmured, 'Goodness me.'

Rhys muttered, 'Oh. Wow. It's . . . it's different live, isn't it?' He nudged his sister. 'Gwennie?' After a moment she turned her head ever so slightly towards him, as if just waking up. Her face was still and solemn and she did not speak.

The music flowed on. Lyriam, always a confident player, had become a consummate performer. He spoke to the crowd, telling of the inspiration behind tunes and sharing anecdotes from the tour. Over a tinkling prelude he said, 'I wrote this for a girl who bought me a cup of tea one day from a place that wouldn't serve me and then stayed to listen to me play. She liked it so much she never left.' A roar of approval welled up as the song swelled into a gloriously lush, romantic piece and he shot a quick look towards the wings. Eli glimpsed movement, saw Bethany's blonde head over folded arms before she stepped back out of sight.

The next tune was ancient, a melody that had made the journey from orchestral to ecclesiastic and back again. It had barely begun when Eli became aware of a murmur in the crowd off to his right, a dissonant droning accompanied by a note of rising complaint. The disturbance was close enough for him to see that a group of half a dozen or so had risen from their mats and blankets, their mouths moving not quite in unison as they appeared to sing along with the tune. As one of the press vidcams scattered throughout the park swung its light around it picked out the symbol of the United Churches, dangling from necklaces and the ropes of beads that several now carried draped over their fists.

'Oh, for fuck's sake,' Callan muttered.

Rhys sat up and squinted at the only one of the group not on her feet. Her fingers were racing across what must be an input screen on the small metal box resting on the mat before her. His eyes flicked from her to the singers, many of whom had bead-wrapped hands pressed to earsets.

'Is that an amp?' he said. 'They're going to hack – oh *no*–'

Gwen was already on her feet and halfway down the slope.

Eli swung round to look at Aryel. She had rolled forward into a crouch, one hand resting on Callan's shoulder, for balance perhaps, or reassurance. His face had gone hard as marble. She looked ready to spring up, into the air, although how that could do other than add to the disruption Eli could not imagine. But she stayed still, watching Gwen.

The girl pushed through the crowd, closing in on the devotees now bathed in the steady illumination of the vidcam. A gaunt man stood at their head and, perhaps realising how few understood what was going on, waved his hands in the air and called out, 'This song is in praise of God! Praise God!' He pumped his arms up and down, as though trying to encourage others to rise and join in.

The musicians on stage seemed to be aware of something happening; they were peering over their instruments into the crowd. The sound the ragged choir was making started to leak through the speaker array, and the music began to falter. Lyriam, still playing, half rose as Gwen stepped into the midst of the UC protest. She looked up and their eyes met. Then her head jerked to the side, one hand coming smoothly up to catch her tumbling earset, the other snapping forward to pluck his from the head of the leader, her last stride taking her over the illicit amplifier as the kneeling woman reared backwards in alarm. The purloined earset slid into place as the young gem came to a halt. It had been one movement, beautiful in its coordination, and blindingly fast.

Another sound rose then, pouring out through the hacked speakers, drowning the shambling, off-key chorus of the remaining UCs with shocking ease: the song as it was meant to be sung, clear and pure and in perfect time, a gloriously rich tone that washed over and silenced them. The extemporaneous preacher's face was slack with amazement. Gwen raised her hands palm up, half placation, half shrug, as if to say, *Isn't this what you wanted?* and then raised them higher as she turned to the stage, a questioning *What now?* directed there as she kept on singing.

Lyriam took one hand off the guitharp long enough to give her a thumbs-up and signal to the musicians. They gathered themselves, recapturing the wavering melody, mirroring their leader's laughing face as he watched the ruby-headed girl down in the crowd. She stood in the vidcam's glow, facing the stunned and speechless UCs now gathered into an embarrassed little knot with the crowd pressing in behind them. Gwen sent an answering thumbs-up to Lyriam, put her hands on her hips and sang it to the end.

Aryel sank back onto the grass, shaking with mirth. Sharon had already patted her husband's shoulder and sauntered off down the slope, her warrant tab now clipped to her own shoulder and blinking blue. Gwen met her at the edge of the UC bivouac, dropped the deactivated amp and the preacher's earset into her hands and strolled back up towards her family through thunderous applause and a pointing, curious crowd.

'Well,' said Rhys, 'I suppose she could have just asked them to sing properly or shut the hell up. But Gwennie likes to lead by example.'

Zavcka Klist was not present at the concert. She would have freely confessed that there was much in Lyriam's music she could appreciate, but really, there were limits. She had gone to a sponsor's reception after the infotech announcement, waded into the scrum of business editors wolfing down free canapés, and skilfully turned the encounter into an impromptu press conference.

When it broke up she drifted casually from one departing group to another as they all made their way to the riverwalk, finally dropping back to stroll alongside her own assistant as others began to make the turn that led towards the park. The two of them did the same, only pausing as Zavcka issued instructions for the next day. When she began to move again, this time heading for the bridge that led to the far side of the river, the assistant hesitated.

'You . . . um . . . you're not going to the show?' he said. He was still making rapid notes on the tablet in his hand, but he threw a plaintive glance in the direction of the throngs moving up the riverwalk.

Zavcka took in the look, bit back a rebuke and instead waved a manicured hand in dismissal. 'No. I have other plans tonight. You go if you like, just make sure everything's taken care of.'

It was an unnecessary instruction, and she knew it. This one was diligent, and talented enough to be worth trying to hold on to. He delivered a compact volley of reassurances, thanks and wishes for a pleasant evening as she strode towards the bridge. She glanced back as she reached the top and saw him hurrying away upriver, already speaking into his earset, tablet still in hand. She thought he would likely try to get everything done by remote in the next half hour or so, the better to relax by the time the performances began.

She sighed. These days it was the best you could hope for.

Her own plans involved going home, wrapping herself in an ancient robe made from real pre-Syndrome silk, and settling down to review the latest progress report from the most sensitive of her projects while the live concert streamed softly in the background. She glanced at the large screen inset in her sitting-room wall every now and then, her gaze pausing there longest when the feed lingered over a close-up of Aryel Morningstar, sitting like some sentimental vision of nirvana with the last rays of the setting sun glinting bronze and gold off her half-open wings.

After that the music and applause and between-tune patter was a half-heard backdrop to her own concerns, until the bizarre interruption by what looked to be an even more ludicrous band of zealots than usual. The shift from the stage to a crowd-cam feed caught her attention, and she watched keenly and with grudging admiration as the young gem woman sang them out of countenance. The girl looked disturbingly familiar, but it was not until the song ended and the camera tracked her as she returned to her seat that Zavcka understood why.

Aryel Morningstar was staring straight at her, for the second time today. At least now she was only onscreen, at the far end of a newstream feed.

Zavcka frowned at the image as the girl sat down to laughter and wryly shaken heads, and what looked like a compliment from Eli Walker. As the feed cut back to the musicians onstage, she called up her messages. She had added Herran to the list of senders who would trigger an automatic alert, but now it occurred to her that this had been short-sighted.

Sure enough there was her own subject line, dangling retransmission tags like accessories. As Eli had expected, her nostrils flared with irritation at Herran's curt directive, but she wasted little time on this. Leaving the message thread attached to the response was no doubt intended to have just such an effect.

Of far greater interest was its result. She read the note carefully, and with a growing sense of satisfaction. It was too early to feel that anything had been accomplished yet, much less grow complacent. But at least things were, so far, going to plan.

6

'Reversionists,' Sharon was saying. 'Not the most hardline I've ever met, but still. It was all about the importance of religious heritage, preservation of traditional values, maintenance of cultural integrity. The usual.'

'In that case, what have they got against Lyriam playing a three-hundred-year-old piece of music?' asked Gwen indignantly. 'They should have been glad.'

'They said what they objected to was it being taken out of its original context. Apparently Lyriam should have made a speech explaining its origins and giving thanks, before inviting the audience to pray while he played.'

Sharon greeted the howls of derision with a don't-shoot-the-messenger shrug. She had arrived late to the after-party, and walked into a storm of questions about the hymn-singing hackers. A quick search onstream while they were being taken into custody had confirmed that the explanation the UC fringe group gave for their actions was backed up by a fairly comprehensive campaign, one which was already being sensationalised by the newstreams. Given that publicity – plus the fact that they'd mostly used their communications privileges to post their statements to public streams – there was little point being tight-lipped about it.

'I wonder,' said Mikal thoughtfully, 'if we shouldn't extend that philosophy to all aspects of life. A lecture on the cultural significance of weaving prior to buying new clothes. An acknowledgement of civilisation's debt to the cultivation of wheat, to be made each time one eats bread.' ·

He eyed a tiny sample of that item, topped by an even tinier cube of meat and slice of olive, the entire confection held delicately between the double thumbs which had swooped down unnoticed to liberate it from the tray of a passing waiter. Laughter erupted around him as he popped it into his mouth, chewed, and swallowed. 'Imagine the level of *appreciation* that would generate.'

'Careful, Mik.' Eli grinned up at him. 'Someone might take you seriously. You're in government now, you know.'

'Oh, is that what happens when you get into government? Someone should have warned me.'

Mikal rolled his eyes, to more laughter. The little group from the grassy bank was now just a slightly denser cluster amid a busy swirl of guests in the largest of the backstage marquees. Lyriam and Bethany had joined them, separately and in both cases momentarily, before being pulled away; in Lyriam's case with a backward glance and many-fingered hands raised in mock despair at the collective groan as he disappeared into the crowd.

Looking around, mapping the movements and mood of the party, letting multiple conversations lap against him as he often did when he wanted to gauge a general disposition rather than plumb a specific exchange, Eli could see that the young musician was, as expected, one of its focal points. Folded unselfconsciously down onto his knees, he was chatting with several chair-bound gems while a standing cordon of mostly norms awkwardly waited their turn to be noticed. The other convergence centred on the twin nuclei of Mikal and Aryel; the one issuing a regular stream of witticisms from two feet above everyone else's head while the other, diminutive in height but clothed in the immense bronze-and-gold glory of her wings, radiated grace, charm, and blue-eyed serenity. Around them the gathering coalesced, passers-by lingering to overhear what others were laughing at, or angling through a sea of bodies in the unspoken hope of catching Aryel Morningstar's eye.

He remembered another gathering years ago, a rare case of interaction in a world where gems and norms were still separate and unequal. Even though she had been shrouded then, her wings unguessed at, he had seen how the centre of gravity tipped towards her; an unexplained attraction that pulled people in, unwittingly and sometimes unwillingly. Once, there would have been sniggers at the notion of gem glamour. Now Eli noted not only the attention focused on Aryel, Lyriam and Mikal, but the knot of music insiders and press that surrounded Gwen, the easy way the gem girl talked and laughed and tossed her glowing, dark red curls away from her face.

It's all about them now, he thought. *There are people, norms, who would kill to be in this room. In these presences.* He felt a vague disquiet at the thought, and Reginald's remark flitted through his mind once again, like the wings of a butterfly brushing against his subconscious. There was something there, he could sense the vibrations of a connection waiting to be made; but his empty glass had just been refilled, and Mikal was winding up the tale of his first day at City Hall to a delightful, devastating punch-line, and Aryel had just caught *his* eye and smiled as she drifted close to him on the eddies and currents of the gathering. The notion, whatever it was, came and went as he let his attention be captured.

'They asked about you,' Sharon was saying quietly to Aryel, under cover of the general hilarity. 'It seems their biggest worry about the operation was what your reaction would be, whether you would get involved, what impact it would have if you did. But of course what happened wasn't anything they expected, and they were desperate to know who Gwen was. Someone found an onstream reference to her as Reginald's foster-daughter, which by their lights makes you sort of her older sister, or at any rate a figure of authority. So they're reading her as some sort of proxy for you.'

Aryel was nodding, her smile now a little grim. 'Positive or negative?'

'They've decided it's positive, on the whole.'

'Why?' asked Eli. 'Their plan failed, and they were humiliated. By a gem.'

'This lot say they don't have any problem with gems as such, and given their reaction I'm inclined to believe them. What they wanted was for the song to be recognised – appreciated – as a hymn, and that's what Gwen's intervention did. Far better than they could have, so they've decided she must have been sent, or inspired, or something, by the Lord.' Sharon glanced over to where the young woman stood chatting, very much the centre of her own group now. Her crowd of admirers had grown, Eli noticed. 'She's got a hell of a voice.'

'She has.' Aryel's eyes rested on Gwen, her face pensive. 'And she loves to show it off. She knows all the old hymns, along with folk songs, opera, pop music. They'll be deeply disappointed, I'm afraid – she sings anything and everything, for the pure pleasure of it. And she's no one's proxy, believe me.'

'Well, she'll want to watch it that the wrong idea doesn't take root. You know what the streams are like.'

'I'll have a word with her, but I wouldn't be surprised if she's ahead of both of us. And I don't think she'll have any trouble getting the right idea out there. Not with that lot clamouring for her comcode.'

*

63

Rhys bit back a sigh as he watched Gwen hold court out of the corner of his eye. He felt unanchored, listening at the edges of other people's conversations, meandering around the fringes of the various clumps that were forming as those who had gathered to listen to Sharon and laugh with Mikal now broke into smaller pockets. He covered his aimlessness by wandering over to the bar to refresh his drink, and found himself well within earshot of the cluster where Bethany held forth.

'They should have been arrested much more quickly. Before it became such a *spectacle*.' Her back was to the rest of the room but she made no particular effort to keep her voice down. Her coterie of four norms and two gems, all painfully chic in razor-sharp haircuts and the latest artfully tailored fashions, were hanging on her every word.

'Oh, I don't know.' Lyriam, back on his feet now, a few paces away and surrounded by the band, turned to interject without moving across to join her. His tone was light, but Rhys' situational sense picked up the edge in it. 'We just heard the streamcast is getting way more hits even than the Beijing show. And Gwen sounded great. I knew she could sing, but wow.'

Bethany stared at him. 'It was *your* show. No one should have inserted themselves into *your* show.'

'True, but since they did I'm glad the story is how they got shut down by a better singer before the cops had to get involved.' He ignored her outraged face, waved past her to where Sharon was slipping back to Mikal's side, and raised his voice to bridge the gap. 'Hey, Shar? Thanks for playing it so cool out there.'

She sent him back a thumbs-up, along with a slightly puzzled look. Rhys, who had been standing next to Mikal when she joined them in the tent, knew that Lyriam and Sharon had already spoken privately outside. This public show of appreciation could only be to make clear to the assembly of friends, fans, favoured journalists and hangers-on that he had no objection to how the matter had been handled, no matter what anyone else might think. Bethany's face was burning, and her group had gone quiet. Rhys winced and hastily moved away, looking for his sister.

He hovered at her shoulder, knowing that her own amplified awareness would have told her he was there long before he came within touching distance. She waited until the man who was talking – one of Lyriam's producers, Rhys recalled – finished a monologue about summer festivals and studio time, and then turned to pull him into the circle, slipping a hand through his arm.

'There you are. Come and help me work out what all these people are trying to talk me into.'

'Like you need help. I should be looking out for *them*.'

She chortled along with the rest, and introduced him to those he had not yet met. The producer said, 'Do you sing too, Rhys?'

'No,' Rhys replied firmly, as Gwen said, 'Yes.'

The group burst into laughter. Rhys sighed and shook his head disapprovingly at her.

'I can carry a tune if I have to,' he told the others. 'But I'm much happier listening. Gwen's the talent.'

'She certainly is,' said a narrow woman with severely cut, dyed blue hair. An agent, this one. She frowned, pencil-thin eyebrows drawn into a deep V. 'Umm . . . it hadn't occurred to me to ask . . . but when you say "talent".' She looked at Gwen. 'It *is* a gem thing, isn't it? I mean your voice, it is enhanced?'

Gwen's smile stayed fixed for a fraction of a heartbeat, then went back to warm and natural so quickly that Rhys knew only he could have spotted the surge of annoyance.

'Not that I know of,' she said sweetly. 'My range and pitch are within norm limits. I can get quite loud without losing tone, but I don't think I'd break any records.'

The woman seemed at a loss. The others in the circle fidgeted and glanced at each other. Rhys felt the firm pressure of Gwen's hand and kept his face still.

'That's fine,' said the producer, slowly. 'It's funny, how we assume— But it doesn't matter. It might even be a better story. So much engineering, but in the end it's an old-fashioned talent. A natural gift. Shining through. Hey, that's *great*.' He grinned at them. 'You mind if I take a minute to post that? Streams'll love it.'

'Go ahead,' said Gwen, as the rest of the group scrambled to concur. He flicked at his earset and began muttering, eyes down and unfocused. Subvocal dictation, state of the art. The others ostentatiously did the same, or pulled out tablets. The skinny, blue-haired norm was tapping away almost frantically.

They are all bloody sheep, Rhys thought. *If he'd said it was a problem, they'd have gone with that too.* He judged them too absorbed for the moment to notice anything in the general hubbub and slid a half-step back, disengaging his arm and grunting softly at his sister.

'Guh. R'gu om.' *Gwen. Think I'm going to go.*

She turned, holding her place in the circle, frowning as she whispered back at him. 'Ah? R'ki?' *Why? I thought you were okay?*

'Ki. Ta. R'nuloh.' *I'm fine, just tired. It's not my thing.*

'R'ki'tay.' *You might feel better if you stayed.*

Rhys shook his head. 'Nhh. R'nff.' *No, I've had enough.* The producer was finishing, eyes up now and looking at them quizzically. Gwen shot Rhys a last, fleeting scowl, eyebrow quirked in her if-that's-really-what-you-want-to-do look, and then her brow smoothed back to perfect and the smile slid onto her face as she turned back into the conversation. Rhys' own proximity sense flared and he turned too, finding Callan behind him, paused in mid-stride and looking at him in surprise.

Rhys opened his mouth, and found he had no idea what to say. He shut it again, and felt his cheeks go hot.

'Sorry,' said Callan, 'I couldn't help overhearing.' His eyes slipped over the back of Gwen's head, and lingered on Rhys' face. 'Twin-speak? I know about it, of course, but I've never heard it used.'

Rhys stared. 'You knew what that was? Oh, of course – your language ability. Most people just hear baby-talk.'

'Not me. What's the matter, are you not feeling well?' He nodded at the drink still clutched in Rhys' hand. 'That stuff's lethal.'

'I'm fine. Hang on, you *understood*? How?'

Callan shrugged. 'Cryptophasia's almost always just mispronounced words from the mother tongue, organised via a very basic syntax. Neither of those factors is much of a challenge for me. But kids usually ditch it young, or else they never learn normal language at all.'

'Da says it was all Gwen and I spoke when they found us.' Rhys found himself rubbing his free hand self-consciously over his hair, and dropped it awkwardly. 'We were only toddlers, so it took them a while to realise it wasn't just babbling. We picked up regular speech okay, but we never completely stopped using it with each other. Sorry,' he shrugged. 'Bad habit.'

'Not at all.' Callan smiled at him. 'I haven't come across a new language in seven or eight years. At *least*. And the UN sends me bloody *everything* these days.'

'Really?' They had somehow fallen into step, moving idly away from Gwen and her group. *Groupies*. Rhys tried to shrug off the dregs of his irritation and thought of setting the glass down – he hadn't really wanted the drink to begin with – then decided it gave him something to do with his hands. 'I thought you just worked with half a dozen or so main languages.'

'There aren't even that many, not any more. The essential ones are English, Mandarin, Hindi and Spanish, and Spanish is starting to fade. But so many of the world's texts have never been properly translated into any of them – even the best apps don't get the nuances right. It takes a person fluent in both, and as the language pool shrinks there're going to be fewer and fewer of us who are. If it isn't done in the next couple of generations vast amounts of literature, history, journalism will just be lost.'

'So you're translating the literary heritage of the planet?' Rhys blinked, and took a sip anyway.

'Yes. Sounds grand, doesn't it?'

'Sounds like something that'll take way more than one lifetime.'

Callan laughed. He had a rich, textured voice, just on the right side of resonant, and a warm chuckle of a laugh. 'I don't have it all to myself, fortunately. They've got a couple of others like me on the project, plus as many multilingual norms as they can scare up. But you're right, there's no way it'll all get done in time.'

'Still.' Rhys was staggered by the enormity of it. 'That entire legacy – whatever survives – will be filtered through just a few of you. You get to put your stamp on it. It must feel amazing, to know that what you do now is going to last for the whole of human history.'

'It does.' Callan's gaze slipped inward, and his expression turned thoughtful. 'It's good to hear you put it like that, though. When I'm cooped up indoors on a sunny day, translating obscure Kurdish poetry, it's easy to forget how lucky I am.' He grinned at Rhys, present again and sparkling. 'How about you, then? I have a feeling your sister is about to conquer the world through song; what are you going to be doing?'

Rhys grinned back, wondering how much was safe to share. He had just decided on a compromise when he again felt the slight pressure, like a prickling in the back of his brain, that told him someone was coming up behind; and detected the vanishingly faint spiced-musk scent and rustle of sound that told him who.

'I'll fill you in,' sidestepping away from him, 'when we're not about to be interrupted.'

'When we're what? Oh.' Callan glanced round, startled, as Aryel came up between the two of them and tucked a small, strong hand inside an elbow of each.

'Good, you haven't left yet.'

Rhys snorted. 'When did Gwen find time to tell you I was going? What with the fan club and all.'

For once she looked surprised. 'You—? I didn't mean you, I thought Callan was getting ready to slip out. And don't be snarky about Gwen, she earned it.' Aryel's voice lowered and filled with concern. 'Are you all right?'

'*Fine.*'

'Oh. Okay, then.' She cocked a reproving eyebrow at him. 'Well, it's about you anyway so I'm glad you're together. Callan, are you around in the morning? I was going to take Rhys down to meet Herran, but I've just had a message. There's somewhere else I need to be.'

'You want me to introduce them? Sure.' Nodding over her head to Rhys. 'Whenever you like.'

'Thanks.' He looked down at Aryel. 'I still don't understand why I can't just knock on his door, though. It's not like we don't know each other. We're not just stream-friends, we're friend friends.'

'Don't I know it, after that stunt he pulled with the alarms.' She sighed, and glanced at Callan. 'It must seem unnecessary given how close you already are, but . . .'

Callan was nodding agreement. 'You'll understand when you meet him,' he told Rhys. 'Herran interacts much more easily, more naturally, onstream than he does in person. There is a . . . pattern to communicating with him in the physical world that has to be followed. It can take him a long time to get comfortable with someone who's standing next to him, and no time at all if they're onstream. It shouldn't be a problem for you, though, since you already have a relationship.'

'Rhys will pick up his cues very fast,' said Aryel. 'I think it'll take five minutes. But you still need a gatekeeper to get you started.'

'It's no problem. I was going to drop in and see him after breakfast anyway.' Callan looked from Rhys to Aryel, the corner of his mouth twitching as though he might be about to break into that warm laugh again. He had been so reserved when he joined them at the concert, almost morose, and then there had been the flash of anger at the Reversionist antics. He had looked too stern to be handsome. But after the music and merriment and a couple of drinks his face had relaxed, was amused and open and very, very beautiful.

He smiled down at Aryel. 'And you're right, as usual. I was about to head home, but then I ran into Rhys instead. So if you want to go soon,' glancing back to Rhys, green eyes catching the light like emeralds, 'I'm ready any time.'

Aryel watched them leave, keeping her own smile sedate, aware that too many onlookers might read too much into it. If his name cropped up in the river of gossip no doubt already flooding out of the evening and onto the streams, Rhys would be mortified. She turned briskly away from the entrance to find that Reginald stood next to her. His own grin was unabashed.

'Well, *that* was quick.'

'Stop it.'

'Oh, please. They were checking each other out before we even got in here.'

'They didn't know they were. At least, I'm pretty sure Rhys didn't. Maybe not Callan either. He's been out of circulation for a long time.'

'So? Stuff happens, whether you're aware of it at the time or not. I'll place a wager on them getting the *circulation* going' – he waggled pantomime eyebrows at her – 'before the week is out. Maybe before the evening's out. What odds are you offering?'

'They're just two young men, walking home on a balmy, moonlit night.' She could not help grinning back at him. 'What could happen?'

'With any luck, a great deal. He needs it.' He appraised her, squinting down his nose. 'I should see if I can't find someone to see *you* home.'

'What'll you do, strap them to a kite?'

'That's a piss-poor excuse to spend your life alone, Aryel.'

'Reginald. My dear Da. Can you imagine the uproar? What this . . . circus . . . would turn into?' She refrained from waving at the room, instead letting her gaze slide absently around it, and back to him. 'My life is complicated enough.'

'He could deal with the complications. More importantly, he *would*.'

'Who would?'

'Don't be coy, girl. You know who.' The bushy eyebrows now arched in the direction of Eli Walker, on the far side of the marquee and listening with every appearance of interest to a commentator from one of the more breathless socialstreams. 'Do you a world of good.'

'It wouldn't do him any.' There was steel in her voice, and

Reginald knew he had finally gone right up to the edge, and possibly slightly over it. 'I've already asked a great deal of him, and I may have to ask more, but I'll neither lie to him nor tell him the truth he wants to know. Not if I can possibly help it. I won't risk the damage to us both.'

DIVERGENCE

There is a moment when she understands that she is different.

She is still very, very small when she knows this, but she is already aware of disparity. She knows that the men and women who care for her, who feed her and bathe her and dress her in clothes poorly adapted for her awkward anatomy, who have gentle voices and kind eyes under brightly glowing hair, are not the same as the ones who instruct them, with their crisp tones and sharp glances. Those ones wear shiny white coats, and their hair does not glow.

Under the coats their clothing varies, and she glimpses different iterations of skirt and suit and boot. Her carers all wear the same shapeless, grey-drab trousers and loose tops, much like her own. But the gap between the carers and the others is not a matter just of clothing or hair colour or even their roles as servants and served. There is something missing from the warmth of those gentle men and women, from the affection she longs for and looks forward to. There is a dullness about the eyes below that brilliant hair. The kindness is real but somehow empty, shallow. Their awareness seems far less acute than hers. They teach her to speak, simple words repeated over and over, and she knows, with a frustration that causes her sometimes to ball her little hands into fists and scream at them in her fury, that she could learn so much more, *so much* faster, *than they are capable of teaching.*

The others watch.

They have more words, those others, and she would like to learn them. Their gaze is as quick and inquisitive as her own, and there is a certainty about them, a confidence in the way they come and go and move and speak, that she is drawn to. But they are testers, not teachers, and they rarely smile or speak to her directly. Mostly they take her to the cold place, where everything is as shiny and flat as their coats, and she is undressed and measured and probed and scanned and twisted and spread and stretched. Some days it hurts, and when she cannot help but cry they call in one of the attendants, a large woman with hair called 'orange' or a thin man topped by 'purple' to comfort her.

So she understands difference, but it takes a particular day for her to understand it in relation to herself. It is a day when they have detoured through the room where they keep the other children. There are four. (She knows this because the orange woman has recently taught her her numbers, first to five, then when she insisted on more, to ten. She could see them stretching on and on in her mind and she wanted to be given the names of all of them, but the orange woman seemed to know no more, and she grew angry and cried, and the orange woman cried, and there were no more numbers.)

Two of the children seem to be asleep, eyes closed beneath the clear plastic hoods of their cots. One twitches and makes muffled mewling noises, through a mouth pinched into a strangely sharp projection. The skin of her back is distended, and beneath it things like cables seem to curl around and about each other in a tangled, terrifying mass. Some days her eyes are open, and then she is propped into a sitting position in her cot; but they are never aware. She has no arms.

The other is still and silent, save for the muffled hiss from the tubes that go into his nose and mouth. His arms and legs are shrunken and twisted, curled into his chest; but his shoulder blades are massive, sharp edges pressing triangles through the skin. More tubes emerge from beneath the blanket that covers him to the waist. She has never seen him otherwise, and his eyes never open.

The other children are awake and out of their cots. One has a sweet, vacant face. There are little flaps for arms this time, and a body that ends abruptly at the hips. She smiles without comprehension when she sees them. The fourth child does seem to understand something, though it is hard to be sure since the face is almost nonexistent. Round blue eyes stare at them over gaps that might be a nose and mouth. That one is able to walk, though his spine is painfully twisted, but they are both strapped into pushchairs for the short trip to the testing room, and the purple man and a white-coat woman are waiting to do the pushing.

The senior white-coat who is taking her today stops and looks them over. His gaze travels across the hissing cots, and then he looks down at her and shakes his head.

'What makes you so bloody special?' he says, in that tone they sometimes use where they don't really expect an answer. He squats down in front of her suddenly, eye to eye, frowning.

She frowns back.

'If it weren't for you we could have shut the whole batch down by now.' He sounds angry. 'But no, we have to keep at it until we work out how the hell we came up with you. You are the fucking anomaly. We can't even manage to fucking replicate you, so I don't see the point.'

'Ano-ma-lee,' she says carefully, hoping he will explain. He blinks at her, a jolt of surprise crossing his face, and then he stands abruptly and they proceed along bright white corridors where sounds fall dull, and into the testing room. She turns what he said around and around, trying to grasp the meaning, trying to fill in the words she doesn't understand with tone and gesture, trying to connect them to something she does understand.

Things are beginning to shift. She can feel it, and it scares her. It scares her so much she wants nothing more than to give up and cry, but she knows that will not help. It will only confuse and exhaust her, and she senses a *potential in the moment that should not be wasted. So she swallows it down, and waits until they have put the sensor pads in place all over her head and shoulders and back, and the white-coat is standing beside her starting to press buttons on the machine, and then she grabs his sleeve and tugs hard.*

'Dok-tor Ow-wen.'

He turns and stares down at her, his face blank with astonishment. She hears the gasps and murmurs from the other white-coats, but she keeps her eyes fixed on him.

'You.' His face is still slack. 'You know my name?'

She lets go of his sleeve and points to the other children, hooked up as she is, waiting. She feels urgent, as though understanding is both close and crucial. As though everything depends on it.

She asks a question to which she already, in that moment, knows the answer.

'Wike dem?' she says. 'Awwel wike dem?'

He squats down in front of her again then, and the customary distaste in his face and voice have been replaced by something else.

'No, Aryel, you are not like them. You are not like anything.'

PROPOSITION

7

The city wheeled below her. She could see pigeons flee for the safety of ledges as they sensed her shadow. Crows peeled up for a closer look, then decided that whatever she was, she posed no threat. This high up the cars and people on the teeming summer streets were no more than specks, and she could take in the tapestry of the city: a chaotic matrix of pale roads dividing the uneven grey of roofscapes from green strips of parkland, punctuated by glistening towers that thrust up into her domain. She glided lazily between them, riding a warm current of air, enjoying the heat that beat down on her barely moving wings. She held the glide for as long as she could before shifting regretfully into a slow, graceful bank that took her left towards an elegant spear of black glass. To her right the brooding steel spike of Newhope slipped behind and out of view.

The bullet-shaped apex of the Bel'Natur building was blunted at the tip, a landing pad intended for the more brutal aerodynamic power of an executive helicopter. She beat hard for a moment to clear the currents that swirled around the tapering tower, then swept her wings back and dropped in from the top.

There were only two in the greeting party, and she silently acknowledged the contradiction of being both pleased to be able to touch down without the usual gawking audience, and knowing it was more likely that staff had not been told of her visit, or were forbidden to witness it, than native uninterest. One of the people waiting for her was a blocky, middle-aged man with lines deeply etched into his face, dressed in a discreet black uniform. His impassive expression slipped for just a moment as he watched her land, and then he flicked a sideways glance at his companion and pulled the mask of professional indifference back into place.

The other was Zavcka Klist.

She watched until Aryel had folded her wings and brushed back a stray strand of hair, as if waiting for confirmation that her visitor had given up the air and become earthbound once again. Then she stepped forward, hand out, crisp and formal.

'Ms Morningstar. Thank you for coming.'

Aryel met her eyes, a grey as dark as smoke. As she took the proffered hand she wondered fleetingly if Zavcka would indulge in the childish spite of squeezing too hard. Instead the handshake was as firm, brisk and brief as her own.

'Ms Klist.' She let the corner of her mouth kink up in time with an ironically raised eyebrow. 'Thank you for inviting me.'

Zavcka's face twitched in response, but she accepted the polite fiction gracefully. 'Shall we go inside to talk? It's a bit windy up here.' She glanced at the silent man, standing a couple of paces back with hands clasped loosely behind him, and added, 'For some of us. If you'd prefer to stay outside that's fine.'

'It's windy for all of us. By all means let's go in.' She thought she caught a flicker of surprise, heard it confirmed in the guard's grunt of approval. Perhaps they had expected her to insist on remaining in the open; if so he would have been unhappy at the thought of leaving his employer unprotected up here. So Zavcka had probably already made it clear that she would be speaking with Aryel Morningstar alone.

As it was the man busied himself with a state-of-the-art identipad that combined finger and retinal scans, and a heavy steel door slid noiselessly back. It looked new, and she thought with amusement as Zavcka ushered her through that they might well have installed it specifically to keep her out.

A short, plushly carpeted corridor led directly to the lift shaft that formed the spine of the building. The man, still unintroduced, stood back to let them enter and looked a question at his boss.

'Thank you, Dunmore. That'll be all for now,' she said, and he stepped back to let the door slide shut on the two women. Alone together for the first time, they regarded each other over folded arms. It took Zavcka a moment to register the shared pose, and she dropped hers to her side. Aryel rewarded her with a faint smile, and stayed as she was.

Zavcka cleared her throat. 'Dunmore is our head of security. He was doubtful about asking you to meet here.'

'Did he imagine I would be a threat?'

'More that you might imagine yourself to be threatened. He tells me there are still gems who fear being disappeared, were they to venture within the walls of a gemtech. An outdated worry if ever there was one. I see I was right to think you wouldn't ascribe to it.'

'Indeed.' Aryel nodded seriously. 'There is also the fact that half of London just watched me land on your rooftop. So no, I'm not worried at all.'

Zavcka's nostrils flared. Aryel smiled at her sweetly. There was a soft chime and the doors swept open. Zavcka said, 'Here we are,' in a tone that, while still impeccably polite, had turned terse.

They stepped into a luxurious lobby, only a couple of floors below the roof level. It swept out on either side of them to the curving glass walls of the building, which let in panoramic views of the city below. Aryel could see that the expansiveness of the room extended into perimeter walkways which appeared to run around the entire circumference of the tower.

Zavcka walked straight ahead, however, towards another corridor which cut through the heart of the building, and was lined with more of the beautifully biocrafted wood panelling that formed the back wall of the lobby. A reception desk guarded it, manned by a fashionable young woman whose poise appeared ready to dissipate when she saw Aryel. She half stood, then sat back down again, and belatedly shut her gaping mouth with a snap as she looked from Aryel to Zavcka. An equally fashionable young man turned with exaggerated casualness from, Aryel was quite certain, only pretending to speak to the girl as he leaned against the desk. He seemed better prepared, smiling and inclining his head graciously to them both.

Just then two more people strolled into the lobby, feigning startled looks that, as always, became genuine wonder within a microsecond. They seemed not to have planned what to do once they'd got their eyeful, and Zavcka glared at them balefully as they paused in confusion and then proceeded hastily across the lobby to disappear into one of the walkways. A high-pitched, slightly hysterical giggle sounded from that direction, swiftly muffled.

The fashionable man shot a disapproving look after them, as Zavcka snapped at the girl.

'Ms Morningstar and I will be in my office. Please see to it we're not disturbed.'

She nodded, speechless and scared. There was a spark of something defiant in the man's eyes, but his tone was pure deference as he said, 'Can I get you anything, ma'am?'

Zavcka managed to suppress an irritated sigh. She had not, Aryel thought, intended to be quite so hospitable.

'Coffee for me, Khan. Ms Morningstar?'

'Tea, please.'

She flashed a smile at the two employees as she followed Zavcka

82

into the corridor, partly for the effect she knew it would have, partly in real sympathy. Without turning around the Bel'Natur head said, 'I do apologise. I can't imagine what my staff are thinking of.'

'I can. Shall I tell you?'

Zavcka glanced back at her, frowning. 'Please.'

'They're thinking that while you'll be displeased, you're unlikely to dismiss or even really discipline them merely for happening to be in the lobby when I happen to walk through it. And that getting that close a look at me is worth the risk.'

They had reached the end of the corridor. Zavcka looked narrowly at Aryel as she raised her fingers to an identipad. 'You seem quite certain of your effect on them.'

'Sadly, I'm used to it.'

The door slid open as smoothly as had the one on the roof, and Aryel stepped into an office almost as big as the lobby they had left behind. The skywalk did not run all the way around the building after all; the rear wall was a sweeping curve of glass-barred sky. Zavcka glanced at the huge biocrafted wood desk and the straight-backed chairs before it, then appeared to make a decision. She led the way instead to a scattering of soft leather furniture and sank onto a sofa. Aryel selected a low armchair that her wings could rest over the back of. Thus raised and arched they were potent, almost a presence of their own as they shifted with her movement.

Zavcka watched her settle, elbow propped on the arm of the sofa, chin on fist. She looked deeply reflective suddenly, as though considering the import of Aryel's words, but there was still something avid in her gaze.

'Yes, I expect you are. But do you really regret your celebrity?'

'Given the circumstances that led to it,' Aryel said evenly, 'it's a small price to pay. But would I have preferred other circumstances, ones that would have allowed me to remain fairly anonymous? Yes, and for far greater reasons than my own privacy.'

That was cutting very close to the bone. Aryel watched her reaction keenly. Zavcka could hardly have expected less, not on this subject, but she still looked away. It was almost a flinch of embarrassment.

'I . . . of course. The circumstances were shocking. A horrendous loss of life.'

Aryel wondered for an astounded moment if it was an oblique apology; if Zavcka Klist really intended, really had the *nerve*, to sit here and offer condolences for those bloodstained days. She thought of Callan and all he had lost; of the damage to Bal and Gaela and Gabriel, and the friends they had had to bury. Her mind finally fixed on Donal, another battle-scarred survivor, and imagined the abuse he would be screaming if only he could hear this conversation. She held on to the picture, channelling her own anger into her mental image of his, and felt it leave her calm, cool, clear-headed. It was a trick Reginald had taught her, long ago.

Zavcka was back to her own cool stare, as though awaiting a response. Aryel sat and stared back, letting the tension build, until there was a soft tap at the door. Khan came in, busied himself pouring and serving, and departed with evident regret. Zavcka regarded Aryel over the rim of her cup, and began without further preamble.

'You must have inferred that my offer to Herran has to do with our infotech programme.'

Aryel sipped before answering. The tea was good, hot and strong. 'We did. Although neither Herran nor I could infer quite what you had in mind. Or why you would imagine he would consent to helping you.'

'Let's deal with the *what* first. I believe the *why* will become evident.'

A touch there of the old arrogance. She was onto more comfortable ground, now. Never look back, eh, Zavcka? The past is another country, a big one, full of peril. If you keep moving forward fast enough maybe it won't catch up with you.

'Virtually all of our current infotech applications require a manual interface,' said Zavcka. 'The most common technologies – tablets, security systems, aircraft and ground vehicles – all of them rely on us to transmit our instructions via some intermediate mechanism like touchscreen or audio input or motion-capture. That requirement is a fundamental limitation.'

She looked at Aryel as if anticipating disagreement. Aryel sipped her tea and said nothing.

'We think we should be able to do away with most of the intermediate hardware, if we can work out how to set up a direct neural link.'

She paused again, expectantly, and Aryel shrugged. 'I assumed as much from your announcement. But you'd still need an interface.'

'We've made great progress there already – we're working on a cranial band that's as light and unobtrusive as an earset. You'd simply think it on, do what you want to do, and think it off again. You could work on the fly, as it were.'

Aryel managed to smile at the pun. 'I rather like not working while flying. As it were. What does this have to do with Herran?'

'Ah.' Zavcka nodded. 'Well. Herran is, as we both know, very special. The core challenge of the work I've just described is the accurate translation of detailed information between binary code and synaptic signalling. And we're pretty sure that Herran is as close to a walking digital–neural dictionary as has ever been.'

'And you think that because?'

Zavcka's lips compressed. Aryel sensed that another flash of temper, like the one she'd seen out in the lobby, was being firmly suppressed.

'Let's be candid with each other, shall we? I think we both know that Herran can access and alter data in ways that no human – gem or norm – should be capable of. In retrospect I suppose it's not all that surprising. He was designed to test the thesis that the human brain could be rewired to mimic an artificial processor. Why you would *want* to change the most subtle and powerful computing device known to humanity into something fundamentally inferior is another question entirely, and part of the reason the programme was cancelled. But we know that Herran had by far the most promising test profile. What he didn't appear to have – then – was anything remotely like normal human cognition, although it now seems his handlers simply didn't recognise his full range of competence. I suppose you know that his . . . departure . . . coincided with a mysterious failure at every level of a complex security protocol, from the sequential disabling of locks and alarms to unauthorised changes in the guard rota.'

She paused for breath and to glare at Aryel, who was smiling gently.

'There was no trace of how that was accomplished. Nothing in the edit logs, no sign of a hack. The forensics team had never seen anything like it. Until three years ago, when they reported to me on how you had apparently hacked a datastream within this company that was so secret and so encrypted only a handful of people even knew of its existence.'

She held up a hand, though Aryel had made no move to speak. 'I've no quarrel with you over the information you accessed, but I wanted to know how you'd done it. And they couldn't tell me. Once again there was no trace. But at least this time they'd seen something like it before. So we looked for what the two events had in common, and the most probable answer was Herran.'

Aryel regarded her for a moment, then put her empty cup down on the low table with a clink. 'That is all very interesting. It doesn't explain precisely what you want Herran to do for you, or why you expect him to agree.'

'We want him to help us. He's got a brain that speaks binary as well as human. We want to work out how he does it, so we can create a translation matrix to replicate it. We won't harm him in any way, or make the process at all unpleasant for him. I said it would be rewarding, and I meant it. We'll pay extremely well for his services.'

'Herran doesn't care about money. He has what he needs. He particularly won't care about helping you make more of it.'

Zavcka nodded briskly to show she had expected this answer. 'At the moment, what we've deduced about his abilities is known only to me and a few of my most senior staff. At the moment, we have no intention of revealing that information to anyone else. Which is fortunate, don't you think? The consternation there would be at the thought of a gem who can infiltrate any data, news or social-stream undetected, find out *anything*, alter *anything*, create *anything*, and leave no trail whatsoever would be – well, it doesn't bear thinking about. The gemtech argument for registration and control of potentially dangerous gems would be back from the dead.'

'That,' said Aryel softly, 'was your argument.'

'It was. It isn't any longer, but there are plenty of others still carrying the flag. And while some people might be comforted by the notion that his expeditions within the streams are likely directed by you, many, I suggest to you, will not be. They'll finally have a credible reason to be suspicious of *you*. They'll wonder who else you've had him spy on. They'll wonder whether Herran, who Bel'Natur records suggest is severely autistic and probably incapable of moral judgement, goes off exploring without your guidance. They'll want him controlled and cut off.'

Aryel leaned back in the chair and resisted the urge to flex her wings in irritation. Instead she looked thoughtfully around the room.

'Was this Felix Carrington's office?'

Zavcka blinked in surprise at the non sequitur. 'It was, yes.'

'It suits you very well.' She caught Zavcka's eyes. Her own had gone hard as an August sky. 'That secret datastream you referred to earlier. Surprising how few other people *did* know about it. The only subscribers besides Carrington had already disappeared or been incarcerated. Of course that's not what *he* said at the trial. He mentioned your name quite a lot.'

The other woman was watching her with a sort of intense calm. There was a note of practised boredom in her tone. 'By then he was trying to implicate anyone he could. Personally, I think he'd become delusional. You know very well there was no evidence in the files you accessed, nor in what the prosecution forensics uncovered later, to suggest I knew anything about it.'

'That's not quite right.' Aryel shook her head gravely. 'The forensics report represents the best efforts of the investigating officers. The files I released represent *my* best judgement. Which is open to revision.'

She paused just long enough to let the meaning come clear, and watched Zavcka's eyes widen and her relaxed posture become rigid.

Then she went on, quiet and relentless, 'What you have to consider, Ms Klist, is that if Herran is capable of everything you claim, one must assume – as indeed you've suggested the public *would* assume – that there are other things he will have discovered as well. And if he is indeed my datastream spy and fixer, it would stand to reason that anything he knows, I know. Your own skills are remarkable; I'm not surprised the authorities failed to pick up your trail. Herran is, as you say, in a different league.'

Zavcka fought for composure, staring back at her like a cornered cat. 'I don't believe you.'

'No?'

'No. If you had found anything to implicate me in the Gabriel affair you'd have included it. I'd be in prison too. You have no reason to protect me.'

'True. You are merely a beneficiary of the situation you outlined a moment ago. If I exposed something the authorities couldn't corroborate independently I'd have to prove that I hadn't simply invented it. And how could I have done that?'

'By . . . oh. You couldn't have explained without bringing Herran into it. Of course.'

Zavcka sat back and drew a deep breath, calming herself, although her nails clicked unconsciously against the arm of the sofa and a tic appeared to ghost across her pale face. The dark eyes were bitter, and Aryel could see the fear flickering behind them. But her voice was steady as she finally said, 'Well. We appear to have achieved a stalemate.'

She looked around the office, as though a way out might appear.

Aryel looked past her, at the wide sky beyond the glass, and longed to be gone. She sighed. 'Yes, but all that means is neither of us can threaten the other into anything. Which is as it should be. I have plenty of reasons to doubt your integrity, but you now have a reason to exercise some. I'll talk to Herran about the project and your offer, and see what he says. It's not for me to decide whether he takes you up on it.'

'Isn't it?'

'No it isn't. I don't have servants or staff, Ms Klist. I have friends.' That did produce a flinch. It was, Aryel thought, the very least she deserved. 'But we had better be clear right now that, in the unlikely event he agrees to work with you, there are going to be conditions.'

8

Sharon Varsi pressed three fingers to an identipad and announced herself, once again running the morning's briefing on the first full day of the Festival over in her head. Everything had run fairly smoothly so far, and if the ragtag troupe from the night before was the worst they'd have to deal with the Met could count themselves fortunate. She could not think what else this summons might be about. The door slid back, and she stepped inside.

The man who had asked to see her was rising from his chair, swinging the tablet on its angled stand to the side, although his eyes still lingered for a moment on whatever he had been reading there. Commander Masoud of the Metropolitan Police shook her hand.

'DI Varsi. All right?'

'Very good, thank you, sir.'

He waved her to a seat. 'How's it going?'

'The Festival? It's early days of course, sir, but there've been no real problems yet. A few hackbot swipes at the infostream, a couple of noise complaints. The usual. There was a disturbance at the concert last night that's got some attention.' Might as well be the one to bring it up. 'The speakers were hacked for a couple of minutes. It was sorted out fairly quickly.'

He looked amused. 'I've seen that onstream, along with your report of the incident. Very well handled, I have to say.'

'I wish I could take the credit, sir. By the time I got to them it was pretty much over and done with.'

'The young woman who faced them down. Friend of the family?'

'In a manner of speaking, though we'd only just met. She's Reginald Morgan's foster daughter.' Sharon wondered if, despite his overall tone of approval, Masoud had called her in to have a word about allowing Gwen to confront the Reversionists. 'By rights it should have been left to the professionals – I told her so, after – but she reacted *very* quickly. By the time I realised what she was going to do, she'd already done it. I thought it best to let her finish the song, rather than disrupt the event further.'

'Mmm. Well.' Masoud gestured vaguely, dismissing her concern. 'You're right of course, though I got the feeling, watching, that she could probably handle herself. And she made them look ridiculous, which is more than we could have managed without blowback from the public. Any worry about repercussions?'

'You mean to her? No, I don't think so. Not from them anyway. They were gobsmacked, but they didn't seem to mind her being a gem. I don't think they're serious troublemakers.'

'But they are Reversionists.'

'Yes, but they're also devout UC – more focused on piety than politics. Which is a good thing, I reckon, or their little stunt might not have been such a shambles. They went on and on about reviving what they called a culture of faith, but they don't seem to be on the bandwagon of returning to a pre-Syndrome evolutionary model.' She shrugged. 'One of them recognised me, but they didn't have a go. The more militant groups would have.'

'I suppose.' He gave her an appraising look. 'Are you still getting a lot of that?'

'Not so much any more, sir. It flares up from time to time.'

'Including here?'

She kept her face carefully impassive. 'You mean at work, sir?'

'Yes, at work. I know not all of your colleagues have been as supportive as they should.'

That's a bloody understatement. It took her back, unbidden, to the early days of her and Mikal's courtship. At first the long hours she was known to spend in the Squats were put down to an admirable sense of duty, and understandable guilt for a massacre she had been unable to prevent. But it had dawned soon enough on her workmates that there was far more to her time with him than could be explained away by mere police work, and the whispers had started. They said she'd had her head turned, gone native, got kinks most folk could barely imagine and no norm would accommodate. Forgotten she was supposed to be doing the job and instead let the job do her. Lost the plot, along with any sense of propriety or chance of promotion. Some of the worst comments had come from people she'd known since her academy days, and worked with side by side ever since.

She kept it from Mikal as long as she could, and laughed it off when he found out; knowing him well enough already to have no doubt that if he understood how bad it was before he understood how tough *she* was, he would walk away rather than let her go through it. And even she had not been entirely sure at first that she was tough enough. It cut her to her soul to find herself suddenly so doubted and disdained in a job she loved and was good at. She would go to him then, dazed with the hurt of it, as though to discover once more what could possibly be worth such damage; and in his warmth and wit and courage, the cleverness of his mind and gentleness of his hands and a resilience of character to match her own, find again the answer. She remembered the day she had set herself the task of deciding which she was most prepared to give up, her police career or him; and concluded in half a heartbeat that she could, and would, do neither.

Aloud she said, 'There was a lot of surprise when I married Mikal, but they've had a couple of years to get used to the idea. Plus he's in the Council now. People have got over it, I think.'

When we have kids, she thought suddenly, it will be back and it will be bad. She pushed the certainty away, tamping it down firmly.

Masoud seemed to catch the edge of brisk dismissal in her tone. He echoed it as he said, 'Good. It goes without saying, you can come to me if things ever get out of hand.'

He glanced back at the tablet. 'Something's come up that needs looking into. I'll be honest, I'm not sure at this stage whether it's going to warrant a full investigation or not, but it's potentially very sensitive and it would benefit from someone with your insight. With the Festival so well in hand I thought you might like to take a crack at it.' He lifted the tablet off the stand and handed it to her. 'See what you think.'

She took it and started to scan, then looked back up at him almost immediately. 'This is from a whistleblower? Any corroboration?'

'Only what was attached. Keep reading.'

It was a short but typically convoluted claim, and she could feel herself frowning as she mentally unravelled the gist of the allegation. She tapped the links to the screenshots that had been provided as proof. They proved nothing, but she could understand Masoud's concern. She returned to the whistleblower's fractured prose, reread a couple of lines, and handed the tablet back.

He was watching her face. 'Well?'

'I'd be very happy to look into it, sir. Thank you for thinking of me.'

He sighed. 'Sharon, you are such a proper bloody cop you make

93

me want to scream. There's no review board here. Tell me what you think.'

'I think—' She considered again what she'd read. 'I think half of what they're claiming is – was – so commonplace it hardly seems worth bothering about at this point. The other half is both very serious and extremely unlikely. My understanding is that security around the central genestock archive is very tight. If there was a breach it should have triggered an urgent, official report. So on the whole the allegation looks dubious.' She paused, working through it. 'Which means that, if it *is* true, then we have three very serious problems. First, who would want this material and what might they do with it? Second, how were they able to break security to get it? And third, why are we only learning about the theft via a whistleblower?'

Masoud was nodding. 'My concerns exactly. Which is why I want someone sensible, who understands the ramifications, to determine whether there's anything to it. It could turn out to be a waste of time. Most whistleblowers are just delusional ex-employees with an axe to grind.'

'I know, sir.' She paused. 'But there's something about this, don't you think? In amongst all of the guff, it feels sort of . . . tangible.'

'I thought so too. I hope I'm wrong.' His fingers slipped across the tablet. 'I'm transferring it to you for follow-up, with a resource allocation. Find out what you can as quickly as you can. And quietly.' He looked up. 'I won't say I don't expect you to mention it to your husband—'

'Of course not, sir—'

'—because I do expect you to.' Sharon blinked at him in surprise. 'I'm not naïve enough to think otherwise, and I understand that his input might be helpful. I'm sure Mikal will be just as aware of the potential fallout from this as you or me.'

He detached a memtab and handed it to her. 'Give him my best, won't you?'

She took the memtab, slipped it onto an intake port on her own tablet. She felt a shiver down her spine as she stood up, as if the tiny, malleable chit of file memory were somehow infectious. 'Be happy to, sir.'

She spent an hour closely reading the file, committing the details to memory and cross-checking what she could against police and public records. The exercise left her feeling no easier.

Genetype hacks had not been uncommon in the old days of intense competition and industrial espionage between gemtechs. Genestock thefts were a different matter. Closely guarded, traded only rarely and at great expense, genestock was the stuff of engineered life itself. A few shadowy tales of internecine robberies and slick substitutions had circulated back in the days before the Declaration; she'd heard them as a young officer, filtering into the post-shift pub gossip via those who'd left the force to work corporate security. But that was before the creation of human beings for profit had been outlawed, and all genestock confiscated by the federated governments. Emancipation had made it both commercially valueless, and virtually inaccessible.

So, at any rate, went the theory.

She pondered the alleged link between the alleged hacks and the alleged heist, hoping to spot some glaring inconsistency that would allow her to dismiss the whole thing with a clear conscience. The more she picked through it the further away that prospect drifted. She checked again for any clue as to who the whistleblower was, but he – or she – had chosen anonymity, and been careful to follow all the protocols that would keep their identity secret even from the police. So, no way of making a judgement based on the credibility of the source. All she knew was that the report had, indeed, originated from behind the firewall of the European Gene-stock Archive.

There were risks to going in hard, not least the blowback if it all proved a false alarm, or, worse yet, a hoax. But if the story was true, too soft an approach might give the perpetrator time to cover their tracks, or to flee. She considered the probabilities there, calculating the least worst option, and fleetingly thought a curse at Masoud. Then she flicked her tablet awake, and began the laborious process of requesting a warrant.

INHERITANCE

He is old and she is still young when they realise that something is wrong.

They did not think it possible at first. Her birthright had been a blessing, a triumph. Its extent was unknown, its implications unclear, but the potential! The power! She feels like the princess she has always known she is, he like the mage he has always dreamt of being. They keep it a secret while they try to understand how it works and whether it will last, though she must sometimes suppress the impulse to throw it in the faces of spiteful friends and inconstant suitors.

Later on she has cause to be grateful for her father's stern admonitions never to indulge so petty a whim.

But that is after he is gone and she is left, as he feared, to make her way in the world alone. Before that they have many years together; more than enough time for him to comprehend, with growing dismay, the consequences of his legacy.

He promises to fix it. He will mend what is broken, he will make it right. He has the knowledge and the resources, his best people are on it – though they themselves do not really understand what it is they are tasked with. That does not matter because he does understand, and he is brilliant, and he will pull the disparate pieces together and find a solution.

He does not.

At the end there are moments when he turns bitter, and jealous, and rages at her youth and strength and beauty. Then he weeps, and is full of apology and sorrow. Then the pain takes him and he wishes again for what she has. She would share it if she could, gladly, though the slow years of his ageing and the indignity of his death slay in her any desire to relinquish it completely. When his eyes turn dark and he leaves for the last time, she can feel only relief that she will not know the same fate.

9

Rhys sat on the stool, trying to make sense of what Herran was telling him. At the edge of his vision he could just see Callan, lounging on a worn, comfortable-looking chairbag, and he found he was having to work hard not to be distracted.

'Parse streams,' said Herran again, patiently. 'Little bits, lots and lots of little bits. I do,' he shrugged. 'Not easy, not too hard. Okay. You do, lots and lots of work. Not get sick.'

'Ri-ight,' Rhys said slowly, looking again at the auxiliary screens where Herran was demonstrating his recommendation. 'So you drop behind the output to the machine code, and drop behind *that* to the base code, and read the output in binary. In real time? Herran, that's unbelievable.'

Herran blinked and rocked a little. It appeared to be his default gesture, taking the place of smiles of acknowledgement and shakes of the head and raised eyebrows. His glowing scarlet curls twinkled. Rhys had never before given much thought to the fact that their onstream friendship had been conducted mostly by text instead of vid or voice. He was now, as Aryel had predicted, coming to terms with the challenges of direct communication.

'Believable,' Herran said. 'I do.'

'But what's the point?'

Herran just stared at him. Behind them Callan said quietly, 'Herran? Why do you parse the streams? What for?'

'To see,' Herran replied promptly. 'Sometimes fix.' He glanced at Callan. 'Only if Aryel says okay. Promise.'

'To fix?' asked Rhys, feeling as if the thing he had just about grasped was slipping out of his reach again. 'Fix what?'

'Let's leave the fixing alone for a minute.' Callan sat up on the chairbag. 'The point is that Herran mostly parses the streams, as he puts it, just for fun. He likes to process the same information in different formats. Doesn't really matter what the information is. Have I got that right, Herran?'

Emphatic nod-rocking. 'Fun. Lots to see.'

'For instance, he's been quite taken with the light sculpture informatics they've put up for the Festival. Not the displays them-selves – he hasn't been to see them – but the datastreams that carry the content. He spends ages hacking the feeds and disaggre-gating them.'

'Not ages,' said Herran. 'Quick quick.'

'Why bother?' said Rhys. 'Once you get into the base code the information is still the same.'

'Yes, but transmitting it that way requires a far more compli-cated algorithm than 2D or even 3D fixed geometry, and that's what Herran finds fun. It's not the information itself but the data-form that conveys it that he likes to drill down into.'

'So—' said Rhys. He had turned on the stool so he could see both of them without squinting. '—so he processes all this information, but he's mostly not concerned with its meaning? Or context?'

'No,' said Callan.

'Mostly not important,' said Herran.

Callan chuckled. 'When Bel'Natur put me through primary lan-guage training they used a similar technique. They'd scroll the same text in different languages across the screen, three at a time. They'd be linguistically unrelated, so I couldn't rely on similarities to help me remember – I might get Mandarin and German and Urdu together, but never Italian and Spanish and Portuguese, for example. But the big difference between that and what Herran's suggesting is that for me, and I suspect for you, it's all *about* meaning. I wouldn't have become fluent if all I took in was the vocabulary and sentence structure. It was understanding the content that was important.'

'What was?' asked Herran.

'Understanding the content—' Rhys began, but Callan shook his head.

'No, he means what *was* the content. Different things, Herran. Most often children's stories at the beginning – twenty-one versions of "The Princess and the Pea" or "Jack Russell's Dog", all translated so that they were culturally appropriate as well as linguistically accurate. Then newstream reports, classroom lessons, stuff like that.'

'You care?'

'Not really. But it was important anyway. The content had to be coherent, to have meaning, for me to be able to grasp the form that conveys it. I know it sounds strange, but it's what my kind of brain needs in order to engage with information.'

Herran made a sound that was as close to a sigh as Rhys had heard from him. His wide, pale eyes contemplated them both.

'Rhys has brain like you?'

'Umm.' Callan looked down for a moment, smiling. His flaming hair fell forward over his face and he absentmindedly pushed it back.

Rhys felt himself swallow.

'I think Rhys' brain is a lot like mine,' Callan said slowly. The smile still played around the corners of his mouth. 'Though in some ways it's like yours too, Herran. He can process a great deal of information very quickly, just like you can. But maybe not in quite the same way.'

Herran's rocking nod seemed disappointed. 'Okay. Sorry not help.'

'What? No, you have.' Rhys waved at the screens, feeling unaccountably flushed. 'This . . . what you do . . . it's amazing.'

'No good for you. Not find genetype either. Not help.'

'No, you *have* helped, Herran. I thought maybe I'd missed something, but if even you can't find our genetypes then I know they're nowhere to be found.'

'Somewhere. Offstream.'·

Rhys shrugged. 'Maybe, but if we don't know where and we can't get to them they might as well not exist. So I have to find the answer some other way.'

'Find quick. Before get sick again.'

'For all I know, I may not ever be ill again. All this worry might be for nothing.' He kept his eyes fixed on Herran, although he could feel Callan's steady gaze from the chairbag. 'I haven't been able to work out exactly what triggers it, or even if there *is* a trigger. It sort of seems like when my brain has a lot of hard, analytical work to do – hacking, solving puzzles, whatever – I'm less likely to have an . . . episode, but I'm not sure if that isn't just coincidence. And sometimes before one comes on I feel upset, or angry, but I don't know if that causes whatever's happening in my brain, or is caused by it. Not knowing is almost worse than the thing itself. You can't imagine.'

He doesn't *imagine*, he thought to himself. It was a sudden, despairing flash of insight, and it damped the warm thrill that had gusted through him a moment before as effectively as a plunge into an icy mountain stream. *That's as hard for him as what he does would be for anyone else.* That's *what they took away.*

Herran stared back at him, impassive as ever. 'Like Syndrome?'

'I – I guess . . . it took them a long time to work out what was causing the Syndrome . . .'

Callan cleared his throat gently. That was not what Herran was asking, and they both knew it. Rhys shot a glance at Callan, knowing he should have explained more last night, wishing he did not have to explain at all. He had nurtured a giddy hope during the long walk home along the river that if he said little and stayed well there would be no need for further detail. But in the hard light of day, in the face of Herran's blunt, guileless questioning, he was forced to conclude that it would neither be possible nor fair to hide the truth of his situation.

He drew a deep breath. 'Yes and no,' he said. 'Most people who had the Syndrome had very mild symptoms to start with, but they were regular, and the damage accumulated over time. What happens to me is . . . I mean it can be, it isn't always like this . . . generally it's more . . .' He hesitated. 'More violent,' he said finally. 'It leaves me tired and achy – I can feel it when I've had a seizure, which a lot of the Syndrome patients couldn't. And it comes and goes. I'll get two attacks in a week and then none for three months. I had one a few days ago – that's why everyone was fussing so much yesterday. But when it goes, it's gone.' He spread his hands as though to demonstrate. 'I'm completely fine.'

'Are you sure?' asked Callan quietly.

'No.' He felt as though the words were being dragged out of him. 'No, not entirely. That's part of what I'm here to find out. Ari got me fast-tracked into the National Neurology Centre, and they've come up with a series of tests to try and work out what's going on.

Whether it's doing any kind of permanent damage. That doesn't start for another week, we came in early to catch the concert and because Da has stuff to do as part of the Festival. It would really help if the doctors had my genotype to look at, as well as me, but,' he sighed and shrugged, and stole another glance at Callan, who was regarding him thoughtfully from the chairbag. 'It doesn't look like that's going to happen.'

'Bad,' observed Herran. 'Need data.'

'I . . . yes, exactly.' He wondered whether it was possible to truly convey his frustration to someone whose emotions had mostly been excised. 'It would be easier to deal with being ill if I knew what I was ill *with*, and how bad it might get. Is it going to stabilise, or go away, or get worse? At the moment I don't know, and I *hate* that.' Herran blinked, expressionless, but Callan was sitting up straight, elbows on knees, looking concerned. 'I hate feeling like it's just happening, and I don't understand, and I can't do anything about it. I guess the good thing is at least now I feel like I *am* doing something. Back home everyone's worried and they want to help, but they don't really get it. They keep telling me to rest.' He raked aggravated hands through his own short ruby-shimmer of hair. 'That's the *last* thing I need.'

Herran appeared to consider this. 'Gwen no?'

'Gwen knows . . .' He caught Callan about to explain, and shook his head at him. 'No, I've got it, I think. Gwen does know, she's the only other person who really understands what it's like for me, but it doesn't happen to her. We don't know why, so part of the worry is that it's just hit me first.'

'You find fix, fix for her too.'

'Maybe. If she needs it. She might not.'

Herran nodded and rocked and blinked at him. Finally he said, 'Need more work,' and turned away to the screens. Rhys watched the lines of code shift and morph for a minute, then turned back to Callan with a sigh.

'That,' he said, 'just about sums it up.'

They left Herran morosely examining the coding minutiae of a museum archive, and threaded their way through the warren of the Squats. Callan had suggested they pick up some lunch from one of the stalls on the high street and go sit by the river. Rhys' assumption that Herran would join them had been met by a blank stare from him and an emphatic shake of the head from Callan, who explained as they trotted down a flight of stairs to the ground floor.

'He doesn't understand why anyone would prefer to sit and look at the water rather than at a tablet screen. He accepts that they do, but he finds it baffling.' He glanced sideways at Rhys. 'Of course in your case you probably won't just be daydreaming like the rest of us. You'll be calculating currents based on eddy patterns, and boat speeds from triangulating the height of the wake.'

Rhys hunched his shoulders uncomfortably. 'It's not *that* bad.'

'I didn't say it was bad at all. I think it's a fascinating ability. I think it's even more fascinating that using it might actually help keep you healthy. That's the *opposite* of the Syndrome.'

'Yeah. But you know, I'm not completely certain that it really does help. I mean, I keep my brain as busy as I can and I still get . . . it. Sometimes.'

They exited Maryam House into a blaze of summer sunshine. Rhys drew a deep breath. 'Callan. Thank you for, you know, not doing a runner.' The other man turned around at that, looking mystified. 'I – I mean, you don't seem to mind.'

'Why would I mind?'

'I don't know. People do. Nobody's supposed to ever have any- thing wrong with them.' He tried to shrug carelessly, felt his shoulders tighten even further. 'Half the time I feel like some kind of deviant.'

Callan grinned at him, mischief sparkling in his eyes. 'There's deviants and deviants, Rhys. If you like . . .' He took in his companion's gloomy face and broke off, shaking his head. 'Sorry, I shouldn't joke about it. Look, whatever it is you have, it's not *you*. If you don't feel it should be the main thing that people think about when they think about you, well, I agree.'

'I can't pretend it's not a big deal right now though.'

'But that's because instead of ignoring the problem, you're trying to solve it. Right?'

'Yes . . .'

'So that's your focus, and it is completely sensible and necessary. And if I can help I will.' They swung onto the high street. 'The way I see it, at some point you'll have worked it all out, hopefully you'll have found a cure, and it'll be history. Just one small part of who you are.'

'That's the plan.'

'So what's there for anyone to mind about that?'

Rhys found himself smiling back, his spirits lifting. 'Nothing, I guess. When you put it like that. I just don't hear it put like that very often.'

They slowed down to peruse the offerings from food stalls and cafés. Callan guided them to the rear of one of the longer queues and stuck his hands in his pockets. He looked pensive, and a little sad.

'I talk a good game, Rhys,' he said quietly, as they edged forward. 'But I was almost killed a few years ago. I lost people who were close to me. It's taken a while – it's *still* taking a while – for that not to be the biggest part of *my* life.'

'Oh. I see. I mean I already knew . . . but I get it. That's why Ari was fussing over *you*.'

'That's right.' Callan's eyes were still distant. 'She doesn't need to, not any more. I, like you, am mostly fine. But I know that feeling, when you're struggling to get well. You need help but you don't want to feel like the *only* thing you are is a damaged— is someone who needs help.'

He was watching the pair at the front of the queue, a squat woman with blazing blue hair drawn up into a bun next to an older gillung man with short, deeply bowed legs who leaned against a walker, breathing heavily as he collected and paid for their food. He handed the parcels to the woman and they moved slowly off. Rhys and Callan stepped forward. Callan sighed and shook himself, and turned to Rhys. The smile was back, the melancholy gone.

'Anyway. So. I get how boring it is when all anyone asks is how you are. How's your sister?'

Rhys burst into laughter. 'She's fine.'

'Enjoying being the toast of the town?'

'I think she's trying to work out what to do with all the attention. Whatever she expected, this has exceeded it.'

'Did she come to London just to launch her singing career, or is she getting tested as well?'

'She did mostly want to go to the concert, I think, meet Lyriam and all her other onstream musician friends and see what might develop. She is going to come to the hospital with me, provide samples for comparison, although,' he shrugged as they moved up almost to the front of the queue, 'with the gender difference and no genetype for cross-matching, I'm not sure how useful that'll be.'

'And she's never had any symptoms? Does she use her abilities as much as you?'

'She uses them differently. She's not much of a hacker, but her sensory awareness is amazing. She processes sound way more than I do.'

'That's handy in a singer.'

'Yeah. We think it might have been what started her off when we were kids. Making sounds for her brain to play with, like scratching an itch.'

Callan took a moment to digest this.

'So by training herself to sing she's actually set up a feedback loop?'

'We think so.'

'And she never gets ill, and you do. It seems to me that what we've got to work out, Rhys, is what'll scratch *your* itch.'

He could think of no response to that other than the flush that washed over his cheeks. He hoped, not for the first time, that the darkness of his skin was sufficient camouflage.

The flirting had started on the way home last night, so gently he had barely registered it at first. Callan's manner seemed calibrated to let him respond in kind, or back away with no hard feelings. But once again he suddenly felt too tongue-tied and clumsy to come up with an equally witty reply. So he stayed silent while they got their sandwiches and drinks and strolled down to the quayside that served the Squats in lieu of a town square, trying to think of something to say without seeming a fool.

'Why three?' he blurted finally.

'Three what?'

'The language feeds you were talking about. The Bel'Natur training.'

'Oh. That's as many as I could process at a time without getting a headache. They'd do different sets of three, though, one after the other.' He looked at Rhys curiously. 'Why? How many do you think you could do?'

'Four or five, I reckon. Maybe six once I got into the rhythm of it.' He took in Callan's expression, and squirmed with embarrassment. 'I mean, umm, I don't know if I'd really learn them . . . I don't have your enhanced language centres, not as far as I know anyway . . .'

'We could try to find out.' Callan straddled a bench and set his food down in front of him. Rhys did the same, more slowly, watching the firebright hair tumble forward again as Callan unwrapped the packages. A real flame would have seemed pale out here in the sunshine, but the glowing red-gold mane sparkled like a jewel. Callan straightened up, shaking it back and frowning in thought as he licked his fingers. Rhys hastily bit into his own sandwich.

'Rhys. Pardon the rude question, but what were you and Gwen for?'

Long pause while he chewed and swallowed the too-large bite. Callan started in on his own lunch, watching him.

'We don't know,' Rhys said finally. 'We were rescued by Da and the others. We were only little and there'd been some kind of accident, a fire . . . I'm not sure exactly what happened, but they found us first and got us away. I know there were no records or anything, and it's not like they could ask around, not back then and especially not with them being Remnants. If word had got out that they were raising gem kids up in the mountains . . .' He shuddered. 'By the time we were older and things had got a bit better out in the world, Da and Ari tried to find out, only the gemtech had gone out of business. Ari thinks we might have been another unregistered experiment.'

'Like her.'

Rhys nodded.

'Did you come from the same place?'

'I don't think so. Ari doesn't like to talk about it, but we know she wasn't rescued, she escaped. She's thirteen or fourteen years older than us, and you know,' Rhys shrugged elaborately to indicate himself, ravaged sandwich in one hand, and rolled his eyes at the sky. 'Not much in common, is there?'

Callan laughed. 'Well, not to look at, no. But she's also very smart.'

'Da thinks she's the smartest person we know, or are ever likely to. I don't disagree. But her capabilities are still normal-spectrum. Gwen and I are something else. Like Herran.' He rubbed at a smear of mayonnaise on the corner of his mouth. 'Like you.'

'I'm mostly normal. My enhancements are very specific. You missed a spot.' He leaned forward and brushed it away, so quickly and casually that Rhys thought he might have managed not to blush. 'And Herran's alteration might be radical, but it's also specific. It seems to me that what you and Gwen have covers a broad range. Very high IQ, acute powers of observation and sensory analysis, and if the way she handled the Reversionists is anything to go by, one or two physical enhancements. Am I right?'

Rhys blinked and squirmed. 'Well, yeah. Although Da says don't assume some of it isn't just the benefits of growing up in fresh mountain air.'

'Maybe some of it is. But I'm guessing not all of it.'

'No, but that part isn't too sophisticated. Speed, strength, coordination. Standard manual labour stuff.' He shifted on the bench, considering whether to say more, and then added, 'Except for the sit-sense.'

'The what?'

'Situational awareness. We don't know what else to call it. It's not really cognitive, more like an instinct. It's how I knew Ari was coming up behind us last night. Knowing exactly where everyone is in a room, even if they're moving around.'

'Are you serious?'

Rhys bit, chewed. 'Mm-hmm.'

'Do you know who's behind you? Right now?'

He swallowed. The sandwich was very good, and almost gone. He spoke softly. 'The Recombin woman and the man with the rickety legs who were two places in front of us in the queue. They were sitting on a bench in the shade. They've finished eating now, and they've just come up to the rail. A couple of norms who were there before them are walking away towards the high street.'

Callan was staring. His eyes flicked up, looking over Rhys' shoulder at the couple leaning against the safety rail, then tracked right to follow the receding backs of the norms. They came back to Rhys' face.

'Wow.' He raised his eyebrows enquiringly. 'Anything else?'

'Not really. You already know about the night vision.'

'Oh yes. Very handy, that.' He crumpled up the empty packaging and stretched, leaned lazily back on propped arms. 'Well, that is one hell of a suite of abilities, way more than I've ever heard of anyone else having. You two must have cost a fortune. I don't know what to make of it.'

'Neither do we.'

They went quiet. Callan looked sideways, out over the river, relaxing into an elegant, indolent profile. It took Rhys a moment to follow his gaze out to the water. He could feel himself doing what he had been teased about earlier, perhaps a little more consciously than usual as his brain seized on the distraction: calculating distances and depth and angles of refraction. He knew that if he had to he could plunge into the river and swim across it at a speed that could probably only be bettered by a gillung. He felt suddenly depressed.

'Does it matter?'

'What?'

'What we were for.'

'Not to me.' It came out absently, and he could see Callan catch himself. 'Not to any of us. But if we knew, we might have a better idea of what's going on with you and how to help. Did the gemtech specialise in anything?'

'Not that we know of, but there was something very weird about the lab where they found us. Da says it was a few miles out of some village that's not even there any more. No one hardly seemed to know it existed until it burned down.'

'Not even him?'

'No, it was well outside their normal range. Too close to civilisation, especially back then. They were passing through for some reason and heard the explosion. Pure luck. Gwennie and I had got out into the woods somehow, and it was clear they weren't going to be able to help anybody else, so they grabbed us and ran. Whoever showed up after must have believed everyone had been killed, but Da kept an eye on the streams for a while just in case. That's how he found out it was owned by KAG Laboratories. As far as we can tell KAG mostly did core R&D at that point, and sold the tech on.'

He shook his head again, frustrated. 'Gwen and I searched, believe me, and so did Ari. There's almost no information on the newstream archives, no corporate datastreams we could find, no one else we've ever heard of who came out of it. KAG didn't have any gestation or crèche facilities, at least none that were registered. They were an old gemtech, they'd apparently been contracting for a long time, so it doesn't really fit. Either they were starting to expand again – we've wondered if we might have been part of the first commercial batch – or they were running this place as a black lab, outside their normal operations and under the radar of the authorities. We don't know, because the whole thing just disappeared.'

Callan frowned. 'That doesn't make sense. Whether it was sold or wound down or went bankrupt, there must be records.'

'I know. But we couldn't find any. When I realised that my genetype might be really important, I hacked every datastream I could. Drew a blank, so I asked Herran if he had any ideas, and *he* searched. And, well, you heard.'

'So what are you going to do now?'

'Rely on the genmed team here, I guess. Ari says I have to stop believing it's all up to me. She thinks the more stressed I am the more likely I am to get ill. She might be right about that part.' He popped the last morsel in his mouth, and wiped his fingers. 'It's just that the more engineered a genome is, the harder it is to understand what's going on purely from sequencing it. You need the modification index, and the epigenetic directory, to see where all the molecular switches are and how they interact with each other. And for that you need the genetype.'

'Blimey.' Callan looked impressed. 'You sound like an expert.'

'I know a lot about genetic medicine now. It's fascinating stuff.' He hesitated a moment then said, 'I'm thinking of studying it.'

'What, properly? Formally?'

'Yes. I already have all the qualifications I'd need, but I haven't said it to too many people yet. I know gems aren't supposed to want to do anything sort of . . . gemtech-y.'

'I guess for a lot of people it feels distasteful,' Callan acknowledged. 'But medicine isn't the same as modification, and anyway, we need to get over it. Otherwise all the expertise will stay with norms.'

'So you think it's a good idea?'

Callan grinned at him. 'I think it's a great idea. I would *love* to know that if I ever needed a genmed consultation you'd be the doctor on call.'

Rhys grinned back, bathed in warmth and a surge of unexpected happiness. His usual sense of being isolated, even in the midst of a crowd, even sometimes from Gwen, was burning away like mist off the river.

He felt well here, sitting in the sunshine in the middle of this huge, complicated, fascinating city, where every smell and sound and glance, every vibration under his feet or glimmer overhead was new enough to give the restless, questing part of his mind something to work on. And the other part of him, the part that cared nothing for the calculus of his environment, felt the pull of the man opposite, felt the flutter in his chest and the tug at the base of his belly; and he thought how easy it would be to fall, and in that moment he could think of no reasons not to.

10

Eli watched the two young men out on the quay, facing each other over their picnic like a pair of beautiful, capricious demigods from some ancient play. Against the silver-grey backdrop of the river their red heads sparkled, one bright, one dark. Gulls dipped and soared over the water behind them, shrieking as they veered ever closer; Rhys tossed a crust to one, intersecting its vector so precisely that the bird snatched it out of the air with barely a twitch of its wings, and said something that made Callan throw his head back and laugh. Eli blinked. To see Callan so relaxed, especially out in the open, was rare indeed.

He was tempted to join them, at least go over and say hello, but he decided against it. Though they were surrounded by others strolling or sitting in the midday sunshine, there was something intimate about the picture they made; an aura of privacy about the way they met each other's eyes and laughed at each other's jokes, and leaned in just a tiny bit closer than necessary to speak. Eli, more attuned than most to the subtleties of human behaviour, smiled and left them to it.

He had other business in any case, and turned his back on the quay as he trudged up the high street to a large and unprepossessing building that squatted at the back of a small plaza, like a lumpen brown package set down to one side but never unwrapped and put properly away. The old leisure centre, long since remade into the town hall and cultural hub of the Squats community, would have won no architectural prizes in any era.

Eli went through to the main foyer, passing Lyriam along the way. The musician was being interviewed, backed artistically against a window with a view of the sun-drenched street behind.

'Of course it was the middle of winter then, before we got here we were always so cold,' Eli heard him say. He glanced over, catching the younger man's eye, seeing the spark of shared memory as for a moment they both relived that refugee's advent. Bethany, standing off to the side, favoured him with a distracted simper. He smiled back, thinking that Aryel had as usual been right, and passed swiftly through.

Mikal was rarely to be found manning the reception desk these days; probably, Eli reflected, never would again. He waved a greeting and mouthed a question to the young woman with shimmering teal-green hair whose hands flickered across a tablet bank as she murmured into her earset. She waved back, nodding and pointing in the direction he was headed.

The giant gem was in his office, multi-tasking with earset and tablet, and he beckoned Eli forward as he hesitated in the doorway.

He stepped inside and dropped into a chair.

'Yes, I understand that, Sharon took their statements.' Mikal spoke into the earset, rolling his eyes wearily. 'No, nothing to do with you, we hadn't thought so . . . we know *you* know any religious association is incidental . . . Lyriam has no intention of being bullied, I'm sure you understand his position . . . Quite.' A longish pause. Mikal's narrow, mobile face twitched with amusement. 'A lovely song . . . yes, there is that . . . very talented. I couldn't say. Always good to talk to you.'

His fingers halted in the act of reaching to flick the earset back to standby. He stared vacantly at Eli, blinking that patient, double-lidded blink. Eli grinned in anticipation.

'The impact of faith is certainly appreciable, if not always appreciated,' Mikal said smoothly, into what must have been a pause for breath on the other end. 'One could hardly overstate it.' He smiled gently, waited a polite half-second in case there was a comeback, and concluded, 'I'll keep you posted, of course, if there's anything further at our end. You'll do the same? Thanks so much. Right. All the best,' and he flicked off and pulled the earset away, tossing it onto the desk with a sigh and shaking his head at Eli's chuckles.

'You shouldn't encourage me, you know.'

'As if you needed it. Who was that, Tobias?'

'Nope, Bishop Maloney herself. Our friends at the UC are quite rattled.' He grinned. 'Also enchanted with young Gwen. Mairead's nurturing a hope that she might actually be a believer. I was simply declining to comment.'

'So what did she have to say about it?'

'The idiots at the concert? Not much. Sharon found out they're from a congregation near Oxford, and the good bishop recalled hearing some Reversionist rumblings from out that way. The usual complaints about cultural shifts and the death of evangelism. No hint of an anti-gem stance, so they let it slip under the radar.'

'Mairead Maloney probably agrees with them.'

'No doubt, but she understands how dangerous any kind of aggressive proselytising could be. It's a very delicate balance for them, given that most of the godgangs were found to have had links with the UC – they're still trying to live down the association. But on the other hand, I think she's also elated that Gwen's inter-vention means thousands of people ended up hearing a hymn for the first time.' He sighed and stretched. 'The truth is she gave it far more exposure than it would have got otherwise. The only bit of the show that's had more hits is the elegy.'

'Not many more. The streams are going mad for her. "*Aryel Morningstar's little sister, with a voice to match those wings!*"' Eli shook his head ruefully. 'If you're trying to revive religion for the modern age that connection doesn't hurt. I don't imagine Gwen realises quite what she's stepped into.'

'She'll work it out soon enough. Lyriam will help. And Aryel knows how to navigate that channel better than anyone.' He took in the look on Eli's face. 'It still really bothers you, doesn't it? Even though you were part of it.'

'Maybe because I'm part of it. It's just . . . the reaction to Aryel is deeply illogical. If you had told me the day before Newhope Tower that people en masse would have such an atavistic response to her, regardless of their backgrounds or beliefs, regardless of history, I would have laughed at you. But when it happened it felt . . . natural. Obvious. Inevitable. It sort of bothers me that it *doesn't* bother me, if that makes any sense.'

'She tried very hard to avoid it.'

'I know she did. She's been completely honourable. And you'd think that her not taking advantage of the situation in all the ways that she could would minimise the impact, that by now she would be just another gem. But she isn't. And it's curious that all the new sects and splinter groups include so few anti-Aryel factions. Almost everyone manages to mould their philosophy into a shape which treats her with enormous respect. Even the Reversionists. *Especially* the Reversionists. I'm glad about that, but I don't understand it. She should be a polarising figure.'

'It is a mystery,' said Mikal solemnly, 'but we'll take them over the godgangs or the gemtechs, thank you very much. Personally I'm quite fond of the religious Reversionists, even though they are less than fond of Sharon and me. They don't want gem–norm cross-overs, but they do want peace and love between all peoples; they think artificial evolution is morally wrong, but they adore Aryel. It's so nice to have incompetent adversaries for a change.'

Eli laughed. 'Speaking of the gemtechs, any word from Aryel?'

'Not yet. She'll message us both, I imagine. I have heard from Zavcka Klist, though.'

'*What*?'

'Oh, not about their meeting. Though given the timing, I think it has everything to do with it.' He picked up the tablet and flicked it awake in one movement, then contemplated whatever was on the screen with the mild distaste of a man peering at something suspect on the sole of his shoe.

'"Dear Councillor Varsi",' he read aloud. '"Just a quick note following our conversation yesterday evening. In addition to the regulatory oversight we discussed, the Bel'Natur ethics and welfare team would welcome your input on appropriate standards and safeguards. I wonder if you would be available to meet with them in the first instance, perhaps to agree an ongoing advisory role? Your perspective, in terms of your public service responsibilities as well as your own personal history, would be invaluable. I hope to hear from you at your convenience. Sincerely, Zavcka".' He dropped the tablet back onto its stand, and brushed imaginary dirt off his fingers. 'Sent half an hour before she was due to meet with Aryel.'

Eli shook his head in bemusement. All he could think of to say was, 'That's how she signed off? "Zavcka?"'

'We're on a first-name basis, apparently. Best mates, I told you.'

'What are you going to do?'

'Go talk to them, of course. I can hardly refuse, can I? But I want to hear from Aryel before I reply.'

*

Gwen's tablet pinged softly, and she raised it in front of her face without bothering to sit up. Another clutch of messages from people she'd never heard of; praise and propositions mostly, a couple of frankly bizarre references to scripture, almost all also requests for an interview. Or an exclusive snippet of song. A few more UC congregations inviting her to Sunday worship, wondering if she could be persuaded to perform for them. She sighed, flicked the tablet back to standby and dropped it onto the bed beside her.

Eli might have been surprised to discover that she was fully aware of the ripples and ramifications of what she'd done. Even as she'd rolled to her feet on that grassy bank in the park, in the first few strides down the slope, she had been calculating probabilities and evaluating options; aware of the placement of every vidcam, sight lines from the stage, the likelihood of the speaker hack working and how she would adjust her response if it didn't. She'd judged the tuneless fools to have no weapons nor to offer any threat of violence, and been right. She'd felt the mood of the crowd around her, euphoria beginning to give way to dismay, and had known exactly what would capture their collective imagination.

But it depended as much on the actions of others, and she'd had a presentiment of folly even as she took the earset that would transmit her own voice. Surely her intention would not be clear to Lyriam; he would not, could not, possibly understand what she planned to do. Much less be willing to facilitate it. She replayed the moment, and felt again the little leap of excitement she'd felt when she realised he did and he would.

Now lying prone in the dim bedroom, alone in Aryel's echoing flat, she was putting her operational calculus to work once more: evaluating the fallout, projecting the next array of possible outcomes. So far things could hardly, she judged, have gone any better.

The furore was very much on the high end of her initial assessment, but almost universally positive. Lyriam's laughing approval, murmured close to her ear, called out over a sea of heads and reinforced in interviews and posts to public streams, had seen to that. She had caught Bethany's glower and knew that the blonde norm did not feel the same way.

She considered briefly whether that should bother her more than it did, and concluded that, right or wrong, she found it impossible to feel any sympathy for Bethany; close though they were in age, similar though some of their experiences must have been – a norm among gems, a gem among norms. But Bethany's life in the Squats with Lyriam had not, Gwen thought, been the only one she had ever known, nor perhaps as stable, simple and down to earth as her and Rhys' upbringing with Da and the rest of their Remnant tribe. Lyriam had listened to their tales from the country, of music made and stories sung around the fire on winter nights, with something that looked like longing. Bethany, visibly bored, had wandered off.

Gwen silently admitted that, in the few moments they had spent together, she had been equally bored by the girl. She seemed to lack the spark of adventure, the anarchic sense of fun, that had enabled Lyriam to appreciate Gwen's intervention. It was her loss – and Lyriam's relationship to manage. All was not well there, that much was evident. She would follow his lead, and if he did not feel constrained by his girlfriend's disapproval, then neither would Gwen.

The only question now was how best to take advantage of the moment she had not-so-accidentally created. She had set a course at the party, followed it up with carefully worded posts and private messages throughout the morning. Now she was waiting to see if the vague plans and half-made promises of the night were real. The inaction chafed at her.

The tablet chimed again. This time, as she read the message, she could feel herself beginning to smile.

He'd said he had to be interviewed for a documentary this morning: something Bethany had arranged, a puff piece on her life in the Squats. He was done with it now, had been able, she read, to *escape*. And he'd been thinking overnight about songs to work on together. Was she interested? When would she be free?

Her fingers slipped over the surface of the tablet even as she swung her legs down to the floor.

Right now, she wrote. *I'd love to. Let's get started.*

She was three strides from Aryel's front door a few minutes later when it slid open and Reginald stepped into the flat. He was frowning as he peered at the tablet in his hand, and there was a testy glint in the sharp eyes as he looked up at her from it.

'You off somewhere?'

'I'm going to meet Lyriam and the band. Were you up in the garden all this time, Da? I thought you'd gone over to the airwalk already.'

'That's where I *should* be. Things to do, people to meet.' He snorted, and waved the tablet at her. 'Instead I've been stuck on this thing. What are you going to do about this mess?'

'What mess?'

'*Your* mess. I keep getting messages from people about your stunt last night. I don't even know who the hell half of them are.'

'Why are they messaging *you*?'

'Blessed if I know. They seem to have the crazy idea that I might have some special insight. Being your father and all.' He scowled at the tablet again, and thumbed it off. 'I've got everyone from priests to politicians asking me about your religious education . . .'

'My what?'

'Exactly. Most of them also imagine I must secretly agree with whatever point those idiots were trying to make. They seem to think being Remnant automatically means being Reversionist. As if.' He snorted again.

Gwen sighed. 'That's a fairly logical conclusion for most people to jump to, Da.'

'And a fairly harmless one, most of the time. Except now they're not just assuming, they're asking. Which means I have to say no, I think they're a bunch of misguided, short-sighted, ancestor-worshipping nitwits.'

Gwen raised an eyebrow. 'You haven't actually said that, have you?'

'Close enough.'

She chortled. 'Well, that should get you lots of attention. You can use it to talk up the airwalk tech.'

'Thank you for the silver lining. Is Rhys still down at Herran's place?'

'No, he messaged to say he and Callan were going out for a bit. He's all right, he's feeling good today.'

'Let's hope he stays that way. Especially while you're up to whatever it is you're up to.'

'What makes you think I'm up to anything?'

'Gwen, love, in the twenty years since you came into my care, you've never not been up to *something*.' The eyes were still piercing, but, along with the voice, had turned gentle. 'Just remember that you are not the most important thing at the moment. Rhys is.'

'Rhys will always be my priority,' she said softly, modulating her own voice to match his, ensuring there was no trace of edge in it. 'But he's going to be fine, I'm sure he is. He doesn't need me to be with him all the time and he hates it when we hover, you know that. He's healthy right now, and he doesn't start at the hospital for almost a week. There's a lot I can be doing in the meantime. You think sitting around here, staring at the walls while you and Rhys and Ari are all out on your various missions is fun for me? I have things I want to achieve too, Da.' She stepped towards the door. 'I'll be there when he needs me. Whenever he needs me.'

'Fair enough.' He nodded acceptance, and then waved the tablet again. 'What are you planning to do about the clamouring faithful?'

'I'm planning to ignore them. Unless I can think of a better reason not to.'

EDUCATION

She often hears them arguing. It is almost always about her, but they do not trouble themselves overmuch to ensure that she is out of earshot. It will be some while yet before they can bring themselves to believe just how much she comprehends. In the meantime, she is learning the wisdom of guile.

She sits on the floor in a far corner, the battered tablet in her hands, and is careful to angle herself so she can see if anyone approaches. She completed the standard curriculum some time ago, working out with little trouble how to access the levels supposedly beyond her capability. Now she is in the encyclopaedia function she is not supposed to know about, flipping from one entry to another, keeping up with the conversation.

'. . . I'm telling you, I think her IQ might even be normal for her age. She hits the average percentiles in every test we give her, she's on track with the modules . . . look at her, she spends every waking moment with that tablet.'

They all glance in her direction. She pretends not to notice, and waits. She already knows what IQ means.

'How bright can she be, if it takes her that long?'

'We don't know that it does. She doesn't have any other toys or learning tools, or playmates for that matter. She might just be going over the lessons out of boredom.' Dr Owen's eyes still rest on her, and his voice is thoughtful. He is the one most interested in her cognitive development – she learned what that was, oh ages and ages ago – and he has never forgotten the lesson

of that first lisping conversation. She works particularly hard to ensure he thinks just as much of her as he should, and no more.

'I say we should open up the modules,' he goes on. 'Let her take a look at the next two or three, see what she goes for. Maybe even give her access to some general reading material. Assess her curiosity.'

Oh good. That would save so much trouble.

Another white-coat shrugs, waves dismissively. She is Dr Panborn, and she is the only one Dr Owen ever needs to get permission from. Things have been changing since she appeared, around the same time that the last of the other children was covered up and wheeled away.

'I don't really see the point of that, but go ahead if you want. Satisfy your own curiosity. It does not, however, address the main question.'

A pause, while they all look at each other. One of the other white-coats, another recent arrival, says, 'Can we be absolutely certain the batch wasn't just contaminated? That would be the simplest explanation . . .'

The lab supervisor, a man named Clark, sighs and rolls his eyes. 'We've been asking that question for seven years now, and I don't think we're going to get any better answers than we've got. What I want to know is, contaminated with what, exactly? A few extra alleles of eagle?'

She already knows what an allele *is. Eagle is new. She gets the spelling wrong on the first try, tries again, and the information rolls up on the screen. She blinks in puzzlement at the picture, some strange brown-black creature perched on the high bare branch of a tree, and then bites back a gasp as it launches itself into the air. She watches, mesmerised by the few seconds of vid, and feels the awkward, naked limbs that flop uselessly against her back twitch and stretch and try to imitate the movement.*

She thought she had already found everything the tablet contained on wings. There is a familiar sense of wonder, and anger, at how much remains to be discovered.

'Obviously why it happened isn't unimportant,' Dr Panborn says, in a tone that suggests maybe it is. 'But it's high time for a shift in emphasis.

We've been working with the Phoenix genestock in other batches, with and without interspecies splicing, and there've been no other aberrations . . .'

'There have,' says Dr Owen.

'They haven't been significant, and they haven't had the upside. Whatever happened in this specimen didn't just incorporate a single radical anatomic transformation, it's carried the mutation throughout the other organs. Systemic complementarity. She's got feathers getting ready to grow, for God's sake, she's got a metabolism that looks like it might actually be efficient enough to power flight. The issue isn't her specific dysmorphism, it's the potential. Reverse engineering the wings isn't so important, I mean what could you ever do with them? But if we can understand how her body has adapted all its systems to support that primary mutation, if we can replicate the totality of that shift . . . that's a gold mine.'

They nod and murmur and glance over at her again, while she taps and swipes at the tablet screen and affects a reassuring placidity. Phoenix, systemic, metabolism, mutation, gold mine. She makes notes, keeping track so she can look them all up later.

This is turning out to be a good meeting.

11

Aryel Morningstar walked through an orchard, and the digital savant Herran walked by her side. In between the neat rows of apples and pears, their spread-eagled, wire-tied branches thick with leaves and swelling fruit, she could see rooftop after rooftop. As they turned from one gravelled path into another the upper land-scape of the city surrounded them, broken only by the line of the river to their right. Amidst the drab grey of cooling towers, power plants, and vent stacks, some of the nearby roofs sprouted gardens too. But nowhere was as thoroughly cultivated and gloriously fecund as the flat top of Maryam House, with its troughs of fruit trees, vegetable beds, and tubs full of flowers and herbs. A gorgeous sunset painted the sky shades of lilac and peach and crimson.

She had brought him up here, out of the familiar confines of his own space, to emphasise what would be required of him if he agreed to go to Bel'Natur. She had more than half expected him to refuse the proposal out of hand, almost hoped he would. Instead he had accepted, it seemed to her too readily.

'You don't have to do it,' she repeated. 'And if I am completely honest, Herran, if I speak to you just as your friend, the truth is maybe you shouldn't do it.'

'I do.'

'It might not be safe.'

'You make safe.'

She stopped and turned to look directly at him. He stopped in tandem, and after a moment he also turned, with that stiff, ever-so-slightly mechanical motion of his, and stared back at her. He never used to be able to maintain this much eye contact, she remembered, and she thought again of how far he had come, and how much he stood to lose in this venture.

'I'll do everything I can,' she said softly. 'I'll have to get some help. You'll need Callan, I think, as well as Eli. But they'll have to agree to it.'

'Bel'Natur say no?'

'I'm not worried about that part. I think Bel'Natur will agree to whatever we ask if it means you'll help them. They want you very badly.'

Herran looked away, his scarred face expressionless as always, his pale eyes taking in the roofscape around them.

'Make pay.'

'Yes, it is a way of making them pay. But don't do this just for that, Herran. Do it if you want to, not because you think you should.'

'Should. Also want.'

'Why, Herran? Why do you want to?'

'My brain,' he said, and was silent for so long that if she had known him less well she would have thought that the entirety of his answer. But she could see the shifting of his eyes as he searched for a way to explain.

'Learn my brain,' he said finally. 'Talking code to people, people to code. No one else can do. Not even Rhys.'

She waited.

'Bel'Natur learning,' he went on. 'Make others talk code too. Build interface, maybe they talk like me. See like me. Think like me.

A little bit. Maybe they *understand*.' He rubbed a hand through his glowing curls, and knocked the heel of his palm roughly against his temple one, two, three times. There was a metronomic rhythm to it. It was something she'd seen him do before, when he was struggling to express a desire or a concept just beyond the language capacity with which he'd been left. Despair washed through her, a tide of recognition and heartache for the loneliness he was unable even to name. Her vision blurred.

'Oh Herran,' she whispered. 'My sweet Herran. That's not what they have in mind at all.'

'I know. I know not same as me, Aryel. But maybe a little bit same.' He cocked his head and looked at her quizzically, then reached out, astonishingly, to touch her face. 'Why tears?'

She took his hand gently, pressed her lips to it, and brushed at her eyes. When she spoke again her voice was rough, but steady. 'Because sometimes I think about the choices that are left to us, my friend, and it makes me very sad.' She let go of his hand. 'Are you sure?'

He nodded. Standing, especially out here in the open, the rocking seemed less pronounced. 'Sure.'

'All right, then.'

When she explained it to him the next morning, Eli was shocked.

'Aryel. Why would you trust her? *Ever?*'

'The only thing about her that I trust is her instinct for self-preservation. She has everything to lose and nothing to gain here. If she harms Herran, or exposes him, she'll take away the only reason I have not to see her thrown into a cell next to Carrington.'

'Isn't that where she *should* be?'

She stared at him, then rustled her wings and looked away, towards the narrow ribbon of windows that let in the morning sunshine and a view of the Squats. She had asked him up to her flat, a cavernous space that took up almost all of the top two storeys of Maryam House, to relate the details of her meeting with Zavcka Klist. Perched on stools in the kitchen, they were more than halfway up the double-height walls that had been created when most of the floor in between was knocked through. From here it was no more than a single long stride to the slender safety rail that prevented the unwinged from falling off what remained of the upper level, and plunging twelve feet down to land on the floor below. The entire apartment was laid out like this, a cavity in which a concealed flyer could stretch, with the living and sleeping spaces arranged as a series of inward-projecting balconies and rooms around the perimeter. She could get from one to another with a couple of beats; visitors had to make do with the narrow walkways that had been left along the edges.

Now she pulled her eyes back from the strip of sky outside the windows, sipped from a mug of tea and grimaced. 'Should she, Eli? Really?'

'I know, I'm sorry,' he muttered. 'The price is too high.' He dropped his chin into his hands and rubbed at his temples. 'And you say Herran *wants* to do it?'

'He does.' She explained why.

'So he's hoping they'll actually replicate the way his brain works? Using infotech alone?'

'Something like that. She wants the same thing of course, but not for the same reasons.'

'I didn't realise Herran felt so isolated. I mean that he's bothered by it. He always seems so . . . contained.'

She circled a meditative finger around the rim of the cup. Her voice was thoughtful, distant. 'I think that most people want to know there is someone else, somewhere in the world, who they can relate to. Who knows who they are, who understands their fears and joys and challenges. Uniqueness is tough, Eli. I think Herran's become a bit frustrated by how slow we all are, and the daft things we find to be interested in.'

He sipped from his own mug and swallowed, watching her closely. 'You must feel like that too.'

She smiled. 'What, slow and daft?'

'That no one really understands what it's like to be you.'

'That is self-evidently true.' Her eyes were back on the windows. 'But at least my isolation isn't mental. And you learn to live with being an aberration, especially when you know how much worse your life could have been.'

'Oh, for the love of— Aryel, you are not an *aberration*.' He stared at her in consternation. '*Unexpected*, I might accept.'

Perfect, he wanted to say, and found it frighteningly close to the tip of his tongue. He bit it back.

She glanced over at him briefly, and looked away at the windows again. All trace of the smile had disappeared.

'Aren't I? You sound very sure.'

'I'm completely sure. And I can't believe you actually think that.'

For a long moment she stared at a spot somewhere in the un-anchored midpoint of the vast room, lost in thought, or memory. Then she seemed to recover herself, straightening up with her usual brisk energy, putting the empty mug down and meeting his eyes. He felt – as he always did – a momentary faltering, a lightning flash of self-doubt that assailed him every time he tried to hold that sky-blue gaze.

'*They* thought that. I never forget that I am not what they were trying for, Eli.' Just the slightest edge had come into her voice. 'I was an accident. There were casualties.'

He put his own cup aside, carefully. This was more than she had ever been prepared to say before, and he felt an almost scholarly sense of obligation to push at the door she had cracked open.

'What sort of casualties?'

'My batch siblings. Others.'

Even one success from a small batch was something most gemtechs would have celebrated, back in the days of radical modification. But she said they had regarded her as an unintended outcome, a fluke.

'What were they trying for?'

'I'm not sure. Something a lot more dangerous than I turned out to be.'

'Is that even possible?' he asked, managing a smile, although the bitter note in her voice was unsettling. He surprised himself with the faint echo of it he heard in his own tone.

'Oh yes.' She arched an eyebrow at him, forgoing the modesty of a denial. 'I think we're all very fortunate that they failed.'

'Who were they?'

'Ambitious proponents of progress. Clever creators of life. Titans of industry. The usual.' The words dropped like stones into the well of the room, with a bitten-off finality that he recognised.

'Aryel.' He shook his head, gave up. 'Are you ever going to tell me where you came from?'

'I hope not.' She sighed. 'So. Herran. Will you help?' And just like that, her voice was back to normal. He blinked in astonishment, and she smiled. It was like the sun coming out.

'Of course. Exactly what do you want me to do?'

'I want you to be his guardian there. You speak their language, you'll understand what it is they're trying to do, if it's unsafe or unacceptable. I'm going to ask Callan to be part of the team as well – Herran will need him for communication, especially at the beginning, and Callan will help him feel safe. But he won't be able to assess the bigger picture the way you can, and you're someone they have to respect. Zavcka already knows she can't bully you.'

He turned this over. 'Callan is highly empathic and very bright, and if he thinks that Herran – or himself for that matter – is being treated improperly he'll pull the plug without hesitation. You don't need us both to protect Herran. You're after something else.' He looked at her expectantly, and she chuckled.

'I am. Although given Callan's own history I wouldn't have wanted him to go in alone with Herran anyway. It's why I've asked you first.' She pulled the clasp from her hair and fiddled with it, frowning.

'The culture change within Bel'Natur that Zavcka talked about. I need to know if it's genuine, or just the usual corporate PR bullshit.'

'I thought you were sure it wasn't real.'

'I assumed so from her speech, knowing her as we do. But now, having gone there and seen her without an audience, I'm less certain.'

'She tried to blackmail you!'

Aryel looked up at him, amused. 'And I blackmailed her right back. Look, I'm not suggesting that she personally is any less unscrupulous than she ever was. But the way she went about it, the assurances she gave around Herran even when she still thought she could force the issue, didn't seem condescending or false. She didn't like having to deal with me, but she did so as though I were an equal with whom she had to do business. And the place did not feel like an old-school gemtech. The staff were mostly young, and the vibe I got from them was what you'd expect from a modern, progressive company. That haughtiness you usually get with the gemtechs, even when they think they're being polite? Well she still has it, although you could tell she was trying to tone it down, and I reckon her security director is a made-over enforcer. But the rest of them weren't anything like that. She's brought in a whole new set. A whole new *mindset*.'

'That,' said Eli slowly, 'is interesting. Carrington carried the can for the Gabriel affair, so why would she have bothered to force through that kind of transformation? She didn't need to.'

'I wonder if she didn't look at the situation and decide she did need to. First of all to give herself some cover against Carrington's accusations, but also because she's clear-headed enough to know the company has to adapt if it's going to survive. Look at Gempro and Modicomm and the others, still struggling to come to terms with the Declaration. Bel'Natur is streets ahead, and that's down to her. Whether she *likes* it or not, she *gets* that gem suffrage isn't going to be reversed. She *gets* that the market in human gemtech isn't coming back. And the old attitudes aren't just wrong these days, they're commercially damaging – because as long as they keep on believing that gems really ought to be products, they're not going to be able to turn us into customers. And yet. What was human gemtech originally for?'

Eli got it. 'Making healthy babies. Which is not a problem for norms any more, but for gems . . .'

'Exactly. You know about Mikal and Sharon's situation, and they're not alone. Procreation is the next big thing that gems are going to have to grapple with. It's not just an ethical debate with the Reversionists, it's a real live existential problem. But we don't know yet if we can stomach the gemtech solution. We need someone we can trust to help us figure that out.'

'You mean me? Aryel, that goes well beyond my area of competence.'

'No it doesn't. It's no bigger than the questions you've already asked, and answered. It isn't just about what's moral, but what's feasible. Whether the gemtechs, or *a* gemtech, are starting to turn into the kind of organisation we could actually stand to work with. Herran being at Bel'Natur gives us access, leverage, and a test case.'

'You want me to assess the shift in the corporate culture of Bel'Natur.'

'I do.'

'What makes you think I'll find out enough just from going along with Herran?'

'Because you being allowed to poke around and talk to people and discover what you need to is going to be part of the price.'

He sucked his breath in sharply, as the full extent of what she was proposing unfolded before him. 'She'll *hate* that.'

'Yes she will. But she'll do it, because she'll hate the alternative more.'

Eli nodded, acknowledging the point, accepting the mission, and aware once again of being subtly, gently manipulated. She had given him many reasons to say yes and none to say no; and no basis whatsoever for the latent sense of unease that coiled at the back of his brain. There was no reason, none at all, to think there was more to this task than he was being told. The implications he could see were quite enough to take his breath away. They had the potential to remake the world. And yet he felt he stood on the edge of a precipice, and could see only a little way down.

12

The director of the genestock archive was convincingly baffled. 'But we haven't *had* a security breach,' he said again. 'How can you be here to investigate something that hasn't happened?'

'If our investigation confirms it hasn't then we'll be out of your way just as quickly as we can, Dr Chang. But it has been reported to the police that quarantined genestock has disappeared from within this facility. I sincerely hope that proves not to be the case, but I'm sorry to say that we cannot simply take your word for it.'

One of the other two men in the room shifted and made a sound in his throat. He stood to the side of Chang, facing Sharon and the detective she'd conscripted from data forensics, and was already proving to be a pain in the arse.

Sharon switched her attention to him. 'You have something to add, Mr Nance?'

'I don't know who reported what to you' – he squinted suspiciously at the warrant, pulsing on the screen of the tablet where she had propped it on the table – '*Detective Inspector*, but this is a waste of time. You don't have to take our word for it. Just check the datastream. You'll see that none of our genestock is missing.'

Nance had been introduced as chief operating officer, an administrative role which freed up Chang to focus his scientific expertise on the research potential and policy conundrums of the archive itself. While Chang appeared bewildered, Nance seemed to feel it was part of his responsibility to deal robustly with any suggestion of malfeasance within the organisation. Sharon was also beginning to suspect that he had a problem specifically with her. There was more than a hint of recognition, and repugnance, in the looks he sent her way; a reaction she had become used to in the years since her marriage to Mikal. For her own part she could not shake the feeling that he too was somehow familiar, but the name had not triggered any alerts from her case files. She had concluded that he was simply yet another example of a type she knew well: middle-aged and middlebrow, a once solid physique beginning to run soft, the customary complacency of a thoroughly respectable life more than a little shaken by finding himself questioned by a senior police officer; and the buttons of his outrage further pushed by the facts of said officer's personal life. He was dealing with the occasion as they often did, veering between pugnacity and defensiveness.

'As I said, Mr Nance, I hope you're right. We'll know soon enough.' She glanced over to her colleague. 'Are we all set?'

He nodded. 'They're in position. As soon as these gentlemen unlock the storage units we can get started.' He chewed at his lip, as though a thought had just occurred to him. 'Of course we could just force the locks. See how hard it is, and what kind of alert it would actually generate.' He gazed past her at Chang and Nance, who stared back, aghast. Sharon maintained her mask of impassive professionalism, but inside she was grinning.

'I'm sure that won't be necessary. Will it?' This directed at the two men on the other side of the table.

'Absolutely not,' replied Chang stiffly. 'We will cooperate fully with the police, of course. Ken?'

Kendrick Nance stabbed at the screen of his own tablet. He

looked balefully back at Sharon. 'You want us to open all of them, then.' He looked ready to proceed, as though eager to prove the pointlessness of their visit.

'No I don't, Mr Nance. We're going to open the units in sequence just as we discussed, and lock each set behind us before we move on to the next. We are also, as detailed in the warrant, going to add me and Detective Sergeant Achebe here as alternate third approvals. As of right now, nothing is accessible without us.'

'I must say, Inspector Varsi, that this seems very heavy-handed—'

'Dr Chang. You want us to confirm that there is nothing wrong here and bugger off as soon as possible. Well believe it or not, that's what I want too. The best way to achieve that is to ensure we have a quick, clean count, with absolutely no loopholes for anyone to point out to us later.' She held his gaze, keeping her voice even but firm. 'As soon as our checks are complete we'll remove the restriction and be on our way. If everything is in order it shouldn't take more than a couple of hours.'

'We can let them crack on while we update the system,' added Achebe, and Sharon nodded again, eyes front on Chang.

They watched while Nance, jaw tight with anger, entered a code and handed the tablet to Chang, who tapped in a series of commands. He then leaned forward for a retinal scan and gave the tablet back to Nance, who tapped some more before staring into the red pinpoint of the vidcam for his own scan. A soft beep sounded from the tablet.

'You should have access now,' Sharon said into her earset. She listened for confirmation and flipped a thumbs-up to Achebe. He stepped forward, reaching over Nance's shoulder to press a memtab against one of the tablet's intake ports.

Nance scowled at the screen as the logo of the Metropolitan Police flashed up. He spread his hands in a theatrical relinquishing of the tablet and stepped back, watching in silence as Achebe pulled up an input panel and added the new layer of security to the existing protocols. Nance and Chang were instructed to authorise it with a second set of retscans, and then Sharon and Achebe added their own scans, and the tablet was finally, politely, handed back to its owner.

'I think we have a right to know,' said Chang, 'who has made this accusation. The suggestion that genestock has been *stolen*, and that we didn't *report* it, is, is a serious one.'

'It is indeed.' Sharon nodded sagely. 'However, you don't have any right to know the identity of the source, and I couldn't tell you even if you did. The report was made anonymously.'

'You're putting us through all this on the basis of a tip from someone you don't even *know*?' sputtered Nance. There was a triumphant note in his voice, as though his indignation had finally been justified. 'I have a mind to call my—'

'Call whoever you like.' Sharon was getting tired of his sniping. She wondered if the real reason for it would boil out and into the open, and how Chang would respond if it did. 'The police are obliged to review every allegation which is properly made and registered.' She reeled off Sections and Codes and Acts of Parliament and was rewarded by the chastened look which descended on Chang's round face, though Nance's pugnacious expression remained much the same. 'It's not necessary for a complainant to identify themselves in a matter such as this, as long as they supply sufficient evidence for us to reasonably suspect that a crime may have been committed. Check with your own legal advisors if you don't believe me.'

She was watching Nance keenly and openly, and saw him register the appraisal in her gaze. To her surprise he appeared to rein in his contempt. Instead he affected a look of boredom, as though he doubted what she'd said but could not be bothered to refute it. So: a private bigot, not quite up to the risk of airing his views in front of his boss.

Chang cleared his throat. 'Can you tell us what this evidence was?'

'No, I can't. But if it proves baseless, rest assured I'll turn my attention to finding out how it was produced and who sent it. I don't like having my time wasted either.' She glanced at Achebe, now seated and busy with his own tablet, sending searchbots trawling through the datastream as he tried to hunt down the source files for the screenshots that had brought them here. She did not tell them that the data detectives generally worked out who a whistleblower was within the first half-hour.

Nance shifted in his chair. 'Look, okay, you're only doing your job,' he said, 'but what this – person – has told you is impossible. It couldn't have happened, and we couldn't not know if it *did* happen. So I'm sorry if we seem a bit aggravated, but it's just, well, you may not know how ludicrous this is, but we do.' Though his words had turned conciliatory, there was still a drawling arrogance in his voice.

Sharon had spent a solid hour working through the supposed impossibilities, and emerged unconvinced. 'How often do you take inventory, Mr Nance?'

'It's taken automatically. Every time a storage unit is opened, by anyone for any reason, it's registered and the system records whether any of the genestock has been removed.'

'Yes, but how often do you actually check the genestock? Do a hard count?'

'There's no need to. Don't you understand? Quantities and lines were verified when the stock came over from the gemtechs, and it was put immediately into secure storage. It can't be accessed without double authorisation – *triple* authorisation now that you've added yourselves – from a very limited combination of senior staff. If anyone was able to open the storage trays without using the proper protocol a whole series of alarms would go off, it would trigger a lockdown. When access is authorised, the date, time, who by and the reasons given are recorded, and notices are automatically routed to Dr Chang, myself, and several others. If what's returned to storage is reduced by more than the authorised research requires, that also triggers the alarms.' He waved his hands, as though at a loss as to how to explain it any more clearly. 'There's no way there could be a problem that we didn't know about. The process is *completely* automated.'

'I understand that. So how would you know if the system failed?'

'How could it fail?'

'I don't know, Mr Nance. That's not my question. How do *you* know, for *certain*, that it hasn't?'

He stared at her, his mouth opening and closing again like some kind of great fish. Sharon could feel her own lips compress into a tight line. *The worst thing about this,* she thought, *is that although he's a bastard he could also be right, and I will be the one who ends up looking, and feeling, like a fool.*

Over in the corner, Achebe inhaled sharply: surprise, discovery and, unmistakably, alarm. She turned to him, registered the hand signal that meant they should step outside.

As she got to her feet the comlink to the search team pinged in her earset. She raised a finger to tell Achebe to hold on, said 'Yes?' and listened.

She let a satisfied little smile settle onto her face even as her heart sank. Across the table, Chang's face was a picture of trepidation. She caught his eyes and held them while the bioforensics officer down amongst the refrigerated units finished her report and pinged out.

'Well,' she said quietly. 'It appears there may be a problem here after all.'

The airwalk ran for more than a mile, parallelling the high walls of the embankment, passing the last crumbling foundations of ancient wharves and lumps of less identifiable marine archaeology. Every hundred paces or so the passage ballooned out to become a wider room dedicated to some aspect of underwater life, from which other rooms or side corridors extended. At each of the nodes there was the closet-sized pustule of an airlock, through which gillungs came and went.

With the tide still coming in, the top of the tubular construction was a couple of feet clear of the water. Late-morning sunshine sparkled as it glanced off wavelets on the surface, a shifting diamond cascade that dazzled eyes looking up from below. It filled the airwalk with natural light, an elongated bubble of submerged brilliance against which the colour of the water column changed from topaz to amber, to the deep silty brown of the riverbed. Tall weeds brushed up against the walls, bent over by the current as though in some silent, peaceful gale. Fish darted past. A shadow detached itself from the murk, the slippery ripple of an eel swimming languidly along beside them for a while before curving away and disappearing behind one of the anchor cables that they could see spearing down into the mud.

Callan was enchanted. Rhys, who had spent much of the past forty-eight hours being secretly awed by the grandeur and casual sophistication of the city, felt a surge of partisan pride for the gillung technology.

'What happens when the tide's out all the way? It'd be too bright and hot then, surely. Not to mention the lack of privacy.'

Rhys shook his head. 'The whole thing is built on a biopolymer

143

scaffold. It maintains rigidity, and it's also photosensitive below about here.' He reached up, his fingers at full extension brushing the inward-curving plastic barrier. 'As the water level drops and more light hits the tunnel, the walls gradually tint darker and darker. But there's also a chemical override that can trigger the reaction without light. Sleeping quarters are generally just left set to opaque.'

'You've slept in one of these? Underwater?'

'Many times.'

'What's that like?'

'Weird the first time. You have the sounds of the water all around, and it's louder on the coast than in a river. You sort of have to convince yourself that it isn't going to collapse and drown you in your sleep. And gillungs generally prefer a lower temperature than us topsiders. But once you throw on an extra blanket, it's fine.'

Callan stopped in another swelling, and tipped his head back to look up at the circle of bright water overhead. The fireglow of his hair shone like a halo against the darkened water-wall of the room.

'It's nice and warm now. Temperature control is built into the walls as well?'

'Yes . . . well, sort of. There are capacitors grouped in amongst the oxygen-exchange cells. They store excess heat to vent back in, and they can also dump it outside if there's an overload. There are more of them along the top in a tidal configuration like this, to capture as much heat as possible. But solar radiation isn't enough, especially in winter or deep water. The tidemills are where the heat mostly comes from.'

They had explored the power generation system in the first of the nodes, peering through the walls to watch a paddle array billow lazily in the river's tidal surge. Rhys pulled up vidcam feeds and interactive schematics that showed how every degree of movement translated into so many joules of energy, captured and directed to the needs of the underwater complex. He had glanced up at one point, felt a moment of vertigo as he found himself gazing into the green depths of his companion's eyes, and then became aware with a start that they were surrounded by visitors. It looked like an amalgamation of two or three norm families, complete with scampering youngsters and a pair of serious teenagers who wanted to know all about everything he had already explained. He had answered politely, found them an infostream module that let them model their own power station and handed them over to the citrine-haired man who swam in through the airlock to the children's shrieks of delight. They escaped while he was patiently explaining why he couldn't put them in it to experience the blasts of hot air from the dryer for themselves.

Now Callan was gazing thoughtfully around the node they were in, this one showcasing offshore permaculture. 'This isn't just about self-sufficiency, is it? Aryel's been saying so for a while, but I hadn't quite got it before.'

'No. It's also how much they can sell to everybody else. These systems, they're incredibly productive and low-impact. And the tech gets better all the time.'

'And the tech is owned by gems?'

'The new stuff is.' Rhys grinned. 'The gemtechs are welcome to the original versions. Less efficient, less comfortable, less safe.'

'What a brilliant new slogan for Gempro.'

Rhys snickered approval. Callan treated him to versions of the phrase in German, Russian and Japanese, each delivered more sententiously than the next, until they were both doubled up with laughter. Other visitors to the airwalk cast bemused glances in their direction. Rhys was wiping his eyes and wishing in a confused way both to stay in the moment forever, and to already be where it felt as though it were heading, when a sealed door leading into a side passage hissed open and Reginald peered around it.

'Good gods. It's that quiet, well-behaved boy of mine. Graca, darling, fetch me my smelling salts.'

Graca stepped out of an airlock into the passage behind him, shaking her quick-dried hair into a shimmering lime-green cloud. 'Sorry, Reg. Wrong century. And Rhys can laugh all he wants.' She padded over to give him a peck on the cheek and look around at the display. 'Although I didn't think it was *that* bad.'

'It's great. We were appreciating,' said Callan, and was introduced. Graca looked from him to Rhys, nodded approvingly and said, 'Well you'd better come and see the rest of it, then.'

She had been putting the finishing touches to a coastal garden, surrounded by a loop of airwalk that kept the briny water and sealife separate from the river while allowing it to be viewed from all sides. They walked around admiring while she unlocked the entrance at the far end and updated the display's infostream. By the time Callan, Rhys and Reginald emerged into the main airwalk again the intervening wall was as transparent as the rest, and the norm troupe they had left behind in the power centre were ooh-ing and aah-ing at a spider crab. Rhys caught Callan's eye and they both turned hastily away. Reginald fell into step beside them, looking amused.

'So the point,' said Callan to Reginald, as if continuing a conversation that had not actually been taking place, 'is to demonstrate all this wonderful stuff to the norms, while in the nicest possible way making it clear that it's not anything they can actually go off and do by themselves. If they want it, they're going to have to work with gillungs to get it.'

He ran his hand along skeins of algae-based textiles as he spoke, soft and fine as silk. The back of his hand brushed Rhys' as his arm fell back to his side, and Rhys felt his fingers twitch towards it in response. Two of them were captured, hooked by two of Callan's, who kept his head politely cocked towards Reginald walking on his other side. The twining fingers tightened. Rhys swallowed and stared straight ahead.

Reginald chuckled. 'That's not exactly how the product info-streams put it, but yes.'

'And what if they don't go for it?'

'They're already going for it. Orders have started to come in. The idea is the bigger the market, the faster the tech can develop. But they haven't had a lot of funding up to now, just the Gempro settlement, and look.' He gestured grandly, barely missing Graca, who ducked as she caught up with them. 'It's happening anyway. The only question is, who wants to come along for the ride.'

A questing thumb had found the palm of Rhys' hand, and was inscribing slow circles in the middle of it. He wondered dazedly if Graca had noticed as she came up behind, and decided he didn't care. The three of them were chatting away about integrated subaquatic villages and five-year action plans; maintaining the appearance of composure was as much as he could manage. He felt almost grateful when an approaching group of visitors forced them out of their four-abreast stroll and into double file. Callan released his hand in an unhurried way as they swung into the new forma-tion and Rhys closed it into a fist, trying to hold on to the feeling.

DISCONNECTION

The world reshapes itself around her.

She is part and parcel of the transformation. Things that have never been bloom and breathe and bleat their way into existence, their cells stamped with the sigil of her father's genius. Life is engineered, adapted, contorted; grafted, implanted, assessed. Aborted or gestated, delivered or declined. That this is acceptable, inevitable – even honourable – is beyond question. Standards must be maintained, output improved; there is no time to waste on products that have value neither in the market nor the laboratory. All must earn their place. She is as proudly and profoundly unsentimental as any of her colleagues, as pragmatic and clear-headed a rationalist as any crisis could require. It is a quality which even those who quail before her admire, a new conviction for a new age.

Yet, though the bitter lash of her tongue belies it, she is never entirely easy inside her own skin, never completely sanguine about her own strange and unlooked-for state. It pins her just enough outside the ordinary that she sometimes seems to herself almost as odd and unnatural a creature as those other creatures, bred and built to serve their betters.

With the one, the crucial difference; the factor that makes all the difference.

Still, something is wrong, and the wrongness must be righted. She is a woman of long memory (and, she fancies, longer foresight), and in the company of her cell-cultured cousins she senses a danger she cannot name.

Though nothing she and her compatriots do need give her pause, she feels a time might yet come when it would be best to sit just a stage or two distant from the blood and sweat and tears of their inventions' flesh-cloaked reality.

The time may indeed be now when the vexatious business of final genesis is best kept at a remove. She has endured enough of it, goodness knows, and it is the least pleasant, most fraught part of her responsibilities. After too many years watching swelling surrogates mill and murmur behind one-way windows, diligently stamping down any tendernesses they conjure, she has had enough. She declares that division dead and sells off, outsources; embraces the quieter clamour of molecular manipulations, the inch-square clarity of the microscope.

She knows the retrenchment is seen as a retreat, and does not care. The dissociation she feels requires a resolution, and removal of the cause seems to do the trick. Besides there is a threat there, she can feel it, however amorphous and infantile it might yet be. It is as minute as the cells and sequences her technicians must now content themselves with, but it is growing. She understands that it may come to life without her, but she will not be the one to give it birth. She is too well acquainted with calamity to be the architect of another upheaval.

She has already seen the world change once. She suspects it may not be beyond imagining for it to change again.

13

Sharon and Achebe sat across from Masoud. She had spent the last ten minutes succinctly relating the day's discoveries at the EGA, and watching his face grow longer with every word.

Now he grimaced at the report infographic on the desk screen before him, splashed with far too many grey unknowns amongst the red and orange high-hazard flags, and rubbed his temples wearily. 'So you're telling me we still have no idea who, how or why.'

'Or when,' Sharon said. 'It could have happened at any time since the EGA was set up.'

'Possibly over a period of time,' Achebe added. 'Since we don't know how it was done, we can't assume it was a single event.'

The police commander glared at him balefully. Achebe twitched and shrank back in his chair. His department's inability to determine how the EGA's security systems had been breached was singularly failing to impress. Sharon cleared her throat, drawing Masoud's attention back, and out of the corner of her eye saw the other detective relax a little.

'My guess is that it wasn't,' she said. 'In order to maintain viability the genestock would have had to be transferred into some kind of temperature-controlled bag or case. It wouldn't need to be large. The vials are tiny.' She held up a little finger to illustrate. 'But enough is missing, and from enough different locations throughout the archive, that I can't see it happening all in one go.'

'So you think – what? Over months? Years?'

'Maybe. Or maybe just every day for a week.' She could hear the irritation creeping into her own voice and reined it in. 'There aren't many permanent staff, and there's been very little turnover. If it's one of them they could have done it gradually. But they also have a steady stream of researchers from various universities and so on, here and abroad, who come in for anywhere from a few days to a couple of months.'

'Crap.' Masoud glared at the infographic again. 'Is there any chance this has got nothing to do with the EGA? That these lines were never sent to them to begin with?'

'You mean that the gemtechs didn't turn everything over? That's what Chang is now claiming, although I can't see that it reflects any better on them since they were supposed to have verified each and every vial as it was checked into storage. And in fact the EGA did find discrepancies at the time, do you remember? A couple of the gemtechs held back some of their most valuable stock, substituted dummy vials, but they got caught out by their own datastream records. So I don't buy it. You'd have to ask yourself not only how they got around those checks, but why so many of them did exactly the same thing. Because the missing stock was originally the property of several different gemtechs.'

'And then,' said Achebe nervously, 'there are the hacks.'

'You managed to verify those, did you?'

'Yes, sir. The trace is very clear, it looks like the same individual broke into the datastreams of multiple gemtechs and searched for specific genetypes in each of them.' He drew a deep breath. 'The genetypes that were trawled by the hacker correspond to the gene-stock that is missing from the EGA.'

'And these hacks happened when?'

Sharon, who knew the answer and knew that Masoud knew it too, tightened her lips and stayed silent.

'Before the Declaration, when the genestock was still with the gemtechs,' said Achebe. 'There was a lot of datastream breaking-and-entering in those days, traces of it are all over the place. Mostly hackbot stuff, very broad spectrum, but some of it was much more refined. Targeted. This hacker follows that pattern.'

'With the added feature,' said Masoud evenly, 'that what our hacker was searching for in the records of multiple private companies four or five years ago has since been stolen from a single secure government facility. Sometime in the last *three* years.'

Achebe squirmed. Sharon said, 'Yes.'

'It seems to me, Inspector Varsi, as though someone is playing a very long game here, and isn't too troubled by minor matters like the confiscation of the genestock they had their eye on.'

'That sounds about right, sir.'

'Or the ban on its use.'

'Well, that's the question, isn't it, sir? We know that they stole from each other, or tried to, back in the days when there was money to be made. But it's tough to work out how anyone could make that stuff pay now. The only human gemtech that's allowed any more is for health reasons, and for parents who can't conceive or have reason to worry how their kids might come out.' She kept her voice rigidly neutral. 'There's no legitimate market for anything else. Every now and then you hear about a back-alley gene surgeon who'll fiddle you better pheromones or make sure you have a baby with blue eyes instead of brown. But this is highly engineered genestock. The EGA's own scientists tell us that kind of shoestring operation couldn't do anything with it. And the cost-benefits around creating a sufficiently sophisticated black lab don't seem to add up.'

'So what do you think is going on?'

'I don't know, sir. I would very much like to find out.'

'What do you propose?'

'We've initiated background checks into everyone who could possibly have had access – the current staff, plus all the people who've come and gone. It's going to be a bit messy, almost everyone who has expertise in this area also has some link back to pre-Declaration gemtech activity. We'll work through them, liaise with local police, see if we come up with any probables. Sergeant Achebe here has begun a detailed systems audit, trying to work out exactly how our thief could have got in and out without triggering any alarms, or leaving a trail.' She glanced at Achebe, who was nodding vigorously. 'I've already spoken to colleagues in bio-crime about the black lab angle, just to make sure we cover it off. They're going to check their sources and get back to me.'

Masoud was nodding, grim-faced. 'The director, Chang. You think he could be involved?'

'I'm leaning very hard on him, sir, and so far my impression is no. He's one of the few who never worked in the industry, came out against it from his student days. I suspect that's a big part of why he got the job. He was speechless when we showed him the counterfeit vials, and he's been scrambling for explanations and excuses ever since. He doesn't seem to have been prepared at all, unless he's a hell of an actor.'

'And the whistleblower?'

Sharon avoided looking at Achebe, wishing she felt less annoyed that this, too, had so far come up a dead end. They were not supposed to go looking for anonymous informants, but in this case finding out who had set them on the hunt would have been a breakthrough worth making.

'Hasn't come forward. And there's no trail in the datastream . . .'

'That's one of the *strangest* things about this whole business, sir.' To her surprise, Achebe had interrupted. 'Normally we'd be able to track back, find the files those screenshots were taken from, or if they were deleted there should be a record in the edit log. But there's nothing. There's no evidence of the theft in the datastream *at all.*'

'So where did the—? Hang on.' Masoud was massaging his temples again. 'So we were sent pictures of files that don't exist, but should.'

'Yes, sir . . .'

'Which provided fake evidence of a crime . . .'

'Yes . . .'

'. . . that really was committed.'

'Yes, sir,' said Sharon and Achebe together.

'So how—?' He took in the look on Sharon's face. 'No, let me guess. *We don't know.*' He flicked at the tablet in exasperation and the infographic finally winked out.

'No, we don't,' Sharon said levelly. 'I'm wondering if it could be one of the visiting scientists, if they were somehow able to mirror the EGA idents and send us something that looked genuine enough to make us go in and find what we've found. I'm told there's all sorts of things wrong with that theory, but so far it's the only one I've got.'

This was not entirely true, but she had no intention of saying any more; not unless it proved unavoidable. She did not look at Achebe, and he stayed quiet. Masoud rested his chin on his steepled fingers and stared across the table at them for a long minute. Sharon met his gaze steadily. She could sense Achebe beginning to fidget beside her.

'Right.' Masoud finally sat back in his chair, shaking his head tiredly. 'Well, this is a deep and stinking pile of shit, Sharon, and we had all better grab shovels and start digging.'

It had been some considerable time since she had last lost her temper quite this badly.

Khan had retreated, gradually at first but with increasing speed, until he stood with his back pressed against the door, face ashen as he fumbled for the release button. Unable as yet to contain herself, she nevertheless knew the torrent of her own abuse to be excessive and unwarranted, and foresaw with a kind of dull weariness the inevitable hunt for a new assistant if she let him get away.

'It isn't your *fucking* fault, Khan!' she shouted at him, recognising the admission to be both incongruous and pitifully inadequate, as the door finally hissed open. She was surprised to see him stop at the midpoint of his escape, looking possibly even more stunned than before. She had a viciously gratuitous vision of the door hissing closed again and neatly bisecting the tablet he was desperately clutching to his chest, his elegant suit, and him.

'It's not?' he ventured, still poised to flee.

'Did you send this?' She ripped her own tablet off its stand and waved it at him. She knew it would take very little for her to throw it at him. She was still going at top volume, and the door was standing open now, with him standing in it. She could feel the pulse pounding in her temples and throat. She needed to calm down.

'Well, *did* you?' Shouting still, fighting for control, not winning. 'Are you that *witch*? Is this *your* idea, to send that *bastard* in here to see how much more *fucking* damage he can do? Well, is it? No.'

He was still standing there. Remarkable. Something about it pulled the plug on her fury. She threw the tablet onto the desk, hard, and collapsed into her chair. 'It is not. So what the *fuck* are you running away for?'

Khan glanced out into the corridor, then stepped back inside. The door closed and he leaned against it, fingers a hair's breadth away from the button. *Really* remarkable. His face was still pale, but he was puzzled now, frowning at her, actually waiting to see if there would be an explanation. She looked away, kneading her own hands together, cracking the knuckles, eyes hooded as she stared at the blank tablet on her desk. Deep. Calming. Breaths. *Yeah, right.*

A small sound, Khan clearing his throat.

'I'm not sure what's happened, ma'am,' he said quietly, 'but I'm certain it can be resolved. I'm going to go and fetch you a cup of tea . . .'

'I don't like tea,' she muttered truculently. She could feel the rawness in her throat, and coughed. Her hands were starting to tremble and she kept them in her lap, wondering if the shaking was going to spread throughout her body, bleakly aware that she should get him out of the office before he noticed. She felt cold and exhausted.

'I'm going to fetch you a cup of tea,' he repeated, with a firmness of tone that made her look up in surprise. 'It'll help you calm down. And then, ma'am, if you'll tell me what's made you so upset, maybe we can find a way to fix it.'

The tea was herbal and surprisingly good. Her estimation of Khan continued to rise. He sat quietly across from her, just out of sight over her shoulder. She had swivelled to gaze out of the panoramic window as she sipped. It probably gave the impression that she was too embarrassed to look at him, which at the moment was just as well. The trembling had receded, helped by the meds she'd swallowed while he was out of the room, but she could still feel the last of the tics and tremors ghosting across her face. She kept her eyes on the sky, watching its colour deepen as the long summer day slipped into evening, while she spoke.

'So,' she concluded, 'he led us to believe he was taking our concerns seriously and would reflect them in his report to the Federation, and then he did the opposite. Quite spectacularly.'

'I see.' That diffident throat-clearing again. 'Umm . . . do you still think his conclusions were wrong?'

'It's not that.' Her mental acuity was returning, and she was aware she had to be careful. Part of the revised brief for Bel'Natur had been ensuring that new staff all had impeccably correct views on civil rights. 'I'm not convinced he was right on that specific point, but the consequences haven't turned out to be as bad as we feared. Not yet, anyway. And I don't object to the way the world has changed, not any more. It was difficult at the time, but I'm over it. I accept that things had to evolve.' She sighed and stretched out her legs, feeling the twinges in knees and hips. 'It's the way he went about it, the duplicity. I don't think there was any doubt in his mind about what recommendations he was going to make, but he pretended otherwise.'

'So you don't think he can be trusted.'

'No, I don't.'

'Does he need to be?'

She glanced around at him, looked quizzical.

'You asked me to familiarise myself with all aspects of the project,' he said diplomatically. 'And I can't see anything about the working practices or the people that he could find objectionable. Mr Herran's involvement will obviously bring a new dimension to it, but if you leave it up to Dr Walker and Ms Morningstar to set the ground rules the question doesn't really arise.'

She looked back at the window, feeling the corner of her mouth twitch into the hint of a rueful smile. He was right, of course, and she'd known it was what she'd have to do even as she read Aryel Morningstar's brusque message. It was the similarity to a previous, disastrous stratagem that had made her so furious.

Explaining that to Khan was out of the question.

Something else he had said struck her. 'Are you familiar with Dr Walker's work?'

'A bit. He's required reading at college now.' She raised an eyebrow at him, and he winced. 'Um. Sorry, I didn't mean . . .'

She swivelled back to face him across the desk, sighed and waved a magnanimous hand. 'It's fine, Khan. My undergraduate days are long past, no use pretending otherwise. I just hadn't realised Eli Walker had become so ubiquitous.'

'He's considered the authority on . . . well, pretty much everything. Everything to do with gems anyway.'

'My understanding was that going to live in the Squats had tarnished his reputation.'

'It depends who you talk to. I'd say it's divided opinion. I know some people think it proves he's gone native and can no longer be considered an objective observer.'

He was nodding gravely as he spoke, as if to emphasise how well this must correspond with her own view. He'd go far, this one. 'But most – including the professor I had – saw it as giving him even more credibility. Reporting from the front line, so to speak.'

'And what do you think, Khan?'

'I think Dr Walker remains hugely influential. Maybe less so among academics these days, but very much so on the streams. People see him as a moral person, even if they don't always agree with his take on things.'

He flicked a nervous glance at her. She thought, with a frisson of satisfaction, that he was worried about setting her off again.

He plunged ahead anyway. 'The thing is, ma'am, it could be

a real positive, him participating in the project. Working with Bel'Natur, bringing a gem and a gemtech back together, brokering a new relationship . . .'

There was a pleading, slightly puzzled look to Khan's face as he described the golden opportunity that Eli Walker represented. This must be what he'd thought when he saw the message from Morningstar, the reason he'd skipped in here smiling with delight only to catch the full broadside of her wrath; and she finally understood how very strange it must be for this young man, filled with the indoctrination and idealism of a new age, to discover that it had not been immediately obvious to her.

The mellow twilight had long since drifted into night by the time Zavcka made her weary way home; a clear, cool stillness washed by the rising moon. She rested her head against the cushioned panel of the car, watching the brighter splashes of streetlamps flash past, and wondered whether the compromises she had been forced to make really would, in the end, be worth it.

On the other side of the city from her plush apartment every light blazed in a small flat close to the river, cluttered with the debris of travel. Bethany poured the dregs of a bottle into her glass and stabbed out another caustic post to her favoured stream. She gulped the wine down as she watched responses ping back, taking lonely comfort in the thought that a great many people were keeping themselves awake so as not to miss whatever she might have to say next.

Down on the streets of the Squats, the bustle and hum of evening revelry was finally fading. Occasional bursts of laughter split the air as the last customers spilled out of bars and clubs to make their way home. Music welled up, a sudden flood of melody as a door opened to let a trio tumble out onto the pavement, turning back to shout slightly drunken farewells at those who remained inside. Gwen waved goodbye to them, catching a glimpse of the moon before the door was pulled shut; turning away to nod at Lyriam and the percussionist and come in on the beat as they ran through the phrase again.

A few blocks away, on a dark and sleeping street, a light breeze stirred the curtains that hung before a bedroom window on the fourth floor of Maryam House.

Rhys came awake so slowly and gently, with a feeling of well-being so completely and utterly enveloping, that it took him some time to realise that he was not in fact dreaming. He became aware gradually of the surface on which he lay, soft next to his bare skin, and the silkiness of the sheet that covered him. The sense of bliss was so complete that he held back from full wakefulness, wallowing in perfect peace.

A sound intruded, someone breathing regular and slow, and he blinked his eyes open into a dimness that was faintly tinged with red. The hue seemed brighter than his own wine-dark glow. Memory washed over him, along with a faint, sour-sweet tang of sex, and he turned his head.

Callan was asleep, his face relaxed, lips parted a little. The scarlet shimmer of his hair cast a flush over his pale skin. Rhys felt his throat constrict at the sight. He rolled over onto his side, acutely aware of his own body, the resting strength of it, the lack of tension or pain. He thought fleetingly that having woken up, perhaps he should now do something; snuggle closer and stroke him awake for more, or else slip quietly away to his own bed in Aryel's flat. He rejected the latter notion in the instant of having it.

Instead he lay quiet, watching, letting the moment cradle him; knowing, without knowing how he knew, that something big and dangerous and precious was beginning, and that he was being swept away by it, and could not have helped it even if he had wanted to.

CONJUNCTIONS

14

Sharon Varsi wondered if it was an inevitable part of every officer's career: for a moment to come when the actions she was obliged to take would appear to contradict the motives behind them. It was not the first time the thought had occurred to her, but as she sat with Mikal and Aryel in his office in the Squats, briefing them on her investigation, the sense of conflict was starting to become acute.

Though she had previously said nothing to Aryel herself, had not even seen her since the concert several days previously, she was unsurprised to learn that news of the genestock theft had already been broken to her. In the same way Masoud had known that she would tell Mikal, she discovered that she had known Mik would tell Aryel. She could not find it in herself to be annoyed. This was the way their world worked. It might even make things easier, although at the moment it did not feel easy. Their reactions so far had been predictable: anger, anxiety, and now, she feared, outrage. She was explaining why she was forced to bring the investigation home, and trying hard not to feel like a traitor.

They were discussing Herran.

'I haven't said anything to Masoud,' she told them quietly. 'And I really hope I never have to. But I can't not ask the question. He put me in charge of this case – put a lot of noses out of joint in the department as well, it turns out – because of my supposedly greater insight. Into the gem situation, quote unquote.'

The words tasted bitter in her mouth. She looked sideways at Mikal, who sat hunched, elbows on knees, hands clasped and pendent in the air above his massive feet, his few fingers and many thumbs woven together in a basket-like symmetry. It looked as though he had folded himself into too small a space, his bowed back on a level with her head and his eyes staring vacantly at the floor. Her heart lurched. She reached out and tucked her hand under his arm.

'Sweetheart, I'm sorry. What can I do? I can't even ask to be taken off it, Masoud would be furious and whoever took over would just wonder why . . .'

'Would you rather not have the case?' Aryel asked curiously.

'It's not that. It's a great case career-wise – assuming I solve it – and I *want* to solve it. I want to know what's going on, I want to track down whoever did this and find out why. If someone's out there doing illegal gemtech with human stock I want to land on them like the proverbial ton of bricks.' She spread her hands in a plea for understanding. 'But I can't be half-arsed about it, Aryel. I'm not saying I believe Herran is involved. I can't imagine why or how he could be. But the fact is, things were done here that as far as I'm aware only he can do. I know if I were any other cop the question wouldn't arise. I wouldn't be aware of his existence, much less be in a position to make the connection. But I'm not another cop. I can't just pretend not to know what I know.'

Aryel met her eyes and then looked away, up at the ceiling, leaning into the low-backed chair she favoured. Her wings brushed the floor behind her and she shook them irritably. Sharon could hear her breathe out, a faint sigh that was almost a snort, over lips compressed into a tight line. It was body language familiar to her friends, a subtle sign of swift and worried thought; rarely visible except to her inner circle. Sharon hoped she still numbered among those few, but it was not her most pressing concern.

Mikal's arm flexed under her fingers as he stirred.

'You're a good cop.'

'Yes . . . ?'

'You're a good cop and I wouldn't want you to be anything less.' He gathered her hand up and interlaced his fingers with hers, gave a brief squeeze and let go. 'I'm sure Aryel doesn't either.'

He wrinkled his brow across the room at her. She replied, 'No, of course not,' as though it hardly needed to be said, while Sharon felt herself go limp inside with relief.

'I don't think Herran has anything to do with this,' Mikal went on. 'Do you?'

'No. I'm absolutely certain he doesn't.'

'But Sharon can't just take our word for it. She has to eliminate him. Properly.'

Aryel was nodding agreement, though a tiny frown had taken up residence between her brows. 'I understand that. I'm just worried . . . how disruptive does it have to be? He can't handle an onslaught of strangers, you know that. He'll shut down. He's already letting himself be put through a lot for the Bel'Natur deal. And we've been keeping his involvement there quiet, for obvious reasons, but if he's suddenly in the frame of a police investigation . . .'

'It'll be kept confidential. I promise. He's a vulnerable person, he'll be very carefully treated, no matter what.' Sharon was aware that she was perilously close to gushing reassurances and checked herself. Things needed to be done, as Mik said, properly.

'He has to be questioned. Protocol says he should come to the station and be interviewed by someone he has no prior history with, but given his autism I can get around that. It needs to be a proper police interview, though. I can tailor it for his condition, but there are things I'm going to need to press him on. I'll have to have another officer there to vouch for me doing my job correctly, and there can't be more than two people supporting him.' She glanced at her husband again. 'And one of them can't be you, babe.'

'Fair enough.' He finally straightened up on the chair, stretching. His spine cracked, and his fingertips almost touched the ceiling. He cocked his head at Aryel. 'Callan? And you?'

'Callan definitely. Not me.' Aryel's posture had relaxed too, arms resting along the sloping back of the chair, slim legs stretched out and ankles crossed. The tips of her wings were fanned along the floor now, but she seemed not to mind. It dawned on Sharon that their earlier anxiety had been no more than fear for Herran, and she felt a stab of guilt for ever imagining otherwise.

You should've known they'd be upset at the situation, not you, she thought, and was comforted. But she thought too that their freedoms had been won as much by the cohesion Aryel had forged, the rock-solid loyalty the gems of the Squats felt for each other, as anything else; and it was perhaps not unreasonable to wonder whether that would ultimately always win out.

Aryel was still speaking, eyes back on the ceiling, thoughtful but no longer tense. 'Eli would be better. That's the configuration Herran's becoming accustomed to, himself with Callan and Eli in unfamiliar situations. This could help to reinforce that, instead of being purely a stressor.' She glanced at Sharon. 'And it would be better for your report if I wasn't there. No undue influence.'

Sharon shrugged and stretched. It seemed to be infectious, as they all eased into a familiar camaraderie. 'It's not like anyone would object, but yes. Callan to help him communicate and Eli as impartial observer are the logical choices. It needs to be today if possible. I'll set it up.'

'Fine. He should be starting at Bel'Natur in another week or two, assuming we get all the terms and conditions sewn up, and it'll be best if there's nothing else he has to contend with by then.' She shot her one-sided, ironic smile at Mikal. 'What do you think? Is she going to throw her toys on the floor and storm off, or stick with it?'

He raised an eyebrow at her. 'Are you referring to Zavcka Klist? The most amenable woman in London? Surely not.'

'I detect a note of sarcasm, Councillor.'

'Only because I keep waiting for the other shoe to drop. I've never been pleased and thank-you'd so much in my life.' He shrugged. 'I haven't seen her again, which is fine by me. The Bel'Natur ethics committee are all puffed up about having executive authority, and they didn't object to anything I put on the table. Not much anyway. I did suggest they endow a chair at Oxbridge especially for Eli, but I knew that was pushing it.'

Aryel chuckled. 'She's not fond of him – I can tell she has to hold herself back every time his name is mentioned. I *am* seeing her, which delights neither of us, but I've made it clear I'm not prepared to negotiate with anyone else. We're on the home stretch now, though. The lawyers will be there today.'

'Who've we got?'

'Jeremy Temple. Dropped everything, doing it for free.'

Mikal hooted with laughter. 'Oh, how she must *love* you.'

Jeremy Temple had been the architect of the legal equalisation of gems with norms throughout Europe; a clever solicitor who freely admitted that his allegiance to his gemtech clients had been turned, along with his head, years before when he met the woman who would later become his wife. They now had a child, who struggled with the legacy of his mother's modifications. Jeremy Temple was, along with Eli Walker, the gemtechs' equivalent of the Grim Reaper.

'I did think that might be the last straw. But she hasn't actually objected to his presence, or Eli's.' She smiled. 'Not so we've heard, anyway.'

'Does it really need to be this complicated, Aryel?' Sharon asked. 'Getting into bed with Bel'Natur for the long haul seems . . .' she trailed off, grimacing.

'I'm not sure about that either, which is where Eli comes in.' Aryel sighed. 'The trouble is that we desperately need gemtech expertise. The reproductive assistance the health services can provide is too limited. You know the guidelines: when they run up against an incompatibility they just strip out the engineering, splice in some baseline genestock and revert to the norm standard. If that's what the parents want, then fine, and goodness knows it makes the Reversionists happy. Most of them. But think about someone like – oh, maybe like Jora. It would be great if her children could inherit autonomic tissue regeneration – but probably *not* the overgrowth that she suffers from. That has as many consequences for her health as it does for her appearance.'

A picture of Jora floated into Sharon's mind: a simple, sweet-natured girl, a face that should have been pretty marred by extra lumps of lip and nose and chin. Aryel was shaking her head. 'And what if her partner's genetype complicated things further? Suppose he was a gillung, for example? And they risked having a child in whom gill tissue might overwhelm lung tissue? Or vice versa? Do we want to have to tell people in that position that their kids can only be healthy if they are as *unlike* their parents as possible?'

'We don't,' said Sharon, with conviction. She felt Mikal shift beside her. 'I just didn't realise it was possible to deal with problems that complicated.'

'Oh, it's possible. The gemtechs have the technology, but no incentive to use it. The government hasn't made up its mind whether to buy it, and we can't afford to, not for a while yet. Public policy is moving too slowly, some of the Reversionists are proving too influential. We need a solution, and we need it quickly.'

Sharon chewed at her lip. 'How long does this intervention go on for, though? If your self-regenerating water-breather grows up and has kids with a high-altitude hyperspectral hybrid, say . . . and then *their* kids . . .'

'Exactly. Either we do what the hard-core Reversionists want, letting our abilities die out – or not reproducing at all – or we face the fact that the legacy of gemtech is going to be with us for generations, and we need an equally long-term strategy for dealing with it.' She shrugged. 'I'm not certain this is it. Bel'Natur may not really be reformed, or reformable. But if they are, it's the quickest, simplest solution I can see.'

Sharon turned this over. Aryel's reasoning, as always, made sense. But she could also see the implications, far-reaching and transformative, as engineered anatomies combined into new forms, and supernormal abilities became diffused throughout the human gene pool. There was a part of her that understood the concerns, the hesitation, the outright fear that fuelled the Reversionists, as well as many more who would not wish to bear that label. She flipped them an ironic mental salute, and moved on. Her own choice in such matters had been made long ago.

'Is Jora seeing a gillung? Just curious.'

Aryel laughed. 'Jora's not seeing anyone, as far as I know. She's only just stopped carrying a torch for Callan, poor girl. But she's only twenty; as long as they harvest her regularly she'll probably outlive us all. It's bound to come up at some point.'

Eli went through his lists again, carefully, thinking that if Aryel really was going to seal the deal that afternoon there would be little chance in the future to fix any mistakes. He had brainstormed exhaustively with her and Callan and Herran, trying to imagine all the possible scenarios, all the protections and guarantees they would need. A reminder began to pulse in the corner of his tablet, but he ignored it for a few minutes, until he was certain that everything was in order. Then he tapped open a vidpanel that he could monitor while he composed a covering message to Aryel.

The interview was being streamed live, but not from the usual chic studio whose ever-changing décor was endlessly imitated by the legions of the hip. Eli recognised the comfortable interior of a decidedly more well-worn club near the Squats.

Bloody hell. She got them to come to her.

The most popular street-culture host on the trendiest social-stream sounded even more star-struck than usual. Eli had for years made a practice of keeping an eye on even the silliest of the streams, having learned too well that that was where changes in moods and attitudes would manifest first. This one was both reasonably intelligent and hugely influential; whatever it touted today was likely to be on everyone's lips tomorrow, and ubiquitous by the end of the week. They had just about given up begging Aryel to be a guest, although that might be about to change.

The host, a waif-thin norm who was known, among other things, for only using his first name, was in full flow. '. . . *she shares with her even more famous foster sister another thing that's rare for gems: a surname. Do you prefer Ms Morgan?*'

'No,' said Gwen. '*Just Gwen.*' She flashed a smile at him. Even through the tiny square of the vidpanel, Eli felt dazzled.

It appeared to stun her interviewer as well. '*Right. Beautiful,*' he mumbled, then recovering himself, '*that's beautiful. Well, I'm not sure it's fair to call this your debut performance, Gwen. Many of us had the pleasure of hearing you sing at the Festival opening a few days ago . . .*'

'*Oh, please.*' She was charmingly dismissive. '*That was an improvised response to an unpleasant situation. Not my usual thing at all!*'

'*Well, you certainly made it pleasant for the rest of us! And you knew a song that was very old and obscure. I think we all found that quite remarkable. Did you learn religious music because of your upbringing?*'

'*I just learned music,*' Gwen replied. She was leaning casually against the vacant bar, elbows propped and long legs crossed, shimmering ruby curls cascading over her shoulders. Her outfit was no longer old-fashioned, but neither was it the current rage; there was an ahead-of-the-curve glamour about it that Eli suspected a thousand young women would immediately attempt to replicate. It was unlikely to look as good on any of them as it did on her. '*Many old things survive out in the mountains. It doesn't mean we think about them the same way our ancestors did.*'

'*I understand there are a lot of traditional sounds in the work you're going to be showcasing for us tonight. But the songs themselves are new, is that right?*'

'*That's right. Almost everything we'll be playing has only ever been heard in rehearsal. And the traditional sounds are not just from one tradition. Lyriam and I are interested in pulling together lots of different influences . . . ah, here he is.*' Another radiant smile as Lyriam walked into the frame, leaned across to shake the interviewer's hand and then propped himself on the bar beside her.

'*It sounds like a real meeting of the minds,*' the host prattled on. '*But I understand you've only recently started collaborating? Tell us about that.*'

Eli concentrated on finishing his message while Lyriam and Gwen tag-teamed the rest of the interview. *P.S.*, he wrote at the end, *I'm watching UnStreamed, and your sister is playing Julius like a violin.* He swiped to send and turned his full attention back to the vidpanel, just as Julius turned his full attention back to Gwen.

'*So, Gwen, I guess we won't be hearing any more hymns from you tonight,*' *then. Any thoughts on the Reversionist reaction to your, ah, "improvised response"?'* He was grinning toothily. *'I understand there was speculation about whether you might have some sympathy for them. Because of your background.'*

'I have a lot of sympathy for anyone who has a hard time working out where they fit in,' Gwen replied sweetly. *'The Remnants know how important it is to learn from the past, but I think there are many people who don't understand – sadly – that that's not the same thing as imitating it. Not at all. We're very clear that the biggest lesson is often what* not *to do.'*

Julius looked slightly stupefied. Lyriam threw Gwen a sideways glance: appraising, and possibly a touch apprehensive. She leaned against the bar, held Julius with her eyes, and serenely waited for the next question. He stammered out something about whether that was part of her approach to music as well, but Eli was not listening to the answer.

That reply went well beyond the show's arts-and-lifestyle remit and he felt a sense of wry admiration for how neatly Gwen had just dismissed the Reversionists and instead placed herself at the centre of the cultural zeitgeist. But more: it took him back to the night in the park, Reginald's cryptic comment, the sense of a shifting landscape that he had felt at the party. He looked down at the tablet in his hands, the plans and protocols he had been working on, the message he had just sent, and thought about the use to which all of that work was about to be put.

Reginald's right, he thought. *Integration isn't going to be a problem, and the Reversionists don't stand a chance. They will be us before we know it.*

Zavcka Klist hated the smell of the lab. She considered it one of the many ironic annoyances of her life that even after the overthrow of all but the most mundane gemtech, the upheavals that had occurred with and without her assistance, the fulfilling of her own ambitions still required her to spend far too much time breathing in the miasma of organic matter and electrolysis, the sweet stink of solvents and waste. She would have liked to come down here less, but she knew too well the dangers of hands-off management; of allowing staff to become isolated, or, worse yet, to believe themselves inviolate. And developments were at such a delicate stage.

Once I get through this part, once I know for sure it's going to work, I'm taking a break. No special security, no sixteen-hour workdays, no fucking labs.

She kept her distaste firmly masked through the few final words of approval and encouragement, and stepped into the lift beside Dunmore. The doors hissed closed, and she breathed a sigh of relief. His face was as stoic as ever, but there was a hint of curiosity in his voice as he said, 'Everything to your satisfaction, ma'am?'

'They're doing very well. Very well indeed. But this deal with the gems is going to happen, Dunmore, and that means the safeguards need to be especially tight. Shift patterns, communications, everything. They need to understand below stairs that nothing, and I mean *nothing*, can be allowed to slip.'

'It won't, ma'am. I'll be drilling them personally.' He cleared his throat. 'Do we know when the gems are likely to arrive?'

'Within a couple of weeks, I hope. There's no time to waste. I'm aiming to wrap up the business end of it today, god help me, and then it'll be as soon as the savant can be persuaded to start.'

He cocked his head at her. It was as close to a look of reproof as she had ever seen from Dunmore. She looked back, puzzled, and then got it.

'As soon as *Herran* can be persuaded to start. Damn. You'd better drill me too.'

'If you like, ma'am, but it won't be necessary. Once they're on site you'll be sharp.'

'I need to be sharp now. Set an example.'

He ducked his head, a fractional movement that conveyed acknowledgement, agreement and approval, but no less deference. Dunmore was a marvel, she thought, a type one hardly ever saw any more. He rarely betrayed an opinion of his own, never balked at anything he was required to do, but he was the sort of servant who would tell you what you needed to know whether you liked it or not, without any diminution of respect. He could be relied upon to read the mood on the streets and streams, and to understand how well it corresponded – or not – with the once-hermetic bubble of Bel'Natur. Though he had neither education nor brilliance, was as stolid and unoriginal as a coffee cup, it was he who really understood how to close the circuit between the requirements of her personal project and the realities on the ground.

How very different from Khan, waiting upstairs for her with notes and calculations for the final horse-trade with Temple and Morningstar. He too had his finger on the pulse of current opinion, but that was because he shared it, he lived it. He was full of creativity and initiative, and enthusiasm for this new, borderless world. She could hold him in her mind's eye as an example, an embodiment of the modern spirit; a marker of how far she had yet to go.

The new and the old, the cavalier and the cautious, the carrot and the stick.

You are a lucky woman, Zavcka, in spite of everything. What you need is at hand when you need it. These two are counterweights; repellent to each other, but equally necessary to your survival. Keep them loyal, use them wisely, and they will get you through this.

15

The club was larger than Rhys had expected, tucked away behind a deceptively modest entrance on one of the still shabby streets that ringed the Squats. They had barely arrived before Gwen dragged him through a door next to the toilets and showed him around a rat-run of narrow passages and odd little offices and storerooms that she rather grandly referred to as backstage. He stuck his head into the noisy chaos of a dressing room to wave at Lyriam and the rest of the band, before he and his sister emerged back onto the dance floor through a different door, this time beside the bar.

Music poured down from hidden speakers, pressing against him like an insistent hand. It sounded Antipodean, at once archaic and oddly modern, a bone-deep bass thrum behind a high, wavering voice that flickered through the notes almost too fast to register. He heard Gwen begin to hum a counterpoint, the subvocal harmonics below the level of most people's perception. She probably didn't even know she was doing it.

The dance floor was a semicircle of clear space in front of a small stage, now bustling with activity as instruments were positioned and equipment checked. It was bordered by seating and low tables, and then there were a couple of steps up to another level, with good views to the front and dark, discreet alcoves further back. Enough to hold a lot of people, even if those who chose the seats at the rear would likely be more interested in each other than in the performance.

But still, it was an impressive space, and it needed to be. With Lyriam as co-star, the show – announced via the breaking-news bombshell of the morning's joint interview, and with the additional cachet of being invitation-only – had within a few hours become the hottest ticket in town. Barely a week had gone by since the concert in the park, and Rhys mentally calculated the degree of hard graft, subtle persuasion and calling in of favours that must have gone into organising it, and concluded that Gwen had been up to much, much more than even he had realised.

Reginald, Graca and Aryel had commandeered a section of plush banquettes on the lower level, close to the stage. Rhys and Gwen made their way over, against the steady trickle of people heading for the bar. Most of the tables, he noticed, were already occupied; the room had begun to fill up just in the few minutes that they had been away. About half the audience for this pop-up performance bore obvious gemsigns, and glowing, jewel-coloured heads made their own light show as they nodded and tossed around him. Many of them called out to Gwen, familiar greetings which she laughingly returned. Despite himself, Rhys had to admit he was impressed. When had she found time to meet them all? Gwen had always been better at making friends; she had the gift of instant charm and effortless popularity, where he generally felt himself having to work at it. But this was remarkable even by her standards.

She slipped seamlessly into the conversation the others were having with a pair of new arrivals who leaned over the railing from above. They said their goodbyes and hurried off to find seats, only to be replaced by others. For several minutes there was a constant flow of people stopping to greet Ari, comment on Gwen's UnStreamed appearance and wish her luck with the show, shake

Da's hand and compliment Graca on the subaquatic technology that was emerging as one of the big stories of the Festival. Rhys smiled and nodded just enough not to appear rude, while he kept an eye on those still arriving.

He spotted Callan as he emerged out of the dim passageway that led to the entrance, and paused to survey the room. Rhys raised a hand, and felt his heart skip as he saw Callan's face light up. He made his way over, arriving just as the last lot of well-wishers were about to depart.

'Twice in one week!' exclaimed the tall albino woman, Aster, as she planted a kiss on both Callan's cheeks. Her skin and hair were bone-white, but her eyes glowed pale purple around piercing violet irises. 'We might almost get used to seeing you.'

'Be careful what you wish for,' he shot back, and there was laughter, a final round of hugs, and then she threaded her imperious way towards the bar.

Her departure seemed to signal the end of the flurry that had surrounded them, and they were finally able to sit. Rhys knew that if his family had not been there Callan would have greeted him with a kiss, wrapped an arm around him as they sat next to each other. Instead he could feel him staying within touching distance but not touching, watching him sideways, waiting to see how he wanted to play it. He shot him a glance back, read the wanting in his eyes, and felt his stomach flip over again as he shifted close enough to clasp his hand for a moment and lean casually against him, thigh to thigh. There was a quick, delighted smile in response, a squeeze of his fingers and a happy glint in the green eyes. Rhys looked back at his family.

Aryel, sitting across from them on a toadstool-like ottoman, arched an eyebrow, shook her wings and smiled. Reginald said, 'Hmm!' and grinned broadly, and Graca chuckled. Gwen stared open-mouthed, blinked, swallowed, and said, 'Callan? Would you mind if I borrowed my brother for a moment?'

Callan looked as though he were considering. 'Any particular reason?'

'He needs to be slapped.'

'In that case, absolutely not.'

'What for?' Rhys, indignant.

'For not talking to me. How did I miss this?'

'You,' said Rhys loftily, 'have not been paying attention.'

'I always pay attention!'

'Apparently not.'

'You *have* been a bit distracted, Gwen,' Aryel observed with amusement.

'Preoccupied, I'd say,' Reginald added.

'Sidetracked, even,' chimed Graca.

'You are all as daft as each other. And you, brother dear, have been keeping secrets.' She sat up straight, scowled prettily at him and drummed her hands on the table as if to emphasise that this was the final word on the matter. Rhys snorted.

'If I – we – were, we wouldn't have been the only ones.' He made a show of looking pointedly around the room and was pleased to see her grin turn a bit sheepish.

'We-ell . . . Lyriam thought it would be better not to trail it too far in advance . . . if we hadn't been ready in time, it's easier to cancel something nobody knows about. And I couldn't argue with that, I'm the one who doesn't really know what she's doing.'

She batted her eyelashes modestly as everyone except Callan howled. He looked a question at Rhys, who stopped laughing long enough to lean over and say in a stage whisper, 'She *always* knows what she's doing.'

'Almost always.' Gwen was still tapping her hands against the table, a faint percussive rhythm that Rhys registered as a nursery song from their childhood. 'The publicity boost from the interview was massive, but it means we've got even more stream coverage than we expected. I don't want to let anybody down.' Her gaze paused for a moment on the door by the bar, and then she smiled at them as the reassurances poured in. 'Right, well. If I'm going to live up to all of this, I'd better go get ready. Callan,' as she got to her feet, 'Rhys is a prat, but that's no reflection on you.'

She shot him an even sweeter smile, stuck her tongue out at her brother and turned to go. Reginald heaved himself to his feet. 'I shall escort you,' he said gravely, 'as far as the bar.'

'I'll help,' said Graca, and they collected orders and made for the scrum that surrounded it.

As soon as they were gone Aryel leaned forward, her face turned serious. 'Cal? How did it go?'

'Fine. No worries at all. It was obvious Herran had no idea what they were talking about. He was as baffled as I've ever seen him.'

'Was he upset?'

'Not really. I mean, you know Herran. He really likes Sharon. He was apologetic.' He glanced at Rhys. '"*Sorry not help.*"'

'What about the other cop?'

'Police psychologist. Had already liaised with social services, apparently, and read Herran's file.'

'Really?' Relief washed over her face. 'Oh, well *done*, Sharon. I should have known not to worry.'

'What's this?' asked Rhys, and Aryel explained.

'A psychologist would be able to make an informed judgement about Herran's mental state, far more than just a regular cop. And it's part of Herran's profile that he doesn't lie. There are things he might keep to himself, or find ways to talk around, but he can't actually tell an untruth. Or break a promise.'

'He can't?' This struck Rhys as almost more amazing than any of the things he knew Herran *could* do. 'I mean, that's good, I suppose, but . . .' He stopped, trying to work through his sense of ambivalence.

'It's a basic human capacity,' Callan said quietly. He sounded sad, and under the table his fingers tightened again around Rhys' where they rested on his knee. 'To be able to make things up, invent a different version of events, justify breaking your word. Herran can't do it.'

Rhys swallowed. 'I thought, when we were with him the other day . . . I mean, the way his brain works is incredible. I was awestruck. And it's not like I think people should lie. But not to be *able* to . . .'

'He keeps things to himself,' Aryel said again. 'And he's gained a little . . . subtlety, I guess you could call it. But sophisticated lateral thinking, leaps of logic, intuition . . .' She shook her head. 'He just doesn't seem to have the wiring for it. That observational analysis you and Gwen do automatically? Way beyond him.'

'That's really why you're sending Callan and Dr Walker to Bel'Natur with him, isn't it? It's not just to help him communicate and feel comfortable. You're afraid they might take advantage of him in ways he doesn't understand.'

'That is a big part of it.' She smiled at him. 'See? Sophisticated lateral thinking. Inference. You just spotted the connections. I wonder . . .' She trailed off, pensive. She was flickering through moods this evening, Rhys thought, the way the aborigem singer had been flickering through notes. It was unlike her. 'Callan, d'you know if Eli's coming?'

'A little later, I think. Said he had a few things to finish off.' He gave her an appraising look. 'It is going to happen, isn't it?'

'Bel'Natur? Yes. We got everything we wanted today.'

Callan pursed his lips and nodded, with the air of a man receiving orders to deploy to the front line. 'Are you really okay with going there?' Rhys asked him softly.

'*Okay* might be a bit strong. But there's a lot at stake, and the neurologist who came to meet Herran seemed really decent. He wasn't put off by her, which I confess is what I thought would happen. So I'm – calm about it, let's put it that way.'

'I think calm is about the best any of us can manage when it comes to Bel'Natur,' Aryel put in. 'And more than some of us *are* managing, when it comes to other things. Gwen, for example, could do with being a bit less spiky.'

'I thought she was pretty confident,' Callan remarked, 'despite what she said. She was great on UnStreamed this morning.'

'Oh she's completely confident about the show, and the interview was never going to be a problem for her. But she went pretty far over the top with you two.'

'She was embarrassed,' Rhys said immediately. 'She doesn't like being caught out.' Surprise flitted across Callan's face and Rhys felt embarrassed himself, as if he were making excuses. 'I mean yes, she was over the top. Did you mind very much? It's just, I know what she's like.' He stopped, because Callan was laughing.

'No, I didn't mind very much. And I think it's sweet that you defend her even when she's the one giving you a hard time. *And,*' his smile took in Aryel now, chuckling softly across the table, 'I suspect that if anyone *else* so much as gave you a dirty look she would crack them open like a nut. So she's okay in my book.'

'You realise,' Aryel put in, 'that potentially that includes you.' She chortled at Rhys' horrified face.

'Oh yes. I recognised the warning shot being fired across my bows,' said Callan serenely. His hand emerged from under the table and snaked around Rhys' shoulders. 'No fear. I'll do nothing to deserve it.'

Much later that night, after the ovations and congratulations were over, the streams had been sent into further paroxysms of excitement with exclusive clips and insider reviews, and most of the crowd had gone home, Gwen cornered him on the upper tier of the club.

'Does he know?'

'Yes.'

'Does he know *really*, Rhys?'

'I've told him.' He felt his gorge begin to rise at the look she gave him, as though questioning whether he really had, or really should have, done as he'd said. 'Look, what do you expect? That I would let someone get close to me, start a relationship, without telling them what they might be in for?'

The worry on her face was clear now, although she pursed her lips and tried to affect an air of carelessness.

'It doesn't need to be a *relationship*.'

'It does and it is. He's not just some boy, Gwennie. He's . . . I've never . . . this is different.'

She stared at him without expression for a long moment. Across the room he could see Callan deep in conversation with Aryel and Eli; somewhere in the dimness behind him he could sense a few other stragglers who would probably have to be levered out of whatever amorous tangle had kept them through the various last calls and general bustle of departure. Graca and Da were nursing final drinks with Lyriam and the blue-haired, narrow-faced agent, staff were upturning chairs onto tables and wiping down the bar. Not for the first time it occurred to him that Bethany had not been seen all night.

'Rhys.' Gwen spoke quietly, and with a deadly seriousness. 'Does he really, *really* understand what happens to you?'

'None of us really understands what happens to me.'

Her eyes bored into him, overturned his attempt to be glib, and he sighed. 'He hasn't seen how I get. When he does, *if* he does, he might run a mile. He might not want—'

He broke off, feeling the uncertainty wash up in him for the first time in days, the fear that he might be doing wrong, for himself and others. This time he could not help but think also of what too much caution might cost him. He watched the line of Callan's throat moving as he spoke to Eli, the lazy curve of his smile and the way he tilted his head to listen to Ari. Nascent desire transmuted, sparking into anger at his sister.

'What do you want me to do, Gwen? Never be with anyone again? Only ever be close to you, and Da, and Ari? Turn myself into an outcast just in case I'm with someone and I have a bad turn and they freak out?' He could feel his shoulders tensing, and a warning whispered in the back of his brain. He shook his head sharply, drew a deep breath. 'I can't live like that. I thought maybe I could, but I can't. Callan says he can deal with it, and I have to believe him.'

Gwen took a step back, hands up for calm, and he realised his voice had risen a little. He saw Graca turn her head in their direction, and kicked himself as he remembered how sharp gillung hearing was.

Callan glanced over at them, still smiling, unaware, and turned back to Aryel.

'Ki,' Gwen said softly. 'R'no sah.' *Okay. Don't get upset.*

'Sorry,' he muttered. 'But look, Da and Ari aren't bothered, so I don't know why you should be.'

'Maybe . . .' she murmured. 'No, you're right. You have to live your life regardless. I want you to be happy, Rhys, you know I do. I just worry.'

'Stop worrying. I'm fine, he's fine, we're fine. I start the tests tomorrow, they'll work out what's wrong, do some gene surgery and fix it. I'll probably never have another attack again.'

'I hope so. For all our sakes.' She was watching Callan too now. 'He's lovely, and I can see how good he is for you. You would never, ever want to hurt him.'

QUESTIONS

She wants to know how old she is.

It is a new obsession, one that seemed to arrive along with the tender bumps on her chest, the tufts of feathers on her wings and clumps of hair elsewhere. She has charted the course of her life as far back as she can, has already calculated minimums and maximums from what she can remember and what she has been able to pull off the datastream. But her tablet access remains clandestine, limited by firewalls she dare not breach, and in any case she suspects the most she would find would be batch cultivation and implantation data, foetal and post-natal development charts. That is not what she wants.

'Why do you care?'

'Everybody else knows their birthday,' she says. 'I just want to know mine. I don't want a cake or anything.' She can still hear the sounds of celebration, faint now behind the closed door of Dr Panborn's office. Someone must have seen her approaching along the corridor, but she'd smelled strange foods and glimpsed red faces over half-full glasses before the door was shut firmly against any closer inspection. She had lingered outside, knowing that Dr Owen would slip out early and find her there.

'"Everybody else" does not,' he tells her, ignoring the comment about cake. 'We do. Gems don't have birthdays.'

She can see crumbs on his lapel. She wonders what they taste like.

'Why not?'

'You don't need them.'

'Why do you need them, then?'

For a moment he appears nonplussed. She is having this effect on him a lot lately. The habit of caution is as strong in her as ever, and she keeps her eyes downcast and her face as blank as she can manage. Still, she is faintly surprised that she continues to fool him.

'It's not a question of why. We just have them. We're made differently.'

'But everybody gets born. That's just a regular thing that happens to everybody.'

'You are not a regular person, Aryel, and you never will be. These things are not important for you. Now,' and he glances ostentatiously at the screen of his tablet, something else he has taken to doing when she perturbs him, 'you have no business wandering about at this hour. Go back to the dorm. You can play with your tablet for a while before you go to bed, if you like.'

And he walks away, flushed with his own magnanimity, and leaves her trembling with rage and hurt.

One day, Dr Owen, she thinks. One day it might be important for you.

16

'It occurred to me last night,' Aryel was saying. 'You said you hadn't been able to work out what was so special about the genestock they took?'

'No. They were older lines, from several different gemtechs.' Sharon wondered why they were going over this again. Her earset had pinged as she was heading out the door, Aryel's mellow tones asking if she had a moment to pop up to the roof. *I've had a thought*, she'd said. *Something that might help*. It was taking her a while to get to it, though.

'Didn't that strike you as odd?'

'Aryel, this whole bloody business strikes me as odd.'

Aryel laughed shortly. 'Indeed. But I'm guessing that makes it even harder to extrapolate who could want it and what they want it for. Especially since the people who have the expertise you need are mostly going to have links either to the EGA or to the gemtechs themselves . . .'

'Or both.'

'Or both. So you can't ask them. But your hacker knew what he, or she, was looking for. If the stock was old then they wouldn't have found it in active datastreams, they would have been breaking into and trawling through archives. Searching for specific genetypes, around which there would have been no current research or chatter.'

'We've inferred from the start that they must have had a shopping list.'

'But what connects the items on that list? You don't just splice random bits of genestock together and hope for the best. If the hacker already knew exactly what he or she wanted and exactly where it was, the hacks wouldn't have been needed in the first place. And you said there are a few hacked genetypes for which the corresponding genestock hasn't been stolen – so presumably the hacker was able to determine that they didn't meet the criteria. What you need is someone who can reverse engineer that search, work out what those criteria were. You already know what they *got*, but it doesn't tell you enough. You need to find out what they were *looking* for.'

'We can't,' Sharon said grimly. 'It's not like I haven't thought the same thing. But it's too specialised for forensics – they're not covering themselves in glory on this one – and the so-called experts they've consulted are no better. The people who understand genetype data well enough to have a chance of working it out are the same ones we can't talk to.'

'I know someone you can talk to.'

'Who?'

'Rhys.'

'*Rhys*?' Sharon stared. 'What does he know about it?'

'He doesn't know anything about your case, apart from that Herran was questioned. But he knows a lot about genetype files, and the data structures that store them. He's spent years hacking into gemtech archives, trying to find particular genetypes.'

'He – *what*? *Excuse* me? *What*?' Sharon stopped in their slow perambulation around the vegetable beds and stared, open-mouthed. 'How does that make him anything but a suspect? What genetypes?'

'His own, and Gwen's. They were the only survivors of a crèche fire, they have no history. At first he was just curious about what they were intended for – they've a wide variety of mental and physical enhancements, but there's no one big obvious thing.' She shrugged deliberately, her wings rising with the movement, feathers softly ruffled by the morning breeze that blew off the river and across the roof garden. 'Then he started to have occasional spells of illness, seizures, and began searching in earnest. But that's only been in the last couple of years, long after the government copied over the datastreams. So his trace wouldn't be any part of what you're looking at. But it does mean he knows how to interrogate genetype data, and he knows the various gemtech archive structures inside out.'

'I see.' Sharon looked out across the Squats, chewing her lip thoughtfully. 'Did he find his own genetype in all his searching?'

'No. But that's because the gemtech that owned the lab which engineered him and Gwen disappeared shortly after the fire, and no public records appear to have survived. This was when the truth about the gemtechs was starting to emerge, the first big scandals, and he found a few mentions of that particular company among those reports. KAG Labs. They had started off as a very big player in the early days post-Syndrome, then had gradually shrunk to being an R&D affiliate and genestock supplier. They weren't registered for in vivo work. So, considering what was going on at the time, it's likely the directors scuttled the company, archived the datastream offline – maybe even wiped it entirely – and ducked out of sight. If there had been anything left to find I am absolutely certain that he or Herran would have found it.'

'Herran helped him look?'

'Enough to confirm what Rhys already knew. He was very impressed, for whatever it's worth. "*Rhys good job.*"'

Aryel took in Sharon's frown and rolled her eyes. 'I assume your interview yesterday cleared him.'

'It did. Which speaking as his friend makes me very relieved, but as a cop helps me not at all. I asked if he knew of anyone else who can do what he does, and he said no. He didn't mention Rhys.'

'Rhys is different. His neural wiring is like yours and mine, but he and Gwen have phenomenally high IQs linked to an enhanced analytical ability. He was hoping he'd pick up the KAG trail in the datastreams of other gemtechs, which would make sense if they'd sold the genestock on when they shut up shop. The point is, he was doing exactly the same thing that your hacker must have been doing. That's why I think he might be able to help.'

Sharon nodded, seeing the logic of it, and trying to reconcile her knowledge that the investigation needed help with her instinctive reluctance to get even more people involved.

'I'll have to run it by Masoud. Cover us both. And of course Rhys may not even be interested.'

'I think he will be.'

'Why do you want him to take something like this on? Especially if he's not well?'

'He is one hundred per cent fine most of the time, and the attacks don't last very long when they do happen. They're scary and they tire him out, but he recovers completely within a day or two. It is worrying, and he's here to try to identify whatever it is and come up with a cure. That starts today – in a couple of hours, in fact. But he won't have to be at the hospital very much and he'll be at a loose end, looking for something to occupy himself with. He has the skill, and it's the kind of problem that will fascinate him.'

Sharon squinted at her. 'Have you already discussed this with him?'

'No, I haven't, I told you.' Aryel took in her look. 'Sharon, come on. I'm not that presumptuous. I'm suggesting this because I think you can help each other, but it's up to you.'

You're suggesting it because you believe Rhys can find the answer, Sharon thought. *That's a thing to take seriously. And it's not like it's the first time we've turned to gem civilians with special skills. That's how you met Gaela, remember?*

What had happened to Gaela and her family afterwards pressed in on her consciousness, and her conscience.

Stop it, Varsi. This is tablet work, he doesn't even have to come to the station. Hardly anyone will know. And anyway, the godgangs are gone.

She looked for more tangible reasons to object, failed to find them, and nodded reluctantly. 'Where is he? I'll need to talk it through with him, before I say anything to Masoud.'

Rhys was at that moment letting himself quietly into Aryel's flat, hoping he could make it to his room and into fresh clothes unnoticed. Not that they didn't all know he had spent the night with Callan, and he was well aware that there could be no escape from the inevitable teasing, but he didn't feel ready for it just yet. His body still thrummed with the pleasure of their early-morning lovemaking, his lips still tingled from the last kiss at the door, and he wanted to let the bliss of it ebb out of him slowly, without interruption.

He knew it was a lost cause the moment he stepped inside. Gwen looked up from the kitchen table where she sat with her tablet and the remains of breakfast, and arched a wicked eyebrow at him.

'Hello, sailor. Finally stepped the mainmast, have you?'

'Oh *god*, Gwen.'

'You shouldn't be saying that to *me*, surely.'

'I'm not going to be saying anything to you, if you keep this up.'

'What do you expect, when you drift in at this hour? Looking . . . well, looking rather the better for wear, to be honest. I said he was good for you.' And she smiled smugly, as if his liaison with Callan had been her idea in the first place.

'You have some nerve. When did *you* get back?'

'Earlier this morning.'

'How much earlier?'

'Early enough to be showered and dressed and fed.' She pushed a steaming cafetière towards him. 'Here.'

'I've had coffee. And eaten. Shut up,' as her face sparkled with mischief. 'Where's Da and Ari?'

'Ari's gone up to the roof to talk to Sharon, and Da walked Graca down to the river. Said he'd be back in plenty of time.'

'He doesn't need to come, if he doesn't want to.'

'Rhys, honestly, sometimes you really are a prat. Of course he wants to.'

'I don't mean it like that. Haven't you noticed how the aquatech is taking off? You probably haven't. Anyway, it's great but it means he's really busy, and I don't want him to feel like he has to choose between helping to close deals and babysitting me.' He shrugged. 'It's not like there's anything he can do, except sit in a waiting room.'

She was staring at him. '*Rhys*. He can talk to the doctors and have a look around, and feel like he knows who's taking care of his baby boy and whether they're up to the job. He's as worried about you as I am.'

'Well, you can all stop. Worrying isn't going to help, and anyway I feel fine. It's been more than a week since the last one.'

'So what's been different this past week? Let me think – *oh yes*.' The wicked grin was back.

'Gwen.'

'How is the lovely Callan?'

'Lovely. Leave him alone.'

'I just wondered . . .'

'Gwennie, if you start asking me things that are none of your business, I'm going to start asking *you* things that are none of *my* business.'

She shut her mouth so sharply that he had to laugh, and felt vaguely triumphant that he had once again managed to catch her out. They were joined by Aryel and Sharon, who looked at him so keenly he felt his spine straighten.

'Something going on?' He remembered the conversation last night. 'Is Herran all right?'

'Herran's fine. It's you I'd like to talk to.' She chuckled at his expression. 'Not like that. You've been recommended. Have you got a minute?'

Gwen looked curious, but Aryel planted herself firmly beside her at the table and Rhys and Sharon went off to the living room. By the time they'd finished, he had barely twenty minutes left to get ready for the hospital. He thought about what Sharon had told him while he stripped, washed, and dressed in something that he hoped made him look like someone who would one day be there as a medical student, rather than a patient.

It was an intriguing problem, and an important one, and he'd said yes almost before she had finished asking the question. He could already feel himself planning how he would go about tackling it: building a mental framework to parse the different elements of the puzzle, organising his lines of enquiry. He found that he was eager, almost impatient for the trip to the hospital to be over so he could get started. The realisation brought him up short as he pulled on a clean shirt.

That's why you suggested me, isn't it, Ari? Give the boy something to work on, something significant enough to really capture his attention, and maybe you can keep him healthy at the same time.

He raked his fingers through his short, tight, ruby-glowing curls and contemplated his reflection in the mirror.

Well, that's fine with me. It could be the most useful thing anyone's come up with yet. And this way, all that trawling through archives looking for things that weren't there won't have been a complete waste of time.

17

Less than a week had passed since Aryel Morningstar and Jeremy Temple declared themselves satisfied with the outcome of the negotiations, but Herran had not wanted to wait any longer.

Eli found his enthusiasm – if that was what it could be called – profoundly strange, given what he now knew about the autistic gem's previous life. He had expected Herran at least to insist that Aryel accompany them on the first day, and was surprised to find him perfectly sanguine about being escorted only by Callan and himself. They sat, three abreast in a Bel'Natur limousine, being conveyed in swift and silent luxury away from the Squats. He glanced over the fiery tangle of Herran's curls to Callan's taller profile, topped by his matching glow. Callan felt the gaze and returned it. The soft smile that had been playing on his lips shifted to something more sardonic.

'Quite an upgrade.' He whirled a languorous finger to indicate the compartment they occupied. 'Wasn't like this the last time I was aboard a Bel'Natur transport.'

Eli looked for any sign of a reaction from the driver, segregated behind his glass partition. There was none. He turned to the diminutive man who sat next to him.

'How about you, Herran? Do you remember being driven around? When you worked for them before?'

'Dark,' said Herran promptly. He sat up straight, his entire upper body rotating as he made a 180-degree scan of the windows. The morning bustle of the city flashed past. He settled back against the plush upholstery. 'Not so comfy.'

Callan chuckled. 'Damn straight.' He shifted, stretched out his legs.

'They certainly seem to be making an effort.' Eli replayed his conversations with Aryel, their speculation about the depth of the Bel'Natur transformation. It had been borne out so far by the alacrity with which the firm had acceded to every safeguard they had required for Herran, and the seniority of the staff who had been sent into the Squats to meet him and be scrutinised by his friends. On the one hand it might indicate just how much of a barrier the digital–neural transcription problem presented, and how many of their hopes were pinned on his being able to solve it. But if that were the only reason then the public announcement of the project – before securing his participation, let alone confirming his usefulness – was more than a little pre-emptive.

'Bel'Natur,' said Callan thoughtfully, 'has never done things halfway. Not in my memory anyway, and Gaela and others who are older than me have said the same thing. I've heard stories about some of the other gemtechs, the corners they cut. Gempro was known for it, and you've heard Mik go on about Recombin. Bel'Natur prided themselves on being different. Whatever they decided to do, they made a total commitment.'

'Same ethos, new objectives?'

'Maybe.'

They were delivered to the main entrance, the driver out and opening the door for them before Eli could move. Heads turned as Herran hopped down after him, and passers-by stopped and stared as Callan emerged. He straightened up, rocking back on his heels a little as he took in the hard black glass that curved away from them. When he looked back down at Herran his smile was crooked.

'Still sure about this?'

'Sure.' Herran was already trotting up the steps to the entrance. Eli took them two at a time and caught up with him.

'Just remember,' he said quietly. 'If you change your mind, if you want to stop, get out, go home, just say so.'

'Home later. Suppertime.'

'Yes, but—' Eli caught Callan's tiny shake of the head, coupled with a grimace. He sighed and let it go. Aryel and Callan had both assured him that Herran knew what he was doing, and also knew he could stop doing it whenever he chose. And anyway, no one could read his cues as well as Callan.

Inside the black glass and white marble of the lobby, another surprise. Striding forward to meet them, Zavcka Klist.

'Gentlemen, welcome.' Her eyes met Eli's. He was conscious that she had not greeted him by name, although, despite the fact that Bel'Natur had engineered both Herran and Callan into existence, he was the only one of the trio she had met before. The enmity that had been between them at their last encounter might be reason enough for that. But she was looking him straight in the face, frank and open, and he knew suddenly that the point was to give no appearance of prioritising her single norm visitor over the two gems.

But he was a half-stride ahead of them, Herran having halted abruptly in the face of her brash advance, and Callan stopping with him. Eli let momentum carry him forward. This was as good a time as any to see if they had taken on board what working with Herran was going to entail.

'Ms Klist. It's been a while.'

She shook his hand, the firm grip he remembered. 'Dr Walker.'

A thin smile. As at their first meeting, it did not touch her eyes. 'Thank you for agreeing to assist us.' He sensed that she had bitten back the word *finally*, as she glanced past him to where Herran stood like a statue, head lowered and hands hanging like stones at his side. Callan, standing close alongside with his own hands thrust into his pockets, gave her a cool stare and looked pointedly past her to another woman who stood a couple of respectful paces back.

She came forward now, moving with the calm unfussiness they had taught her, flicking a look at Zavcka as she went past. She greeted Eli and Callan first, then stood in front of Herran, just out of reach and with her own arms quiet at her sides.

'Hello, Herran. Are you well?'

A long pause. Herran peeked up, pale eyes glinting behind surprisingly long lashes. He nodded, rocking a little at the waist. 'Sevi. Good.'

'I . . .' she glanced back at Zavcka. 'My boss would like to meet you. Is that okay?'

Zavcka had gone still and quiet and watched keenly as Sevi Romero, senior neurolinguist, had taken point. Now she stepped forward as Sevi had done, her movements turned measured and slow, tone pitched low and reassuring. 'Hello, Herran. I am Zavcka.' Eli saw Callan register the given name and altered body language with the same twitch of surprise as himself. 'Are you well?'

An even longer pause this time, the rocking more pronounced, but Herran's eyes through his lashes steady on her face.

'Zavcka,' he said finally. 'Herran. Well.'

'Thank you for coming. We're really looking forward to working with you.' They watched each other for a moment longer. She straightened up just as Callan cleared his throat gently to signal *Enough*.

Her eyes lingered on Callan's face too, as the final introduction was made; a face still beautiful, but no longer completely perfect. Callan kept his hands in his pockets and pinned her with that cool green stare. It was a look so knowing that Eli, had it been aimed at him, felt he would have had to take it on somehow, or else flee in embarrassment. Zavcka betrayed nothing but the same professionally polished politeness she had shown throughout.

She shepherded them swiftly through the registration of tablets and fingerprints. Eli could tell from the bewildered looks they got that the chief executive's personal attention to such minutiae was not common practice.

But then neither, any more, was the sight of gems within the walls of a gemtech.

The word must have gone out, he decided, as an urbane young man who had materialised apparently out of thin air to assist now ushered them into a lift. There was no blatant staring. The girl on reception had smiled timidly at Callan, and not gawked at Herran. If comments were being made people were waiting until they were well out of earshot.

They stayed silent as they were whisked upwards, their awareness of Herran, facing into a corner with his back to them, a palpable thing. Callan leaned against the wall beside him in an elegant, protective slouch and Eli flanked Herran on the other side, feet apart and hands together in what felt uncomfortably like a sentry's pose. He watched Callan and the assistant, Khan, size each other up. Khan looked away a moment later. What Eli could see of his face was tinged a delicate pink. Callan tipped his head back and gazed up at the mirrored ceiling, the wry smile twitching back onto his lips, the red shimmer of his hair the only blush about him.

Four floors of the tower had been given over to the new info-tech division, but their first view of it was not impressive. A blank wall greeted them, unbroken save for the faint outline of a door and the identipad inset beside it. Eli glanced back into the empty lift before the doors slid closed, certain that the call buttons had already been fingerprint-sensitive.

'Double screening,' said Sevi, following the look. 'In case someone who doesn't have authorisation gets out alongside someone who does.' She stepped up to the identipad, eyes and fingers aligned to the scanners as she spoke into the device. 'Hold for group entry.'

They all shuffled forward, Herran up on tiptoe to get his face high enough. Eli went last, and felt his tablet thrum faintly as its signal was scanned and accepted in tandem with his own. The door slid open.

What greeted them on the other side was not what he'd expected.

They stood in a well-lit, casually disorderly lobby area, surrounded by scattered clumps of low, comfortable-looking furniture. He could feel the dead air of a damper field, located there no doubt to minimise the disturbance of people coming and going from the floor as much as to provide a place for private conversation. Beyond it, rows of screens and workstations radiated away in every direction, manned by what he immediately thought of as a motley crew of technicians. A few looked to be his age; most were younger, and none older. Although there was an air of intense busyness about the place it nevertheless felt informal, in a way that Eli recognised from his own university days. It was far removed from his memories of typical gemtech ambience.

'No white coats,' Callan murmured. Zavcka looked over at him.

'No. Some of the work requires clean rooms and suits, but apart from that we thought it would be better if it didn't feel like a traditional lab.'

Eli kept his eyes on Herran, who had walked without hesitation out of the damper field and made straight for the nearest empty workstation, which had an overlarge monitor and integrated input screen. A couple of people working beyond it looked up, startled. They took in Herran's hair and scarred face, the taller, similarly flame-haired figure of Callan in the background and Sevi shaking her head at them with a finger to her lips, and went back to their own work, although they continued to cast interested glances in Herran's direction. He stood stock still in front of the screen, ignoring them all as he scanned the feed.

'Is that a recent decision?' asked Eli, still watching him. In his peripheral vision he saw the two women exchange glances.

'Yes,' Zavcka said. 'Some of the researchers did wear them, although there was no real reason for it. Force of habit. But,' her eyes flicked between Herran and Callan, 'we didn't want you to feel like you were back in the old Bel'Natur.' Behind her Khan smiled a little. Eli felt certain that this touch had been his idea.

'I see.' Callan's tone was flat.

Eli jumped into a stretching silence. 'I was surprised you'd located the project here.'

'Yeah.' Callan, not looking around, frowning a little as he regarded Herran. 'Labs and dorms used to be way out in the sticks.'

Zavcka stepped in beside him, so that they stood companionably side by side just within the damper field, watching the small gem. Herran had pulled his own tablet out and was doing something with it, without taking his eyes off the main screen.

'The agricultural divisions still are, of course,' she said. 'There were pragmatic reasons for locating this project at headquarters – we have a lot more empty space here now and the location is convenient. But I am also determined to ensure that we – the administrative staff, the executives – never again allow ourselves to become divorced from what it is that we actually do.'

She turned her head, speaking quietly now to Callan's profile.

'I understand how hard it must have been for you – both of you – to decide to come here. I know that as far as you're concerned we are on probation. I know that we are not likely ever to be forgiven. I get it. I can't change the past, Callan.'

He looked back at her, arms folded across his chest, eyes like hard green stones. Eli wondered if she was going to finish the speech with *I can only try for a better future* or some similar platitude, and whether Callan could contain himself if she did.

Instead he dropped his arms and strode away from her and out into the room, his attention back on Herran. Eli moved instinctively after him, and felt the others follow. Callan's voice was low and steady as he left the noise suppression of the damper field behind, but it carried the hint of a huskiness that Eli recognised. 'Hey, Herr. So. What d'you think?'

'Okay. Not bad.' Eli realised that the feed scrolling across the monitor had changed subtly while Herran had been standing there. 'Mostly not stupid.'

Sevi's jaw dropped. Callan looked over at her. 'That might not sound like a compliment, but it is.'

'Um. Herran.' Sevi was visibly working out how to structure what she wanted to say. Eli turned around, caught Khan throwing his boss a worried glance and Zavcka Klist opening her mouth to speak. He was almost relieved to see a flash of the old, peremptory arrogance in the crease between her brows, the flare of her nostrils and the tilt of her head.

Eli held her gaze and shook his head deliberately. He mouthed, *No.*

'But—' Khan started, eyes darting between them.

Eli spoke quietly and evenly, conscious of the audience of staff now obviously paying attention to them and the need both to explain and to reassert the ground rules. 'This is what it means to work with Herran. Looking at your systems to him is like looking around this room for the rest of us. It's how he orients himself, how he knows where he is. He's not going to do any harm.'

Zavcka's jaw tightened. Her eyes bored into him. Beside her Khan fidgeted, but neither spoke. Behind him Eli could hear Sevi, with help from Callan, get a monosyllabic version of the same reassurance from Herran. He turned around.

'All set?'

'Set.' Herran's small fingers slid across the workstation input. His other hand clutched his own tablet to his chest. 'Put back. Quick quick. See?' The feed now looked as it had when they first entered, although Eli would have been hard pressed to describe exactly what the difference had been. Herran looked up at him, face as devoid of expression as ever, pale eyes innocently blinking.

Callan's tightly controlled anger of a few minutes ago appeared to have been replaced by a coiled, toxic amusement. He looked over Herran's head at Zavcka.

'We can continue,' he said, 'if you'd like.' Although his voice was measured and calm there was a whiplash edge to it now that reminded Eli of Aryel.

She took them through the ranks of programmers and past the prototyping rooms, pausing here and there for explanations and to let them meet key personnel. It had been made clear that a mass introduction would be counterproductive as far as Herran was concerned, and not particularly useful for anyone else. But there seemed a determination to display every element of the project, and to ensure that everyone who was a part of it was subjected to the visitors' scrutiny. Eli remembered Mikal's comment about transparency, and the way he too appeared to have been welcomed into the organisation.

He decided they must really be serious when she let the technician who was leading on development of the cranial interface explain exactly how they thought it could work. He lingered over the mockups they had been shown, feeling a little sick, and sensed Zavcka pause beside him.

'You're using what you learned from Gabriel.'

'Yes.' Her eyes met his for a moment, before they slid away to rest on the delicate headbands arrayed on the bench. She spoke as if to the equipment. 'We still don't understand – I don't think anyone does, even now – his ability to experience the thoughts of others. Some kind of synaptic hypersensitivity, although how that's not completely overwhelmed by background radiation . . . Anyway.' She shook her head. 'He showed us it was possible. If you boost the signal and damp down the interference, thoughts are transmissible. The problem is understanding them.'

'That hasn't been his problem.'

'No. Quite the opposite. Poor child.' She stepped briskly away from the workbench. 'Fortunately, deactivating the interface at will has proved to be fairly simple for us. I imagine he must wish for a similar switch for his own ability.'

'I imagine he must.' He did not try to keep the acid out of his voice.

She strode ahead without responding. Callan looked back and raised a questioning eyebrow. Eli scowled at him and shook his head.

They ended in Sevi's lab, a light, open space that bore little resemblance to the testing chambers of old. It was full of neurolinguists and psychologists eager to meet Herran. Eli watched keenly as Sevi showed him the ergonomically padded, articulated chairs, with their sensor arrays draped like gossamer diadems over the high backs.

Herran poked a finger into the upholstery. 'Comfy.'

'Yes, everyone thinks so. We've all taken a turn. Part of setting up the baseline.'

Herran inspected the arms and footrest of the chairs. Callan smiled grimly, as though he knew what was coming.

'No straps.'

Sevi looked genuinely horrified. 'No, of course not.'

'Good. Straps bad.' He looked up at Eli, rock-nodding. 'New chairs.'

'I should think so. Looks okay to you, Herran?'

'Okay.'

'Excellent. I wonder,' glancing first at Callan, then at Zavcka, 'if I could have a quick word with Ms Klist? There are a few things we should clear up.'

If she was annoyed there was no sign of it. They left Khan hovering around the edges of the group as Herran hopped up into one of the chairs and pulled out his tablet, and Callan settled down to discuss the details of the next few days with Sevi and the rest of her team. Zavcka led the way to one of the huge parabolic windows that made up the skin of the building. There was the same relaxed scattering of low furniture that appeared to be ubiquitous throughout these floors, and the falling away of external sound as they stepped inside another damper field. She folded elegantly into a chair, watching as he lowered himself to one opposite.

'We haven't yet discussed my role here. The others must know I'm going to be doing more than taking care of Herran.'

'Your broader remit has been made clear to them. I admit I wasn't thrilled at first—'

'I imagine not.'

'—but I've revised my opinion. You and I did not part as friends, Dr Walker, and as much as anything that was down to your absolute willingness to speak your mind, regardless of the consequences.' She frowned. 'Aryel – Ms Morningstar – says she wants you to assess the ethical framework we now abide by and see if it stacks up, with the understanding that if you think it doesn't, or if there are steps you recommend that we're not willing to take, Herran will pull out immediately. That's only a threat to us if we haven't done as well as we think, and aren't willing to try to do better. Well, we have and we are. I've decided to think of you as a sort of external auditor. You'll have access to all the personnel and files you need. All I ask is that you look at where we are now, not where we were four or five or ten years ago.'

'That's what Aryel specified as well.'

'And that if you do conclude we're on the right track you allow us to quote you.'

He sat back and regarded her. The charm offensive of the past hour, the deference of the past ten days, began to make sense.

'That's a big *if*. And if you misquote me, or take me out of context, I'll embarrass you. Badly.'

'I understand. I've had my fill of underestimating you, Dr Walker.' She smiled thinly and gathered her legs beneath her to rise, the dismissiveness of the gesture a subtle counterpoint. 'Sevi is in charge of the science, of course, but I'll stay in close contact . . .'

'I am not at all sure that's a good idea.'

She was arrested in mid-motion, comically startled.

'I beg your pardon?'

'Sit down, Ms Klist. We're not done yet.'

She sank back onto the chair, casting a quick glance towards the suite where the others could be seen but not heard, having what looked like a sober but perfectly amicable discussion. No one was paying attention to them, and the face she turned to Eli was hard. He gave her no opportunity to speak.

'I know that you and Aryel have had candid conversations, and I suggest you and I continue in that vein. Bel'Natur might indeed be a changed institution these days, with staff who had either no or very limited responsibility for the abuses it committed. I can't deny that Sevi and Khan have a fresh new look about them. But you are not peripheral, Ms Klist, and Callan knows that as well as Aryel or Herran. Or me.'

She licked her lips. He found the involuntary gesture immensely satisfying.

'Does Callan think I was responsible for . . . he must know how distressed I was . . .'

'Your distress then was as much a public relations stunt as the one you're hoping to pull off this time, with me. Callan is no more an idiot than I am. He knows the part you played in what happened to him. What happened to the others, after.'

'I never meant—'

'I can believe you never meant for it to go as far as it did, considering how close it came to destroying you. If the outcome had been different I seriously doubt we would be seeing any of this remorse from you now.'

She stood, then, swivelling sharply to face the window, her fingers gripping the sill.

He rose more slowly, turning to look out as well, as though they were enjoying the view. 'Callan is here,' he went on evenly, 'because Herran needs him to be. Herran is here because he has made a rational decision to earn as much help as he can for those who need it, in the only way that is available to him. I am here to make sure that the assurances you've given are genuine and the promises you've made are kept. I am not certain any of that can withstand your ongoing, personal hypocrisy.'

Her face had gone white as marble, lips compressed into a thin line. Two red spots shone on her cheeks, and her eyes were black and dead as coal. Her hands, he noticed, were trembling and she clasped them together tightly. They stood side by side, as she had stood next to Callan earlier, and gazed out of the window. He felt strangely peaceful. He could hear her take one shuddering breath after another as they watched birds swoop past.

'Khan will act as liaison,' she said finally. She managed to keep her voice level, but there was a raggedness to it he had never heard before.

He nodded thoughtfully at the faint outline of their reflections against the glass. 'I think that would be best.'

There was no reply except for the sound of her heels, clicking rapidly away.

REVOLVING

She learns to remake herself.

It is a necessity of her condition. It is, by its nature, conspicuous; not immediately, often not for a considerable while, but over time, inevitably, those around her begin to notice, to question, to wonder. To whisper behind hands and cast eyes askance. She discovers that no landscape can long endure her presence. She resists the signs, always, not wanting to leave behind what she has built, exhausted by the thought of having to start again. Again.

She develops a weary fortitude, and strategies for coping. She teaches herself the skills she needs to create a shred of continuity in this unanchored existence, a framework that will allow her to maintain some sense of identity as she steps out of one life and into the next. She notices herself shift, subtly, with every incarnation, into someone who is a little bit more like the person she must now be; and she forgoes resentment in favour of sanity.

She learns that she can lengthen the intervals between her own reinvention, reinsertion, by minimising those with whom she must share space and time. Relationships become shorter, more perfunctory, easily discarded and eventually dispensed with altogether.

This is not loneliness. This is survival. This is what she tells herself.

But she finds complete seclusion beyond even her powers. It does not take long for her to feel herself again locked away, a precious princess imprisoned in a tower, looking at the swirl of life outside the windows. She descends, engages, forms connections, attracts attention. Time passes. The whispers start.

She leaves before they begin to suspect.

18

Callan left Herran at home, settled comfortably back in front of his own screens with Aryel for company. He trudged up three flights of stairs, ignoring the lift in favour of the mindlessness of movement, thumbed open the door of his own flat, and walked straight into Rhys' arms. It was like falling out of a rain of knives and biting cold into warmth and gentleness and comfort. He held him close and did not speak until he could trust himself not to weep. As they stood there wrapped together in silence he detected the faintest tremor in Rhys' limbs, and in the fingers buried in his hair. It occurred to Callan that the younger man might well have reasons of his own for distress.

He relaxed his grip, pressing his cheek and then his lips against the side of Rhys' face, and felt himself blinking back the traces of his own upset as he pulled away enough to look at him.

'Sweetness.' He forced a smile. 'So how was *your* day?'

'Not any more fun than yours.' Rhys' face was wan, his answering smile just as tentative. 'Lots of poking and prodding.'

'Really? I could do that. Better.'

That got him a chuckle, and a bit of sparkle back into the indigo eyes. 'You definitely could.' Rhys shook his head. 'Never mind. Tell me. Was it horrible?'

'Yes. Well, not entirely. It was weird.' Callan had turned his own micro-balcony into an oversized, opulent window seat and he flopped onto it, tugging Rhys down with him, noticing with unease how carefully the other man lowered and arranged himself, his sigh of relief as he settled into the cushions. 'You could tell they'd been briefed to be nice to us, but they were *really* nice. Bending over backwards. The people, the place, they weren't anything like I remember.'

'You'd been there before?'

'Once, when I was about fourteen, I guess. They were shopping me around for my first indenture and they brought me in to demonstrate to a client. Some Asian conglomerate. In through the service entrance, up in the goods lift, speak only when spoken to. The rest of the time they talked about me like I wasn't in the room. I'm pretty sure where I was taken to then was on the same floor as today.'

'Oh, *Callan.*'

'No, it's fine. I mean it's not, but, you know.' He frowned. 'It was completely changed, and I don't just mean the space. The difference . . . it wasn't only the fancy car and going in through the front door and being spoken to like a real person. I was all set for that to be window-dressing. But remember I told you about Sevi? How she seemed all right? Well, she was pretty typical.'

'So why did your message sound so pissed off? And you looked wrecked when you came in.'

'Because this entire symphony of reconciliation was being conducted by Zavcka Klist. In person.' He rubbed a weary hand across his face. 'What those men did to me . . . I don't think about it most of the time. I've learned to put it away, I had to. But it's there, Rhys, and she was behind it. I'm sure of that, even if she didn't issue the instructions herself, or target me in particular. To be expected to stroll along, politely chatting about how times have changed . . . as though it had nothing much to do with either of us . . .'

Rhys was aghast. 'She *spoke* to you? She had the *nerve*?'

'You'd think we were old friends, the way she spoke to me. You should have seen her, Rhys, touring us around, showing off her shiny revamped company like some sort of badge. It's like she thinks if she surrounds herself with sincere people her own insincerity won't matter.'

'What did you do?'

'Held it together, just. Eli finally sent her packing.'

'He did? In her own place?' Rhys grinned in appreciation, though it still looked like an effort. 'I like him.'

'Yeah, Eli's good people. He told her if she wanted us to be able to stomach working there she'd have to shove off, and she did. Which was another piece of weirdness, come to think of it, but a good one.' He patted Rhys' knee, now propped comfortably against his own. 'Your turn. What happened?'

'Oh, you know. More tests.'

'What sort of tests?'

'Nerves. Reflexes. It's not important.'

'Yes it is, sweetie. You're moving like you're hurt. Are you in pain?'

'A little . . .' Rhys' eyes slid away from Callan's face. 'I shouldn't load any more of this on you. Not with everything else you have to deal with.'

'Rhys, don't. Don't you *dare*.' He leaned forward, cupped a hand against Rhys' cheek. 'Dealing with you is the best thing in my life at the moment. The best thing for a long time. I want to know what's going on.'

Rhys looked back at him, blinked hard and swallowed, and gazed away again across the sunset-streaked city. His fingers crept up to press Callan's hand to his face.

'I've been really well since I got here and they needed to see what an attack does to my muscles and the control centres in my brain, so they gave me some stuff today to try and trigger some of the symptoms. It worked. It's wearing off now but everything sort of aches. It's hard to describe.' He shifted against the cushions. 'It's like every muscle has been strained, not a lot, just a little. Just enough. I feel bruised.'

He looked back at Callan, managed a smile, kissed the cradling palm and pulled the hand away from his face with a pretence at briskness. 'It'll probably be completely gone in a couple of hours, and at least it didn't mess my head up as well. I've been working on Sharon's problem and I'm finally getting somewhere. Want to hear my theory?'

'I want to know why you look so scared.'

Rhys stared down at Callan's hand, still clasped in his lap. Callan tickled his palm lightly, urging, feeling a tremor of fear hum along his own nerves.

'They're worried that whatever I have looks like it's degenerative.' Rhys spoke to the tangle of fingers. 'They . . . they're not completely sure yet. But the pattern of the attacks and the test results they're getting . . . and what they did today to switch it on, it all sort of confirms . . .'

Callan felt the tremor turn into a shiver, a hard humming like a frozen spear through his guts.

'They think it's going to get worse? How much worse?'

'We don't know for certain. They might come up with a treatment. I might find better ways to control it. It might stabilise on its own.' His voice was shaking now. Callan tried to keep the terror he heard there from echoing in his own.

'And if they don't and you don't and it doesn't?'

Rhys looked up at him then, finally. His eyes pooled and spilled over. 'Then they think it'll kill me.'

Aryel Morningstar perched on a stool in Herran's small, tidy kitchen and watched him eat. They sat across from each other over a worktop that doubled as a dining surface. Herran mostly used his fingers, moving them with metronomic regularity from dish to mouth, pausing every now and then to clean them fastidiously with a biowipe before returning to chase down every morsel of the meal she had prepared. From time to time Aryel stabbed a fork at the contents of her own plate, without enthusiasm.

Herran's pale eyes flicked up at her, observing. He rocked a little. 'Not hungry?'

'Not very much today, no. Is it good?'

'Good.'

'Well, that's Bal's teaching for you. Want some more?'

Herran pushed the empty plate ceremoniously towards her and gave his fingers another wipe. 'More.'

It pleased her greatly that he had learned to enjoy food, instead of treating it as no more than a tedious refuelling that took him away from his tablet and screens. They had formed an instinctive, unspoken rota back in the beginning of the Squats, making sure he had a tasty meal and company to eat it with every day if they could; prising him gently offstream and into the more visceral interactions of meat and bread and touch and speech. She had watched him change over those lunches and suppers, bit by infinitesimal bit, could almost map each new word or glimmer of expression that he gained against a taste or texture that gave him pause, and fired a new, old pattern into the altered web of his brain. Some deeply buried instinct for humanity had stirred with every bite.

Now he watched her spoon seconds onto the plate and again spoke without prompting. 'Problem?'

'I'm worried about Rhys. And a little bit about Gwen, but mostly Rhys.' She put the plate back in front of him. 'And you, of course. I'm worried it will be too hard for you.'

The fingers plunged in. 'Not hard. Only time.'

'It might take a long time, Herran. You might be there a while.'

She had to wait while he chewed and swallowed and blinked at her.

'Not long,' he said with certainty, as he picked up the wipe again. 'Setup okay. I do testing, Callan does talking, Eli asks questions. All together. Quick quick.'

'If you say so. What did you think of Zavcka?'

'Scared.'

'That's not good. That's not good at all. Will she be a problem for you?'

'No. Maybe. No.'

'Herran . . .'

'No problem.'

'And you're sure it will be okay with Sevi?'

'Sure. New chairs. No straps.' He was rock-nodding again, with the subtle emphasis that she knew signalled satisfaction; although she could not be certain whether his contentment had to do with the Bel'Natur arrangements, or the meal.

Dinner was in the early stages of preparation a few floors away, in a larger and less orderly apartment. Like Aryel's, this flat had also been altered to accommodate a gem with a need for more than the average amount of headroom. In Mikal's case it had meant raising the ceiling by close on three feet, salvaging extra-tall doors from derelict public buildings and constructing extra-large furniture.

On her first visit Sharon had felt like a doll propped onto a grown-up chair, and had laughed about it with him. On her second she was disoriented to find, when he sat down, that his face was almost on a level with hers and his legs, stretched out under the table, emerged on the other side.

She had poked her head down to look, observed that his chair legs had been cut away almost to nothing, got to her feet and shoved him unceremoniously off the seat. He'd sat on the floor and watched as she manhandled the mangled chair into a corner, replaced it with a properly giant-sized one, and with a flourish invited him to reseat himself.

'I think,' he'd said from the floor, 'that I might be in love with you.'

'Good. I love you too. Don't ever do that again.'

They'd married in less than a year. The amputated chair stood against the wall: a reliable source of amusement, and the anticipated throne for children who would one day use it to haul themselves upright, balancing on unsteady legs before clambering up and plopping their nappied backsides down, cackling in baby glee. It had become a tiny ache in their hearts, that chair, an empty seat waiting to be filled.

Now Sharon sat with her back to it and half listened to Mikal's droll account of the day's doings in Council, the earnest proposals for cost-saving schemes that would save at best half what they cost to set up, the hands-off pomposity of career civil servants and personal shenanigans of politicians.

'You want to watch how you make fun of them, dear. It could be you next.'

'I'm not worried. My laundry is aired, and carries a warrant tab.'

'What a lovely image. Thank you.'

'I try.' He opened the freezer cabinet, regarded its contents for a moment, then shut it again.

'You're just doing that to get cool.'

'Guilty as charged. Salad?'

'Sure.' She was scowling at her tablet. 'You know, the more of this we manage to unravel the less the whole thing makes sense.'

'The genestock?'

'Mm.'

'I thought you were making headway, now that Rhys is on board.'

'We are. He's a genius. Achebe doesn't know whether to be jealous or worship at his feet.'

'So it makes no sense in the sense that . . . ?'

'Well, we already knew that the hacker and the targets didn't fit the usual pattern. Generally, supposing you didn't know where to find what you wanted you'd use hackbots to do a broad-spectrum search, and then follow up with a targeted intrusion. But this was a single hacker trawling a dozen different gemtechs right from the start. And what they were targeting – well, you'd expect it to be new models, really innovative genotypes, that sort of thing.'

She glanced up at her husband, conscious that she was speaking unsentimentally about matters both exceedingly painful and too recent to yet be history. He blinked back at her, the thoughtful half-smile that told her this was all right, and returned his attention to the tomatoes he was chopping. 'I'd have thought so, yes. But you said they were old?'

'We inferred they weren't current because Achebe could tell that the datastreams they were in had already been archived before they were copied over to the EGA. But Rhys has deciphered the filetags, and it turns out most of them were *really* old. Not just a few years, more like two or three generations. I mean, that would be considered obsolete, right? So then I started to wonder if this was some weird historical voyeurism, maybe they're looking for dead ends, famous disasters. But none of them were like that. The main area of interest seems to have been a bunch of fairly innocuous genetypes – transitionals, Rhys calls them – that were engineered between twenty and forty years ago.'

Mikal set the knife aside and frowned. 'That is strange, not to be going after a marketable end product. Mind you, that was when the big shift happened – thirty, forty years ago. Less low-IQ brute-force labourers, more . . .' He picked up a lettuce and gestured vaguely at himself with it, while the double thumbs of the other hand popped open a jar balanced on his palm.

'Charming, intelligent and erudite?'

'I was going to say highly modified, but okay.'

She blew him a kiss. 'Okay, so the main focus of this hacker happens to be a really interesting time for gemtech. I hadn't thought about that, but you're right. It produces the first fully functional gillungs, and you, and Aryel, Bal and Aster . . .'

'Yeah. *Anatomic innovation for prosperity and security.*'

She stared up at him in dismay.

'That's not one of *mine*,' he hurried to assure her. 'Recombin marketing slogan. We came up with several very rude versions. Anyway.'

'Anyway . . .' She steepled her fingers and rested her chin on her hands, distantly aware that it was a Masoud gesture and annoyed by the fact. 'But it's not as if innovation stops. I mean, Gempro goes on to perfect the gillungs, Bel'Natur makes a big push into neurological and sensory abilities, we get people like Gaela and Callan and Herran—'

'Bel'Natur were all-rounders.'

'—and the gemtechs keep on pushing the boat out; right up until the government put a stop to it they were— What?'

'What?'

'Say that again. Bel'Natur?'

'Hmm? Oh, I know their publicity was all focused on beautiful, brilliant redheads who norms would be happy to have around – your Gaelas and your Callans, and all the sexual subtext – but the truth is, they were at the forefront of all kinds of enhancements. They even had a hand in the gillungs. Reginald told me they discovered when they were working out the settlement that Bel'Natur had sold Gempro a lot of the early technology. They didn't want to be bothered with developing it, they had so much else going on.'

Sharon picked up a neatly sliced carrot, tapped it against her teeth and then bit into it thoughtfully. 'That's really interesting. Because none of the hacks were aimed at Bel'Natur, and none of the stolen genestock was theirs.'

'Maybe whoever was doing it already knew all about them.'

'You mean it originated there? Maybe. But then why would they be looking at what their competitors had done way back when? Wouldn't you be trying to spy on the *latest* research from Gempro, Recombin, Modicomm?' She waved the remains of the carrot. 'That's another weird thing. Although the gemtechs were different, Rhys says the genetypes appear to have things in common. He's going to focus on that, see if he can nail down a pattern. But I think that's another reason why this can't be about black-market gemtech. You'd go for variety, surely. The bottom line is, the stock that's been stolen corresponds to the oldest genetypes that were hacked, and had been in storage for at least – *at least* – a quarter of a century. Stuff that old might not even be viable, it definitely wouldn't have any street value. So why would anyone want it? I mean, if you've found a way to infiltrate this incredibly secure storage facility and steal whatever you like, why steal *that*?'

Mikal prodded thoughtfully at the salad. 'And you still don't know how they pulled off the theft?'

'Not how, no. But Rhys has an idea about who it might have been.'

Mikal looked up sharply. 'What? Who? Why aren't you out arresting them?'

'He doesn't know their identity, although he's going to take a look at the profiles we ran and see if he can spot anything we missed. No, get this. He thinks the whistleblower might also be the thief.'

Mikal was dumbstruck. He stared openmouthed for a moment, then clasped his hands on top of his head and described a slow turn, as if the pressure might keep his cranium intact and the rotation reorient the world into its proper orbit. When he came back to face her Sharon was grinning at him.

'Now you know how I feel.'

'I'm beginning to think that compared with police work, politics is actually sensible. He thinks this why?'

'He says look, what do we know about the whistleblower? Nothing, except they must have known about both the hacks and the thefts, plus have the ability to mirror the EGA datastream to create a trail for us to follow. What do we know about the thief? Also nothing, except they too must have known about the hacks, plus have the technical expertise to subvert the EGA's entire security system – which is fully integrated with its datastream. Same knowledge base, same skill set. Same person.'

'I . . . right . . . okay.' She watched him digest this. 'Do you buy it?'

'I think it's mad, but it fits the facts.'

'But *why*? You pull off the perfect heist, get away without a trace, and then you *tell the cops*?'

'Like I said, the more we find out the less sense it makes. Maybe he was feeling unappreciated. Wanted to show off.'

'In that case he should go work for the city. No, scratch that. We've got enough worries without a criminal mastermind with self-esteem problems on the payroll.'

She laughed. 'Anyway. Whether he's right or wrong on that score, young Rhys is turning out to be worth his weight. I should message Aryel a thank-you.' She got up to set the table, and a shadow passed over her face. 'Have you heard how today went, by the way?'

'I had a message from Eli to say reasonably well. No hostility, no backing off.'

'I think,' she said, her voice suddenly distant, 'that sounds like very good news. I think maybe we need to talk about what happens if it keeps on going well.'

'It's a good start but they've barely started. What's wrong?'

She gave him a weary, eye-rolling, what-do-you-think look, put the glasses and cutlery down on the table with a tinkling thump, and disappeared in the direction of the bathroom. Mikal heard a soft, heartfelt curse, followed by the vacuum hiss of the toilet flushing. He finished arranging the table with care, trying to push back a familiar sense of disappointment.

Sharon reappeared several minutes later, leaning against the doorframe. Her gaze slipped over the ridiculously truncated chair against the wall before she looked back at him, shaking her head.

19

Three days in, Eli found himself wondering if he had been too harsh with Zavcka Klist.

He had not seen her since their conversation outside the neural transcription lab, and his slightly juvenile sense of satisfaction had not much waned. But the sea change she had claimed for Bel'Natur was becoming undeniable, and everyone he spoke to credited her for it. Wary of any dissimulation that might be spreading ahead of him he had quickly busied himself beyond the bounds of the infotech programme, finding his way into the airless offices of building services and striking up conversations with engineers and administrators in the canteen. He had yet to discern any overt anti-gem feeling, or much pride in the company's past. Veterans tended to mutter disavowals pitched somewhere between moderate embarrassment and outright shame; newer staff spoke earnestly of transformation. A purge had taken place; the most staunchly regressive following Felix Carrington out the door, and the remainder reformed. He struggled to reconcile the magnitude of the change with the unabashed bigotry – if not the ruthlessness – of the old Zavcka.

But any guilt he might have felt for the way he had handled her was allayed by the presence of Callan, whose normally unruffled demeanour was tempered by an undercurrent of disquiet unlike

223

any Eli had seen in him before. He could not be certain that it was entirely down to the memories their being here must have triggered, but he didn't imagine it would help.

Herran by contrast seemed fine. By the second day he was accepting the greetings of the technicians who worked with Sevi, before climbing with equanimity into the testing chair to occupy himself with his tablet while they went through the specifics of the session with Eli and Callan. He would peek up through his lashes as the sensor net was placed carefully over his head, issuing gnomic comments that at first only Callan understood, but that on translation suggested he had been paying attention to the conversation as well as to whatever he was amusing himself with on the streams. Sevi and one or two of the others were quick to pick up on his patterns and quirks of communication, to understand and interact without Callan needing to mediate. So far the whole thing was proving much more collegiate than Eli had anticipated.

Returning from one of his forays into the nether regions of Bel'Natur, he stuck his head in at the door of the lab. Herran was reclining with a tablet stand angled a comfortable distance from his eyes, watching the lines of code that flashed up on it. The lacy skullcap, through which fiery curls poked in every direction, read and routed his synaptic activity to banks of screens before which the neurologists shook their heads in bemusement. Callan sat nearby, monitoring, every now and then getting Herran to say aloud the meaning of what he saw. The scientists scanned that brain activity too, and compared it with the unspoken interpretation, and looked even more baffled.

Eli caught Callan's eye, raised a quizzical eyebrow and mouthed *Okay?* Sevi looked across anxiously. Callan nodded, gave him a thumbs-up, and Eli retreated to the seats by the window.

Now that he was fairly certain there was no active campaign of

deceit at the staff level, it was time to become a bit more methodical. He pulled up directories on his tablet and started to work
through them, checking policies and programmes, working documents and personal communications. He set up a searchbot to look
for gaps where offending files might have recently been deleted,
and another to check edit logs for hasty revisions. The sheer size of
the system was overwhelming. He got lost in side-shoots of African
agricultural communes and a tangle of Middle Eastern tax shel-
ters, found his way back through a network of Asian subsidiaries
as exotic and mysterious as any Silk Road trail.

Hours passed. He noted with wry appreciation that almost everything prior to the Temple Act affirming gem and norm equality
had been archived. So. A line had been drawn under that event,
and the records that would have reinforced a mindset now deemed
defunct were hidden from casual view. He wondered if anything
else had been hidden there as well.

Unsurprisingly, his access did not extend to probing archived
files. He called Khan. The assistant's visual came up on his tablet
at once. He listened politely.

'I understand, Dr Walker, but you can't expect that old stuff to
be representative any more.'

'I don't. I've seen a lot of it before, remember, when I interro-
gated the gemtech typology criteria for the Federation.' He sighed
inwardly, hating how pompous he must sound even as he played
the expertise card. 'It's the transition that I want to examine.'

That was feeble, and he waited for Khan to call him on it. There
was a long pause.

'And you'll want to confirm what's on the other side of the firewall,' said Khan meditatively. 'Of course. Sorry, that was a bit slow
of me.'

'I . . .' Eli was momentarily nonplussed. Then he recovered

himself and plunged on, 'Look, everyone's been at pains to tell me there's no double dealing or hidden agendas here, and so far I've found nothing to contradict that, but if I'm to confirm it then I need to see everything. I'm not trying to drop you in the middle, Mr Khan. I'll explain it to Ms Klist if you prefer.'

'No, don't do that.' Khan looked alarmed. 'There's no need to – um – disturb her. She's authorised me to see to it you have everything you need. I'll have your tablet's access level upgraded immediately. And, Dr Walker?'

'Yes?'

'My name's Arthur.' He cleared his throat and glanced away from the screen, as if slightly embarrassed. 'I – ah – I know Ms Klist is very formal, and if that's what you prefer, then—'

'It isn't. Thank you, Arthur.' He did not return the invitation, and sensed that the young man would be sharp enough to notice.

The access clearance came through within a couple of minutes, and Eli plunged into the archive. If the systems he'd been trying to parse before felt like they contained a planet-worth of information, this was a galaxy. He reminded himself that he was only looking for anomalies, files added too recently or carrying the wrong date stamp, and set up more searchbots. But the archive was so vast that he found it impossible to capture what he needed to know with a few simple commands, and ended up delving again down wormholes, replicating his earlier efforts as he struggled to grasp the shape and size of the thing. Bel'Natur was an old company, one of the first gemtechs to emerge out of the black days of the Syndrome, and it had absorbed many others in close to a century of existence.

It occurred to him, as he got ready to launch yet another searchbot, that the sub-archives of alien and mostly ancient records were a particularly unlikely place for anything of interest to be located. He hesitated, weary of the task. The chance of finding anything was remote. But then, so was the likelihood of there being anything to find anywhere at all. He had seen enough already to be fairly certain that if a grand deception was being orchestrated, it was offstream and tightly contained. The point was to be thorough, to satisfy himself – and be able to assure Aryel – that he had left no stone unturned; to be able to live with the increasing likelihood that he, Eli Walker, once the gemtechs' harshest critic, would be the one to certify their redemption.

Bile rose in his throat at the thought. He swallowed it down, grimacing, and swiped the searchbot live.

He left the bots running, knowing they could take hours to turn anything up, and checked on Herran and Callan again. The chair had been fully reclined and the little gem was lying flat out on it, sensor net still in place, eyes closed, small hands clutching his own tablet to his chest. Callan looked up as Eli came in and paused at the sight of Herran.

'Nap?' he whispered.

'No,' Herran and Callan answered together.

'They're doing a scan of his brain at rest,' Callan continued. 'Although it isn't.'

'Thinking with no looking,' said Herran. Through the customary flatness of his tone, Eli thought he detected a note of annoyance.

'Try not to do any thinking, Herran.' Sevi was standing before one of the monitor screens, shaking her head at the patterns that morphed across it. 'You're supposed to be having a break. Would it help you relax if we took the net off?'

'No. Relax with tablet.'

'Really?' She looked from him to Callan and Eli. 'We've done a lot today, I thought he could do with some rest . . . Okay, Herran. Chill out onstream if you prefer.'

Herran promptly sat up, cross-legged on the gurney-like surface, and activated his tablet.

Eli strolled over. 'Want to turn this back into a chair?'

'Okay.'

Eli waited a beat to see if he would do it himself, then reached for the controls. 'You doing okay today? Not tired?'

'Okay. Not tired. Not night.'

'You could get tired in the daytime too, Herran.'

He looked up at that and blinked, considering. 'No.' He adjusted himself against the chair as the back came up and the leg-rest folded down. 'Not sick. Not sleepy.'

'Hungry?'

'Not yet. Not suppertime.'

'He had lunch,' Callan interjected. He did look a bit weary, Eli thought. 'We went up to the canteen today. Someone said you had just left. It wasn't bad, eh, Herran?'

'Not bad.' He was absorbed in the tablet.

Eli stood by him for a few seconds longer, trying to work out what he was streaming. It looked like Festival news and social-stream commentary, but interspersed with code in the weird mashup that only Herran could decipher.

He shook his head and went over to Callan. 'How about you?' he said quietly. 'You don't seem quite so chipper.'

'I'm fine.' The answer came out on reflex, then he caught Eli's look and sighed. 'I'm a little tired, that's all. Didn't sleep so well.'

Eli tilted his head to indicate they move out of earshot. Sevi turned politely away to her screens as they stepped clear of the lab.

'What's going on? Is this bringing too much back for you?'

'No. I mean, the first day wasn't great but since then . . .' They had reached the damper field by the window. He stared out of it. 'It's like that old story, you know, about falling through a mirror and everything on the other side is sort of the same but not really? Takes a bit of getting used to. But I can't fault Sevi or her people. They're trying really hard.'

'I know you used to have nightmares . . . If this is bringing them back . . .'

'No, it's nothing like that.' He hesitated, took a deep breath. 'You know what's happening with Rhys, right? This condition he has?'

Eli began to understand. 'Aryel told me about it. They're trying to identify the illness? Work out how serious it is?'

'Yes. And the news isn't good so far. It looks like just about as bad as it could be.'

'You mean—?' The look Callan gave him was confirmation enough. 'Oh, Callan, I'm so sorry. That must be so hard on you. Both of you.' And on Aryel, he thought. And Gwen, and Reginald.

Callan looked steadily out of the window for a long time. Eli got the feeling that whatever he was seeing was elsewhere.

'I've only just met him, you know?' His voice was hardly louder than a whisper. 'Onstream doesn't count. I've only known him, in person, in . . . in the flesh, for a couple of weeks. So maybe it doesn't make sense for me to be this torn up about it. But I . . . he . . . it feels like I've only just *found* him.' He twisted his hands together unconsciously. 'He makes me feel connected.'

'You're in love with him.'

Callan nodded. 'Completely.' He glanced sideways at Eli. 'Am I mad?'

'Don't ask me, my friend. I once managed to marry a woman I'd known for so long I thought I must be in love with her. Turns out I wasn't.' He shook himself clear of the memory and rested what he hoped was a comforting hand on the other man's shoulder. 'No, I don't think you're crazy, and I think Rhys is lucky to have you. Do they know what it is he's got?'

'Not really. It looks like some of the old neuromuscular diseases, things that shouldn't show up in anyone any more, gem or norm. But it's not exactly the same as any of them.' He rubbed a distracted hand through his hair. 'They're running profiles on his genome, but it's so highly engineered they're struggling to match it to anything they recognise. If they had his genetype, the genealogy and all the modification markers, that would help. A lot. But they don't.'

He raised his shoulders, let them drop, and Eli took his hand away. 'Do you want to get out of here? Go and be with him?'

'No. I mean I can't yet. He'll still be at the hospital. They kept him in last night so they could pump him full of drugs and see what happened. He's spending the day getting scanned too.' He glanced back to where Herran was busy swiping and tapping at his tablet. 'He gets home in a couple of hours.'

'Well let's get ourselves home before then if we can. And if juggling that and this gets to be too much, don't try to do it. We'll work something out.'

'Thanks, but I want to be part of this. Not just for Herran's sake.' He smiled wearily. 'Rhys knows what we're doing here. How important it could be. We both want it to work.'

The bots were still trawling when he got back to the survey, after a word with Sevi and another, almost cheery assurance from Herran. He spent some time organising interview notes before he checked them again.

A string of alerts flashed up, and he scrolled quickly through. Mostly on the current system, nothing recent or too serious. Some derogatory language, quickly slapped down; a couple of questionable proposals similarly rejected. A few more from the archive, innocuous and easily explained: cancelled projects, defunct departments.

The last item on the list had been thrown up by the mergers and acquisitions bot and he realised with irritation that there must have been a mistake in the setup. It pulsed invitingly, though the icon was the dull grey of an inactive link. He tapped at it. Nothing happened. Back into the archive, copy over the linkcode, wait an unfeasibly long time for it to come up . . .

File not found.

He blinked at the banner, and went back to the searchbot panel. The file icon was still there. He tapped it again, waited, again went back to the archive. This time he typed the link in manually.

File not found.

So whatever the searchbot thought it was flagging up wasn't actually in the archive, though the dead link still pulsed on the panel. Had to be an error of some sort, a system-generated glitch, a ghost in the machine. Such things used to happen, pre-Syndrome. Get rid of it, run another searchbot in the morning. Eli yawned and swiped in a deletion command, and frowned. It wasn't responding to that either. Nor would the tablet now respond to any other commands. He stared at it in frustration, dreading having to call Khan, already thinking guiltily of asking Herran for help instead. His finger tapped a steady tattoo as he considered the options.

The icon bloomed under his finger, and he jerked back in surprise. A cascade of links shot into life, one after another, file text flashing across the screen and disappearing faster than he could read. A few words and phrases popped out of the maelstrom and stuck in his consciousness, even as the links that contained them were lost in the whirlwind.

Extreme modification tolerance.

Weapons potential.

Batch cull.

Klist.

The torrent stopped, finally, on a link that flashed blue before expanding into a message, in a format that felt oddly archaic.

1503114AS

TO: Zara Klist

FR: Jonah Wycliffe

RE: Phoenix Project – CONFIDENTIAL

Appreciate your surprise at learning of this. Assure you it was news to me as well. Circumstances unique to say the least! How it has been kept embargoed this long remains a mystery, though no doubt Dr Panborn can shed some light. She does not quite seem to grasp the necessity of this – autonomy has become rather a bad habit, I fear. I think she feels entitled to keep the details a secret even from you and I, although she has hinted at modifications I frankly cannot credit. I am making haste to gain some clarity, and to make clear to HER that the fiefdom she appears to have enjoyed is now at an end. However, the little I have been able to gather suggests it essential to maintain absolute secrecy until we know exactly what we are dealing with.

I will revert soonest.

Eli read the message again, twice, feeling his own surprise harden into suspicion. Another link pulsed at the foot of the message. He slowly reached out, and tapped it to life.

PLANNING

She has the shape of it now.

She glances at the map openly but without expression, knowing that they are more likely to notice her if she appears furtive. So her blue eyes blink in studied disinterest, while the brain behind them analyses and memorises, filing away contour lines, river courses, place names.

The name of this place.

She already knows a great deal about it. Its outer walls describe the limits of her existence, its inner corridors and compartments the ambit of all her days. She knows every nook and cranny, every line and seam; even the forbidden spaces are familiar shapes, their boundaries explored under the guise of play or aimless wandering.

She knows some of what goes on in them; she knows that the upper reaches of the complex house more freaks than her, that others have replaced her long-dead batch siblings, though she is rarely permitted to see them. She suspects that some at least may be destined for a life beyond the laboratory, and precautions must be taken to ensure no knowledge of her departs it with them. She knows the lab itself has been here a long time, from well before her own inexplicable advent. And she knows that it is secret – so secret that the world beyond these walls is largely ignorant of its existence. She gleaned this first from diligent eavesdropping, and confirmed it when she learned to daisy-chain her truncated tablet to less limited devices and access the infostream that flows invisibly through walls as wide as the span of her arms, past the double-locked doors with their retscanners and armed guards, up the lift shaft she has never been allowed to enter. Up and out, into the world.

A world in which the place she inhabits appears to be both named and unknown. The irony amuses her.

She contemplates this, knowing it helps her remain detached, helps hide any hint of excitement. She has dreamt of escape for as long as she can remember, but the edges of the dream have always been indefinite, amorphous. Escape into what? Where? She realises now that this has worried her far more than the mere mechanics of departure, the difficulties of how to get out. She has been planning for how since she broke the first level of encryption on that first tablet, maybe since she first took hold of Dr Owen's lab coat and called him by name. She has cultivated forbearance, and accumulated knowledge, for just this reason.

Now, finally, she knows that above her head is a strangely named forest, and anticipation makes her lift and rustle the newly fledged wings on her back. No teeming city in which she would be spotted and brought down before she has gone two steps, no wired encampment patrolled by armed guards. They have no need of a secondary prison. Forty yards of earth and rock beneath fifty miles of wilderness is more than enough.

They have wandered away from the map, and she listens to them talk loudly about expansion, reallocation of space, improved access. Even now it never occurs to them to consider what they say in front of her, and she almost shakes her head in wonder. She knows so much more than they imagine, and this buried citadel is not as impregnable as they think. She has been planning for a long time, observing and calculating, assessing habits and shift patterns, compiling a mental inventory of what she will need and where to find it when the time comes. Teaching herself the chemistry of damage.

She takes a last look at the map. There are other names on it, names she recognises from her illicit excursions by tablet. Outlaw places that promise sanctuary to such as her. Places she can disappear into.

She will have to act quickly, before the plans they are making can alter the patterns that she knows. She drifts towards the door, the dorm, her tablet. She is already composing the messages she will encrypt and send, seeing in her mind's eye the steps she must take, the risks she must run, to win herself a life.

There will be casualties. Of that she has no doubt. But then, there already have been. She remembers a boy with a twisted spine and barely a face, and eyes as blue as her own, and she has no qualms.

The shape of it is clear to her, and she knows what she must do.

20

Rhys tucked a pillow behind his back and tried to find a comfortable position in the endlessly adjustable, perfectly ergonomic institutional armchair he'd dragged over to the window. The pain was not as bad as the first time they'd found the formula that would trigger his muscles to spasm out of control, but the trembling and residual twitches seemed worse, and there remained a pervasive soreness throughout his body that made him want to do nothing more than curl up and sleep it away. He kept his back firmly turned to the hospital bed he'd vacated as soon as the doctors had left the room, and focused on his tablet.

The pattern was about to reveal itself; he could sense it, like a word just out of reach on the tip of his tongue, like the cacophony of a crowded room the instant before sit-sense rendered its actors discrete and comprehensible. The genetypes were ready to give up their secrets.

He had delved down, past the shorthand of labelling systems and lists of key features that told only what the gemtech engineers had considered important, down into the core language of amino acid sequences and the subtler cues of the epigenetic control switches. And found nothing; layered one atop the other they neither merged nor strongly contrasted. These were, as he had explained to Sharon, transitional genetypes – the intermediate stages before the final assembly, the spectacular splices, that would result in a supernormal human. They were in themselves both crucial and unimportant.

That shared insignificance, the realisation that each sample of stolen genestock represented no more than a thing on its way to becoming another thing, was the first connection between them he had found. Then there were the haunting similarities between certain chunks of code, random alignments of sequence that were neither baseline normal nor identical to each other, but that felt like echoes, seeming to repeat and recur with variations major and minor across the archaic genestock of half a dozen gemtechs. If you looked at the genetypes in their entirety the resemblances appeared coincidental. But if you popped those sequences *out* of the chromosomal array, mapped the engineering markers not just back to baseline but *against each other* . . .

He had it.

The sequence strings he had isolated slid across the surface of his tablet, organising themselves into a hierarchy, a fractal pattern with antecedents and dependents. There were gaps in the structure, pulsing question marks where further links should logically occur, but the overall shape was clear. He felt the breath go out of him.

For a long moment he sat there stunned, the ache in his back and legs forgotten. He knew he needed to check and double-check, run tests to audit the relationships he had found, prove whether or not they were robust. He also knew, with a certainty that he recognised as the subconscious calculus of his own altered brain, that what he was looking at was right, it was real. The audit would be for the reassurance of others, not for him.

He tapped more layers of information into being. Provenance, possible avenues of transcription. The missing pieces, the gaps, sprang into sharp relief.

And began to tell their own story.

He had the full picture, and more, when Gwen arrived half an hour later. He looked up as she slipped into the room, blinking in surprise as she pushed back the hood on one of his larger and more shapeless jumpers. Instead of springing free, the long curls of her hair had been pulled back and pinned up. It made their glimmer almost as tame and constrained as his own short locks.

'What's that for?' He glanced out of the window, then back at her. 'It's not raining.'

'It's raining fans. Well, not exactly, but I keep getting recognised and, you know, you have to stop and talk to people. I didn't want to be late.' She dropped her satchel onto the bed and unfastened the jumper. 'How're you feeling?'

'Okay. A lot better than this morning. Where's Da?'

'Airwalk. The meeting's running late. Apparently the aquatech buyers don't see why they should be required to maintain the same environmental standards in their onshore operations as well. Don't think it should be any of the gillungs' concern. Da needed to stay and be the voice of moral authority, and I guess he's taking you at your word about prioritising the contracts.' She sat on the edge of the bed. 'He did say he's really sorry, he'll see us back at Ari's. As long as you're cleared to come home, of course.'

'Yeah. I'm supposed to take it easy for a couple of days.' He caught her look, and shrugged. 'Even easier than usual, which would be bloody difficult.'

'You're not exactly doing nothing.' She jerked her chin at the tablet. 'When they say *complete rest* I don't think they mean *spend hours investigating a criminal conspiracy.*'

'If I were staring into space doing nothing I'd be a hell of a lot worse off, I think. And it's incredible, Gwennie, what I've found . . .'

He trailed off under her steady stare, a look he knew to mean she was not remotely interested in what was swirling on the screen of his tablet, and was not about to allow the subject to be changed. He decided to wait it out, pointedly settled himself deeper into the chair, and stared right back.

She blew out a sigh, mouth quirking into a startlingly accurate impersonation of Aryel's ironic half-smile. 'So. What's the verdict? Or are you going to tell me second again this time?'

'That's not fair.'

'How d'you work that out? It's what happened.'

'Gwennie, I already know you're going to stand by me to the end of time, come what may, all of that. That's us, that's who we are.' Rhys did not mention how absent she'd been even when they were together, how often he'd thought over the past weeks that he was little more than a distraction as she focused on building her career, how much his words felt like hope instead of certainty. 'Callan – it's like I told you before. I can't just assume the same things about him. You weren't around, you were off doing music stuff, Da was down at the river . . . Callan was there and he wanted to know what was wrong and I needed to tell someone. Plus I didn't think it was fair to keep it from him.'

'Were you worried he wouldn't be up for it after all?'

'I guess I was, a little. I didn't know, not for certain.' Rhys did not try to downplay his relief at the memory of Callan's reaction. 'I couldn't just go on what I hoped would be true. Will be true. Sticking around through this – it's not going to be pretty, Gwen. He may change his mind yet.'

Her face went still as she registered the implication. He could hear the struggle as she tried to keep her voice light.

'Do they know anything more now than they did yesterday? Or the day before?'

'They're even more certain now of what they thought yesterday and the day before. It's degenerative. If they can't find a treatment soon, it will become terminal.'

He heard himself deliver the news in a voice as flat and even as if he were describing a programming problem or projecting the latest algae harvest, and wondered at the calm he now felt after his terror and tears of only a few days ago. He knew in a vague way that it had something to do with the unfolding puzzle of the genestock thefts; something about it which both diverted him from his own prognosis, and gave him hope. It too had the whiff of pending inspiration, of a connection waiting to be made. But one that would have to wait a bit longer, because now it was Gwen whose face was crumbling from apprehension into anguish, and who was starting to cry.

He hauled himself out of the chair, leaving the tablet behind and pulling her up into a hug. He was mortified to feel how limp she was, as though she had suddenly found herself a weight too heavy to bear, and how she shook against his chest.

'Gwennie, I'm sorry. Don't. Stop. Gwennie, it's okay.'

'It is *not* bloody okay!'

It came out muffled, shouted through sobs. He stroked her bound-up hair and murmured to her in twin-speak, and was relieved when she pushed away from him with her usual supple strength after a few minutes, drying her eyes on the jumper.

'I'm sorry,' he said again. 'Maybe I shouldn't have said it like that . . . but Gwennie, it's no different from what they told us before, it's just confirmation . . . and . . . and you weren't so upset then, I didn't think you'd . . .'

'I didn't believe it could be true. How can it be true? You don't seem any worse.' She sniffed loudly, glaring at him now, still wiping her eyes with the backs of her hands. 'You get better, you go right back to normal, you always *say* you feel fine . . .'

'I do, but it takes me longer each time. They understand why now.'

She had herself under control, finally, and he spun the heavy chair back into its accustomed position and sat down. She sank back onto the bed, listening.

'Every attack makes the next attack more likely. The more often they happen the less time my muscles and nerves will have to recover, which means the damage will accumulate, which means the next attack will do even more damage.'

'So the key is to stop you having attacks in the first place.' Her focus was coming back, she was thinking about solutions. Good. A distracted, self-absorbed Gwen might leave him feeling neglected; a weeping, shaking, panicking one threatened to throw his entire world out of balance.

'Exactly. They think the cure – if there is one – will have to be some kind of epigenetic therapy, a drug that suppresses the right molecular switches in the right order for the right amount of time. It would need to be very precise, or it might do more harm than good.'

'Do they know how to make it?'

'They're pretty sure they could if they had my genetype, and comparing your genome with mine is helping them work out where the trouble spots are. But it's not isolated to one chromosome, it's not even just in the DNA. It's the whole protein environment.' He could feel his own frustration mount, a coil of anger and fear in his chest as he described the problem. He sighed it out, leaning forward with elbows on knees, running his hands over his hair. Another version of a classic Aryel gesture. He was annoyed rather than amused by the flash of insight, but even as aggravation overtook him he knew it for a warning.

'We are *so* engineered, Gwennie. We're so fucking altered. Anyone else with genetics this weird would have some obvious *purpose*, they'd be able to breathe water or read binary or fucking fly. The doctors could look at their phenotypes, their physical reality, and say Aha! We can compare you to this gem or that gem, someone else that they *do* have the full assembly manual for. As it is, working out what they need to know from the genome data alone is like trying to reverse engineer a . . . a . . .' Rhys looked for a simile, failed to find one. 'I don't know what. A planet, a galaxy. There's nothing else living that's as complicated as we are.'

'What are you going to do?'

'Work with the doctors. Do my own research. Stay as busy as I can. Try not to get into the frame of mind where I have an attack.' He fished the tablet out from beneath him, dropped it onto the bed beside his own overnight bag. 'This helps, believe me.'

'What I can't believe is that you're taking it so well. Staying so calm.'

'I have to stay calm. I'm not saying it's easy. I cried my eyes out with Callan, the other day.'

'Are you sure – are you absolutely certain – that you're safe with him?'

'I'm sure. I know it sounds bizarre with this hanging over us, but underneath it all he makes me so happy. I'm safer with him than with anyone else, except you.'

When they got home Sharon and Callan were both waiting on Aryel's spacious balcony-living room. They took in Gwen's red-rimmed eyes and subdued greeting, and looked alarmed. Aryel herself, leaning casually against the finger-thin safety rail along the edge of the drop, closed her own eyes for a moment in silent acknowledgement of the story Gwen's told, though her face did not change. Rhys felt the tension in the room like a blow against his already aching body, and sighed.

'Stop it, all of you. It's not good news, but no worse than it was, really.' He dropped his bag on the floor and let Callan pull him into an embrace. They held each other tight for a long moment, before Rhys pushed gently away. 'I've got some stuff I need to tell Sharon, then I'm all yours. In the meantime, Gwennie can fill you in, okay?'

Callan nodded wordlessly and kissed him, the soft smooch on the corner of his mouth that had become habit, that filled him with such a surge of contentment it seemed impossible he could ever be ill again. Over Callan's shoulder he saw his older sister's expression shift, bright blue eyes shadowed in thought and the firm lines of mouth and jaw that told him she was already scoping, assessing, casting the net of her own ferocious intelligence wide in search of a solution.

I'm not sure you can fix this one, Ari. But please, please try.

He watched her usher Gwen and Callan towards the kitchen, then turned back to Sharon.

'I headed over when I got your message,' she said tightly. 'But I didn't expect you to be working while you were in hospital, Rhys. It can wait . . .'

'Thank goodness I did work. Kept me from going crazy. And no, I don't think it can.'

He flopped onto a sofa and pulled out his tablet. 'I know what the link is. I know why these particular stock samples were taken, and I think I know who may have taken them.'

Sharon sank down beside him as he activated the tablet. The tree-like structure reappeared on the screen. 'There *is* a relationship between the genetypes, and this is it. It's a genealogy.'

'What?' She shook her head. 'That can't be right. We checked to see if any of the stock had been traded between gemtechs—'

'Maybe the stock hadn't, but these key sequences have. Traded or stolen, I don't know.' His fingers slipped across the screen, pulling up infographics to demonstrate. 'We're not talking about normal parent-to-child transmission or sibling-to-sibling variants here. The relationship is limited to specific segments which have been spliced into otherwise completely unrelated genomes, engineered for completely different purposes. If you organise those sequences by the genetype file dates you can see how they change subtly, over time, as more and more alterations are made.'

'So you're talking about something like generations? Parent, child, grandchild?'

'Exactly, but generations as defined by manipulations in the lab, not natural procreation. Think of it as a genealogy of the engineering.' He tapped back to the original schematic. 'The majority of the genetypes lie in parallel, not in sequence – like lots of kids out of the same parents – and came onto the gemtech datastreams over roughly a fifteen-year period, which ended roughly twenty years ago. The sequential ones are iterations, subsequent tweaks of the same segments of code. That's why there were three Gempro samples missing, two Recombin, and so on – even though *within* Gempro, *within* Recombin, the samples were from completely different product lines. Which tells us something about the sequences themselves – they must have been incredibly powerful, incredibly important for *something*, to be used this much over this long a timespan.'

'So someone was trying to get hold of . . .' Sharon stopped and thought. 'Of all the descendants from a single sample? One individual?'

'I think so. The similarities at the point they enter our picture here' – he tapped at the trunk of the tree, a mangrove-like structure with multiple lines that split and split again – 'are very close indeed, sometimes just a couple of base pairs. But it's not every descendant, it's not going all the way to the end of the line. This is the main difference between what the hacker was looking at and what the thief ultimately stole. They followed up on some lines for a generation or two, stopped right away at others, but whenever they lose interest it seems to be because the next stage is a major transition. Sometimes it's an end product and sometimes a dead end, but either way something completely transformative happens. I was able to check most of them. This one was a gillung precursor. This one forms part of the Recombin super-sensory lines. And this came from the archive of one of those cybernetic graft labs that was shut down around eighteen years ago.'

Sharon shuddered at the memory. 'Who was the ancestor?'

'You mean the original genome? I don't know. The lab was probably working from a cultured cell line, it's impossible to tell anything about the individual it came from. Whoever they were – and bear in mind we're going back at least forty years here, maybe longer – they must have had some mutation that proved particularly useful in a whole range of alterations. So much so that the gemtech that owned it kept on modifying and supplying the same sequences for literally decades. You can see how the engineering markers accumulate over time.'

'Can you tell what the mutation was?'

'No. I'm guessing for such a wide range of applications it had to be something really subtle that would have an impact throughout the organism, something that enhanced the primary modification. Or complemented it. Maybe it made metabolism more efficient, or sped up neural development. Something like that.'

The thought that had been nagging at him, unshaped and

inchoate, nagged at him some more and then fled again. He resolved to focus on it, try to bring it to the surface and understand what his enhanced intuition was trying to tell him, later that night when the business of the day was done. For now he held himself upright against the cushions and stayed quiet, watching Sharon's face as she did her own processing.

'Right,' she said finally, slowly. 'So the point of the hacks was to identify and locate every engineered version of a particularly potent set of genetic sequences that somehow got distributed throughout the entire gemtech industry. The point of the thefts was to secure physical samples of each of those versions, right up until the point where they got amalgamated into an end product. They don't want the end products, but they do want all the steps along the way.'

She looked at him for confirmation. He nodded. He suspected she was rehearsing the report she would be making to Masoud.

'Okay, so. Who took them, and why? What use are they to anyone now?'

'That last one I don't have an answer for, but I think they were taken to complete a collection of the entire genealogy. And I think the key to *who* lies in the sequences that aren't here. Look.' He tapped in a command and pointed to the gemtech logos which now pulsed above each avatar of stolen genestock. 'Who's missing?'

She scanned them quickly. 'All the big gemtechs are there, except for Bel'Natur. We knew that already.'

'Yes, but Bel'Natur should be there. And I know that because of this.' He pointed to three mangrove trunks that arose at a later point on the time axis from the main clump, and bloomed into the logo of Gempro. 'The obvious assumption is that Bel'Natur simply never acquired any of that stock, so there was nothing for our hacker-thief to steal from them. But thirty years or so ago Bel'Natur supplied the key sequences for these genetypes to Gempro. And the stock from Gempro's work with those three *was* stolen. They're the same sequences. Bel'Natur *did* have them. I've got them showing as a gap in the genealogy.'

'Why weren't the Bel'Natur versions stolen as well, then?'

'They couldn't have been, because they were never at the EGA. I checked. And the genetypes aren't in the Bel'Natur datastream archive either. But they have to exist.'

'Fucking hell,' she muttered. Her face had gone a bit grey. 'They would have had to be pulled out of inventory and excised from the records before the confiscation orders were even issued.'

'They must have been. There would have been a window between the date of the hacks and the government clampdown. A narrow one, but enough.'

'So either Bel'Natur is behind the whole thing – or they just withheld their own samples of that stock and tampered with the datastream, knowing there was some value in it worth the risk. In which case the thief will probably try to steal theirs too. If he hasn't already.'

'I think the first of those is far more likely, though I don't know if the culprit is the company itself, or a former employee. I've got you a suspect.'

He swiped the screen with its jungle of genetypes away and called up another app. A face appeared on the screen, and Sharon started. The dossier of facts from the Met's own investigation scrolled up beside it.

'This one always felt a little weird to me, a little too obviously in the clear, so when the rest of it started to fall into place I went back and did some digging. Technical director of a highly regarded integrated-ops datastream company gets hired by the new European Genome Archive, nothing strange there, except it was his old firm that installed their system in the first place. He knows it inside out. And look at where he worked before.' He tapped at some links that were not part of the Met file Sharon had supplied, and sat back in triumph.

'That's just another private company. Wait, what—?' She leaned forward, squinting in disbelief at what had popped out of the opened links.

'It's a wholly owned subsidiary, once you track it back through a couple of shells.'

'Holy. Fuck.'

The face continued to swivel slowly on the screen, left-profile to full-face to right-profile: square, self-satisfied, thoroughly respectable. Sharon stared at it as though it had just sprouted horns.

'I need to haul him in. Work out what his angle is, if he's working for someone . . .'

'Yes.' Rhys squirmed, looking and feeling momentarily embarrassed. 'I did almost hack his credit account, see if I could find evidence of a payoff. But then I thought you probably wouldn't be okay with that.'

'*Rhys.*' Sharon barked out a laugh with little humour. He could see the tension in her shoulders and hands, the way she sat poised on the edge of the sofa as though about to spring into action. 'No, I'm afraid I would have had to disapprove if you did that. Leave the breaking and entering to the professionals.'

'Yes, ma'am.'

Her smile held real warmth now. 'This is amazing. You've cracked it, do you realise that?' She grinned. 'Achebe will be beside himself.'

'Thanks, but I'll feel better about it once we know what he's done with the stock.' Rhys frowned at the tablet. 'I still can't work out why anyone would want those sequences *now*.'

'Where did they come from in the first place? Who was the

supplier? We need to hunt through their archive, see if we can understand what makes them so important.'

'That's another mystery. It's a gemtech I've never heard of. They're not in the EGA datastream archive, and I couldn't find any record of them other than what's right here. There's no trace at all.'

Sounds a lot like KAG, came the whisper in the back of his brain, and part of the connection he had been groping for clicked sweetly into place. It startled him so much he almost lost the thread of what he was telling Sharon. 'Some outfit called Phoenix.'

FIRESTORM

21

1703114AS

TO: Zara Klist

FR: Jonah Wycliffe

RE: Phoenix Project – UPDATE – CONFIDENTIAL

The audit has been accelerated as per your instructions, though I am of the view that, so far at least, it raises as many questions as it answers.

To summarise: the Phoenix Project appears to have begun as an attempt to understand, exploit and mediate the properties of a uniquely mutated genome. There is no indication of where your late great-uncle procured the original Phoenix genestock; the corresponding genetype did not bear any obvious engineering tags, certainly none that identify it as a product of Klist Applied Genomics. It has been suggested that it may have been developed by a rival establishment and come into his possession under questionable circumstances, and that this would explain the truly remarkable arrangements he put in place in order to keep it a secret. I must say I consider this explanation to be unlikely. As a stratagem it is far in excess of requirements, but more pertinently it does not accord with my memory of Dr Klist, who was a man of unimpeachable char-acter. I cannot imagine him stooping to such unsavoury practices.

What is clear, however, is that he was aware of the remarkable regenera-tive power of the Phoenix genome. It appears that it was this which allowed it to accept ever more radical modifications, many of which we have indeed seen filter back into the broader KAG genetype pool, to our undeniable benefit.

(Though some, I fear, may also have filtered OUT, and made their way into the inventories of our competitors. While it was Dr Klist's edict that any commercially useful discoveries be returned exclusively to KAG – mirroring the standing order he left with Finance that any such offers from the Phoenix Project be accepted without question and fairly compensated – there has in practical terms been no mechanism in place to ensure that his instruction to THEM would be carried out. From the reports I have received regarding their ambitions for expansion, I have doubts as to whether what they earned from KAG over the years constituted the entirety of their commercial income.)

Dr Klist's directive to the original Phoenix team clearly did not anticipate that they might become independently ambitious. According to the rediscovered charter documents, their objectives were meant to be twofold: to maximise the commercial potential of the genome, yes, but equally to find a way to allow the Phoenix to reproduce. His notes indicate that early attempts at cloning her failed. However there is no indication of any outstanding ability possessed by this female phenotype that would explain the desire to simply replicate her unmodified; still less to produce viable ova, and thus circumvent her native infertility.

So the motivation behind this aspect of the Phoenix Project remains a mystery. Dr Klist left a sealed protocol to be followed in the event of success, but no explanation. I confess I can understand why the researchers became increasingly focused on pursuing the more interesting, and more lucrative, avenues of enquiry presented by so remarkable a mutation, and why this trend became the norm as years and decades passed. Dr Klist's other priority would have become increasingly remote as the original researchers retired and new ones arrived; to the extent that this objective of Phoenix appears to have become forgotten.

Eli leaned back, rubbing his eyes, and tried to think through whether what he was learning about the nested-doll history of Bel'Natur had any relevance at all to the task Aryel had set him. It was becoming clear that this had been a particularly strange episode, and that efforts had been made to delete all records of it – but whether that cleansing had been ancient, from before the KAG datastream had even been placed in Bel'Natur's archives, or was of a more recent vintage he could not tell. He was following a trail of ghosts, imperfectly resurrected from a digital graveyard, and he had to admit it was the mystery of the thing that intrigued him.

Part of that mystery was why they had been resurrected at all; he was no master programmer, and his standard-issue searchbots should not have been able to reconstruct whole communications from shreds of data. Had the Phoenix correspondence been trashed but not wiped, were the bots struggling to pick related bits from some invisible midden of Bel'Natur detritus? There must be an explanation for the ephemeral nature of the ancient messages; it had thrown him badly, the way the files he closed after reading more often than not disappeared as though they had never been. Some popped open again when he frantically entered search terms composed of half-remembered phrases, others did not. But format conversions and name changes had finally done the trick with those he did pin down: allowed him to mirror copies to his private stream so he could access them again. He could only assume that the deletion process itself had somehow undermined the safeguards that would normally prevent files being copied offsite.

He had grabbed as many as he could that way, focusing first on preservation and deferring consideration of the contents, until Callan's worried face in the corner of his vision told him it was time to go; and had then sent up a silent prayer, that he would be able to find his way back in on their return tomorrow. He hoped for that even more strongly now. The story he had unravelled so far, mostly told in fussy, verbose reportage from the unknown Jonah Wycliffe and punctuated occasionally by acerbic responses from the equally unfamiliar Zara Klist, was tantalising in its incompleteness; it felt as though he were reading some gripping pre-Syndrome thriller, and had had to pause halfway through.

So twenty years earlier, more or less, KAG Labs had discovered that its founder had left behind more than a Nobel Prize, the gratitude of a planet and the foundations of early gemtech. Eli knew of Jarek Klist of course. Every schoolchild learned by rote the names of the scientists who had saved them from the Syndrome: a modern-day communion of saints. He knew too that the current chief executive of Bel'Natur was descended from the legendary geneticist, but he had never heard of Zara. If Jarek was her great-uncle she would be what to Zavcka, a second cousin once removed? So there was no more than a generation's difference between them. Zara and Zavcka must know each other. The older woman had been at the helm of KAG when the Phoenix Project came to light, judging from the memos between her and Wycliffe. But it seemed she was not long to remain; filetags suggested that the messages had been deposited in the Bel'Natur archive within a year of being sent. Had the outgoing leader got her younger relative a job with the megacorp to whom she had just sold the family business? Perhaps Zavcka had inherited some sort of sinecure? If so she had certainly made the most of it.

He shook his head sharply. *Focus.*

Zavcka would know that her family's heritage was woven into the fabric of the company she now commanded, but it did not follow that she knew about Phoenix. Or that it was more significant than any other sordid, secret project in the tarnished history of gemtech. But what had happened to it, and what indeed had become of Zara?

He could learn no more from reading the correspondence yet again. He tapped up another searchbot and began to look for Zara Klist.

*

He was almost ready to go to meet Herran and Callan outside Maryam House the next morning when Aryel came in over his earset, sounding weary.

'Eli, I'm so sorry. I should have got back to you last night . . .'

'Don't worry about it. How's Rhys?'

'The news is bad, but he seems okay. He's dealing with it better than the rest of us. Gwen's been in a state, Reginald isn't much better. I think it's just hit, you know? How serious his condition is.'

'Can't they do anything?'

'They're trying. He's staying calm and rational about the whole thing, but I'm not sure we're helping. Things were a bit fraught. He finally got away – I don't blame him – and went to spend the night with Callan. The rest of us stayed up late talking round and round and round it.'

'Callan's not going to want to come in today, is he? That's okay, I can take Herran on my own, he's communicating really well now. Or we could just skip it, take the day off. That might be better.' He felt a pang of regret at the thought of the delay.

'I think you'll find Callan ready and waiting. Rhys is back here now. Somehow in the middle of everything he managed to make a breakthrough in Sharon's case and he's working on tying up loose ends.' She paused as though considering whether to say more, and evidently decided against it. 'He says the distraction is helpful.'

'He ought to take it easy.'

'Yes, that's what we all keep telling him. He says surely we have better things to do than stand over him, fussing.'

'Is there any way I can help?'

'Tell me what you called to tell me last night. I could use some distraction myself.'

He explained about the searchbots and the mystery they had unearthed, read her some of the messages. There was a sharp intake of breath at the subject of the memos, a small sound of incredulity at who they had been written to. Then a silence far too intense for mere polite attention.

When he stopped there was a long, long pause before she spoke.

'Eli, you don't know how important . . . I've been trying to find out what happened to KAG Labs for *years*. And this discovery they made, this secret project, it was called Phoenix? You're sure?'

'Yes. Why, does that mean anything to you?'

She was talking over him, a thing she almost never did, not hearing or not answering his question. 'And KAG didn't know about it? Seriously?'

'Seriously. Up until the date of these memos, KAG thought Phoenix was just an obscure little lab out in the wilderness that every now and then offered them some really innovative R&D. They apparently didn't know they were supposed to get exclusive access to its findings. Even though it was nominally deeded to the corporation, it was also shielded from any interference or oversight. Funding was via an endowment that Jarek Klist set up before he died.'

'So, until these memos, KAG wouldn't have been aware of what Phoenix was up to.'

'Not beyond what the researchers saw fit to sell back to them via the arm's-length arrangement Jarek created.'

'I see.' Another long beat. He imagined her blue eyes narrowed in thought, the absentminded nibbling at the inside of her lip. 'How was it discovered, in the end? How did they find out?'

'By accident. It seems the Phoenix people wanted to expand the facility, and the reply to their application got copied to KAG. Who of course had no idea they were a trustee of the property until that point. The whole thing unravelled pretty quickly from there.'

A short, musical laugh in his ear. 'Municipal bureaucracy

uncovers gemtech black lab. How delightful. What happened then?'

'I don't know. That's as much as I was able to get before we had to leave. I'm going to see if I can find out more today. But Aryel, all this stuff is more than twenty years old. I mean, whatever Phoenix was up to, however bad it was, it doesn't tell us anything about Bel'Natur, then or now. It's interesting, but it isn't the part that's important.'

'I'm not sure about that,' she murmured. 'But tell me the part you think is important.'

'I've been trying to find out about Zara Klist. The woman who was in charge of KAG when Phoenix came to light.'

'What about her?'

'It seemed strange that I'd never heard of her, given how famous the Klist name is. I'd always thought that KAG Labs folded after Jarek Klist died, but it turns out it went on for another twenty-five years . . .'

'That much I did know.'

'Did you? Well . . . then you probably know they increasingly focused on core research, in vitro splices and sequences, just a link in the gemtech supply chain. Solid, but not spectacular. A big departure from the ethos it had when Jarek was around.'

'And you think that was down to Zara Klist?'

'Not just Zara. Jarek had a daughter, another Zavcka, who worked with her father for many years until she was killed in a skiing accident. Some time later *her* daughter, Zytka, joins granddad Jarek. He's in his eighties by then. Zytka runs the company alongside him, just as her mother did, and takes over after his death. It would appear that Zytka is our Zavcka's grandmother.'

Stone silence on the earset. 'Aryel?'

'I'm here. Where does Zara fit into this?'

'She appears to come from a South African branch of the family – Jarek had a brother who went out there as a young man. I remember reading a print interview with Jarek while I was a student, from when he won the Nobel Prize. He was talking about his grief at how his brother's family was devastated by the Syndrome, and I'd got the impression that no one had survived. But clearly someone did, because a hundred years later up pops Zara and takes over KAG.'

'From Zytka?'

'No, from a caretaker board. There appear to have been provisions that kicked in whenever there wasn't a Klist available. So Zytka steps down after fifteen years or so, they run things for a while, and then Zara shows up.'

'Interesting. I take it Zara disappears after the sale of KAG?'

'Not right away. She sticks around for a year or two as a Bel'Natur board member before she resigns and returns to Africa.'

'And the current Zavcka?'

'The current Zavcka shows up on the Bel'Natur executive management team around ten years ago. She's notoriously private: apart from what's on her CV no one knows much about her. And that is pretty much all I could find out on any of them.'

'Curiouser and curiouser.' Yet another meditative pause. 'What do you think it means, Eli?'

'I . . . honestly, Aryel, I don't know if it means anything. The Klist patriarch clearly set things up to ensure a member of his family would always have the top job in the company he founded. Nothing too strange about that, but it bothers me that there is so little sign of them anywhere *else*. I tracked down a few records, just enough to verify marriages, births and deaths, but I couldn't find anything deeper than that. Anything personal. Or social. There are a few business-related mentions, but nothing that's purely about *them*. There're hardly even any pictures. I found a few of Zavcka the First, mostly taken in company with her father, and there've been more of Zavcka the Second since she took over Bel'Natur. But the only ones I could find of the others were a media shot of Zytka at Jarek's funeral, and a portrait of the Bel'Natur board of directors during the time Zara was a member. Even their husbands don't seem to have much of a life onstream. Hardly any pictures or posts from them either.'

'Is it only husbands? I mean, are all the Klists women?'

'It appears so. There's no mention of any of them having sons.'

'Do they look alike?'

He was confused for a moment, as much by the urgency in her tone as the question. 'You mean the women?'

'Yes, the women. Zavcka the First, Zytka, Zara, Zavcka the Second. Do they resemble each other?'

'Not really. Well, hang on.' He flipped through the images on his tablet. 'Come to think of it, they do. Different hair colours, but the faces are very similar.'

'Can you send me what you've found?'

'Sure.' He tapped up her comcode. 'On its way. Apart from the fetish about female names starting with Z, the thing I can't wrap my head around is how does a dynasty as rich and powerful as the Klists go through generation after generation and leave so little trace of themselves behind? That doesn't just *happen*. It feels intentional.'

'I'm sure it is.'

'But why? What are they hiding? I always thought Zavcka's reclusiveness – our Zavcka, Zavcka the Second – was just a quirk. Now it looks like a strategy, one that's been maintained for over a century. And I can't imagine any good reasons for that.'

'Do you think it has anything to do with the Phoenix Project?'

He bit back the reflexive dismissal, and reminded himself that Aryel Morningstar never asked stupid questions.

'Well, it obviously started long before the secret lab came to light – wait, you mean maybe Zara wasn't really surprised? Something like it might even still be going on?'

'I don't know yet either, Eli. But I think you're right to worry.' Her voice had gone reflective, tired again, a little sad. 'Let me think about it, see if I can come up with anything else. And . . . and if you learn anything more about Phoenix, please come and talk to me.'

22

Sharon kept her smile tight and hard, and as devoid of amusement as a training sergeant on examination day. She knew that the sleepless night had left lines and shadows around her eyes, and counted it an advantage for this particular interview. Let there be no illusions about just how much trouble her guest was in.

He did not look much better; few people arrested before dawn and taken into custody without the benefit of shower, shave or coffee did. She could see, in the way he twitched against his rumpled shirt and ran his hand over a chinful of stubble, all the while glancing at the silent young witnessing officer who stood at the rear of the room, that he was trying to work some sympathy out of his state of general dishevelment. The façade of embattled and indignant innocence had been fairly well kept up, but cracks were beginning to show.

Sharon rested her hands on the table, absentmindedly flicking a thumb against the curve of her wedding ring before she noticed the motion and stilled it.

'Tell me about the genestock.'

'What about it? I don't know anything, I told you. I didn't even know it was missing until you showed up.' Combative as before, and with the same air of disdain; but there was a touch, just the faintest shred, of fear about him now. She knew he would be trying hard to conceal it.

'Come now, Mr Nance. If anyone was in a position to know *everything* about it, including how to remove it without triggering the alarms, it's you. The only reason you took the job in the first place was in order to steal the genestock, isn't that right?'

The barest flicker of recognition before his face went back to a carefully blank hostility, but it was enough. She knew she had him.

'I don't know what you're talking about.'

'Why did you conceal your previous employment?'

'I've never lied about where I used to work. And anyway, it's not like it was illegal.'

'It might have had some bearing on whether the EGA decided you were the right person to install their security and run their operations.'

'I never worked for Bel'Natur.'

'Let's not get bogged down in technicalities. They owned the business, they funded the operations, they were the primary client.'

'There's nothing illegal about that.'

'So you agree that you did work for them.'

'No, I said—' A pause. He would be replaying the conversation, trying to avoid catching himself in a contradiction.

Sharon made her smile even flintier and pressed the advantage. 'I wouldn't want you to get confused, Mr Nance, so let's recap what we know, shall we? You earned an extremely generous bonus payment during your final year, really remarkable considering that human gemtech had been severely curtailed, the Declaration was about to be issued, and Bel'Natur was in deep financial and legal trouble. But you helped them out in turn. You used those funds to buy out the subsidiary you worked for, transitioning its intellectual property and technical expertise into a new firm under a new name, a firm in which you had a major stake. You then won the contract to set up the EGA's integrated datastream and security systems, based largely on, and I'm quoting here, "remarkable insight into the inherent weaknesses which the Archive must be aware of, and the potential threats against which it must remain vigilant". The irony of that statement is really quite breathtaking.'

She paused for breath herself, and took stock. His fists were clenched on the table, and his mouth was clamped shut.

'So then, having made such a huge success of your new venture's first big commission, you immediately wound it down in order to take a much more modestly paid position running the system you'd just installed. My guess is you got that job based on the premise that no one else could understand it and take full advantage of its capabilities as well as you. I suspect that was absolutely true, though not in the way the EGA imagined. What I find fascinating' – she made a show of leaning forward and tapping up information on her angled tablet screen, though everything she needed was already there – 'is that your partner in the business, JKE Investments, didn't seem to object to this at all. In fact, even though the whole thing ended up posting a considerable loss, they've since made several rather large payments into your Abu Dhabi credit account. Which I notice isn't mentioned anywhere on your European Federation tax return, by the way, but we'll leave that aside for now.'

She looked up, held his eyes and let the last vestiges of the smile slide off her face. 'Who is JKE, Mr Nance?'

He managed a smirk. It was fairly unconvincing, and there had been no mistaking the spark of worry at the mention of that name. 'You tell me, since you know so much.'

'I'll be able to do that very soon. One way or another. I admit the datasearch is taking a little longer than expected – they're very well shielded, far more than is reasonable for an ordinary private investment trust. But we're closing in. We've already gone through the first layer of extra-territorial satellite registration, down to the Caribbean, across to Dubai, back up into space and now over to' – she squinted at the feed scrolling up the edge of the screen – 'Eastern Europe. Almost home. You need to consider, Mr Nance, that if I find them and find out what they've done with the stock before you get around to telling me, I'm not going to have any reason to go easy on you.'

He tried to cover his unease with sarcasm. 'Oh, is that what you're doing?'

'So far that is exactly what I'm doing.'

'I don't know what happened to the genestock. I can't tell you something I don't know.'

'Who did you hand it over to?'

'Who says I handed it over to anyone?'

'So you still have it.'

'No I don't.'

'Then who did you give it to?'

'No one. I told you.'

She regarded him gravely for a long moment. 'A dead drop? Is that what you're trying so hard not to tell me, Mr Nance?'

'I'm trying not—' He stopped, shook his head and spat, 'I'm not trying to tell you anything.'

'Yes you are. You've been trying to tell us how clever you've been for a couple of weeks now. You just didn't expect us to turn out to be as clever as you.'

And there it was at last, the reaction she was looking for, shaken out of him by the shock of her ambush: a wash of pallor, jaw slack for a moment with surprise, a jolt of real fear. Rhys had been right. And how interesting, that it was this revelation which concerned him most. Sharon sighed, putting a little theatre into it. Time to drop the final bomblet that Achebe had uncovered last night while they were pulling the case together for the warrant application. 'You know, Mr Nance, when I met you I thought you looked familiar but I couldn't put my finger on why. Turns out it was because I'd met your brother only a couple of days before. You resemble each other. He's taller and thinner, of course, and he hasn't changed his surname. You have. Why was that, Mr Nance?'

He stared at her, bewilderment at the sudden change of subject sliding quickly into fury, then into something else. For the first time there was naked hatred on his face. Sharon could hear the other officer react to it, a sharp intake of breath and a shifting of stance. 'I decided it was for the best. I don't have to explain why.'

'Were you trying to distance yourself from your family, or shield them from your anti-Declaration activities? Or just make it harder for anyone to work out what you used to do for a living?'

'I wanted a new name. A new start. People do that all the time.' He spat it out, struggling for composure.

'They don't, actually. It's quite rare. Also, most people don't have a brother who leads an evangelical UC splinter group. Did his actions at the concert that night have anything to do with why you decided to let the police know that a major theft of highly engineered genestock had taken place under their noses and there wasn't a damn thing they could do about it?'

'I didn't—' He stopped. She thought he was trying to work out whether it could be to his advantage to admit blowing the whistle, while still denying the theft, and was unsurprised when he apparently concluded it wasn't. 'My brother's activities are embarrassing.'

'Are they? Is that why you spent an hour onstream with him the night he was arrested, and why you posted his bail?'

'He's my brother.'

'He's never done quite as well as you, has he? Never had the grades, the career, the sense of conviction. He's a fairly ineffectual character, really. But still you've supported him, like a good brother should – although if he embarrasses you it could only be by not taking as tough a Reversionist line as you would like. You share a lot of his views, Mr Nance, and you hold them far more strongly even than he does. We've been taking a look at your life onstream, all your handles and the forums you post to. It's been very enlightening. Your brother made a fool of himself that night, but it's clear from the comments you made that that's not how you saw it. You felt he had been humiliated by a pair of gems and the institutions that now protect them, and it made you angry. It made you want us to know we were being made fools of in turn. So you pointed us at the stolen genestock, you gave us the finger, because you wanted to see us run around in a panic; and you were certain we could never trace either the theft or the tip-off back to you. But you were wrong, Mr Nance. And here we are.'

He was breathing hard now, face red, teeth grinding behind white lips. The explosion was close, and after it the collapse.

She needed to push just a little harder. 'History's going to repeat itself, I'm afraid. Your brother will get a slap on the wrist, a telling-off from the judge, a hundred hours or so community service. You, on the other hand, will get the full whack. Criminal conviction, custodial sentence, seizure of assets . . .'

He came up out of his seat, teeth bared, slamming his body against the table so that it and the tablet shook. The chair fell over behind him. Even though she had been expecting something like it, it took all Sharon's self-control not to flinch as he screamed into her face.

'You think you can do anything to me? You nasty, unnatural, traitorous *bitch*! You can't fucking touch me! You think I don't know who you are? What you're married to?'

Sharon's right hand was up and clenched, the signal to the officer who had surged forward behind her to hold position. She resisted the urge to punch Nance with it. Hard and fast in the larynx, be weeks before he could speak again.

'You think I'm *afraid* of you?! I have *protection*, you hear me? You can't prove anything! You—'

'Sit down, Mr Nance.'

'You don't deserve to carry a warrant! Call yourself police—'

'*Sit down!*'

It was a controlled shout, honed by years on the beat: low and sharp as a whip-crack, and with all the command she could put into it. He stared in amazement as she sat at ease, as though nothing had happened, and then took in the officer standing behind her with stinger baton half drawn.

Sharon said, very softly, 'I'm not the one you need to be afraid of.'

She let the moment stretch, let the reality sink into him, until he stepped back from the table with his hands open and raised. A flood of invective continued to tumble out, low and vicious, as his eyes stayed fixed on Sharon's face. She flicked two fingers up and the officer moved, hand still on the baton, to right the toppled chair.

'Shut up. That's *enough*.' The chair slammed back into place. 'You can't talk to Inspector Varsi like that.'

'It's fine, constable.' Sharon spoke peaceably, fingers laced together on the table again, posture deliberately relaxed. 'Mr Nance is entitled to his opinion. Sit down, Mr Nance.' She injected steel into her voice. 'I won't tell you again.'

The chair was prodded against the back of his knees, none too gently. He went quiet and folded down onto it. The constable stood behind him, fists on hips, until Sharon gave her the nod and she strode back around to her place, the colour still high in her pale face.

Guess it's okay to dish shit out to our own, but no one else is allowed. Good to know.

She returned her attention to Nance.

'You've made a very big mistake, Mr Nance,' she said, quietly, so that he had to stay quiet himself in order to hear. Use the adrenalin crash, dangle the possibility of a way out. 'And I think you know that now. You might have had protection once, but you won't any more. If you hadn't sent us that message there's a good chance no one in the EGA or the police would ever have discovered the theft. And I think, Mr Nance, that's what JKE wanted. And expected. It was never part of their plan to have the Met hot on their trail. I think whoever's behind them is going to be very, very pissed off when they find out just how badly you have screwed things up. And they *will* find out. They're not going to be looking out for you then, are they, Mr Nance? No, they're going to be getting as far away from you as they can, they'll be finding ways to drop the whole thing on *you*. Isn't that right, Mr Nance?'

He was shaking his head, whether at her or himself she did not know. There were traces of spittle on his lips. 'They won't . . . they can't—'

'Oh, I think they can, and I think they will. And you think so too.'

He sat there for a while, shoulders slumped, head hanging down. He would finally, she thought, be taking in the entire depth and breadth of the hole he had dug for himself.

When the words came, they were bitter and broken. 'What do you want?'

She sat back and let out a long, silent breath. Her reply was no less bitter. 'I want details on how you beat the system. I want to know all about JKE. And I want you to tell me about the dead drop.'

*

Their icons snapped into place, the hair-thin lines that linked generation to generation glowing bright as the program he had written matched up sequences, measured the infinitesimal shifts of mutation and manipulation, and confirmed the suspicion that had nagged at him all night. Rhys stared at the screen as he and Gwen slotted with the neatness of inevitability into the genealogy he had worked out the day before. He did not know whether to howl with rage or dance for joy or cry.

He had formed the conviction that it would be worth checking, worth testing, probably pointless but just in case, no reason to think they were but no reason to believe they weren't. Then he had fallen asleep while wrestling with the paradox that unless he already had his genetype for comparison, he had no way of finding out whether an analogue of it sat somewhere on the Phoenix ancestral tree. A circular conundrum, an insoluble riddle.

Until he woke up with the answer.

A full genetype included the huge, unwieldy dataset of the underlying genome; but without the index of engineered mutations and the epigenetic directory of intricate molecular switches that regulated their expression, it was barely useful. Everyone relied on those registers; every analytical tool was keyed to them. They extracted meaning from millions of base pairs, translated the information, organised it. They told engineers and doctors and desperate young gems not only where problems lay, but where solutions could be found. Having the genome alone was like having a complete set of grid references, but no actual map. And that was all he had of himself and Gwen: just their genomes, decoded by the hospital, a string of six billion inscrutable indicators.

And the genomes into which the Phoenix sequences had been inserted, sitting like bedrock beneath the rest of the hacked data, so obvious he had been unable to see it. And the indices that mapped those sequences back to their insertion points, that he could use to compare with the same points for himself and his sister.

And there they were.

He traced the lines with his finger and mulled over the implications. So KAG Labs had also been a Phoenix client, and like Phoenix had disappeared. On its own this information was of little use. But he was connected to Phoenix, and by more than just coincidence. The segments of his own genome that the medical team had identified as being where the problem most likely lay were a tidy subset of the sequences he had found embedded in stolen genestock. Somewhere in the layered history of splices and recombinations, something had gone terribly wrong. Somewhere in that same history, in the panoply of variants that the thief had taken, would be the key to putting it right.

Think, Rhys.

A rustle on the edge of hearing, a hint of spice and musk, a sense of presence. He said, 'Hi, Ari,' and looked up.

'Hey.' She stopped at the threshold where the narrow perimeter walkway opened into the expanse of the living room and leaned against the wall, surveying him. 'I've got some news.'

So have I, he thought. *But you'll tell me to back off, Ari, leave the business end of it to Sharon, get permission before I hand these genotypes that Gwen and I are related to over to the analysts. I'm not sure I can do that. But I'm not sure what else I can do.*

'What news?'

'I've just found out where KAG Labs went.' She told him.

'Hang on. You're telling me KAG is now part of Bel'Natur?'

'Yes and no. Bel'Natur absorbed them completely; there's not even a listing on the datastream. The messages Eli's searchbot found were resurrected from trashed files.'

'Think there might be some trashed genotype files there too?'

'If there are it'll be more than he can do to search them out. He said he saw no sign of any filetype other than messages. It'll take some proper forensics work to see if there's anything else there.'

'Can we ask—?' He stopped. His mouth had gone dry with fore-knowledge of what the answer would be.

Aryel was shaking her head grimly. 'Yesterday, certainly. I needn't even have mentioned Eli – he's not sure how he accessed this stuff, and clearly he wasn't meant to. But it wouldn't have mattered. I could've just said that after much research we've learned that KAG Labs was acquired by Bel'Natur almost twenty years ago, and we've a KAG gem with a serious medical condition, and would they like to further enhance their reputation by helping to save his life? And the head of the company would have had no choice but to say of course, anything we can do to help. But today . . .'

'Today the gem who needs saving is the same one who just impli-cated them in a criminal conspiracy.' He felt panic rise in his chest. 'But maybe it's not them, maybe this guy Nance was working for someone else. Maybe they're in the clear and they'd still be willing to help.'

She sighed deeply. 'I have a horrible feeling that they are involved, Rhys. Maybe not the whole firm, but the person at the top, the person I'd have to ask. I can't go to her directly now, not without compromising Sharon's investigation. We have to wait.'

'For how long?'

'Until the threads she's tugging at unravel a bit. Until Bel'Natur is either under formal investigation themselves, in which case we can get a warrant to search the archive under an imminent-threat clause. Or until they're cleared, in which case we're back to where we were yesterday and I can approach Zavcka Klist.'

'You don't think that's the way it's going to turn out, though.'

'I doubt it. And an investigation creates all sorts of problems –

for the infotech project and what we hoped to get out of it, for Eli, potentially for Mikal. It's going to take a little time to work through, Rhys. Probably a couple of weeks.'

I don't have time, Ari. I'm close to another episode, I can feel it. I might not have two more weeks.

She came away from the wall and lowered herself onto a chair opposite, reaching out to ruffle her fingers through his hair as she sat. The gesture reminded him of how he and Gwen used to cuddle up on either side of her when they were little, one under each wing, while she read them stories or taught them their maths. Or let them amuse themselves, playing beneath and behind her while she buried herself in her tablet, her focus complete as she studied the world into which they already knew she would one day venture. Ari, the adopted big sister, always loving and caring but always with a bigger mission.

'I will get what you need from them, I promise. I won't fail you. But you need to be patient and to trust me. And whatever happens, you need to stay well.'

He nodded soberly, not meeting her eyes. All these other considerations, all these other people and priorities. A spark of rebellion flared in him.

It isn't just Dr Walker. Herran's there. If he knows what to look for he can find it, easy. They'd never even know.

23

Getting back into the deleted KAG sub-archive proved easier than Eli had expected. He had the trick of it now, and Rhys would have been interested to know that he had already spent a minute or two trying to determine what else might be accessible, and disappointed to learn that he had found no trace of any genetype files. There were indeed other dull grey links into what would once have been its datastream, but these really were broken; no amount of tapping and typing would prompt them into life. Eli was almost relieved. What he most wanted to pursue, the message files, were still there; still evanescent, but capable of being cornered and copied if he worked fast.

As he grabbed and mirrored, grabbed and mirrored, he realised they were not as jumbled as he had at first thought; he might not be seeing every exchange between Zara and her army of minions, of whom Jonah Wycliffe appeared to be the commander-in-chief, but what he was getting was clear and chronological. It was also very limited in scope. This was not a random selection of retrieved messages from the lost datastream of KAG Laboratories. They were restricted to a narrow timespan around the discovery of the Phoenix Project, and had two other things in common: every one was a communication from or to Zara Klist, and every one had Phoenix as a subject line. It was as though the searchbot had gone looking specifically and exclusively for evidence of how the chief executive had dealt with the discovery of the secret lab.

Finally he had another half dozen or so messages, neatly stacked below those from the day before. The first appeared to be a direct response to the explanation Wycliffe had sent.

1703114AS

TO: Jonah Wycliffe

FR: Zara Klist

RE: Rv1: Phoenix Project – UPDATE – CONFIDENTIAL

Reports appreciated but fail to address primary concern: what are these people up to NOW? Regardless of one's opinion of JK's instructions, the fact remains: they should have been followed to the letter, they were not, and enormous funds have been spent instead on – WHAT? Nguyen has advised that sequences acquired from Phoenix, while generating high value output, were probably inexpensive to develop. Meanwhile cryptic references to breakthrough modifications and extreme tolerance levels (with which I am becoming progressively less amused) suggest in vivo experimentation, for which neither they nor we are registered. Are they growing live prototypes down there? If so how many, what's the cost-value, and what are the legal implications? If they don't want to be shut down immediately they had better start explaining what it is they've got that's so special.

The tone of that felt both familiar and passé; like something her younger relative would once have said. Eli shook his head as he tapped up the reply. The more of her he read, the more Zara reminded him of the Zavcka he had met four years ago. It made him wonder again about the transformation, about whether it was really possible for someone so entrenched in a particular way of thinking to change so much.

1803114AS

TO: Zara Klist

FR: Jonah Wycliffe

RE: Rv2: Rv1: Phoenix Project – UPDATE – CONFIDENTIAL

I have finally extracted a bit more from Dr Panborn, who reacted with much indignation when informed that without specifics we are not inclined to treat her claims as anything more than hyperbole; and with horror at the realisation that, unless they give us reasons to think otherwise, she and her colleagues are at this point entirely dispensable. Reasons have been duly advanced.

She confirms that in vivo experiments have indeed taken place, though somewhat irregularly. This has been alongside the in vitro work which we knew about. They have been attempting to develop marketable applications of what she insists truly is a breakthrough. It began with an initial test batch back in 100, which was (as is generally the case) largely disastrous; the lead researcher at the time used an inter-species splicing technique as a rather flamboyant method of assessing the degree of anatomic plasticity which the Phoenix sequences could render tolerable. The resulting dysmorphia was as extreme as could be hoped, but the integrity of core organ systems was nevertheless largely preserved. One of the subjects in particular displayed none of the typical indicators of cognitive or physical deficit, despite a vastly altered physique, and indeed has appeared to develop more or less normally. Attempts to replicate her have failed, though Panborn insists this is beside the point. In her own words:

'The prototype is a female juvenile who has a functional pair of additional limbs. Furthermore, her overall anatomy, metabolism, hormonal and neural function appear perfectly adapted to what is an unprecedented modification. This systemic cascade of complementary mutations has been a scientific treasure trove, and has informed our understanding and further refinement of the relevant sequences and switches – several of which KAG has already had the opportunity to work with. The extra limbs, though functional, are not in our view inherently useful (there are some in the team who consider them to have aesthetic value, though that is a matter of opinion). However, their core architecture should be amenable to the design of a platform with significant industrial and combat applications, and we are actively developing the relevant modifications to test this. As a parallel development, we have had significant success recently combining a variety of metabolic, sensory and neural enhancements within a standard physique package, and are within a decade of bringing the results to market.'

So there you have it. Cybernetics is a fashionable field at the moment, and one in which we have only a peripheral stake – if Panborn is not being overly optimistic then there really could be some 'significant' value in their current research. I gather there remain about a dozen live specimens from a total of 4 batches (50% survival rate, not bad), mostly late infancy to early pre-adolescent. The exemplar prototype is of course already adolescent. The resident expert on her is a Dr Owen, who was part of the original batch design team and has carried primary responsibility for its results ever since. They seem to consider the lack of registration an irrelevance, given the current low levels of enforcement.

Panborn continues to insist that Phoenix should and must be left alone, though I sense with somewhat less conviction. How do you wish to proceed?

Eli read the quotation from Dr Panborn again. Premonition settled over him like a cloak, like the charcoal-grey shroud a diminutive gem with sky-blue eyes and a face as delicate as porcelain had once worn. He reached to tap the next file open, slowly, like a man in a dream. His finger shook.

1803114AS

TO: Jonah Wycliffe

FR: Zara Klist

RE: Phoenix – Site visit – CONFIDENTIAL

Advise Panborn, Owen etc to expect us at 17:00 on the 20th. Non-negotiable. Industrial and combat? Based on that am inclined to arrive with hazmat and full security detail. They have 24hrs to convince me to make it you and me on the XJet instead.

Supplementary limb pairs have been attempted before. Spectacular failures. If they've managed a neuromuscular infrastructure compatible with combat implants it would be well worth developing, though I am not inclined to alter our own registration status in order to do so in-house; there are reputational issues to consider, and I am not convinced that the public's newfound interest in gem welfare will dissipate soon. But in any event, such a breakthrough is not compatible with Panborn's refusal to provide images or a more detailed description. Suspect we may be going to visit the circus. Does this prototype of theirs have a second pair of working arms, or does she gallop on four legs like a horse?

Anger now, at the contempt, the callousness, the gratuitous nastiness of it all. Whoever she was, whatever she was, no fourteen-year-old girl deserved this. And shame, because none of it was ancient, none of it was beyond responsibility, he was already a young man in university when these words were thought and said and sent. He had read and heard such things before, many, many times, and shame took hold of him and shook him like a dog shakes a rat, every single time. Shame, and anger, and disbelief.

It can't be, he thought. Not her. No one could ever have spoken so of her.

He had almost convinced himself as he opened the reply from Wycliffe. It was uncharacteristically short.

1903114AS

TO: Zara Klist

FR: Jonah Wycliffe

RE: Rv1:   Phoenix – Site visit – CONFIDENTIAL

They are expecting us, and are pretending to be pleased about it.

When asked for details on the prototype, Panborn shunted me to Owen. Owen refused to respond and shunted me back to Panborn. I was finally able to get them both on a voice conference, which has just ended. They attempted to explain their reluctance by claiming that sending any visual or audible record offsite would prove too great a security risk; but said they were worried that if they simply described her I wouldn't believe them. This went on for some time. I finally extracted a verbal description, though they were not wrong – I can hardly credit what they have told me.

They say she has wings.

Callan glanced out at Eli, hunched over his tablet in the sound-dampened seating area, and turned back into the lab. There was a spring in the step of the researchers today, and Sevi wore a broad smile, though the circles under her eyes told of a sleepless night.

'You understand it now? Seriously?'

'I think so. There's a lot more to do, but that went exactly the way I hoped it would.' She was beaming as she stood beside Herran, half-reclined in the chair with the sensor net on his head. 'Was that okay for you, Herran? I know it was a little different from what we've done before . . .'

'Okay.'

'Do you mind if we run a few more tests like that?'

'Not mind.'

'If we get the results I expect we can refine the parameters pretty quickly, but we'll have to stop in between to recalibrate. It might get a little boring for you.'

'Not boring. I work.' He raised his tablet, clutched as always in his small fist, and waggled it slightly.

Callan lifted an eyebrow in response. These last few days of disruption, filled with the things Herran normally disliked – being tested and endlessly talked to, being taken away from home – appeared to have had the unexpected effect of making him more expressive. They had been greeted this morning by Sevi's bubbly conviction that the neural translation team had finally made a breakthrough in their attempt to decode the binary structure of his mind, and Herran had reacted with more than his usual remote equanimity: he had engaged in the conversation, he was interested.

For the first time Callan found himself questioning whether he really understood how Herran's compromised psyche functioned at all.

Now the little gem did his half-body turn towards the doorway, though from his seat he was unable to see through it. But he looked pointedly in that direction, before turning back towards Callan.

'Eli okay?'

'Yeah, just busy.'

'Working.'

'Mm-hmm. Something came up yesterday, I think. But he's fine.'

Herran gazed at him steadily for a long moment, then blinked hugely and solemnly. As the long lashes fluttered down and up again Callan realised with a start that it had become a gesture, an element of body language, like another person's shrugged shoulder or his own raised eyebrow.

Where did he learn that? From Mikal?

'Eli fine. Rhys not fine.'

'What did you hear? He's okay, he hasn't become ill.'

'Could get ill very bad. I know.'

'I . . . he might, Herran, but he hasn't yet. There's still time.'

'Need find genetype. Quick quick.'

'Yes . . .' Callan wondered if Herran had been hacking Rhys' medical files. He wouldn't put it past him.

A shadow fell across the door, and Eli poked his head in. 'How's everything going?'

'Really well today. Sevi,' nodding in her direction, 'thinks she's cracked it.'

'Have you? Oh. That's good.' He looked dazed, distant, a little sick and not really interested in what Sevi might or might not have cracked. Herran looked at him, unspeaking, and blinked. Callan looked from one to the other and thought, *Something is going on here. I'm missing something.* But Sevi was too elated to notice.

'Looks like it.' She grinned at Eli. 'We were thinking about it wrong, layering our own assumptions over Herran's reality. We thought he must be like a person with primary and secondary languages, and that binary would be the secondary one. But it's not, it's as native for him as human-speak. More so, maybe, because more of his brain is dedicated to it. Now that we understand how he organises the information we should be able to move a lot more quickly.'

'That's good. Eh, Herran?'

'Good.'

'Do you think—?' Eli looked from Herran to Callan to Sevi, as though searching for something. He seemed lost, disoriented. 'If everything's okay here, do you mind if I step out for a bit? I – I have to see Aryel.' Again that stricken look. 'Something's come up that I really need to talk to her about.'

Callan found himself suddenly afraid, for no reason he could name. He nodded dumbly, unable to formulate even a basic question. Sevi chirped, 'Fine by me!' and turned away to set up for the next test.

Herran blinked. 'Go,' he said. 'Aryel explain.'

LEGACY

She is a cousin this time. She resolves to be a daughter in the next incarnation – it makes things so much easier – but the maternal link had begun to feel dangerously overused. So she made herself distant, thrice removed, and wonders now how much else has escaped her notice while in exile.

He hid his gift to her, from her, and he hid it in plain sight. A strategy not unlike her own, and she is as aware of that irony as she is of the sick feeling in the pit of her stomach at the other uses to which he has had it put. So she was this to him too, and she swallows down the knowledge, and tries not to mind.

There are more immediate concerns. His covert enterprise was never intended to stay hidden so long, and she must take steps, quickly, to ensure that the discovery of one secret does not reveal the other. That irony would not entertain. Especially not now, when she is long accustomed to her isolation, long reconciled to the fact that what had mattered most to him matters not at all to her. She is content with fictional procreation.

How strange, she sometimes muses, that one possessed of such vision could not think of legacy other than in the old, tribal terms: ancestral blood in the veins, familiar features on bright young faces, wisdom whispered through the lengthening night. She has no need of such distractions. She is her own birthright. Even if his wayward disciples had remained true to the task he set them, even if they had found the solution he so longed for, she is far from sure she would have availed herself of it.

But they succeeded at something. *They have fashioned a different prize, it seems, unsanctioned and unexpected, but no less valuable for that. The mystery of it excites her, and in this at least she has no doubt that her father would be of the same mind as herself: it is his gift to her, and she wants it.*

24

'Here's the thing,' Sharon was saying. 'I don't believe he didn't know who hired him. Even if he never dealt with them directly, which is what he's claiming, it does not make sense to me that he'd take those kinds of risks unless he knew who was behind it and he was confident they were going to hold up their end of the bargain. Not to mention that, as a hard-line Reversionist, he'd want to know he was getting it for people who weren't far apart from him in terms of ideology. But he will not name names.'

She gazed up at Rhys out of the screen of his tablet, her brow still creased in annoyance. Her voice came directly into his earset, and he had activated its damper field so he could not be overheard either. Not that they were likely to be; he was in his bedroom with the door closed, and a strangely pensive Aryel had gone up to the roof garden. But Gwen could come back at any moment from whatever recording session or publicity opportunity had been scheduled that morning, and he knew too well how sharp her hearing was.

'Why is he refusing to talk, if he's got no reason to be loyal to them any more?'

'I don't think it's loyalty, Rhys. He's scared. He's so scared he's not even constructing good lies any more. He tried to convince me that it was all done onstream and for the final phase he was sent

285

a list of the stock they wanted, but then he got caught out trying to explain how he knew about the hacks.'

'Do you think he was also the hacker?'

'He may have been, although we don't have any direct evidence for that. But he definitely knows his way around gemtech datastream security – seems he developed a good chunk of it. And considering that the whole point of turning anonymous informant was to show off what a bunch of mugs we are compared to what a talented little criminal he is, it's possible he only included the hacks because he was responsible for them too.'

'That part, the whistleblower thing, that was because of Gwen? Seriously?'

'Believe it or not. Small world.'

'It just seems really stupid.'

'People do stupid things when family is involved. He got so angry about his brother, he lost the plot.' He could see her frown deepen and her eyes slide away before she set her jaw and looked straight at him again. It was a cue Rhys recognised from their work together, the thing she did when she was uncertain but about to plunge in anyway. 'I wondered . . . I know I should be leaving you alone, Rhys, and if you'd rather just step away from this now I'll understand. Gwen's involvement was a complete fluke, but I thought I should tell you . . . and you said having something else to concentrate on was helpful . . .'

'It is.' Actually he wanted to be focusing on the problem of disinterring his genetype from the bowels of the deleted Bel'Natur archive, but he had learned more about what he was looking for from working the case than in all the previous years of searching. Instinct told him to keep that avenue open; and besides, he had grown too fond of Sharon simply to tell her no. 'Is it his Reversionist links you want me to look into?'

'No need, Achebe has that covered. And anyway it's not illegal, just – indicative.' She grimaced slightly. 'It's trying to uncover who he was working for and what happened to the dead drop that has me stumped. It feels like it's all right there, you know, but I can't pull the pieces together. I thought maybe you could spot whatever it is I'm missing.'

'I'll do my best. What was the dead drop?'

'A disused postbox set into the wall of an alley in the financial district.'

'A what-box? What's that?'

'It was a pre-Syndrome message distribution system, back when everything had to be printed and sent to geographic addresses. They'd get pushed through a slot and fall into a chamber behind, and then an official would come along with a special tool to open the chamber. They were made of metal, waterproof, fireproof . . .'

'So it would hold temperature.'

'Yep, I thought that when we opened it up. Very cold, even though it's a blazing day.'

'They're still accessible?'

'They're not supposed to be. There are only a handful left in the entire country, mostly inset into buildings or walls of historic value. The slots are supposed to be sealed shut, but this one's been tampered with. It's rigged with a catch: if you know where to press it'll open and then snap shut again once you let go. Nance said the genestock vials were sealed inside a super-insulated flexcase; it would have slipped right in. He made two deposits. He also said his instructions were via ghost message, you know, the kind that auto-delete? One way only, so he had no way of telling anyone when he'd made a deposit. And he was explicitly instructed not to try, just to drop whatever he had whenever he had it. And I do believe that, because he seemed truly baffled about how anyone was going to know it was there, much less get it out.'

'Hacked security vidcam. Easy.'

'Except there aren't any eyes on that alley. It's not really a shortcut to anywhere, just a dogleg between buildings with major roads at either end. Sheer walls on both sides, London brick. As for getting into the thing, one of my guys had to borrow what we needed from a museum.'

'There must be something. A microcam.'

'We scanned for vid signal and found nothing. But guess which building is right around the corner – literally fifty yards or so from the end of the alley. I couldn't believe it; I hadn't realised it would be so close until we got there.'

'Bel'Natur.'

'Yep. Bloke even strolled up and introduced himself as head of security, asked if there was a problem in the area he should know about. I checked he was who he said he was and we had a little chat. Said they didn't have any cams on it, seemed surprised the city doesn't either. But he said it was far enough away from their building, and anyway they haven't had any security concerns for a few years now. Hope nothing's changed in that respect, Inspector, if we can be of any assistance, blah blah. It was like all the stories Mikal's been telling me about the new and improved Bel'Natur.' She paused.

'But.'

'But. Seems a little too close for coincidence to me.'

'How did he know you were there? If he doesn't have eyes on it?'

'Said he was just passing by, glanced into the alley and noticed us . . .' She caught his look and shrugged. 'I agree, it feels very convenient. But it's also completely plausible.'

'A distance cam? Inside the building itself, high up?'

'Angles are wrong for the postbox. We checked.'

'Damn.' He thought. 'Was there anything in the chamber? When you opened it?'

'Just a layer of dust. Disturbed, as though something had been there and been removed.'

'Okay . . . and it's just around the corner, hang on, let me work this out . . .'

How does a layer of dust get inside a sealed box?

On his screen, Sharon was frowning again.

'There's a risk in being so certain it leads back to Bel'Natur that we ignore other possibilities. Or discrepancies. Like, would they really have gone to the trouble of creating an investment trust, sheltered behind a daisy chain of shell companies that appear to take advantage of every corporate secrecy provision on the planet, just so they could pay off Nance? The truth is they wouldn't have needed to set up anything so complicated. But that's how JKE Investments is structured.'

'That's what it's called? JKE?' His heart sank. Ari had been right, again. 'That's her. Zavcka Klist.'

'Her *personally*? How do you know?'

'I've had Klists on the brain today. Ari thought she was involved – don't look like that, I had to tell her, you know she won't say anything. Good thing I did, too, because now it's all coming together.' He explained what he had learned from Aryel. 'According to the files Dr Walker found, there was a big blow-up about some secret project called Phoenix – remember them? – and shortly afterwards Klist Applied Genomics was merged into Bel'Natur. The person who now runs Bel'Natur is a direct descendant of Jarek Klist and therefore probably controls whatever remains of her ancestor's legacy. JKE could stand for a lot of things; "Jarek Klist Estate" is one of them.'

'That's a hell of a leap, Rhys.'

'It's what I do. I know it's all circumstantial, but it fits.'

'She'd have had her eye on Nance for a long time.' Sharon's voice was distant, her eyes staring off the edge of the screen as she thought it through aloud. 'She'd have been grooming him, whether he knew it or not. Maybe she snuck the hunt for the Phoenix gene-types into a more general portfolio of industrial espionage. So she found out where the stock was, in half a dozen different gemtechs, and maybe she even had a plan for getting it. Buying it. Such old stuff, they'd have been happy to sell it. But then human gemtech is suspended, the stock is confiscated, the Declaration comes along, and all of a sudden it's a much bigger challenge.'

'To which she engineers a solution, using Nance. Even if she didn't instruct him herself, when he got the nod he'd have had a pretty good idea who was behind it. That's what gave him the con-fidence to go ahead, like you were saying, and it's what's making him scared now.'

Wouldn't she be scared? That's a lot of exposure – both to Nance and to whoever's her go-between. She must have some kind of insurance. I wonder if Nance knows what it is. 'Maybe you just need to lean on him a bit more.'

'I would so love to do that, but he's been taken ill. By the time I got back from the alley he was being rushed to hospital. Some kind of breathing difficulty, the medic here says it was probably stress-induced . . .'

'Is it serious?'

'Very. I've just had a message come in while I've been on with you; he's in intensive care and deteriorating. Bugger goes and dies that'll be another fucking headache.' She winced. 'Sorry. That's not very professional of me. Of course I hope he'll make a full recovery.'

'I wouldn't count on it.' The search Rhys had begun running

when Sharon said *head of security* was scrolling up results in a side panel on his tablet. Bruce Dunmore. He'd been there well over a decade, through revolution and regime change, and his rise to head of department paralleled Zavcka Klist's ascension to the top post in the company.

Not part of the purge Callan's been talking about, then. He's old school. And you don't need vid on the box, you wouldn't want it, nothing that could be scanned for so easily. All you'd need is a radio signal, and it hasn't got to travel more than fifty yards or so in a straight line, so it could be weak. Tough to spot in the general stream traffic. Stick a transmitter at the right spot and anything falling through the slot would activate it. You'd coat it in an obsolescence gel that's triggered by the transmission, so if your operative was rumbled and the wrong person opened the box all they'd find is dust. If the drop goes smoothly you just stick a new one in when you make the pick-up. Same tech they used to spy on each other, and to get around the government prohibition on tracking runaways. Old school.

And then one day you get a signal, and when you rock up there's a bunch of cops wrestling the thing open. So you have a friendly chat with the officer in charge, stroll back to your office, and activate the insurance policy. Breathing difficulty? That's a nanite bug, the same ones they used during the gem riots in Bangla back in '22, back when Bruce Dunmore was working retrieval for Bel'Natur in southern Asia. Respiratory paralysis. Nance will be dead inside an hour. And he didn't know. Sharon could never have made him talk if he did.

He explained it to her. 'This Dunmore character is part of it, he has to be. Nance is being eliminated. They know how close you are. They're going to be getting rid of all the other evidence too – the genestock, if it's still in the building, any remaining traces of KAG, any links to Phoenix.'

'You said Eli had copied some records? They won't be able to wipe his stream.'

'No, I don't think they know about what he found. But he doesn't know anything about this either, and the stuff he mirrored has nothing to do with it, it was just a bunch of old correspondence. It's not important, that's not what—' He heard his voice rising and stopped. *Deep breaths, Rhys. Calm down.* She was staring anxiously out of the tablet at him, and he knew he had to explain.

'Sharon, I've got a personal stake in this. A big one. Gwen and I are KAG gems, that's why Ari came to tell me what Dr Walker had found. We'd spent years trying to find out what happened to that company.'

'I know, she told me about that. She said you wanted to know what they'd designed you for, and then you were trying to find your genetype—' She broke off, and he could see the comprehension wash over her face.

'I need it. I need it badly, it's probably the only chance I've got. And now I know where to find it.'

'As long as it's still there, and as long as they don't wipe everything before we get to them. Oh, Rhys.'

'Can you help me?'

'I can try. Everything you've laid out – as you said it's all circumstantial, it's not ideal for a warrant, but I can argue that the risks are so great they need to make an exception. Let me get on to the hospital, tell them what we suspect is wrong with Nance. If they can confirm that part it'd be a big help.'

'How long?'

'I've got to pull lots of things together and get Masoud on board. It's past noon already – probably tomorrow morning.'

'Tomorrow.'

'At the earliest. I'm going to move as fast as I can, Rhys. Look, they know Nance is out of the picture, and they know he can't have implicated them, otherwise we'd be banging on their door already. We were at a complete loss in the alley, Dunmore will have seen that. They don't know about you, they don't know how we got on to Nance; they'll assume it was the EGA who spotted the theft, that he screwed up somehow and got caught. They don't know that we know about the hacks, or Phoenix, or KAG. They've got no reason to rush.'

No, but they will, Rhys thought. *No one who is this careful, this meticulous, this ruthless, is going to leave anything to chance. Not even for a day.*

Sharon was already pulling back from the screen, eyes darting and urgent, worried despite her own reassurances. He knew there was nothing more he could say, nothing more she could do beyond the task she was already leaping to. The Metropolitan Police would be inside Bel'Natur within twenty-four hours, and it would not be fast enough. He swallowed.

'Okay, Sharon. Whatever you say.'

When his earset buzzed Callan thought for a moment it must be Aryel, or Eli calling to offer some explanation for his strange behaviour. When he heard Rhys' voice his heart skipped.

'Hi, sweetie. You okay?'

'I'm fine. I was wondering – what's going on there today?'

'What?' Callan was nonplussed. 'Nothing. Apart from Eli going home to talk to Aryel about something, and Sevi finally working out Herran's wiring. So yeah, I guess there's a bit happening. What do you mean?'

'I just wondered if . . . if Herran had a minute to check messages . . . Dr Walker's on his way back here?'

'Yes, should be with you in the next few minutes. You said you needed Herran?' The unease that had begun earlier with an uncharacteristically assertive Herran and flustered Eli deepened and strengthened. *What is going on?*

'Yes . . . I mean, I messaged him a while back, I was hoping he'd have one of his breaks . . .'

'He's had a couple.' Callan looked over at Herran. The little gem had been sitting up for the past ten minutes, feet stuck straight out in front of him and fiery curls tumbling unconstrained by the sensor net as he hunched over his tablet, tapping and swiping and ignoring them all. Now he was being lowered back into position for the next test run, but he turned his head towards Callan. Again he felt a jolt of surprise, as if someone he barely recognised was beginning to look out of Herran's pale eyes.

'Tell Rhys okay,' Herran declared. 'I send.' He tapped the blank screen of his tablet significantly.

'Send what?'

'Directions. Secret. Rhys knows.'

'Oh *well*. In that case.' Callan pretended an exasperation that was not too far from the truth. 'Forget I asked.'

Into his earset, to Rhys, 'Did you get that?'

'I heard. Callan, I . . . it's not that big a secret. I can explain later. Okay?'

'Okay.' He paused, wondering again at the gnawing fear that was beginning to growl and rumble around the base of his ribcage; wondering what the connection was between the nervous tension in Rhys' voice and the expression on Herran's face that was almost like a smile. 'See you later, then. And Rhys?'

'Yes?'

'Love you.'

'I love you too. So much.'

25

Zavcka Klist spun on her heel at the last instant before she would have crashed headlong into the wall of her office, and the delicate piece of shimmering glass sculpture mounted on it. Her fury was such that she would have been pleased to break something, even something as expensive as that, but not quite at the cost of her own skin. Instead she paced back, panoramic window on her right side now, the expanse of sky and steel punctuated by smudges of deep, bluish grey. The oppressive heat of the past few days seemed finally ready to summon up a storm.

Dunmore had seated himself in one of the chairs on the other side of the mammoth desk, and was watching her impassively.

'It's all very well to say he's not going to do any more talking,' she snapped. 'The problem is you don't know what he's already told them.'

'If he'd told them about me I wouldn't be here to tell *you* about it. We have time.'

She spun round again, this time at the midpoint of the great table with the great window behind her blazing too, too much light into the room. The shadow it threw onto the polished surface before her was sharp and small as she grabbed the back of her own chair and leaned over it to glare at him.

'How *much* time, Dunmore? Can you tell me that?'

'No ma'am, I can't. Most likely several days, maybe several weeks. They might never make the connection.'

'Or they might be making it right now. That's a risk I'm not prepared to take. We need to clear out. Get the staff and every last piece of the experiment off site and far away from here.'

He regarded her with his usual stolidity before nodding agreement. 'I can get the staff out now, but we can't move anything else during the day without attracting attention. It'll have to be tonight. Late. I'll make the arrangements.'

She felt a surge of relief, and the rage that had been on the cusp of boiling over into aches and trembling began to subside. Dunmore's unflappable demeanour was a strange palliative, she thought; it always seemed to help pull her back from the brink. Not for the first time, she wondered if he had already associated her condition with the enormous costs and risks of their illicit project; and if not, what he thought they were doing it for. 'You agree we need to move fast, then.'

'Strictly speaking I don't think it's necessary to move *this* fast, but there's no harm in being careful. That Inspector Varsi might not have a clue, but she's no fool either. If she got pointed in the right direction . . .' He shrugged.

'I could probably slow her down. For a while at any rate, before Masoud got wind of it and took over.'

He looked momentarily surprised. 'Oh?'

'By all accounts she's very fond of her husband.'

'I see. Well, she'd have to be.' He heaved himself to his feet. 'I'd better get on. Is there anything else I should be taking account of, ma'am?' He looked pointedly at her tablet where it sat angled for reading on the desktop, and glanced towards the door through which Khan had been summarily ejected when he came in to make his urgent, private report. Even though their instinctive dislike made them wary of each other, it would have been impossible for someone as sharp as Dunmore to miss the younger man's bubbling excitement.

She dropped into her chair and swiped the message from Sevi back onto the screen. 'No, not really. It's our other experiment of the moment, the neural to digital study. Seems they've finally worked out how Herran's language centres do the processing. They're already modelling a translation matrix that they think will mimic it.' She smiled up at him faintly. 'That one's excellent news, Dunmore. Nothing to concern you.'

Instead of turning away with his usual barely articulated grunt of acknowledgement, Dunmore looked thoughtful. 'Glad to hear it, ma'am. Although I'd got the impression you weren't as interested in that project any more.'

'Not at all. I just decided to let them get on with it. They didn't need me hovering.' The memory of how she had been dismissed by Eli Walker still made her want to grind her teeth, but she stopped herself. If Dunmore picked up any hint that her withdrawal had not been voluntary, there was no excuse or assurance on earth that would prevent him from wondering what could possibly have been important enough to compel her to swallow such an insult. As far as he knew the secret project and the public one were unrelated, and she could not risk him, even him, suspecting otherwise.

No one can be allowed to know everything. No one can ever be trusted that far. Once this is over, what do I do about Dunmore? So valuable, so reliable, but the truth is he already knows too much.

I wonder if he knows that I can do to him what he did to Nance. I wonder if he's arranged some insurance of his own.

No hint of her thoughts showed on her face as she flicked Sevi's breakthrough off the screen, as though it was a matter of little moment. She nodded a brisk dismissal to the security chief, channelling full, cool command as she issued instructions. 'Take every precaution, Dunmore, and any resources you need. As of now this is your only responsibility. I'll expect an update every hour.'

He gazed back at her, equally imperturbable. 'Of course, ma'am.'

The doctor Sharon had spoken to via tablet met her at the entrance to intensive care, and helped her into an isolation suit.

'I didn't realise this would be necessary.'

'It probably isn't. I doubt we can save him. But just in case the antivirals we cooked up manage to make any headway against his pathogen load – bloody enormous, I've never seen anything like it – he's going to be very vulnerable to secondary infection.'

Sharon turned round. Dr Ohoruogu had round, kind brown eyes in a round, kind brown face. Both eyes and face looked very worried.

'So this isn't for my protection, then? There's no risk of it jumping from him to someone else?'

'No, there's no transmission vector. Once it's woken up the artificial virus maps to the host's epigenetic matrix and starts replicating. It'll kill whoever it finds itself in, but it can't infect anyone else.' He shrugged helplessly. 'Trouble is, anything we use to hit the virus also hits his immune system, which makes it harder for him to fight the virus. Or anything else that comes along. It's a race to the bottom.'

'How long does he have?'

'If things continue as they are? Not long. If we hadn't had that call from you, worked out what to give him, he'd be dead already. But we're not winning, Inspector. We're just slowing things down.'

Sounds a lot like police work. Sharon kept the thought to herself as the doctor guided her under the sterilisation lamp. She stood on the mat, closed her eyes and remained still for the first burst, raised her arms and turned slowly for the second. He repeated the process on himself and ushered her through into the room where Nance lay, barely visible beneath a mass of tubes and sensors. A clip in his nose directed oxygen-rich air down into labouring lungs. He did not move and Sharon dropped her voice to a whisper.

'I thought you said he was conscious?'

'He's in and out. More out than in, to be honest, but I don't think you're going to have any better chances.'

She moved over to the side of the bed and looked down at the dying man. His skin had taken on an unhealthy, greyish pallor. He looked half the size of the suspect who had bluffed and prevaricated and sworn at her just a few hours ago.

'How would he have been infected in the first place? Food? Drink?'

'Possible, but this has moved so fast I'm more inclined to think he breathed it in. The nanites could've been sitting in the bottom of his lungs for years. They aren't pathogenic themselves, they just contain the instructions. The body doesn't notice them until they're activated.'

'And how are they activated? I thought the victim had to be exposed to something else, a trigger?'

'Generally, yes. My guess is he would have breathed that in too. Would explain why the onset was so sudden.'

The man on the bed shifted. His eyelids twitched, and twitched again, and finally fluttered open, as though with enormous effort. Sharon bent over him, hoping he could see her clearly through the tight bioplastic mask that covered her face.

'Mr Nance? It's Inspector Varsi. Can you hear me?'

A nod that was more a suggestion than a movement. His breathing was so loud Sharon had to speak above it.

'Mr Nance, your brother's been informed that you're ill, he's on his way. Do you understand what's happened to you?'

Again the fractional acknowledgement, and she looked over at Dr Ohoruogu in surprise. He spread his hands. 'We haven't told him.'

'Heard,' Nance whispered. It was a croak, as though just saying the word had cost him several breaths.

'You heard us talking?' A nod.

'Then you know what your situation is.' A dull, dark stare, full of exhausted resentment. She wondered if it was still all aimed at her. 'Mr Nance, I'm sorry. I truly am. We had no idea, and I'm guessing neither did you.' She pulled up a chair and sat, leaning forward so that her masked face was only inches from his own.

'You know what's at stake here. You know who did this to you. I can make sure they don't get away with it, but you need to help me out, Mr Nance. You need to tell me who you think put these things inside you.'

He opened his mouth and tried to speak, but all that emerged was a rasping croak. 'Duh . . . duuh . . . duuhhn . . .'

The effort dissolved into a fit of coughing and Dr Ohoruogu moved to the other side of the bed, tilting it up slightly and adjusting the flow of oxygen. His eyes met Sharon's and she nodded to acknowledge the message.

He can't take too much of this.

The spasm eased. 'Take it easy, Mr Nance,' she said, as soothingly as she could manage. 'Don't wear yourself out. Now I'm going to say a name, and I want you to nod or shake your head to let me know if I've got it right. Okay? Okay.' He was so limp she wondered if he was even still awake, until she caught the glint of eyes peering at her through slitted lids. 'Dunmore? Is that the name you were trying to tell me?'

A nod, tiny but unmistakeable.

'Thank you, Mr Nance. Thank you very much.' She sat back, took a deep breath. As deathbed accusations went it wasn't much, but everything would help when it came to the warrant.

Warrant. Paperwork. Station. She leaned forward again.

'Mr Nance, I need to ask you something else. About this morning, while you were at the police station.' That dull stare again, flat and emotionless, too tired now to be angry. 'After you and I spoke, but before you were taken ill. Did anyone come to see you? Anyone who wasn't a police officer?'

He looked away and she thought he was shaking his head *No*, but his eyes were wandering, vacant and unfocused. His lips moved.

'Raj,' he mumbled.

'Who's Raj? A friend?'

A nod. 'Solic . . . soli . . .'

'Raj is a solicitor?'

A blinked *yes*.

'Did he bring you anything? Give you anything? Any medicines, inhalers, anything like that?'

A shake of the head.

'Come on, Mr Nance, think. Someone at the station this morning gave you something that triggered this. Something you would have breathed in, smelled—' She broke off because his eyes were resting on her again, and this time seeming to see.

'Cof-*fee*,' he managed, and coughed. 'Raj . . .' And he was out of breath again.

She waited through the recovery, thinking, and made a leap. 'You've known Raj since the old days, yes? He worked for the company too?'

He was halfway through another painful nod when the realisation hit him. This time the coughing, sputtering spasm was so bad she stood up and moved the chair back to give Dr Ohoruogu room to work.

When he straightened up there was no question of continuing the interview. Nance's eyes were closed and he was breathing in harsh, whooping gasps.

The doctor lowered a mask over his nose and mouth, increased the oxygen flow again, checked the monitors and shook his head. 'I'm afraid that's all you're going to get from him, Inspector.'

'It might be enough. I'm sorry—' She broke off with a sigh. The brother would arrive just in time to hold his sibling's hand at the end, maybe; but any last words he might have heard had been spent instead on her. And she was not sorry. She needed them more than he did.

She went back through to the clean room, ripping at the isolation suit in her haste to get out of it, get out of here, get to somewhere where she could work through the implications of this latest twist.

An old friend who just happened to be a lawyer. Someone who could find out what he'd told the police. Someone he would trust to defend him. *What a clever fucker you are, Dunmore. Or do I have Zavcka Klist herself to thank for this?*

The sound of a throat being gently cleared whipped her around. Dr Ohoruogu stood there, gazing at her with his warm, worried eyes as he peeled off skinpaint gloves. He pitched them into a recycler festooned with biohazard labels and rubbed his hands together. No, *wrung*. This kind, conscientious doctor was literally wringing his hands at her.

'Inspector, can you tell me . . . is this a gang thing? I mean I know maybe you can't say, but this . . . this pathogen . . . we're not prepared for this. If this is the start of something . . .'

She could almost have laughed. *Oh, ordinary criminals! Violence for profit! Vendettas! How I wish.* Instead she peeled off her own and chucked them after his. 'No, doctor, I think it's the end of something. I just don't know exactly what.'

Rhys slipped along the alley Sharon had described to him earlier, noting the metal panel and apparently sealed aperture of the defunct postbox, his own enhanced awareness checking for and confirming the lack of surveillance. He reached the corner where the passage emptied onto the bustle of the street, slouched casually with his back against the wall that ran between him and the Bel'Natur building, and pulled out his tablet. It was no different from the pose seen at any hour of day or night all over the city, that of one who had simply paused to check messages or directions; but he had pulled up a reflective surface and was using the tablet as a mirror, scoping the side approach to the round black tower. He located the security cams, calculated angles, observed the patterns of foot and vehicular traffic. The heat was oppressive, and he could feel the pressure building in his eyes and sinuses. Thunder rumbled in the distance, well below the hearing of most. He wrinkled his nose at the prickling that told him rain was on the way.

I'll be long gone before it gets here.

It took only about five minutes for him to find the combination he needed, moving at the right relative speed to ensure the cover they provided would be complete, and he felt a glimmer of satisfaction. Gwen would no doubt have accused him of being excessively cautious, but no one ever came to grief that way. He did not look up as a group of office workers, hurrying to or from some meeting perhaps, came towards him along the main road. They were bunched up on the narrow pavement, chattering away, and he was confident that most were completely unaware of him swinging without fuss around the corner of the alley as they passed, and falling into step behind them. One young woman, trailing on the outside and to the rear of the group, glanced across with a flicker of interest; he kept his own gaze vacant, unseeing, and her attention shifted away just as quickly. It might not have if the ruby glow of his hair had been evident, but he had reclaimed his hooded jumper and it was as concealed as Gwen's had been.

He was keeping an eye on a passenger van that was coming towards them, and a delivery lorry paralleling their progress on the other side of the street. The one should slow down just *there* at the intersection, the other speed up right *now* as the road widened slightly. Here was where the group he had hidden himself in would spread out as the pavement broadened, but here also came the big man he had spotted, hurrying along so that he cut across their path at exactly the point that allowed Rhys to slide up on the inside and peel unnoticed away from the group, the man, the vans – the lenses of the cams perfectly if only momentarily blocked – and into the sudden gloom of the Bel'Natur service entrance.

He was moving fast now, because there would be at least one more cam set into the ceiling that he could neither avoid nor risk glancing up to locate. He needed to be no more than a shadow himself, easily missed or dismissed as a trick of tired eyes if the cam was being monitored. A watcher would have seen only a blur, like a bird whizzing through on the wing, gone before it could be brought into focus. He judged the first infrared beam to be about knee-height and jumped it without breaking stride; the second was at around the level of his chest and he went through it as he had been instructed. The jump had barely slowed him down but he had to brake sharply for the door, heart in his mouth. *Here's where it could all go horribly wrong.* He had crossed twenty feet of monitored space in the blink of an eye, but if it took more than that to get inside all his speed and subterfuge would be wasted.

The glass panel slid aside, instantly but only partially, just enough to let him slip through. He twisted his hips to clear the narrow opening as it whooshed back and sealed shut again. It would likely not even register on the system as having been opened; like his passage across the entryway it might at best be recorded as a glitch, a gremlin in the system.

Thank you, Herran.

He had been let into a small lobby, with the drab, utilitarian look of back offices the world over. It was deserted, and he heaved a sigh of relief. Herran's message had given him a narrow window within which he could enter without risk of immediate discovery, but he did not understand how the little gem could have been so certain. Now, though, he saw that the blast doors across the central corridor were closed, and heard muffled swearing beyond them. A flashing light on the control panel to the side of the doors, another above the lifts. Herran had sealed this entrance off from the inside, probably made it look like a fault in the fire safety systems. A minor annoyance, easily corrected and therefore unlikely to arouse suspicion, but guaranteeing a few precious, unobserved minutes.

He glided around the side of the bank of lifts, found a door with no lock. The stairwell. He pushed it open gently, crouched low and slipped through, blurring again into a flattened sideways leap that took him across the landing and halfway down the first flight of stairs. It was a jump that should have sent him pitching headlong to crash, bruised and broken, on the landing below. Instead he touched down with perfect balance, feet spread three risers apart, and peered cautiously back up at the space he had just crossed. The cam was aimed at head height on the door he had come through. He reviewed the line he had taken, the angle of the jump, and was satisfied that he would not have been seen. But there were voices, clearer than those in the corridor and growing louder, along with the tramp of feet descending from above. He turned, still crouching, and slipped down the stairs.

Genetype not in datastream or archive or trash, Herran's message had said, so quickly in response to his question that he wondered if Ari had already asked the little gem, if he had already looked. *Not deleted; not there. Somewhere else, maybe.*

Any idea where? he had asked, as hope faded in him, and he had had to wait for the answer. But when it came it had kicked him out of the apartment and across the city, and down here.

Empty under ground. Empty but full. Lots of space, lots of secrets. Too much power for no use. Something to not see. No cams, no streams, no good for me. Maybe you look?

The stairway curved down and down, and he followed it into the dark.

ESCAPE

It is both easier and harder than she imagined.

There has been a distraction in the air of late. Something has them worried, and it is not her. Unease ripples through the underground laboratory; indignation, embarrassment and, yes, she knows the scent of this one well: fear. It hastens their steps as they hurry to and from the lifts and in and out of meeting rooms, prods them into a shuffling half-run that looks like panic. Recriminations echo behind closed doors.

She has tried to learn what has happened, concerned most of all for how it may impact on her own plans. She senses danger in the way Dr Panborn looks at her, and then looks away as though pained. There is no more fellow feeling in it than there ever was; it is the customary look of avarice, merely uncoupled now from ownership. Panborn is not the strident, cocksure chieftain that she was. Dr Owen, who should be gratified by this, is if anything even more anxious. He mutters some bitten-off complaint about interference, and explains in small words that they are part of a bigger company and the bigger company has decided to take an interest in their work. Then he adds, 'But nothing whatever to concern you, Aryel!' with a false heartiness that is anything but reassuring.

So change is coming, and she has no desire to be there to meet it. She does not for a moment entertain the thought that their unknown overlords might disdain her captivity as much as she does; her secret excursions on the infostream have taught her better. She has learned enough of the world to know that liberation does not lie on that horizon. But the upheaval has won her one advantage: their preoccupation has made them less vigilant than usual.

So she slips from her bed in the early morning darkness of the complex, which she knows mimics at this hour the pre-dawn gloom of a sky she has never seen. A strip of tape salvaged from a rubbish bin has kept the door unlocked. She makes a brief stop in the closet where the cleaning fluids are kept, then on to the small lab crowded with centrifuges and incubation trays, and the old autoclave which is never used any more. The lab itself is set aside for blood tests and tissue sampling, the grimy wet work delegated to the most junior researchers. Except no one is junior any more, there have been no new staff for years, and everyone thinks themselves too important for so mundane a task. It has become a petty punishment of Panborn's to assign it to whoever is out of favour. Even so they have managed to make it only a monthly chore, and the rota will not come up again for weeks.

She mixes what she has carried from the closet with what she has pilfered over months, carefully hidden behind the panels and in the crevices of machinery. Then she sets the autoclave, time and temperature selected for maximum effect, and pauses by the door, listening for any sound in the corridor outside. All is silent. From where she stands she can look back and see the numbers on the face of the machine, counting down. She whispers a benediction, and slips out.

It is the waiting that proves hard. The chemicals cooking behind her need to come to the point of full, explosive potency just when the layers of security between her and the surface are dependent most on people, who can be panicked and tricked, and least on locked doors with the finger- and retscanners that she knows she cannot fool. She can do nothing with the time but fret about the risk of discovery, and ponder the unknown into which she is about to step. But she has picked a good day, it seems: as the hours pass oh so slowly she notes that their agitation is even greater today than it has been. There is a scurry and a bustle and an anxiety that builds *as the day goes on, until it borders on hysteria. It is almost as though they know something is going to happen.*

'It's sent,' she hears Panborn say to Owen, brusquely but with a note of defeat in her voice, and glances over to find herself being glared at with such fury it gives her an excuse to slink meekly around the corner as though on her way back to the dorm, where she is supposed to stay until she is required to present herself for inspection at the odd hour of five o'clock. She has spared no curiosity for this new indignity, whatever it may be. She will not be available.

It is early afternoon, and she checks the countdown on her tablet. Five minutes to go. Time to get into position.

Back in the utility closet and suddenly paranoid, she wonders why she imagines there is the slightest chance of this working. Surely they know all about it. Surely at any moment the door will be pulled open to reveal guards with stingers drawn. Owen will appear behind them, hands clapping sarcastically, eyes grave and disappointed. Surely, surely, after all these years, after an entire lifetime, it cannot finally be about to end.

She pulls the grey blanket she has hidden here earlier up over her head, hugs it tight around her shoulders and nervously twitching, utterly useless wings, and clamps her jaw tight on her own uncertainties. It will end, and end today, because she will not have it otherwise. Her resolve floods back and wraps her even tighter than the blanket: a potent thing, and deadly.

The blast is louder than she expected. The shockwave rips along the corridor, sending her staggering into the wall. Something pungent is knocked over and begins to pool along the floor. She peers out, into a corridor filled with smoke, screams, confusion. Trousered legs charge past. She can hear the shouts, people urged to assemble, cries that some are trapped behind the fire.

Those will mostly be service staff, gathering in the old canteen further down the corridor as they always do at the end of the lunch break, to spend a few minutes exchanging reports and gossip from up above and down below. Most of the guards, most of the others. They can only get out if they force the fire door that will have sealed them in, and if they do that the rush of air will feed the fire. Either way, they are out of the way.

Everyone else will be gathered in the safe room close to the lifts and stairwell, ready to evacuate, or to seal themselves off if the fire prevents it. She wonders if they will notice that she is not among them. She wonders if they will care. She is out of the closet now, and running.

Owen sees her through the clear panel on the heavy blast door, and shouts, arm raised in fury. She cannot hear him, not least for the roar of hungry flame behind her, although the backdraught's shockwave slams her forward and into it. She hears shrieks, of pain this time as well as panic.

The fools did try to force their way through.

She meets Owen's eyes through the panel as her hand slams down on the emergency switch. With the fire safety system activated it moves easily, and she hears the hiss as the door seals, and sees his face change as he finally understands. She is already turning away, without a pause or a look back. What she seeks is in front of her.

The main entrance, the one that opens onto lobby and lifts and stairs, stands as she has never seen it: wide open and unattended. She is through it like a ghost, and gone.

26

He found her on the roof.

She was waiting for him under the arching sprays of the apple trees, just beginning to bend with the weight of swelling fruit. Her seat was one of the many bits and pieces of waste material that the people of the Squats had recycled to new purpose, sparking a wave of retro-industrial chic: an old piece of metal ventilation tubing, capped and upended into a stubby cylinder. Normally it served as a stool for stepping up to harvest from the higher branches, or sitting beneath them to rest. Now it formed a plinth for the still life she made, leaning forward with elbows on knees and chin cupped in fists, wingtips skimming the ground as though some great artist of a bygone age had chosen an angel's form to personify deep meditation, or perhaps the desolation of grief.

She brushed a hand across her face, and for a moment he thought that she was weeping.

His footsteps crunched on the gravel path. When she turned to face him her eyes were dry, but her expression told him there was no need to disguise his own upset.

He stopped five feet away, full of discovery and remonstration, and found he did not know how to begin. 'Aryel.'

She smiled faintly, tiredly, with a sadness that tore at his heart. 'Eli.'

'Why,' he began, then stopped, swallowed, started again. 'Why didn't you tell me?'

'Do you think this is a conversation I wanted to have any sooner than necessary?'

'It's *me*.' The hurt was welling up in him now. 'You could have told me. You didn't have to leave me to find . . . to find . . .'

Hands up and over her face again, pushing back her hair. It was loose for once, a heavy dark fall that hung still in the oppressive heat under the trees. 'I was hoping against hope that you wouldn't find anything else.'

Calm as always, but instead of calming him in turn he felt his frustration start to rise, and his voice along with it.

'No. *No*. I *told* you it was about Phoenix, and you pretended not to know—' He stopped. She hadn't, not really. She had done what she always did, changed the subject, misdirected. 'You *knew* I knew enough, then, to tell me the truth. And you knew I was going back to look for more. You even said . . .'

He remembered what she'd said, and trailed off again.

She might have hoped otherwise, but she had known that, ultimately, they would end up here.

'I never thought I would hear the words "Phoenix Project" again,' she said. Her hands were spread now, pleading, trying to explain. 'I know you think I'm never surprised by anything, Eli, but you're wrong. I was . . . I was shocked that it had surfaced, that there were any records at all, and . . . and I was sick to think you would learn about what happened there. I knew I couldn't – shouldn't – prevent it, but I couldn't bear to be the one to—'

She straightened up on the stool abruptly, shaking her head and her wings back, as though something unpleasant was descending upon her and she wished to be rid of it. Eli stayed quiet, leaning against the espaliered tangle of twigs and leaves, and watched her over folded arms.

'And what you told me about KAG not knowing about Phoenix, not being in control of it, I didn't know that part. I truly didn't. And it's important, really important. It explains so much that I could never work out.'

'What did they have to do with anything? What happened at the lab was before their time.'

'Nothing was before their time, not really, that's what you told me this morning. Jarek Klist set the whole thing up. But that's not what I mean, I meant Rhys and Gwen and . . . and the others. I couldn't be certain, until now, what it was they were trying to do. Or why they . . . we . . . why any of us were possible.'

'But you knew about the research, that they were on to something extraordinary. You must have done, you were the proof of it.'

'I thought I understood. I thought I knew exactly what was at stake, I thought I had it all worked out, but I knew *nothing*. Gods and monsters, Eli,' she spat, in a sudden rage that he recognised as self-recrimination, 'if I had known what could happen, if I had understood the consequences, do you really think I would have? My own people, my own—'

'But it – I— What *did* happen, Aryel?'

He caught the flickering sideways glance that told him she had herself under control and was thinking through her answer, framing a clever response. He found himself moving from disbelief to a slow-burning anger of his own.

'No, you know what, *that's* what I want to know, and I want to hear it from you. *Now*. Don't try to divert this, don't you dare. Don't ask me what I read in the memos, or to tell you what I *think* I know first. *You* tell *me*. Tell me what happened.'

She looked up at him then, more than a little startled, he thought, and full of a kind of quiet despair. And she told him.

Afterwards he found himself sitting on the ground, his back against one of the long troughs that held the trees of the apple orchard, facing her across dappled shade. Sweat trickled down his back and he felt exhausted, as though he had run a long, long way. She looked just as weary: drawn, and worn, and tiny. Even her wings seemed shorn of their grandeur. The silence stretched out between them, while he tried to digest it all.

That was what happened, she had said at the end. *And I was responsible for all of it.*

He knew it for the truth, but perhaps a truth more harshly felt than was necessary. She had been born into captivity, after all, her awareness limited and her sensitivities cauterised; and in the single-minded pursuit of her goal to wrest control of her life she had managed to acquire just enough knowledge to be truly dangerous.

'So you *couldn't* have known,' he said finally. 'How it was going to turn out, what all the risks were. And at least Rhys and Gwen survived . . .'

'Yes, they survived. Is that my saving grace, that I accidentally managed not to get *everybody* killed?'

He let that one go unchallenged, although the words dropped like acid into the drowsy air. Instinct told him it was best to let their force spin out, dissipate against the lazy buzzing backdrop of bees heedless among the wildflower tubs, rather than try to take her on in this mood.

She was being hard on herself, very hard, and for once he could understand why.

'Do they know?' he said finally. 'Rhys and Gwen. They don't, do they?'

'No. They don't. When they were little it was for their – our – protection. And then they grew up and there seemed no reason to revisit it.' She sighed, and tried to shake herself free again. 'The truth is, I haven't had the courage. It – it's not how they think of me, any more than it's how you thought of me, and I haven't—' She stopped, looked him straight in the eye for a moment, then shrugged, looked away, bit her lip. 'Can you blame me for that? Not wanting them to know there was ever a different Aryel from the one they grew up with?'

'No, I guess I can't. But I don't think you're being fair to yourself. The Aryel they grew up with is the same Aryel who had the wit and courage and strength to break out – just a bit older and sadder, I reckon. Wiser. And they wouldn't have grown up free and safe and loved if you hadn't. What happened there was a tragedy, and you were one of its victims.'

'I don't feel like a victim. I walked away. I *ran* away.'

'Thank heavens for that. Or you wouldn't be sitting here now, under an apple tree, in the middle of a city full of gems who are only free and equal citizens because of you.'

That seemed to bring her closer to tears than any of the horrors she had related, or anything else he had said. She looked down at her lap, muttering, 'And you.'

'And Jeremy Temple, and Gabriel, and Gaela . . . we could make a list. The point is, you go through what you go through to get to where you are. I understand that this is a terrible thing to live with, but it's not what you intended to happen. That *matters*, Aryel. And what you've accomplished since then – it makes up for it. It more than makes up for it.'

'I don't know if anything can ever make up for it.' A muscle worked along the side of her jaw. 'I don't think the rest of world would be as . . . as generous about it as you're being.'

'I'm just trying to be fair. And we live in a fairer world than we used to. People might surprise you, if you give them a chance.'

She shook her head, eyes still fixed on the hands clasped in her lap. She needed something else to focus on, he realised. Some action she could take, something outside herself.

'What are you going to do about that part?'

'I don't know.' She drew a deep breath and finally shot him a crooked smile. 'I'd like to say that it depends on you, but it doesn't entirely. After it was all over KAG came in and swept everything up and Phoenix was never heard of again. Reginald and I always assumed either that KAG was behind Phoenix all along, or that it was a business transaction – KAG knew Phoenix had something valuable, so they bought up the datastream and whatever other assets were left from whoever did own it. Either way we thought they were going to build on Phoenix's work, maybe pretend it was all their own – revive the legacy of Jarek Klist and all that – but then KAG itself disappeared, for reasons still unknown.' She rubbed a weary hand across her brow. 'Until you found those trashed messages in the archive. I told Rhys this morning – I had to, his life might depend on it.'

'I didn't see any other kinds of file, certainly nothing that looked like genetypes, but I'm no expert. He must be desperate to get at it.'

'Yes. Things are complicated because the breakthrough he's made in the EGA case potentially implicates Bel'Natur. So we have to let that play out a little longer, which he's not happy about. I suppose the only upside is it gives me a bit of breathing space before I have to tell them what else is in the files. And my worry there – it's not just about me, about what it'll do to our relationship. Rhys shouldn't get upset or angry. It exacerbates his illness. And this is going to make him very upset, and very angry.'

'I see.' He didn't really, but before he could ask what she meant she started and reached a hand up to her earset; then hesitated, glancing at him.

'I have to answer this, it's Sharon. She might have some news.'

He nodded, and she flicked to receive. On another day he would have gestured to ask if she wanted him to step out of earshot, or simply have done so anyway; but not today. He had felt the buffering mass of secrets between them unravel as she spoke, stripped away until it seemed to him that for the first time there were no barriers between them. That emptiness was desolate now, filled with the echoes of her sorrow and regret, but it was lighter too, uncluttered; a clear space in which something new might be built. He had no mind to let it fill up again.

She was frowning as she listened. 'That's odd. I left him downstairs – no, I'm up in the garden with Eli. I suppose he might be asleep, although I thought he was too wound up. What's happened?'

More from Sharon, and he became aware of a different kind of tension in Aryel: knotted hands and hunched shoulders mirroring clipped, one-word questions and a deepening line between her brows. The stillness of intense concentration. Her eyes flicked up and caught his for a moment. They were full of alarm.

It was infectious. He found he had shifted into a crouch, and the sweat on his back had gone cold.

'He's going to do *what*? Hang on. *Hang on.*'

She was on her feet now, and he came up with her, feeling the ache in his own shoulders as he saw how her wings had gone rigid with stress. 'Have you both gone mad? Why—?' And she listened again, and listened, and finally nodded reluctantly, although her lips were compressed into a white line and there was no hint of relief in her glance.

She flicked off at last and met his eyes. 'We have a serious, serious problem. We need to find Rhys.'

Rhys had descended four floors below ground level before he found the door he was looking for. The dim stairwell illumination had ceased two storeys above, and it was only night vision that let him negotiate the rest of the route safely. There were no cams here, not down in the dark; instead infrareds were cleverly positioned at the midpoint of each flight, requiring further acrobatics on his part. He cleared the last of them with a high, arching backflip, coming lightly to rest on the final landing. Blank walls faced him on three sides. He turned to the fourth, and contemplated the door.

It was heavy, with no transparent panel to peek through, and rough with the dust and grime of years of disuse. But it had a lock that would have done a bank vault proud: a mostly mechanical contraption with massive cylinders inset into the jamb itself, fronted by an old-fashioned alphanumeric keypad. His instinctive calculus told him that the potential combinations ran into millions. And next to the input panel a fingerprint identipad, and above that a retscanner. Security in triplicate.

It took him no more than a few moments' work with his tablet to confirm that, as Herran had predicted, the lock was completely isolated; no hint of a signal, wired or streamed, extended beyond the device's own impregnable shell. His fingers searched along its edges and found an input slot on the lower rim, no larger than one of Da's ancient darning needles. Not a standard memtab port, not at all, but he had come prepared. His fingers worked through the kit of parts tucked away in his jumper and found a matching connector, then danced across the surface of his tablet again, dropping the right apps onto the right memtab. He pulled the memtab loose and attached the connector to it, slid it into the lock, and he was in.

Uploading his own biometrics was easy, as easy as it had been on the day they first arrived in London and he had, at Gwen's insistence, broken into the Festival's concert hall. With no central server command there were no alarms here to worry about tripping, but neither was there a conduit by which Herran might hack in and sort the third problem, the alphanumeric code.

I shouldn't need him for that. But it took a little longer than expected, and he felt himself twitching with anxiety as he watched the combinations spin past.

Then the app started to find matches, and as each character was identified and locked into place he realised he was shaking his head in recognition, and rueful disbelief. He reached out finally, stilling the spinning icon and tapping in the final entry.

PhO3nix2.

The lock turned with a soft thunk. He put his shoulder against the door and pushed it open a fraction, listening intently. Faint light showed through the crack, but there was no sound at all; no murmur of voices or hum of equipment, nothing that made his sit-sense prickle. He pushed the door wider, and slipped silently inside.

He was in another lobby that fronted the lifts, its layout not that different to the one just below street level where he had first entered; but he knew from Herran that this floor and the one above it appeared nowhere on the lift's control panel. *No reason for any visitors – even the regular staff – to suspect it's here, and no access unless you have special keys or control codes.* But there must be some workers who had been around long enough to know, to remember. He thought about conversations with Callan and Ari, the way the old guard seemed to have been almost entirely replaced, and another piece of the puzzle slid into place.

She kept Dunmore, though, and he's old guard through and through. He'll know all about this place.

The thought gave him an extra frisson of caution, though the basement seemed deserted. Dim lights brightened as he moved into their ambit.

So there is a control system down here. Isolated from the building's main datastream, self-contained. But they kept the emergency door isolated from that too. Which means the system could never be used to lock you out, you could always get in via the stairwell.

Interesting.

Now if I were a quarantined server running an illicit underground lab, where would I be?

He turned slowly, thinking. The lift shaft ran from where he was standing straight up through the core of the building, creating a spine that supported not only the structure itself, but all its services: the stairwells, wet and dry risers, ventilation and communications. And this was deep underground, too deep for normal streaming. So there would have to have been a satellite hub down here once, boosting the signal from the building's control centre far above. It would have been located close to the main shaft; somewhere optimised to relay a strong signal throughout this subterranean labyrinth. For that reason it would make sense to have located the new hub in the same place.

In other words, close by.

He found it in a spacious closet off the main corridor, just a few steps away from the door through which he had entered: a small, hi-spec unit encased in crystalline bioplastic, hard-wired into its power source. No integrated input screen; no one without a tablet of their own could access the thing.

Also interesting. So you can't just stroll up and start tapping, and it's probably got a preregistered list of the tablets that it's allowed to grant access to. Wonder if they still bothered to tell it not to talk to strangers?

It did and they had, but the identity safeguards were no harder to crack than the stairwell door had been.

And the beauty of a sequestered server is that it can't tell anybody it's being breached.

The directory read like a smaller, more focused version of the many gemtech datastreams he had hacked: endless iterations of protocols and parameters, reams of experimental data, obscurely titled reports. A messaging platform, unknown to him and heavily encrypted; project and financial management apps that he recognised.

Genetype archives and inventories of genestock. KAG, and Phoenix, and others.

A glance through those sub-directories told him that easily half of them were, or were derived from, the files he'd spent the past few days working with. The rest were new to him, but he felt his pulse quicken as his fingers swept the list up his screen. He and Gwen were in here somewhere, he knew it. But there were hundreds of files. It could take hours to find what he was looking for.

Priorities, Rhys.

His own signal was weak, too unreliable to support transmission to the surface; but strong enough to wake the disused relay circuits, piggyback his tablet, and send a message to Herran.

I'm in. I found it. Can you help?

The response was almost instantaneous. *Yes. Show me.*

He swiped in the permission, thinking wryly that Herran could have bowled over his own defences, taken control of the signal and looked at whatever he damned well liked within a few seconds. As it was he watched the data zip lightning fast across his screen, morphing subtly as machine code overlaid output; mirroring what Herran was doing on his own tablet a dozen storeys up.

The message panel popped back to the surface.

Plenty lists. Genetypes, genestock. Need time to find yours.

They don't just have mine, he tapped back. *These are the people who stole the genestock Sharon questioned you about. There's something very bad going on here, Herran. Someone has already been killed to try and keep it secret. We need to preserve this datastream. We can't risk them getting rid of the evidence.*

Barely time for a breath before the patterns of data changed again, streaking less swiftly but somehow more purposefully up his tablet screen.

Okay. Slow link, take a little time.

Do you HAVE time? Then, after a moment's thought: *Are you secure up there? No one can know what you're doing. We don't know who else is part of it.*

Okay here. No one know unless tell them.

Don't tell Callan, please. He'd just worry. Promise?

Promise. Not asking, not telling. You safe.

The reassurance made him smile. Herran onstream was a different being: direct, fluidly communicative, completely confident. And more in tune with normal cares and fears than most people would credit. Rhys watched the datastream spin away to whatever safe haven he had devised for it, and breathed a sigh of genuine relief.

It would take another ten minutes or so, he calculated, and wondered that there had still been no hint of any other life in this place. Perhaps they had already cleared out, called off whatever experiments were being conducted here, destroyed the evidence? The datastream was incriminating, true, but without the genestock it would have less potency. Sharon would no doubt have told

him to leave any further investigation to those qualified to con-
duct it, but he had already well and truly ignored her orders. He
poked his head out of the door and listened to the silent passages
beyond, considering.

His situational sense was still quiet, but there was a scent on
the air that troubled him. It had a hint of the hospital about it,
and of something else as well – something older and deeper, like
the memory of fear, and other emotions he could not name. He
hesitated, reluctant to leave his tablet behind. But Herran needed
the link, and did not for now need him; so he left it running, and
went to find the source.

27

'I've been thinking about the excellent progress we've made,' Mikal said airily, 'and it occurs to me we may be lacking in ambition somewhat.'

'Really?'

'Really. Bel'Natur is so clearly ready. And with the Festival's closing ceremony only a few days away, I believe there's no time to lose.'

'Time for what, Councillor?'

'To end with as big a bang as you began.'

Zavcka Klist glared at him from the far side of her vast desk. She had consented to this impromptu meeting as much to maintain appearances as out of concern for how close DI Varsi's investigation was getting. But, if they had learned anything to link that fool Nance back to the firm, surely the wife would have told her husband to keep his distance? Put an end to all contact, run no risk of a taint to his reputation? Instead here he was, sitting relaxed as a lord in one of her leather armchairs, halfway across the room. She had been greatly surprised to see him there when she turned to take her own seat; she wondered if he had not understood that he was supposed to follow her, and sit where she indicated. Nothing else about the conversation so far was making much sense either.

'I don't follow.'

'Bel'Natur's reputation is in a delicate state at the moment, Ms Klist. Despite our best efforts,' he smiled at her gently, 'things could turn out quite badly, if an impression forms that the company is being less than ethical, or equitable, in the pursuit of its current goals. But it seems to me that all the ingredients are in place for the very *opposite* conviction to take hold in the public imagination.'

Caution prickled along her nerves. 'You're worried about our reputation? That seems . . . unlikely.'

'On the contrary. I've been impressed by your response to the concerns I raised when you made your announcement two weeks ago. Since then our priorities seem to have become more and more aligned.' He crossed one impossibly long leg over the other, and spread his bizarre hands for emphasis. 'Not only do you now have gems working closely with your own staff, you've committed to providing us with reproductive therapy, possibly for a great many years to come. Anything that damages Bel'Natur has the potential to harm that relationship, and deprive us of its benefits. I am very, *very* keen to ensure that doesn't happen.'

'I see.' A hint finally, of what this was about. And so obvious she could have kicked herself for not understanding sooner. 'Do you mind me asking, Councillor Varsi, if you have a *personal* interest in this at all?'

His smile was munificent now, as though she had just won a prize.

'Indeed I do. It's something,' he said with elaborate casualness, 'that my wife and I have discussed.'

She sat back in her chair and repressed the urge to heave a sigh of relief. A straight-up mutual-interest negotiation, couched in terms as subtle as she could wish. And *he* had come to *her*. This was so much better than blackmail.

'I believe I'm beginning to understand you, Councillor. You're worried that any – concerns shall we say – could undermine the Herran compensation package?'

'Indeed. And if not the package itself, then certainly Sharon's and my ability to take advantage of it. Given our positions we have to be very careful about what we allow ourselves to be associated with.'

'Naturally. Tell me, do you have any thoughts on how to mitigate those concerns?'

'I do.' He looked as pleased with himself as any other two-bit politician she had ever met.

'You said the opposite outcome was possible,' she prompted. 'That suggests something that enhances our reputation, instead of diminishing it.'

'Something that enhances your reputation, and improves your balance sheet even further.'

'What would that be?'

'Your commitment to absolute fairness, to ensuring complete parity between gems and norms. The thing is, Ms Klist' – he leaned forward conspiratorially – 'there's no question that what Herran is gifting to the gem community in exchange for his assistance to you solves an immediate problem. However in the longer term it has the potential to present us with several more. An accusation of unequal treatment is quite possible – inevitable, the more I think about it.'

'*Unequal?*' Her temper flared as she recalled what access to Herran had cost. 'Aryel Morningstar and Jeremy Temple negotiated over a million credits in Bel'Natur human genome expertise! Exclusively for gems!'

Mikal was nodding sagely. 'So they did.'

'The credit line is going to run and run until it runs out. It could last well over a decade. Compounding the unexpended value over that time will triple the total from what it would have been if we'd just paid Herran what we were prepared to. At least. Plus a share of profits from the products we develop as a result . . . It is an *enormous* amount of money!'

'Perhaps over the long term,' Mikal murmured. 'The present value is slightly less enormous. But my concern is who and what that credit line will be paying for.'

'Bespoke reproductive engineering – not just enough for embryo viability, full-on compatibility analysis and design. Available to any gem who applies. How is that *unequal*?'

'Because it's not available to norms.'

She stared at him in disbelief. He let his dangling leg swing gently and pressed his hands together, steepling the four thumbs and six fingers and pointing them at her for emphasis.

'Ms Klist, you made that deal under a certain amount of duress and we all know it. The fact that you made it at all tells me you think the value of Herran's involvement will more than merit that *enormous* amount of money over that *extended* period of time. But the deal also means Bel'Natur needs to maintain its human gem-tech expertise in order to hold up your end of the bargain. Now that's a fairly big investment, and I can't believe you wouldn't want to find more ways to leverage it. In the meantime, norms are going to be aware of what's on offer to us, they're going to be aware that instead of the numbers of gems – or at any rate our peculiarities – diminishing over the next few generations, our population is going to grow. The Reversionists will, if you'll pardon the pun, completely freak out. And will gain popular support, because people who do not share in an entitlement are more likely to turn against it.'

'Why would norms want to share it? They don't have trouble reproducing, and when they do systems are already in place to help.'

'Yes, but they don't get to have *special* kids, do they? *We* will. They're not going to appreciate the fact that we get all the help we need to have ever more extraordinary children, and they don't. Haven't you noticed how glamorous we've become? People are enchanted by the thought of having a child like Lyriam. Or his lovely friend Gwen. Perhaps not another me, but certainly another Aryel. There's a boom in children's stories about living under the sea with gillungs or up in the air with flying people. The popular imagination has already gone there.' The fingers jabbed at her. 'And why shouldn't they be able to realise it? Under the tightest controls, of course, the very highest ethical and welfare standards.'

'And,' she said slowly, still not quite able to believe what she was hearing, 'for a price.'

'Absolutely.'

'Those tight controls and high standards,' she mused, 'will be affirmed by our ongoing association with gems. Which will serve as an endorsement.'

'Precisely.'

This was too good to credit. Time to be blunt, and see if he would backtrack. 'Councillor Varsi, you are proposing a way back in to human gemtech.'

'Ms Klist, you are already doing human gemtech, and if all goes well you are going to be doing it for a long time to come. I want to ensure that everything you engage in is aboveboard, and that it doesn't backfire on gems. You want to make money. I'm suggesting a way to accomplish both our goals, and I'm suggesting you announce it at the close of the Festival. It would be proof of the new ethos of partnership and equality between gems and norms, it would put paid to any lingering doubts about Bel'Natur. Not to mention being an elegant bookend to your earlier performance.'

She sat in stunned silence for well over a minute.

'Out of curiosity,' she managed finally, 'do your associates in the gem community share this view?'

'Some will, some won't. The view that matters most to me is my wife's.'

'Your wife is – on board?'

'Completely.'

The black tower reared above him like a missile, its blunt, bullet-shaped tip threatening a sky now heavy with storm clouds. Not even on their first day here had it seemed so menacing. Eli affected a nonchalance he was far from feeling as he crossed the gleaming lobby, reminding himself to make eye contact and smile as he passed the girl on reception. He recognised two young men from the coding team exiting the lift as he entered it, and he managed to return their nodded greetings without, he thought, any hint of the knowledge that now pressed down on him like a weight.

Alone in the lift, he leaned against the wall, feeling the weariness that had descended under the apple trees of Maryam House wash over him again. *I should be used to this by now, revelation piled on revelation.* But there was no preparing for such moments.

He checked the time on his tablet. Late afternoon already. A couple of hours at the most, and he could usher Callan and Herran home to the safety of the Squats; hopefully innocent of the day's developments, quite possibly never to return. He glanced around, eyed the tiny slits of air vents up in the ceiling panel, and wondered how Nance had been infected in the first place. Another cup of coffee, taken casually from the hand of a trusted colleague years ago, nanites inhaled with the steam? A packet of biowipe tissues left on a desk, perhaps, or a ride alone in the lift?

If they want me, they've got me. It's not like this is the first chance. The opportunities and possibilities spun out in his memory, increasingly lurid, and he was grateful when the lift came smoothly to a stop and the doors slid open.

Callan met him at the entrance to the lab, tablet in hand and green eyes troubled. Eli read the look and sighed inwardly. He let himself be redirected towards the sound-dampened seating area. As soon as the air went dead around them Callan spoke.

'I've had a message from Aryel. Looking for Rhys.'

'She still hasn't found him?' That was bad. Eli had left her pretending to be less perturbed than she was at the emptiness of the flat, and her inability to raise Rhys on his earset or tablet. 'She thought he might have gone to be with Gwen . . . she's recording today, apparently, he'd have had to switch everything off . . .'

'He's not with Gwen, or Reginald either. Aryel spoke to the studio, but I could have told her that. I don't know where he is, but I think it has to do with something he and Herran have cooked up. They said it was a secret.'

Eli stared at him, then twisted round to peer in at the open door of the lab, where another test was being run. Herran was sitting up this time, clutching his own tablet to his chest as he read text off the angled screen that was part of the experiment's apparatus. Sevi stepped into view by his side, asked him something, and one of his hands came away to jab at the screen. That was evidently not fast enough, and he tucked the tablet securely into his lap and used two hands, working with astonishing speed. He looked up at Sevi a moment later and they could see his mouth form the word *Done* as he swung the screen away. She looked startled, glanced at a monitor, and then nodded and smiled and said something to him as she stepped away. Herran's nose was already buried back in his own tablet.

'What's he doing?'

'I don't know. He's been weird for the past hour or so, ever since he got Rhys' message. He's usually quite placid about the tests, he doesn't mind how complicated they are or how long they take. But this afternoon it's become – urgent, as though something critical is happening somewhere else that he needs to attend to. I almost thought he was going to refuse this last one, but while Sevi was explaining he *interrupted* her. He *never* does that. He was doing something while she was talking – you know what he's like, tapping away no matter what else is going on – and then he just said, "Okay. Five minutes. Quick quick." And he *meant* it. They had to scramble.'

'You think he's in communication with Rhys?'

'Yes, but when I asked him he said, "Can't tell. Promised."'

'He has to. This is important.'

'So I gather. Eli, what's going on? I messaged Aryel back – I wasn't too worried at that point – and this is what she said.' He spun his tablet round and swiped it awake. Eli saw a text panel with Aryel's comcode, and the words *NOT GOOD. Need to find him. Talk to Eli, don't be overheard.*

He looked back into the younger man's anxious face.

'What's happened to Rhys?' Callan demanded. 'Is he in trouble? Is he ill?'

'He's—' Eli stopped, squinted suspiciously around at the low, comfortable chairs, the curved wall with its panoramic view to one side and the ceiling with its ambient lighting and other unobtrusive panels and projections, and led the way out of the field and into a cramped corner away from the neurolinguistics lab. Callan followed, his worry palpably growing with every step.

'What are we doing?'

'Being paranoid, most likely.' Eli kept his back to the room and sketched out what he had learned about the case, Rhys' discoveries and their implications for Bel'Natur as well as for him. 'Whoever's behind this is ruthless as hell, and Sharon is hot on their heels. All thanks to Rhys. Sharon's concerned about what the lawyer might have found out from Nance before he collapsed. Nance never knew about Rhys, but the lawyer was at the police station, he knows his way around the system, he might have picked up a rumour of him there. Not,' he said quickly, as Callan's eyes widened in alarm, 'that it would serve any purpose whatsoever for anyone to want to harm Rhys. But it's a new development that he doesn't know about, and Aryel doesn't like not knowing where he is, not with all this going on.'

'Neither do I. And I don't like us being here, either. Shouldn't we be going?'

'We can't. If we suddenly packed up and went home it would prove that we think there's a problem. Sharon says she and Mikal have a plan to get everyone safely out of this – including Rhys – but it's only going to work if Zavcka believes that no one besides the two of them knows anything. So we have to keep a low profile, leave at the usual time, that kind of thing.'

'Act like nothing's wrong.'

'Exactly.'

'Eli, Rhys has uncovered a crime that could sink this company for good, put people in prison for the rest of their lives, and now he's disappeared. Something is *very* wrong.'

'He hasn't disappeared if Herran knows where he is. But we're going to have to get him to tell us, and we're going to have to do it in a way that doesn't raise any suspicions. Has Sevi noticed he's acting strangely?'

'She's no fool, she must have done. But she's also really wrapped up in this breakthrough they've made. I don't get the sense that she's focusing on anything else.'

'Good. Let's use that, then.'

They made their way back into the lab. Herran looked up from his tablet the moment they entered. Though his scarred face was as expressionless as ever, Eli noticed that he was blinking rapidly.

'Okay, Herran?'

'Okay.' He did not sound it. Callan strolled over to him while Eli went to talk to Sevi. She was sitting in a huddle with two of her team, voices low but animated as they pored over the datastream outputs on the monitor screens around them.

He judged it best not to call her away and squatted down beside all of them instead, speaking softly. 'Hey, Sevi. Mo, Kwame. All still looking really good, I take it? That's fantastic. Listen, Callan's been telling me he's a bit concerned about Herran, have you noticed anything?'

They looked at each other. 'He's been more communicative than usual,' Sevi said, just as quietly. 'But also more – how would you put it, Kwame? Sort of impatient.' The man nodded. 'I worried whether we were asking him to do too much too fast – we're all really excited today, you can tell – and he keeps saying he's okay. But his reactions do seem a little off.'

'Callan thinks so too. It might just be his way of sharing in the excitement, or maybe he *is* tired but doesn't feel he can say so for some reason. It's not easy for us to tell either, believe me. We're going to take him out into the lounge for a few minutes, give him a change of scene and have a quiet chat. All right?'

'Of course. Dr Walker, he's been an absolute champion, what we've got today—' The colour was high in her cheeks, and her eyes were shining with discovery. 'We've unlocked it, I'm certain. If Herran wants to take a break for a few days he really shouldn't feel badly about it. He's given us so much to work with.'

'I'll make sure he understands that. Thank you, Sevi.' He stood up, knees creaking. *Thank you so very, very much, Sevi. You just gave us a way out. And I even believe you mean it.*

They tried to lead him towards the far corner, but Herran headed straight for the chairs within the damper field and they had no choice but to follow. The little gem came to a stop in the middle of the field, blinked at the windows and their astonishing view, and then turned aside so it was out of his field of vision. He did his 180-degree whole-body swivel, looking from Eli on his left to Callan on his right.

'Okay here. No bugs.'

Eli felt his mouth fall open in astonishment, saw the expression mirrored on Callan's face. 'How do you know?'

'Checked. First day.'

Eli chuckled. 'Herran, you are a wonder. That's very good to know, thank you. But listen, there's something else we need to ask you about.'

'Rhys.'

'Yes. Where is he, Herran?'

He looked from one to the other of them again. He was rocking and blinking and as close to agitated as Eli could imagine him. 'Said wouldn't tell. Rhys said don't tell Callan, Callan will worry. Promised.'

'Herran, it's too late for me not to worry. I'm already worried.'

'Worried,' Herran repeated, and Eli realised with a jolt that he was talking about himself. 'Rhys not answer. But said wouldn't tell.' He was rocking harder now. His fingers clenched and unclenched around the tablet.

'I know you promised, Herran, but this is really important, sometimes promises—' Eli broke off as Callan held up a hand to silence him.

'No, that's not going to work. We need to solve this on Herran's terms. Herran, it was me Rhys didn't want you to tell, wasn't it?'

'Yes.'

'Did you promise not to tell Eli?'

'No.'

'And Eli didn't promise anything, so he can tell me. Right?'

Herran blinked at him. Callan walked away, stepped outside the damper field and stood there with his back turned. Eli shook his head sharply and sank down onto one of the low seats. Herran sat opposite him, back straight and eyes wide.

'Herran. Where is Rhys?'

'Down below.'

'Below where?'

'Here.' He realised Herran's stubby forefinger was pointing between his feet, straight down at the floor. 'Basement. Minus four.'

'He's *in this building*?'

'In building. Minus four.' Herran waggled the tablet. 'Link good. But not answer.'

'Why is he there? How did he get there?'

'Find genetype. I help.' He explained in his clipped, disjointed style, until Eli understood it well enough to call Callan back to them.

'I've got to go and find him.'

'One of us must. I'm not sure it should be you; they're used to me poking around the building . . .' But the mutinous look on Callan's face told him that line of argument would get him nowhere. 'Okay, fine. How do you get there, though? I thought I'd gone to every part of this building, and I had no idea that floor existed.'

'How did Rhys get there?'

'Stairs,' Herran responded. He was completely sanguine now that Callan had heard the story from Eli, not from him. 'Hard to pass. Cams, beams, locks. Okay for Rhys, not okay for you. Take lift.' His fingers flew across the tablet. 'I make code.'

WINGS

Even her father could not have dreamt of this.

Acceleration pushes her back into creamy leather upholstery. Outside the engines rise from whine to bellow to roar, and there is a soft thump beneath her feet as the executive jet leaves the ground. She barely feels it, barely hears it. She has eyes only for the image that rotates on the screen of her tablet.

It is an anatomical rendering only, but it is enough. She squints at the complex articulation of the shoulders, the angled planes of bone where powerful muscles connect and contract. The musculature itself is amazing, interweaving and overlapping across the back, the neck, the chest. The schematic flexes, showing how the systems are isolated, each pair of limbs acting independently of the others.

She admits now that she had given little credence to the claims Jonah extracted. There are no six-limbed vertebrates. There is no template, no genetic framework on which to hang such a creature, no model outside of myth. The building blocks do not exist. She had expected at best a malformed, monstrous thing. But this thing is perfect.

They were right to keep it a secret, she thinks, and wonders if she is going soft. Patience has never been her virtue, and they made her wait. But it would have been too easy for word to filter out via assistants and infostreams. Even now details are sketchy; the file was sent only after Jonah had assured Panborn they were on their way, and the illustration is not a photograph.

But they will be there soon enough, and there will be no further need of proof.

She glances at him, sitting opposite her across the polished bioplastic of the table, staring at his own tablet as though thunderstruck. He feels the gaze and looks up. She raises an eyebrow, a small indicator of her own amazement. He shrugs massively, hands spread, as if to say: Who could ever have imagined?

Indeed.

Six limbs. A pair of arms, a pair of legs and a pair of wings.

It is almost enough to rekindle her sense of wonder.

28

It was, Rhys thought, like that ancient story of a ship inexplicably abandoned, with sign of neither struggle nor madness; everything left just so, as though the inhabitants might return at any moment. To be sure, some rooms had the cold hollowness of spaces surplus to requirements and long ago emptied out, but most were well stocked and tidy, and scrupulously clean.

There was a succession of laboratories, each with a purpose he recognised. Here was where the modelling would have been done, the virtual selection of sequences, the datastream shuffle and splice preparatory to the manipulation of actual molecules. The researchers had only to step across the hall to deliver their projections to colleagues in charge of doing that molecular excision and reassembly for real; he moved down the banks of equipment, checking off sequencers and centrifuges, thermocyclers and spectrophotometers. At the back of the room he found the cold storage necessary for genestock, checked the labels on a few of the tiny vials, and nodded to himself in satisfaction.

In the next room along, the wet work: microscopes and microsurgical equipment for the incorporation of engineered genomes into living gametes, incubation trays for nurturing newly created embryos, more tissue storage. Ova only, he noticed, all identically labelled. A single donor? He moved on, stuck his head inside a bright white room. The examination table with its stirrups and restraints, the neatly racked specula and ranks of pipettes, told the next chapter in the story. Implantation, involuntary. He shuddered and ducked out, still chasing the elusive scent.

He found a kitchen with fresh milk in the fridge, half a loaf of bread, fruit in a bowl on the countertop. Next to that and strangest of all: a room full of gaily coloured mats and cushions, soft toys and bright bioplastic construction blocks. A rugged, rudimentary tablet, loaded with picture books and nursery rhymes, left on a low table next to a bed. Its coverlet was starred with orange-petalled daisies, between which full-throated bluebirds appeared to twitter a silent song. *Is this a crèche?* But there was only the one bed, and although narrow it was sized for an adult, not a child.

Where's the dorm? There must be space for surrogates, and a birthing room, and a nursery. They wouldn't need a crèche for toddlers yet, surely, the stock wasn't stolen long enough ago. Maybe not the nursery either. But if they're doing the implantations here they'd need the rest of it. You wouldn't risk bringing them in just to smuggle them right back out again.

He stood in the corridor and turned in a slow circle, testing the air, straining his senses to the limit. Still no hint of another human moving anywhere nearby, but he thought he caught a sound this time; something so faint he could not be entirely sure he wasn't imagining it, a hissing pulse on the edge of even his hearing. A few steps in that direction and both the sound and scent seemed stronger. He headed along the passage, calculating as he went. How many people would it take to staff this operation, when it was at full flow?

Depends on how many surrogates, but you wouldn't need more than a handful to do the science. Four maybe? Six?

Where are they?

What the hell is that sound?

It led him to a side passage that ran back towards the lifts, and the door of a room that he was certain, the moment he rested his hand against the touchpanel, held a living person. There were low, slow breaths beneath that pulsing hiss, and a hint of human warmth and musk mingled with the unpleasant clinical smell. Beyond that he could read nothing, but he knew what the sound and the smell were now. He pressed the panel, and the door slid back.

The room he stepped into could have been in the hospital where he had awoken just the day before; but a critical-care suite, not the homely facility for ambulatory patients in which he had stayed. A vital-signs monitor and life-support unit throbbed against the wall in the barely audible rhythm that had led him here. Tubes disappeared under the blankets of an articulated bed in the centre of the room, delivering hydration and nutrition, and drugs too, no doubt, and collecting waste. Though sealed and sterile, the aroma of illness still hung over the equipment; a whiff of intimacies exposed, of incapacity and despair.

On the bed was a girl.

He moved silently to stand beside her, and felt the breath go out of him.

She was young; certainly no older than himself, he thought, though it was hard to be sure. Her face had been burned, badly but not recently. The melted flesh had long since fused, set and gone pale. The scarring ran down the side of her neck, spread across the patch of shoulder he could see, and disappeared beneath the light blanket that covered her body. Her undamaged skin was the same warm brown as his own; the fuzz of hair covering her scalp glowed the same ruby red.

He knew, with a sick certainty that turned his stomach over and made his head swim, that if she were to open her eyes they would be the same midnight blue.

Though her breathing was regular and deep, there was something in the girl's stillness that told him this would not happen, that her tranquillity was not that of normal sleep. Sensor pads dotted her skull and chest, and a slim clip on her nose held the faintly hissing oxygen supply in place. But these were not what shocked him most.

It was the swelling low down on her torso, pushing the blanket up into a round flannel hill that he suddenly wanted to touch, to rest his hands against as though giving or receiving a blessing: the unmistakable bulge of a woman in the late stages of pregnancy.

There was a pair of chattering office girls in the lift, who fell silent but smiled politely when Callan entered it. He smiled back, and pressed the button for the canteen: the only floor, apart from the lobby and exit, that he had legitimate reason to visit. He could feel them eyeing him up, bursting with the giggles and gossip that he knew would include him the moment they were safely out of earshot. The taller of the two, pale and freckled with elaborately curled ginger tresses, kept having to pull her eyes away from his hair: glowing, flame-red, tousled and in need of a cut.

Carelessly sexy, that was what Rhys had called it. He'd come up with the line that first morning, as they lay in bed and he combed through it with his long, clever brown fingers.

What makes you think it's careless? Capturing the fingers, kissing them, while Rhys laughed.

So it was part of your plan, was it, to seduce me with your beautiful hair?

Whatever works.

Callan felt the breath catch in his throat at the memory, felt his own fingers flex as though caressing silky skin, heard his exhalation turn into something close to a moan. A rush of warmth at his groin. This would not do at all, not now, not here. He shook himself and ran deliberately rough hands back through the mane of hair: clearing it away from his face, clearing the image of Rhys laughing amid a tangle of sheets, clearing his head. Across the lift the girls exchanged glances.

They got off two floors above the canteen, much to his relief. If they had still been there when the doors opened he would have had to disembark, pretend he had actually come for something, wait for another lift and try again. As it was, the moment the doors closed on their whispers and backward glances he stepped up to the control panel and rapidly pressed floor numbers in the sequence that Herran had instructed and he had memorised.

The lift descended, not stopping at any floors though all the buttons were now lit. It shot past the canteen, where Bruce Dunmore waited. He was idly watching the numbers on the inset panels count down and up, the better to plant himself before the sliding doors most likely to open for him, and he came alert as a down count flicked past that floor without pausing. He glanced at the waiting passengers, wondering if anyone else had noticed. If they had they made no sign. The doors of another carriage slid open almost immediately, and they piled into it without complaint.

His own arrived and he stepped inside, thoughtful. He was the only one in it and he glanced up at the ceiling, towards the executive suite to which he had been summoned, and considered changing direction. There were only two lifts that ran the full length of the building, from top floor to lowest basement, and this just happened to be the other one. He could short-circuit the cryptic message that would no doubt be waiting for him, redirecting him to meet her below stairs instead, and just go directly there. But Zavcka Klist had told him to come to her office, and she disliked presumption. Best to stick to the script, collect the message, retrace his steps. He let go of the tiny key he had been fingering in his pocket, the one that would override the other controls and send the lift straight down to the hidden floor. Follow orders, put up with Herself's idiosyncrasies, collect the reward. The reward in this case would be well worth it.

He relaxed, as much as he ever did, and kept going up.

As soon as he went past the second basement level, housing the less-than-executive car park and bowels of building services, every light on the panel went dead. For a moment Callan thought it had all gone wrong, and waited for the lift to shudder to a halt between floors, and demands for identity and explanation to crackle through its inbuilt comlink. But it kept going, smooth and swift, and he barely noticed that the ride had ended before the doors slid silently back.

He stepped cautiously out of the lift, and into a dimly lit space. It brightened in response to his movement and he saw a small lobby, undecorated and desolate. Corridors branched away from him, all empty as far as he could see, all silent as far as he could hear. He dared not call out.

Herran had had no idea where else Rhys might have gone down here, but he had known roughly where the tablet was located. Callan spotted a door that looked about right, only a few steps away. He edged towards it, had his hand on the touchpanel ready to slide it back, when another right hand came down on top of his. Immensely strong fingers wrapped around his mouth from the left, clamping it shut.

Rhys' voice hissed in his ear. 'Cal, what are you doing here?'

He could neither answer, nor even move. The slim body that had him pinned against the wall, that had been pliant and warm in his arms the night before, might have been made out of steel. Rhys whispered, 'Shh, no noise.' The fingers on his hand and mouth relaxed and that unyielding body stepped back, releasing him.

Callan turned around. 'I'm looking for you.' He could barely speak for the hammering of his heart. '*Shit*, Rhys!'

'Sorry. Did I scare you? Oh honey, I'm sorry.' He looked mortified, but the tension was still in him, his eyes flickering from side to side, along the corridors, across to the lifts, back to Callan's face. 'I didn't want to risk you shouting, I wasn't certain yet if you were on your own . . . but you are, aren't you? How did you get here? Why are you looking for me?'

'Because you need to get out of here. This genestock business is blowing up, Rhys. Herran's got what you need, he's got the datastream and he got me down here, but we need to go. Grab your tablet, come on.' He stabbed at the call button. It lit up, and stayed lit, and his heart sank. The doors did not open. The lift was gone.

Rhys had not moved. 'We can't.'

'What do you mean we can't? You got what you came for. These people are *killers*, Rhys. If they find us—'

'How do you even *know* all this? I didn't want you involved! Herran promised he wouldn't tell you I was here, and I didn't even tell *him* everything . . .'

'He didn't. It's complicated. I'll explain on the way.'

'There's someone here. We can't leave her.'

Callan spun round and stared at him. '*What?*'

Rhys held out a hand. 'There's only us and her down here, and I don't think she can hear us. But we can't leave her. Come on. I'll show you.'

The fingers that wrapped around his and tugged him along were gentle again, though he could feel the suppressed power in them now, like a river in spate, dammed but barely held back. And more: there was a tremor in the hand he was holding, faint but constant, a distant earthquake deep inside the muscle. Callan swallowed.

'Rhys – Rhys, sweetheart. You're not very well, are you?'

'I'm fine.' Callan could hear the lie in his voice. 'I'm a hell of a lot better than she is.'

It was a bit late in the day, Zavcka Klist thought with annoyance, for Dunmore to get the fidgets.

The stolid security chief had actually looked surprised when Khan showed him into the office, and as she gave him a brusque synopsis of her conversation with Mikal Varsi, his unease appeared only to grow.

'I take it, ma'am,' he said when she paused for breath, 'that you're not in any doubt about this proposal?'

'Are you joking, Dunmore? I have huge doubts about it. Norms wanting to have gem babies – the whole notion is farcical.'

'But – I'm sorry, I got the impression you believed him.'

'The fact that the idea is idiotic doesn't mean *he* doesn't believe it. He's looking for a way in.'

'Or pretending to.'

'Or pretending to. But why would he? Why tip us off to how much they know if he and the wife aren't trying to work an angle for themselves?'

Dunmore shot another glance at the door, as though he had somewhere better to be, before he looked back at her.

'I've met a lot of cops in my time, ma'am. You can usually tell the ones that are inclined to bend.'

'That wasn't your impression of Sharon Varsi?'

'No, it wasn't.'

'Maybe he talked her into it. The problem's got to be with him, after all . . . if they really have a problem . . . or maybe . . .' She trailed off, frowning.

'Maybe he just wanted you to think you can trust them.'

'What would that get him?'

'It might get *you* to make a mistake. To feel more secure than the situation warrants.'

'You're the one who said there was no immediate danger . . . what is the *matter* with you, Dunmore?' as he appeared almost to edge towards the door.

To her amazement, he responded with a question of his own. 'Ma'am, have you instructed any of the below-stairs staff to return? In light of your conversation with Mikal Varsi, maybe?'

'No, of course not. I did think you were right and we needn't have moved quite so quickly, but no point slowing things down now. Why?'

He explained about the lift. 'I thought perhaps you'd gone down yourself, to check on the surrogate. It's probably nothing . . . an override from maintenance, bringing it down for servicing . . .'

'Isn't that one of your people?'

'Yes, ma'am, he is. And he hasn't messaged me the way he should if he was taking it out of service.' He tapped at his earset for emphasis. 'It's probably just a glitch in the building control systems, nothing to do with any of this. There was another one half an hour or so ago, it partially activated the fire safety lockdown on the service floor for a few minutes. Maybe it's related, but . . .'

'But you had better go and check, Dunmore. Now.'

A couple of miles away Aryel Morningstar once again climbed the stairs that led to the roof of Maryam House, speaking low and fast into her earset as she went. Events were moving swiftly now, with more in play than even she had anticipated, and though much remained uncertain the risks to Rhys were clear. By now they might be clear even to him, and she quickened her step as she issued final instructions.

Once again the stakes were higher than she had imagined, but at least this time she had learned that early. At least this time there was something she could do about it.

And this time, my weapons are not so crude.

She slowed for a heartbeat as she passed beneath the apple trees. There, the stool where she had waited for Eli; waited to confess, be judged and found wanting. Here, the spot he had stood and then sat to listen, to witness but not to blame; and in that gentle absolution, opened up a world.

The past was indeed another country, full of peril and doubt; and she had been moving so fast for so long she had failed to notice how far she had left it behind.

Now she strode for the lip of the roof, fingers reaching down automatically to check that her tablet was secure in its squeeze-pocket on her thigh. The memory came to her of Zavcka Klist, high in her tower, boasting about how such physical interactions could become obsolete. Think it on, think it off. Work on the fly.

Maybe that too. But that's not all, is it, Zavcka? I know what you want now. I know almost all of it.

I wonder what I would have done, had I been you. Would I have been tempted?

The thought made her pause for a moment, just a moment, one foot up on the coping, wings rising to catch the wind. Such a prize, a thing sought and yearned for, a thing killed and conquered for. A gift beyond price. She looked down the long drop between buildings to the ground below, a narrowing, darkening tunnel with death at the end, and considered the question.

Her story is not mine. I know what I am. My gift is enough.

And leapt.

EPIPHANY

She stands on the lip of the gorge that bars her way and finally knows despair. The torrent of water that carved it plunges down, down, down, pulling her gaze with it and her body off-balance. She totters, exhausted and awkward, and almost loses her footing on the mist-slicked turf. Instinct flings her arms and her other limbs wide, a frantic flapping to haul herself upright, and the torn, soot-blackened blanket is flung free to twist and billow lazily into the white churn. She is exposed now as well as trapped, but there is little logic any more in concealment. The pursuit is too close for another path or another plan. In her mind's eye she sees what is behind her, and with eyes the colour of sky she looks at what is before, and the choice seems less an outcome than a method.

It comes to her then, whispering on a wind through the trees: a sigh softer than the grass beneath her trembling feet, louder than the roar of the water. It is seductive and majestic and insistent, and it catches her and holds her fast. There are shouts in the forest now, and the distant scream of a helicopter wheeling to the hunt, but she no longer hears them. She is listening too hard to something else, something below and above and beyond these distractions.

It is barely a pattern but almost a melody, and it murmurs a truth that she feels in the roots of her soul. She is not instructed so much as reminded, revealed to herself. The song that is not a song pounds through her veins now, like fire and ice and the wind between stars, and in this newest of creatures under the sun there blooms a knowledge older than time. There is chaos in it, and order, purpose and madness and a pulsing certainty. The song that is not a song sings to her the language of flight.

'I understand,' she whispers, and leans forward, and falls free.

29

Callan stood at the foot of the bed, his shock at the sight of the pregnant, unconscious girl overcome for the moment by a greater worry as he watched Rhys fussing around her, checking monitors and intravenous supplies, mumbling almost inaudibly to himself about foetal heart rates and blood oxygen levels. It seemed the barely discernible tremor of just a few minutes before was becoming rapidly worse, fuelling his restless, nervous, constant movement.

'We need to get back to the others,' he tried again. 'Eli and Herran are upstairs waiting for news, Aryel's desperate to know that you're all right . . . once we get out of here we can send paramedics and police to take care of her . . .'

'Can't leave,' Rhys muttered. 'Look at her, *look* at her, look what they did to her, and then they just left her here. She's all alone, Cal, look. Look at what they did.'

'I see, sweetheart, I see her. I see what they did. We need to send people who can take care of her properly, who can make sure she's safe.'

'I'll keep her safe. She's all alone, look, they left her, they left her all alone. We can't leave her alone.'

'We're not going to abandon her, of course we're not. But she's stable, Rhys, you said so yourself. Whatever's wrong with her, she's not getting any worse lying there. But you are, sweetie, you're falling ill. You know you are. We need to get you out of here.'

'What if they come back? They might come back. They might hurt her. Or – or take her away.'

'Rhys, please, I know your head isn't feeling too clear right now, but try and think. Think it through with me.' Callan drew a deep breath, thinking it through himself, trying to express it in a way that Rhys' fracturing intellect could grasp. 'Whoever left her here went to a lot of trouble to set up the life support so her condition wouldn't deteriorate while they were gone. They wouldn't have done all that if they were going to come back and do her harm.'

Rhys had stopped beside the bed, bending forward a little with his hands held in a painful pose up against his chest, fists spasmodically clenching and unclenching. Though he was staring fixedly at the girl, his head was tipped towards Callan. There was a frown of intense concentration on his face, and for the first time since he had heard his lover's voice out by the lifts, Callan felt a tiny surge of relief.

He was listening, and Callan realised that he *was* trying, trying hard to focus and to think.

'She can't walk,' he went on, keeping his voice low and even. *Stay with me, Rhys.*

'They'd need a medical transport to move her. That means transferring the life support to a mobile unit, and that takes time. There's no way anyone could get her out of here in this condition faster than *we* can get out and get help.' He had an idea, palmed his tablet, and aimed it at the still figure on the bed. 'Sharon's not going to need to wait for a warrant once she knows there's a comatose gem surrogate locked away in the basement. She'll be down here with an ambulance crew and half the Met in ten minutes flat. And the moment we get to where there's a signal, I can send her proof.' He waved the tablet at Rhys. 'But we need a signal. I can't get onstream from here.'

'I can.' He came towards Callan, his gait strange and shuffling, hands extended for the tablet. 'I'll get you onstream.'

'What? How?'

'Relays,' Rhys said. He spoke quietly, and appeared to be trying to mimic Callan's calm, methodical tone; but with a great deal more effort. 'Same way mine is talking to Herran. Need to give yours access.' With the clearer speech had come a sharp drop in coordination, and he practically clawed the tablet out of Callan's grasp. 'Call from here. Won't have to leave her.' He stabbed at it awkwardly.

'Rhys.'

'I can hold it together,' he whispered, but Callan could hear the strain in his voice, and this close he could see the tics and tremors that chased themselves across his face and hands, like insects swarming just beneath the surface of the skin.

When the lift deposited Dunmore in the drab little lobby of sub-basement four, his first thought was that nothing whatever seemed amiss. The lights were reassuringly dim until he stepped into their radius, and the place was silent as a tomb. He sighed, and relaxed his grip on the hard, comforting handle of the gun. Check the surrogate first, then the rest of the floor; report to Herself, and go lean on his plant in maintenance to find an explanation. These glitches, if that's what they were, could not be allowed to happen again.

The cheeky sod had already had the nerve to suggest he might have imagined the ghost-passage of the lift. Dunmore had given him a right earful for that, but in truth he was beginning to wonder himself.

He was already half a stride past the server closet when he

noticed something, a wrongness that tugged at the edge of his vision and brought him back around.

There was a gap between the edge of the door and the jamb, a line of darkness no wider than the thickness of his palm; as though the release had been pressed and then pressed again quickly, before the door could slide completely open. Or closed. Could it have been left like that earlier, in the rush to evacuate, to get to the new premises and prepare them for the night-time transfer of surrogate, supplies and equipment? But none of the staff on duty this morning were responsible for the lab's datastream, they would have had no business in there. He pressed the release himself, and the door slid back.

The lights came on. What they illuminated this time brought him up short. A tablet sat next to the server, its bright yellow memtab connector flashing slowly; and the gun was tight in his hand again, as a cold, still alertness descended. No glitch, this. And was that a murmur of sound now, deeper in the bowels of the building? He listened, but if it had been there it was gone.

He moved over to the tablet, and swiped the blank screen awake. A complex, shifting design filled it, a morphing web of colours and shapes. Whoever had got in here was using a pattern password, and he was taken aback for a moment. Those were generally the province of data geeks, not cops or corporate rivals. He would have to scrawl a sigil across it, connecting points within the slip-sliding hues and geometries in just the right order and at just the right instant to gain access. Impossible. He scribbled a finger experimentally over the screen. It flared bright white for a microsecond, washing out the wriggling pattern; then it came back up again, now even more complicated, and moving faster than before.

Dunmore did not try again. Instead he hooked his fingers under the connector, and tugged. It came away, and he slid the tablet inside his jacket. It would take time to destroy it properly, and Herself might want to have someone take a look before he did so. No telling what else might be on there.

He stuck his head out of the door, listening. Now he was sure he heard something. Voices, so more than one; maybe many more, but waiting would not improve the odds. He held the gun in both hands like an old friend, and went to find them.

Two hundred feet above his head, Eli sat with Herran in the dead zone of the lounge, pretending to work on his own tablet while the little gem rocked and tapped and swiped. Sevi and the others had been perfectly accepting of his explanation that Herran was in fact a little stressed and in need of a longer break and some refreshment, which Callan had gone to fetch. But as the minutes ticked by without his return, Eli began to wonder how long it would take before one of them came out to ask if he had got lost on the way to the canteen; or worse yet, put a call in upstairs to report the absence. He was trying to work out a way to forestall this when a touch on the arm made him jump almost out of his skin. Herran, who never ever touched anyone except for the brief, ritualised handclasp at greeting, had reached out and poked him.

'Eli.' The pale grey eyes were enormous. 'Server link gone. Broke.'

'The link from Rhys' tablet? It's gone down?'

'Gone down.'

'That's good, right? He must have collected it, they must be on their way up.' But there was something in Herran's demeanour, the agitated rock-nodding and staring eyes, that told him this was not the news he hoped for.

'Not Rhys. Not disconnected. Broke. Wrong password, then broke.'

Eli felt his mouth go dry. 'Okay, Herran. This is what we need to do.'

Higher still in the tower, Zavcka Klist swivelled into yet another sharp turn before the glass sculpture on her office wall, and stopped abruptly. This was ridiculous. She was wearing a hole in the carpet, not to mention her shoes. Dunmore had messaged from maintenance with the news that all looked to be in order; there was no record of a lift being taken to the lower floor since he himself had done so to slip the staff offsite during the lunchtime crush. He was going down to double-check, and would report back.

She was seized by a sudden unease at the thought of him, alone down there with the girl. What if he tripped over a tube, or touched the life-support settings? What if he touched *her*? How much did she really know about Dunmore anyway, save that nothing appeared to be beyond or beneath him? And even if the surrogate was perfectly safe as far as he was concerned, was it really a good idea to have left her, unconscious and alone, hooked up to a machine that had no way of alerting anyone if something went wrong?

Khan jumped in surprise as she came through the door at speed, blowing past him without a sideways glance; then recovered and was on his feet, hurrying after her.

'Ms Klist?'

'Stay here, Khan, I don't need you.'

'You've that conference in—'

'Cancel the conference.' She strode past the startled receptionist without a look or a word. 'I need to check on something below stairs. I might be a while.' She stepped into the lift. Khan could see a tiny metal key in her hand. He stopped, staring, as she stabbed the button for the basement level as though it were an enemy. Her eyes were like black stones in a face gone hard as marble.

The doors slid closed and she was gone.

Rhys looked close to tears when Callan finally took the tablet gently away from him and slipped it back into his pocket.

'That's it, that's enough. You've done all you can. It's okay.'

Rhys' head was down and he was shaking it as though in defeat. His whole body was shaking, hands tight up against his chest again, and his breathing came in short, sharp gasps of pain. Callan went to wrap an arm around him, and felt him flinch.

'She's going to be all right, we just need to—'

And then Rhys was rearing back in alarm, away from Callan and the door, a look of horror and profound shock on his face, and Callan, startled, recoiled as well.

Into a small hard roundness, pressed into the small of his back. This time the voice was one he did not know.

'Don't move. Put your hands on your head. If you make a sound I will shoot you.' And over his shoulder, to Rhys, 'You too. Hands on your head. Who else is here? How many?'

Zavcka Klist enjoyed no moment of false confidence as she stepped out of the lift. Though she could not make out the words, there was no mistaking Dunmore's voice. The shouting was coming from the direction of the medical unit. And now a second voice shouting back, one that she thought she recognised. She had an inkling, then, of how her security might have been breached; and cursed herself for a fool as she ran.

'He can't!' Callan yelled. Dunmore had shoved him further into the room, staying close to the door and covering them both with the gun. It was a blunt, ugly, deadly thing and he felt his guts quail at the sight of it. Right now it was pointed at Rhys, who stood swaying, ash grey and drenched with sweat, his hands still curled into fists and pressed up against his collarbone. Callan's own hands were clamped on top of his head as ordered, but Rhys seemed unable to comply. 'He can't,' Callan said again, trying to inject some calm into his voice, into the situation, even as the room seemed to spin slowly around him. There was a hiss followed by a hollowness in his ears. He wondered if he was about to pass out.

You had better fucking not.

'He's ill, can't you see? He's . . . finding her, finding her like this, it's sent him into shock . . . he's no threat to you. He's no threat!' And he found himself stepping in front of Rhys as the gun was raised and steadied.

'If he can't talk he's no fucking use to me, but you might be. Get out of the way.'

Callan looked at the big man, heard the death in his voice, saw it in the small black cavity of the barrel and knew he was in a place he had been before. It washed over him for a moment: the certainty of his own destruction, the memory of pain and terror and utter helplessness, the roaring, screaming horror of it.

He felt Rhys' warmth at his back and heard himself say, 'No.'

And as Dunmore stared at him in amazement, heard something else – heels clicking along the corridor outside, moving fast, coming closer. Dunmore swung round, gun coming to rest on the doorway as Zavcka Klist appeared in it. Callan, his muscles tensing to try something, anything, froze as though paralysed.

It was partly the look on her face that stopped him, ice-hard and implacable, and the black fury in her eyes. They widened in surprise for the merest instant at the sight of Rhys, and then she was all arrogant, aristocratic command.

'Dunmore, do not point that thing at me. Point it at them. What's the situation?'

'Found them in here, with her. And a tablet, downloading data from the server.'

'You have that?'

'Yes, ma'am. Right here.' He tapped at the chest of his jacket and she nodded briskly, stepping into the room beside him.

'Are there others?'

'Don't think so, ma'am. They'd have turned up by now if there were.'

The black gaze fixed on Callan. 'Is it just the two of you?'

He considered for a moment whether it would be better to lie, try to convince her that the shadowy recesses of Sub-Basement Four were swarming with infiltrators. It was an attractive prospect, but not one that would stand up to much scrutiny. On the other hand if he told her that he and Rhys were alone she would see no reason not to have them shot immediately.

'Yes,' he replied, and added, 'For now. More are on their way. They'll be here in a few minutes.'

'I very much doubt that. I assume Herran got you in here somehow, but he's hardly going to be charging to your rescue.'

'He might surprise you.'

'Not again, he won't. There's no stream access down here. You know that; that's why you were trying to copy the datastream to your tablet. All Herran, or Eli Walker, or anyone else who's in on this adventure of yours will know is that you disappeared. We'll cooperate fully with the search, but all anyone will find is a vacant floor that hasn't been used for years. If they pull out, so be it. We've got what we need from him.'

He opened his mouth to reply, but she forestalled him by stepping a little to the side to peer around him at Rhys, and the still, silent girl on the bed. 'Rhys, I take it? I expected something more impressive, after everything we've heard. What's wrong with him? Why isn't he talking?'

'He's ill. He has a – condition.'

'Not for long. Get away from her!' Snapping, as Rhys' swaying shuffle took him a half-step closer to the girl. 'What were you doing in here? If you've hurt her . . .'

'If *we've* hurt her?' Callan was incredulous. 'We're not the ones who burned her, or who have her locked up and *unconscious*, in *a dungeon*, being used as a *surrogate*. It's not us who's hurt her, Ms Klist. That's on you.'

She cast a sideways glance at him, looking oddly, bitterly amused. 'The burns have nothing to do with me.'

Dunmore shifted deliberately in the doorway and she nodded and stepped back, closer to him, further away from the two captives. Callan saw that in the distraction of her arrival he and Rhys had become separated. Rhys stood across the room now, two long strides away, and his heart sank.

'How do you want to handle this, ma'am?'

'You seemed to have matters in hand when I arrived, Dunmore. What were you going to do?' The bitter amusement had seeped into her voice as well.

'I was going to question this one, shoot them both, get rid of the bodies and then come and report to you.'

'I see no reason to change any part of that plan except the last bit.'

Callan, watching Rhys and thinking hard, imagined that he saw the younger man's hands flex for a moment before the import of her instruction dragged him back. 'You won't have time,' he said, keeping his voice deliberately light. Maybe it would give them pause, make them wonder. 'The others are too close. You don't have time to kill us and dispose of our bodies before they get here. So you need to consider whether that's the kind of evidence you want to be found with.'

Zavcka shook her head. 'Nice try, but you haven't been down here long enough for anyone to—'

And then Rhys moved.

Although Callan was looking at him as it began, looking with the intensity of a man who wishes his last sight to be of the thing he cares for most, he could not afterwards say exactly how it started, or what he did, or in what order. One instant he was standing there, arms just starting to come down to his sides, head just starting to come up; then there was no more than a blurred streak of skin and clothing with a smeared ruby shimmer at the top. Dunmore gave a strangled shout as he was borne over backwards.

Then came a series of images, strobe flashes on his consciousness: Dunmore's arm yanked straight, the hand with the gun still in it pointing up at the ceiling, and another, crushing hand wrapped around the wrist. The report of the weapon, shockingly loud within the enclosed space, and the thud and skitter as it fell and skated away somewhere. Rhys on top of Dunmore, the dead man's hand with its shattered wrist flopping away, Rhys' other fist slammed into a throat gone strangely flat. Dunmore's eyes popped halfway out of their sockets, his mouth open in a half-finished scream.

Callan had barely begun to take his own hands down from his head before it was all over.

Rhys slumped back against the wall, staring at his hands as though in disbelief, face stunned and racked with pain. For a moment his eyes met Callan's. 'Cal,' he said. 'I didn't mean—'

The spasm took him, arching his body from the soles of his feet to the crown of his head, twisting him away from the wall to fall hard to the floor. Callan was by him in an instant, trying to grab the flailing limbs and hold them still, then simply to cradle and protect Rhys' head as it beat out a tattoo on the cement. He felt the skin on his own knuckles crack and break. It could have been no more than a few seconds, but it felt as if hours had ticked by before the convulsions subsided enough for him to bring his own weight to bear and hold Rhys down. It still felt like he could be thrown off at any moment.

A metallic clink against the hard floor, and the sinking cold in his belly again. He twisted his head around. Zavcka Klist was straightening up, the gun in her hand. He could see the shock on her face transmuting into fury and a hard, merciless hatred.

'If anyone's planning to show up,' he said aloud, 'now would be a fucking good time.'

30

Even in the swirling chaos of the moment, Zavcka Klist thought it was a strange kind of humour that would make a young man struggling to contain a foaming, thrashing lunatic, who had just witnessed one death and was seconds away from his own, speak sarcastically to the aether as though spirits might step out of it and come to his aid.

She thought that an instant before she was hit from behind, the impact sending her staggering forward, the gun ripped from her hand. She caught herself against the edge of the hospital bed and spun round.

The girl, the one from the concert, the beautiful girl with polished brown skin and curling, glowing, dark red hair, and dark blue eyes sparking a fury to match her own. Droplets spinning off the hem of a raincoat as she moved, almost too fast for the eye to follow. The gun shredding in her hands, not just pulling the magazine out, *breaking* it out, the trigger spinning merrily away through the air under the snapping force of her fingers. The mangled weapon was tossed into the furthest corner and the ammunition tucked safely into a pocket as she moved with the same blurring speed to where her brother lay beneath Callan on the floor.

Behind her, wings filled the doorway. Aryel Morningstar stepped over Dunmore's body, and into the room.

She took in the scene in an instant, periwinkle-bright eyes scanning every inch in a way Zavcka knew would miss nothing. Her dark hair was also damp, and beads of water dotted the surface of her wings.

'Move away from the bed, Ms Klist. Over against that wall, please. Now.'

And Zavcka felt herself obey, too stunned to argue, because hanging back in the corridor, retching at the sight of Dunmore's lolling tongue and displaced eyeballs, was Arthur Khan. The only words she could find were for him.

'You *bastard*.'

'On the contrary, Mr Khan is here precisely because he is *not* a bastard. And we would have got in without his help anyway, but he did save us time.' Aryel crossed to the bed, but her attention was on the trio on the floor. 'Gwen?'

Gwen was lying half on top of Rhys, helping Callan to hold him, her greater strength containing the worst of his convulsions. She held his jerking head under the crook of her jaw and was muttering to him, baby talk it sounded like, soothing, pleading. His eyelids fluttered over eyes rolled up so that only the whites showed.

'He needs help, Ari, he needs a sedative . . . something . . . it's not . . . stopping . . .'

'She has medicine,' Khan said hoarsely. 'Pills in . . . in her pocket. She gets fits sometimes . . . she didn't think I noticed . . . but not so bad as him, not nearly so bad . . . I don't know if it would help?'

'Thank you, Arthur, I think it might help a great deal. Zavcka, your pills, please.'

'Piss off.'

Aryel frowned and Gwen looked up, but it was Callan who was on his feet and slamming her back into the wall with his left hand, his right feeling along her jacket. He found a pocket, dipped into it, came out with a little bioplastic tube half the length of his finger.

'This?'

Khan swallowed. 'Yes.'

Callan let go and turned back to Rhys without another look or word. Gwen had rolled him round and was sitting braced against the opposite wall, holding him from behind. Her arms were wrapped tight around his, hands gripping her own wrists to hold them in place as he twitched and spasmed, with her legs crossed over his thighs. That was less effective, and Callan had to rest his own weight on Rhys' shins as he knelt, to keep him from kicking himself free. He grabbed Rhys' chin with one hand and popped the tube open with the other.

'How many?'

'At least two, I imagine. Zavcka, how many do you take for an attack?'

She stayed furiously silent and Aryel rounded on her, wings arched and eyes blazing. Her voice was like the crack of a whip. 'Zavcka! Do you think watching him suffer instead of helping is going to help *you*? *HOW MANY?*'

For the first time, Zavcka Klist flinched. 'One if it's just coming on, two if I don't catch it in time. They said I could take up to three if it got really bad.'

'Callan, give him four.'

He looked up, startled. 'You sure?'

'He's heavier than she is, and this is worse than bad.'

He nodded, and then they had to watch while he tried to wrestle Rhys' clenched jaw open.

'Squeeze,' Gwen said. 'Hard. Harder.'

'But I'll hurt him.'

The look she gave him spoke volumes.

He clenched his own teeth and ground thumb and fingers into Rhys' face until his mouth opened enough to pitch four of the tiny pills inside; then held his jaw closed and tipped his head back, massaging his throat until he swallowed convulsively.

'How long?' Aryel asked quietly. She was still standing by the bed, a hand resting on the blanket. 'Before they take effect?' She raised an enquiring eyebrow at Zavcka.

'A minute or two.' She resisted the urge to spit curses or rub her bruised shoulder and instead pressed both hands flat against the wall behind her, trying to still the trembling. Her brain felt sluggish, caught in a loop of shock and rage that was making it hard to think; and she needed to think, needed to try to work a way out of this. Refusing to volunteer the pills had been a mistake. There was nothing to be gained by antagonising them as long as they held the balance of power. She needed to reverse that. What did she know, and how could she use it?

Khan was with them. Had he always been? Was it just him, plus the two upstairs? If so that made it – she calculated rapidly – seven people she had to try and contain. What levers did she have, what kinds of pressure could she bring to bear? And if it went beyond them who else would they have brought into the loop, what could she . . .

Across the room, Aryel Morningstar had stooped to retrieve the plastic tube from Callan and was walking towards her with it, shaking it over her palm.

'You could use this yourself, I see,' she said quietly, and held out a tiny white pill at arm's length. Zavcka stared in astonishment, as behind her Callan growled a protest. Aryel's eyes never moved from Zavcka's face as she replied. 'No point letting her go downhill as well, Cal. Sharon's going to need her to answer a lot of questions.'

She waited until Zavcka had reached out hesitantly, taken the tablet and gulped it down before saying pleasantly, 'You can also save yourself the trouble of coming up with an offer – or a threat – to try to prevent that. Detective Inspector Varsi and half a dozen officers are currently in the lobby, all trying to pile into the lifts along with a paramedic team. Another ambulance and goodness knows how many more police are on their way— Oh, they're here now? Just arriving. Thank you, Eli. Sharon, note that Ms Klist has just taken a dose of her medication.'

Zavcka felt her jaw drop. Aryel was listening, she was *speaking*, into her *earset*. She nodded, apparently at something only she could hear, and pinned Zavcka with those eyes again. 'Are you confused, Ms Klist? Let me explain. Rhys' tablet wasn't copying your server, it was linking it to the streams via your own old relay system. He linked Callan's as well. Herran used that link to activate Cal's earset, including the microphone's ambient pickup function, and conferenced in Eli, me, Gwen, and Sharon and Mikal Varsi. We've all heard every word that's been said since you stepped into this room.'

By the time he got down into the bowels of the Bel'Natur building, Eli Walker was beginning to think he too might be in need of something to settle the tremble in his hands and help him catch up with his sense of ever-expanding astonishment.

He had barely been able to credit the sheer audacity of Aryel Morningstar, plummeting down onto the roof of the tower through bomb-bright cracks of lightning and sheeting rain as the storm burst around her; calling Arthur Khan as she did so to tell him that an express lift was being sent up for her, that it would stop and the doors would open on the executive floor for five seconds on the way, and it was his job to get all of the passengers out of it.

Then Khan not only doing as he was told but riding up to meet her, saying, unprompted, 'Something's happening. I don't know what but I think it's bad. She's just gone below stairs and she said it in front of me and I'm not supposed to know there's anything down there.'

Aryel gave him two chances to get off, put as much distance between himself and the unfolding scandal as he could: first when the lift stopped to pick up Eli and Herran on the way down, and again when it deposited them in the lobby. Gwen had raced in at that point, a blur of brown and red and wet, almost knocking Eli off his feet as she streaked past and slammed into the lift next to Aryel.

He had not thought it was physically possible for a human being to move so fast.

Following her, his own considerable speed torpid by comparison, the looming, comforting presence of Mikal, borne in on a sound wave of approaching sirens. 'Sharon's almost here. Maybe you should wait—?'

But Aryel had said, '*Herran, now!*' and the doors had barely closed on the three of them before the shot rang out in their earsets, along with Dunmore's strangled shriek.

By the time Sharon screamed up with two patrols and the paramedics, even though he knew the worst of it must be over, he was living on the edge of his nerves.

'Herran, are you okay to stay with Mik? I need, I *need* to get down to them.'

'Okay with Mik.' Nodding and rocking over his tablet, cross-legged in a corner of the lobby, ignoring or oblivious as he had been all along to the babble and bustle of clusters of curious employees, their numbers growing and anxiety peaking as the police herded them back.

Sharon sighed and said, 'I really shouldn't allow you to do that,' and he gave her a look, and she said, 'Oh, what the hell. In for a penny, in for a pound,' and waved him into the lift.

And all the way down, they listened. Eli wondered whether Zavcka didn't realise she was still being heard by others – even more others, as Herran linked in more earsets. He knew Masoud was en route now and listening in, as were the officers in the lift with them. Maybe she thought they had killed the connection, or maybe she just didn't care any more.

'You might have made him worse, you know,' she was saying savagely. 'That medicine isn't a generic, it was specially formulated for me. What makes you think it'll work on him?'

'It is working, look at him.' Aryel's voice, serene in response. 'Where do you think he got this condition from anyway? This is *your* illness, Zavcka. Mutated, early onset, and far, far worse, but fundamentally the same syndrome. He inherited it from *you*.'

Gasps from the police in the carriage as Eli and Sharon exchanged bewildered glances, echoing a muttered, '*What?*' in their ears from Callan. Gwen was silent, save for the murmured, unceasing baby-talk.

'What do you mean *inherited*? He has nothing to do with me! I never had any children!' Snarled, but with a note of doubt, Eli thought, as the doors slid open and they tumbled out. 'And if I did, they wouldn't be—'

He could hear her voice in his other ear too now. He flicked the earset silent as he and Sharon led the charge down the corridor towards them.

'They wouldn't be gems? Zavcka, please. Rhys and Gwen are Phoenix products. And Phoenix is *you*. You are the one— Ah, the cavalry.' Aryel looked up as they appeared in the doorway. 'Watch your step.'

She stood by a hospital bed, on which lay the girl: unconscious, heavily pregnant, horribly burned, but the undamaged parts of her face and her stubble of hair so like Rhys' and Gwen's that Eli felt the breath go out of him. A batch sibling – she must be. There was another survivor, then.

Backed up against the right wall, Zavcka Klist as Eli had never seen her, could never have imagined seeing her: face venomous, composure irretrievably cracked, the angles of her tall frame more contorted than elegant. She looked shockingly old.

Against the left, down on the floor, Rhys, and Callan, and Gwen. If Rhys was better now Eli shuddered to think how bad it must have been. The young man's skin was terribly pale, its normal warm brown tinted a sickly green. His eyes were closed and his jaw slack; Callan was wiping away a spot of drool. Limbs and torso twitched in a constant, jerky, dreadful rhythm, but at least his entire body was not convulsing out of control. Eli supposed that had to be the improvement.

At his feet, Dunmore's corpse. He saw the injuries, registered the force that must have killed him, and found himself unsurprised. He had seen Gwen in action twice now, and if anything her brother would be stronger.

The police and paramedics poured in around him. A hand pointlessly pressed to Dunmore's crushed throat, the medic rising with a shake of the head and stepping swiftly on to bend over the girl on the bed. His colleague had gone straight to where Rhys was propped up, cradled between Callan and Gwen. She held a monitor unit, and Eli could hear her asking questions, low and urgent.

Sharon Varsi took one sweeping look and issued a stream of orders: two officers detailed to begin searching the rest of the floor, two more to remain in the room with her, the fifth sent back to stand guard and direct traffic at the lifts. Cams on at all times. 'Medics have priority. Stay out of their way unless you need to render assistance. Mr Khan, I'm going to need a statement from you back at the Yard, but for the moment please accompany Constable Farah here. Farah, keep an eye on him, he looks a little peaky.'

She turned to the blonde woman standing with her back to the wall. 'Zavcka Klist, you are under arrest on suspicion of illegal human genetic modification, aiding and abetting the theft of human genetic material, kidnapping, forced surrogacy, false imprisonment, attempted murder, and aiding and abetting the murder of Kendrick Nance. I must warn you that you do not have to say anything, but it may harm your defence if you do not mention when questioned something which you later rely on in court. Anything you do say may be given in evidence. And if you don't want to be physically restrained I suggest you stay exactly where you are until I tell you otherwise.'

Aryel had retreated to the opposite wall, as much out of the way as she could get in the crowded room. Desperate though he had been to reach them, now that he was there Eli did not know what to do. He crossed to stand beside her, sidestepping the paramedic who had finished checking the unconscious girl and was now joining the other one crouched in front of Rhys.

'You all right?'

'Fine,' she whispered back. 'But Rhys, I don't know about Rhys. And Gwen and Callan . . .'

He looked down at the cluster of heads at hip-height beside him, Callan's orange flame and Rhys and Gwen's ruby casting an incongruously cheerful sunset glow against the white wall.

'Herran started running a search as soon as he got access and he thinks he's found his genetype. He's found a batch anyway, and he says it looks about right.'

She nodded acknowledgement and said softly, into her earset, 'Herran, are you hearing me? Can you package up what you've found with Rhys' own Phoenix research, and send it ahead to the hospital?' She listened. 'Thanks. Yes, he's very, very ill. They'll be bringing him up in a minute.'

One of the officers was shaking a cover out over Dunmore's body, as the paramedics angled their gurney into the room. Aryel frowned.

'Sharon?' she said. 'Rhys' tablet is still on Dunmore, I think.'

'Good point. Ennis, record me, please.' The officer stepped closer, shoulder cam angled to capture her movement as she rifled inside the dead man's jacket and came out with the tablet. She slipped it into a clear plastic evidence sleeve and kept hold of it. 'We have his position, yes? Let's shift him, then. The medics need to get these two out of here.' She looked a question at the one who had checked both the girl and Rhys.

'She's stable,' he said. 'Vital signs are good. His aren't so good, we're going to take him first. The rest of the crew are on their way down for her; she'll be fine. Just don't touch anything.'

They manhandled the gurney next to him, then watched in amazement as Gwen straightened up, one arm under her brother's knees and the other beneath his shoulders while Callan supported his head. She placed him gently on the gurney, stepped clear so they could secure him, and turned into Aryel's embrace. Gwen hugged back, but she was staring over Aryel's shoulder and the arch of her wing at the girl on the bed. Eli realised it must be the first time she had focused on anyone but Rhys. She extricated herself and moved closer to look.

'Ey-a,' she said softly, amazed.

'Do you remember her, Gwennie?'

'I don't know . . . I think . . . Ellyn. I think her name might be Ellyn.' She turned back to them, her eyes bright with tears. 'I have to go with Rhys, Ari.'

'Of course you do. You and Callan both. Go on. Da will meet you there, and I'll come as soon as I can.'

Callan's head came up a fraction at the mention of his name, but he did not look around. His hand was still cupped against Rhys' face as the little procession made their way out of the room, and his eyes were so fixed on it that Eli did not know how he could tell where he was going.

Love, he thought. *It doesn't matter where you're going. You just go.*

He looked down at Aryel and found she was looking across at Zavcka Klist. The second set of paramedics were here now, their own gurney next to the bed as they bustled around it disconnecting and reconnecting the monitors and tubes attached to the girl Gwen had called Ellyn. They had folded back the blanket and he could see that the scars extended all the way down her left side. Her hand had been almost entirely burned away, leaving no more than melted stubs where the fingers and thumb should be.

Zavcka Klist came a half-step away from the wall. She looked tense enough to snap. 'What are you doing?'

One of the medics glanced over his shoulder. 'Getting ready to move her. We can't take that with us.' He jerked a thumb at the life-support unit and went back to what he was doing. She stared at his bent back, her mouth working and hands hooked into claws. Sharon, standing by the door listening to a whispered report from one of her officers, raised an interested eyebrow.

'Wait. What will happen to her? Who's going to look after her, now?'

'She's going to the hospital, Zavcka,' Aryel said quietly. 'They'll look after her. They'll take very good care of her.'

'No. *No.*' Suddenly words were tumbling out of her, desperate, frantic. 'You have to let me take care of her. Whatever else happens, you have to do that. I have everything – everything she needs. I've got more money than you can imagine. You have to let me give her what she'll need, everything she'll need—'

'The state will take care of her,' Eli said, bemused. 'She'll have everything.'

'The *state*? That's not enough. It's not nearly enough.'

'For fuck's sake, Klist, you want us to believe you *care* about this girl? After everything you've done to her?'

It felt good to snap, release a little of his own rage and outrage. But Aryel placed a hand on his arm to calm him, the soothing touch and gentle shake of the head telling him there was, once again, something here that he did not understand. She moved to stand at Ellyn's head, looking down at her scarred, sleeping face.

'She doesn't mean the girl we're looking at, Eli. She means the girl inside of her, the baby girl she's carrying.' Her eyes drifted down to Ellyn's distended abdomen. 'That's you in there, isn't it, Zavcka? A whole new you, now that the old you is finally wearing out. You with your one imperfection removed, or so you hope. Tell me, have you also fixed the thing Jarek was trying to fix?'

They stared at her: Sharon, the officers and medics in complete bafflement, Eli with the familiar sense of pending revelation and Zavcka with the cornered, desperate expression of a hunted animal finally run to ground. 'You can't,' she whispered, and the horror and despair in her voice were such that he could almost have felt sorry for her.

'I can't know, or I can't tell? I'm sorry, Zavcka, but I do and I will. It's time this particular skeleton came out of its closet.'

'Aryel,' Sharon said politely, 'what the hell are you talking about?'

'You should know exactly who it is you're arresting, Inspector. Let me introduce you to Zavcka Klist. Zavcka the First, Eli. Daughter of Jarek. Born in the year 2042 of the old calendar.'

'That's impossible,' he sputtered. 'That's seventeen After Syndrome, that's almost a hundred and twenty years ago!'

'Indeed. That's how old she is, though I agree she generally doesn't look a day over forty-five or so.' She cocked her head critically at Zavcka, who had shrunk back against the wall as though hoping to fall right through it. 'A bit more than that today, but then it has been a rough one. That chain of Klists you described to me this morning, Eli – the daughter, the granddaughter, the distant cousin, the great-great-granddaughter – they have all been the same woman. Childless and ageless, disappearing and reappearing and manipulating her own stream records to maintain the illusion of a dynasty when it was just one person all along.'

'That,' said Sharon in the same polite tone, as she watched Zavcka pin herself to the wall, 'is bonkers.'

'Yes.'

'Can you prove it?'

'Yes.'

'And what does it have to do with the child this girl is carrying?'

'The child is a clone. It turns out that Zavcka here is not going to live forever after all. About five years ago, I reckon, she discovered that she has a degenerative neurological disorder, not unlike the Syndrome. You've seen it at its worst in Rhys. It's moving slowly, probably because of her longevity mutation, but it will kill or disable her eventually. She did not consider that to be an acceptable outcome, so she set out to alter it. Now it also turns out – and the proof of this part is on that tablet in your hand, by the way – that her genome formed the base stock for a truly vast amount of gemtech research. Her father set up a black lab, codenamed Phoenix, to unpick its potential, commercialise the findings via Klist Applied Genomics, and along the way try to solve an unfortunate consequence of the mutation. But after he died Phoenix started experimenting on its own account. One of those experiments resulted in me; later work delivered Rhys and Gwen, and poor Ellyn here. Isolated sequences found their way into end products right across the industry. There may well be a bit of her in Mikal; there certainly is in Bel'Natur gems like Gaela and Callan and Herran. Zavcka decided to track down all of them, correctly figuring that somewhere along the line the flaws would have been identified and engineered out. She set up this lab, she retrieved the genestock and she set about creating a healthy clone of herself. That clone is the baby growing inside this girl.'

There was a long, long silence. There was so much wrong with it that Eli didn't know where to start. He did know that Aryel was neither stupid nor insane, and he noted that Zavcka was neither ridiculing nor denying. She looked sick, but not stunned. He glanced across at Sharon, and saw that she was eyeing Zavcka, and Aryel, and no doubt thinking the same thing. The paramedics and the other police officers were eyeing each other, as though wondering how they had wandered into this madhouse, and how to get out.

'But,' he said.

'Only one but?'

'A clone isn't the same person. This Zavcka will still die. You're saying – what? She wanted a baby version of herself she could raise to be as much like her as possible?'

'I wish she were that selfless. What has her other big move been, the thing she's risked her reputation and huge amounts of money on? The infotech programme. The ability to encode human thoughts and memories into a digital format, into binary. We were told it's meant to create a more seamless interface, to be able to manipulate electronics directly with the mind, but think about it. Think about the implications of that research. In ten or fifteen years, when that baby is a young girl, where do you think the technology will have got to? What could you do with it then?'

Sharon got there first. Eli watched the colour drain out of her face, as the full horror of it dawned on him too. 'Holy fuck,' she whispered. 'She'd – *replace* her? With herself?'

'I think so. So does Herran, as it happens. He thinks it's possible, and he should know.'

The moment stretched out, frozen, until one of the paramedics loudly cleared his throat and said, 'We need to take her now,' in a tone that brooked no dissent. They had the desperate look of people who would do just about anything to get out of that room, and away from the lunacy that seemed to fill it. The two officers shifted from one foot to another, and looked as though they wished they had an excuse to go with them.

As they moved Ellyn from her bed onto the gurney and covered her up again, Zavcka Klist started to speak. Her head was still down but she was looking up through her lashes at Aryel Morningstar; a pose that, bizarrely, reminded Eli of Herran.

'You unnatural, unholy bitch.' Her voice was low, and thick with hate. 'You think I don't know who *you* are? What *you've* done? You think I won't tell them?'

'I'm sure you will.'

'No one, *no one*, needed to get hurt here. If you'd all just stayed out of my way, let me have what I wanted, no one would have got hurt. You think I'm the one who damaged that girl? She's an imbecile, none of this matters to her, she doesn't have any idea what's going on. I didn't do that to her. *You* did.'

'Ms Klist,' Sharon said sharply, 'I've arrested you for kidnapping, forced surrogacy, attempted murder and a whole lot more.

Defamation of character might not seem like much in comparison, but I'll happily add it to the list.'

'I wish she were lying,' Aryel said quietly. 'For once, she's not.' Her voice was heavy with sorrow, and she ran her own small hand up the blanketed ridge of Ellyn's arm, brushed the melted skin along the jaw, then touched her fingers to her own lips and pressed them gently against the sleeping girl's cheek. Eli glanced at Zavcka Klist, and for the first time he thought he saw the fight go out of her.

The paramedics took up position at either end of the gurney, moving with a suggestive briskness, and Aryel stepped back to let them wheel it away. She looked across the blanketed mound of pregnant belly at Sharon. 'In a way I *am* just as responsible for what's happened here as Zavcka Klist is, and I'm done with keeping secrets. I have another story to tell you, Inspector Varsi, and there are a lot more dead people in it.'

SCORCHED

Nothing is left.

The scars lap up to her feet, shockwaves of soot and debris in spreading semicircles, as though discarded by a retreating tide. The eruption point is a jagged, blackened hole in what remains of the front façade of the building. The explosion must have blown out the main entrance, she guesses, judging from the broad tier of steps that lead up to the mouth of the cavity. Their surface is pitted and buckled, and the firefighters and police who swarm up and down them do so carefully, for the too-white brightness of the emergency lights casts harsh shadows, concealing as many hazards as it reveals. The starkness of that glare has the contradictory effect of making it harder, instead of easier, to identify what it illuminates. In front of the steps she notes two similar, oddly sculptural masses of twisted metal slats, spears of glass dangling haphazardly from their grooved edges, and wonders briefly what they were, before her mind draws the tortured shapes into perspective.

The doors.

She remembers her own fierce imaginings as she waited out the obfuscations of Panborn and Owen, of simply blowing the doors off this place and taking control, and her shock is replaced by anger. Someone else had the will, the invention, the audacity to do what she only dreamt. And not in order to take possession, but to leave it.

A small sound like a sob from the functionary who accompanied them.

379

She looks around, wrinkling her nose at the heavy smell of burning – burnt plastic, burnt wood, burnt flesh – and notes with disapproval the traces of tears on the young man's face. He touches her arm wordlessly, gestures towards shapes laid out on the grass, clear of the furthest traces of the blast. Light pours onto them from even more high-lux lamps, their spindly frames telescoped tall, square heads lowered as though in prayer, beaming down an indictment.

Beyond all is dark, dark. The night-time forest reaches up almost to the very edge of the primly paved, neatly trimmed square that lies before the burnt-out shell. Outside this blasted oasis the silhouettes of trees march away in every direction, dense and impenetrable, towering. It seems to her that they lean in, as though to reclaim it already.

Between the drawn lines of trees and trauma the bodies lie side by side by side, some already in bags, most only hastily covered by a sheet. She counts twelve, fifteen, twenty. Some of the mounds look too small, incomplete, but then she recalls there were children here too.

Jonah trudges back towards them, carefully skirting the edge of the blast radius. Beyond him men and women in uniform shift and murmur and stare, and then go back to the hurrying business of interview and investigation. She sees the orange flight suits and green camouflage of the retrieval teams, corralled behind police vehicles and barricades, and thinks that steps must be taken to ensure the tale of this disaster does not spread.

Jonah stops in front of her, face a mask of bitter disbelief.

'Survivors?'

'Not as such. They say one of the juveniles is still hanging on.'

'I want it kept alive. Whatever it takes. What about the staff? Panborn?'

Jonah shakes his head.

'Are all the gems accounted for?'

'They're not sure. The . . . the one we came to see . . . they think she's dead, but they haven't found a body. The others . . .' He gestures wordlessly

at the shrouded piles behind him. 'It's hard to say. And none of them are certain how many were here to begin with.'

She pushes back another surge of irritation at the unprofessionalism, the cobbled-together unaccountability of it all. 'If they didn't manage to retrieve her why do they think she's dead?'

'They tracked her to the edge of some kind of cliff, a river gorge. No way down.' They exchange glances, the thought flashing unspoken between them, and Jonah shrugs. 'No reason to think that . . . She never had before, and the physics of it . . . it just doesn't work. The retrieval team believes she must have thrown herself off rather than be captured. Not that they know exactly what they were hunting . . . they'd never seen—'

He breaks off at the look on her face. She breathes deeply, controlling her temper. No point taking it out on Jonah.

'The explosion was secondary to the fire?'

'Apparently there were two. The first one was small, contained within the underground facility. They're still not sure how she caused it, but the way she used the chaos to get out . . . it's clear it wasn't an accident, she must have had a plan. She released the others and led them outside but she didn't stay with them, she headed off on her own.'

She nods, picturing the disoriented gems stumbling through the forest in every direction, delaying and misdirecting the trackers while their liberator pursued her own escape. She appreciates the ruthlessness of it. 'So the retrieval team went after them.'

'Yes. They say Panborn ordered them to go, said rounding up the gems – especially her – was top priority, not to worry about the fire, they had it under control. They picked up the others fairly quickly – seems they were mostly quite young – and returned them here, then went back out to support the unit on her trail. So the helicopter and foot squads were all miles away, the other side of the hills, when they heard the second explosion. By the time they got back—' Jonah breaks off again, surveying the destruction.

'So what caused it? The second explosion?'

'Nobody's sure yet. The pilot says there was a fuel dump down there, in one of the old mine chambers. His theory is that the fire must have burned through.'

She thinks through the unfolding stages of crisis, understands how it could have happened. There is one small mercy, at least: that she already knew about this place, was already on her way here with Jonah, has already used the hours they spent halted by flashing lights and barricades further down the mountain to begin to manage the disaster. There will be no leadership gap within which rumours can circulate, no delay in the actions she must take. The damage can be limited, contained.

How fortunate.

A thought strikes her. 'Did she know?'

'Sorry?'

'The gem girl, the prototype. Did she know I was coming today?'

'What? I don't know. Why would she? But they might have told her, I suppose . . .'

She feels her jaw tighten as she files the question away. One more piece of a puzzle she senses she may never solve. It hardly matters, not any more. Time to get to work.

She steps well inside the damage zone and turns in a cool, deliberate circle, making it plain she is watching as the heads of assembled officialdom snap round. To her left a big man in a soot-stained firefighter's rig with a badge on the chest, to her right a small woman with a police captain's epaulettes. As one they break off their conferences with subordinates and stride determinedly in her direction, a pincer movement. Good.

Let them come to her, the better to understand who is now in charge here.

She strolls a few steps forward and stops to wait, ignoring first the murmur and then the hush, glancing around at the wasteland as though conducting her own investigation.

Near her feet, more twisted metal. Gold this time, bright lights picking out the gleam through the rust-rainbow patina left by the explosion. Letters, *a sign still legible despite the damage. From the size and where it has come to rest she surmises it must have hung above the shattered doors; an announcement, a proclamation. A mockery.*

   Phoenix.

REMNANT

31

'When I was a child,' Aryel said, 'I used to hear the researchers talk about the "fertility problem". Sometimes they called it the Phoenix problem. It was something they said I had inherited. A lot of the tests they did on me when I was little had to do with it, but as the years went by they talked about it less and less. When I was older and broke into my own files, I found out that I'd been born without ova, although I didn't really understand what that meant at the time. But it wasn't until Eli found the memos that I put two and two together. You see, I also knew that they'd tried to clone me, over and over, and always failed. They'd make it through the first few hundred cell divisions, and then . . .' She blew a raspberry.

Eli found the crude expression out of keeping with her usual grace, and thoroughly endearing.

They were in her vertiginous living room, himself and Mikal and Reginald and Herran and Gwen, draped over the furniture in the exhausted sprawl of puppets who have had their strings cut. Even Herran was sitting back a bit, tablet largely dormant on his lap. Midnight had come, and long since gone. From where he sat, slumped with his head tipped back on a sofa, Eli could see shreds of cloud whip by on the dying eddies of the storm, dark and ragged against the night sky.

'And that was the same story with Zavcka?' Mikal asked. His arms were extended along the back of another sofa, hands drooping over the ends, and his legs stuck so far out in front of him that they were almost hanging off the edge of the drop. 'So much for engineering out imperfections.'

'You have to remember what an early stage gemtech science was at. The clock was ticking for Jarek and his wife: she had the Syndrome, they knew she only had a few years left to live. Whether he intentionally tampered with the embryo beyond what was necessary to try to make their child Syndrome-safe or whether it was just an accident of the early technology, I don't think we'll ever know. But at some point Jarek and Zavcka discovered that she had come with two extra features: she couldn't conceive, and she didn't age. They may have believed she was literally immortal. Can you imagine? The holy grail of human desire: never to age and never to die. Only if you can't have children you can't pass that gift on, and if you can't clone yourself you can't even create another you for company. There's no one to live forever *with*. I'm not sure that's ever bothered Zavcka as much as it bothered Jarek, but I think it consumed him. One of his reasons for creating Phoenix was to try to solve the problem.'

'And Phoenix created you.'

'And Phoenix created me. Not on purpose, I hasten to add. They were experimenting with cross-species splicing, seeing how far the reparative aspects of the mutation could be pushed. They didn't expect the batch to be viable.'

'It worked, though, didn't it?'

'What worked?'

'Jarek's plan.' He rolled his head towards her, his tone droll. 'Phoenix created you, and you have fulfilled his mission. Zavcka's going to have company for the rest of her life, however long that is. Granted, it's probably not *quite* what he had in mind . . .'

She chuckled wearily. 'No, I'm sure it's not. She's already begging them not to make her own story public, to keep pretending she's Zavcka the Second. Got her lawyers all over it.'

'Why care?'

'I think there are a few reasons, Herran. One, she's spent a long time being afraid of what would happen if people found out: of how they might try to take advantage of her, not to mention uncovering all the ways she's used it to take advantage of others. Two, she would have had to do a lot of manipulation of the family assets to remove them from the identity she was leaving behind, and transfer them into the identity she was creating. If Zavcka the Second is acknowledged not to exist, she risks losing control of a vast fortune. It's still hers, remember, even though she'll be in prison, and she might yet outlive whatever sentence they give her. And three, to admit it means admitting she is highly engineered, that she is the thing she's spent her entire life looking down on.'

'Gem.'

'Exactly.'

'What'll happen now?' asked Gwen. She was uncharacteristically subdued, though Eli supposed it was understandable under the circumstances. 'To Bel'Natur? The research they were doing with Herran, and – and everything else?'

Aryel raised an eyebrow at Eli, a gentle hint that he had managed to sink himself into the cushions and avoid being part of the conversation for quite long enough. He pushed himself wearily upright.

'The company will continue,' he said. 'She's a major shareholder, but not the only one. And we want it to, because the deal Herran made with them still stands. The infotech programme has real potential, but it'll need very stringent public oversight. Now that we know what her intentions were, the gatekeepers need to be on guard. Complete transparency.' He shifted, trying to get comfortable again, and jerked his chin at Mikal. 'That's your area, Councillor.'

'Indeed. All that time I spent in their ethics committee meetings might not be wasted after all. Of course,' he mused, staring at the ceiling, snapping his fingers with both thumbs in a softly syncopated quadruple beat, 'pimping myself, my wife, an oblique promise to divert a police investigation and a truly daft scheme to bring back gemtech may not be the best advertisement of my fitness for the role.'

Weary laughter from everyone but Herran, who blinked his grey eyes solemnly at them.

'I'm not sure it was that daft,' Aryel murmured. 'What did Masoud say?'

'Masoud was apoplectic. I think it's his reaction to a tactic that he can't possibly approve of, even though he thinks it's really, really cool.'

'Is Sharon going to be in trouble, do you think?'

'What, for drafting in two civilians, one a seriously ill young man with no experience of police work and an inclination to go off-piste, and the other an unorthodox city councillor to whom she just happens to be married? She's already offered him her warrant tab. He asked what the hell he was supposed to do with it.'

'I have another question, Ari,' said Gwen, though she sounded hesitant. Her tablet was also on her knee, inactive but near to hand. She trailed a thoughtful finger over the blank surface.

'You can have as many as you like. What is it?'

'I'm not going to shout at you and Da for letting us think you were with him for years and years before he rescued us. Not yet. I'm too tired and there's too much going on. But I want to know something.'

'Thank you for not shouting. Yet. What do you want to know?'

'What were we for?'

An expectant quiet then. It was, Eli realised, one of the few remaining mysteries. For some. He saw Reginald close his eyes and shake his head a little, as though in resignation.

'What do you think, Gwennie?'

'I think a lot of things. I want you to tell me.'

Aryel sighed, and pushed back her hair. She had loosened it again and it fell heavy around her shoulders and over the arches of her wings. Eli saw the metal clasp glint in her fingers as she gestured helplessly at the air.

'You were meant to be combat models,' she said. 'Soldiers. I've thought so for some time, and I suspect we'll find confirmation in the Phoenix archive once Herran finishes resurrecting it. It was the big thing around twenty-five years ago – there were endless, nasty wars all across North Africa and the Middle East, all the tribal factions trying to secure what was left of their fossil fuel reserves. Plus flare-ups in South America and Southeast Asia that looked as though they might go the same way. The military focus was cybernetics, and they tried that too, but I think Panborn was clever enough to realise that if no one could make mechanical grafts work then whoever turned out a literal super-human – speed, strength, agility, night vision, acute hearing, proximity awareness, high operational IQ, all the things you and Rhys have – could make a killing.' She heard herself, and winced. 'Sorry. Poor choice of word.'

'It's okay. That's . . . that's kind of what I thought.' She was silent for a moment, picking at a pillow on her lap, the waiting tablet still on her knee. 'It doesn't matter if that's what they meant us for, as long as it's not what we are. It's just . . . as long as nobody *thinks* that's what we are. What Rhys did . . .'

'What Rhys did saved his and Callan's lives, and quite possibly

Ellyn's as well. It's a miracle he was able to do it at all, the effort must have been . . .' Aryel trailed off, shaking her head. 'There's no way he could have controlled his own strength, not in that state. The doctors will confirm it. There'll be an investigation, there has to be, but don't worry about it. No one will hold it against him, or you.'

'Good,' she whispered.

'Now I have a question for you. Have you spoken to Lyriam?'

'What on earth do I say to him, Ari?'

'Having dropped him in the pot,' rumbled Reginald, 'you might want to let him know whether you'll be leaving him there to stew on his own.'

'Da.'

'Or fishing him out, or joining him. Extra spice never went amiss.'

'*Da!*'

'What? It's only what everyone else is saying.' Grins, guilty snickers and meaningful glances shot around the dim room. 'Don't get me wrong, he's a nice lad. I like him. But it's a shame there's only one Callan.'

Eli had been perplexed to discover, when they were finally able to make their way to the hospital, that the crowd of newstream journalists and socialstream commentators ranked outside was not only several times larger than it had been at police headquarters, but also far less interested in them. They were there for Gwen, who rumour declared to be at her sick brother's bedside. Or not. He heard one hack excitedly reporting a piece of half-heard gossip, to the effect that it was Lyriam over whom she watched, laid low by the violent hysterics of his newly ex-girlfriend.

As he and Mikal made their way in with Herran trotting along between them, microphones and vidcams were thrust at them from every direction; but the scandal they were being asked to comment on had nothing to do with Bel'Natur, Zavcka Klist or Aryel Morningstar.

'What on earth,' he said, as they finally made it through the scrum and into the hospital's foyer, 'is going on? Something's happened to Lyriam?'

'Oh, a great deal has happened to Lyriam,' said Mikal, 'and I hope he has his head on straight enough to handle it. You haven't heard? No, I suppose you wouldn't have. You either, Herr? I thought you always kept an eye on the streams, no matter what.'

The little gem's head, shoulders and torso swayed precisely forward and back in his signature emphatic rocking nod.

'Streams say Gwen did a bad thing. Also Lyriam. Also Bethany. Also Lyriam did a good thing, and Gwen, and Bethany.'

'It's very confused,' Mikal sighed, as they took the stairs up to the next floor, having all apparently decided, by mutual and unspoken agreement, to avoid the lifts wherever they could. 'I haven't quite worked out the details . . .'

'Lyriam playing with Gwen, Bethany not know. Aryel calls Gwen, come quick quick for Rhys. Gwen goes quick quick. So quick people at music place find out. Tell Bethany, tell streams.'

'People at music place find out what?' Eli asked, thinking that even after two weeks of being almost constantly in his company, decrypting Herran's tortured syntax was as difficult as any other mystery he had had to unravel.

'Gwen and Lyriam playing.'

'But they would have known they were playing together.'

'He doesn't mean,' said Mikal, waiting for them from where his longer legs had carried him, half a flight further up, '*that* kind of playing.'

393

'What kind—? *Oh*.'

'*Oh* indeed. As far as I can make out they were in some kind of break room, and when Aryel told Gwen what was going on at Bel'Natur she got out of there so fast she left poor Lyriam with his pants down. Literally.'

'Oh god.' Eli could picture it, and had to fight back the urge to dissolve in hysterical laughter.

'Banged out past a bunch of musicians, who would probably have kept their mouths shut, and a gaggle of studio flunkeys who unfortunately didn't. By the time she got to where I was waiting in the alley, it was all over the streams. Rude jokes from the studio techs, histrionics from Bethany, you can imagine. But then Lyriam went onstream to say he and Bethany had split up a couple of days after the concert in the park, he hadn't made an announcement because it's a personal matter and he wanted to be as sensitive to her as possible, give her time to make the adjustment and tell people in her own way. Pointed out that they haven't been seen together since then, and the people close to them all knew. It had been on the cards for some time, long before he met Gwen. So on and so forth. His friends are piling in to confirm that this is true, hers to say it's not.'

'Bloody hell. Where does this leave Gwen, then?'

'Everywhere from cold-hearted home-wrecker to innocent caught in the crossfire. And I do mean everywhere.' He jerked a pair of thumbs over his shoulder, vaguely in the direction from which they had come. 'Witness the media mêlée.'

'Oh well, it's not like this family has anything else to deal with just now. Does Aryel know?'

'I don't know. Don't see how she'd have found the time, but she always manages to know a bit more than seems reasonable, doesn't she?'

It was said without a hint of rancour, a simple statement of fact that Eli knew for truth. And indeed there she was when they finally found their way to the waiting room on the critical care wing, her straight flight from the station having brought her here more swiftly: standing at the window with an arm around Gwen, her voice a soft murmur of reassurance as they gazed down at the cluster of uplink vans and milling journalists in front of the hospital. She must know that their attentions would turn to her soon enough, and his heart ached at the thought.

Herran spent an hour with the genmed team, walking them through the Phoenix genealogy Rhys had constructed, and the genetype data that he had found and matched to it. They were as unused to him as he to them, and the conference would have been impossible without help from Callan. Nothing less than the possibility of finding a cure would have enticed him away from Rhys' side.

'It's the Syndrome,' he said quietly, when they were wrapping up. 'It is, isn't it?'

The doctors and geneticists glanced at each other. 'It's very close,' one of them said eventually. 'Not identical. A variant.'

'But you can fix him. You know enough now.'

'We should be able to design a treatment. That epigenetic suppressant he was given is a good start; if we can get access to the development work on that it'll save us a lot of time.'

'It was private research,' said Aryel evenly. 'Bel'Natur's pharmaceutical division. I'll have it to you by lunchtime tomorrow.'

'You can do that? I mean . . . I understand the company is in some turmoil at the moment. They probably won't release anything until the lawyers . . .'

'Herran?'

'They don't give, I get.'

'Quite.'

Rhys was stable, heavily sedated, and would not be waking up any time before the middle of the morning. They were all urged to go home, get some sleep and come back then. Callan point-blank refused.

'I might sleep a little here, I won't there. And I don't want to know anything more about anything right now. I just want to be with him.'

Reginald blinked hard, sniffed and clapped him on the shoulder, and Gwen hugged him tight, and they left him sitting in the glow of his hair and the winking lights of the monitors, Rhys' hand clasped between both of his own, murmuring sonnets to him in French.

Now Gwen chucked the pillow across the room at Reginald, sighed and departed, tablet in hand, while Aryel shook her head reproachfully at him.

'That's being a bit hard on her, don't you think?'

'She can take it. You know full well she could've moved just as fast but with a lot more finesse if she'd wanted to. At some level she'd decided it was time to get things out in the open. She let Rhys be the excuse, and now she's feeling bad about it. And so she should.'

Aryel opened her mouth for a rebuttal, considered, and closed it again. Reginald gave a little snort of triumph. 'Tell me about the girl, their sister. Ellyn. Apart from the burns – and the belly – is she all right?'

'No she's not. Severe brain damage.' Aryel rubbed a hand across her brow. 'Zavcka took great pleasure in telling us that she has a mental age of around four.'

Eli could remember cases like it, too many, from his studies of the gemtechs. 'That's why they put her in a coma.'

396

'Yep. Hard to tell a rambunctious, immensely powerful toddler that she's seven months pregnant and she needs to take it easy.'

'She's due in about two weeks,' Mikal said. 'I've been talking to the doctors. They're in a quandary, because normally the ethical thing to do would obviously be to bring her out of it. But the reason Zavcka had her sedated in the first place is – I hate to say it – it's a real reason. She'll be confused and traumatised, she might hurt herself or the baby. They'll deliver her surgically either way, but they're thinking it would just compound the atrocity of what's been done to her to wake her up now. I tend to agree.'

There were murmurs of reluctant assent from Reginald and Aryel, and Eli himself. Herran blinked. 'The choices that have been left to us,' he said in an oddly formal, stilted tone, as though quoting, and then in his normal voice said, 'bad.'

Aryel smiled tiredly across the room at him. 'Yes, Herr, it's another one of those.'

'And the baby is really Zavcka?' asked Reginald.

'The baby is a baby,' Aryel said firmly. 'She isn't anybody yet, and she'll get to keep her own mind now. She'll grow up to be herself. How much of the old Zavcka will come through in her, we have no way of knowing.'

'That's a hell of a thing to be saddled with, though,' Eli mused, head tipped back against the cushions again. 'It'll be a matter of public record, it'll be . . . huge. People will know she's going to grow up, but not grow old. She'll need protecting.'

'The burden of being a Zavcka is going to be no joke,' Mikal agreed. 'Even for a Zavcka.'

'She'll be fine if she's raised right,' Reginald grunted. 'What d'you think, Ari?'

'I might have an idea,' she said meditatively. 'Maybe a solution

. . . a way to keep her safe, from the world and herself . . .' She stifled a yawn. 'Don't know yet. Need to think it through.'

'Something else I've been trying to think through,' Eli said, keeping his voice as uninflected as he could, 'is how I found those messages. I checked my searchbot. Nothing special about it, and the search terms I used had nothing to do with KAG or Phoenix. There's no way it should have been able to find, much less resurrect, much less reconstruct them.' He stole a glance across the room at Herran and caught Aryel doing the same thing. The little gem's face was as expressionless as ever.

'I've been wondering about that myself,' Aryel said, and waited. Herran did not react. Mikal had caught their focus and was looking from Eli to Aryel to Herran with puzzled interest, while Reginald grinned and nodded to himself with an air of quiet satisfaction.

'Herran,' said Aryel. 'You gave Eli's searchbot a bit of help, didn't you?'

'Yes. Searchbot stupid. Couldn't find.'

'Why'd you do it like that?' Eli asked, perplexed. 'Why make it look like something I'd stumbled over by accident, instead of just telling me?'

'Couldn't. Promised.' He blinked solemnly at Aryel.

'You promised—' Eli broke off, thinking, pulling the pieces together. 'You were poking around in the archive for a reason and you'd promised not to tell anyone but Aryel what you'd found.'

'Yes. Breaking rules. Not supposed to tell.'

'But you told . . . no, you *didn't* tell me anyway. You altered the base code of the searchbot so it could find what you'd found, and you let *it* tell me.'

'Yes.'

'I'll be damned,' Mikal muttered. He was sitting upright now, and his look of mild surprise had given way to full-on amazement.

'Why, Herran?' asked Aryel. She sounded as baffled as Eli had ever heard her, and a little hurt. 'You knew the messages were about me, you knew there were bad things in them. Why send them to Eli at all? Why didn't you just let me know what you'd found?'

Herran regarded her steadily. 'You tell Eli?'

'I . . . no, I wouldn't have told Eli.' She stared at Herran staring back at her, face blank, long lashes blinking hugely. 'You . . . you knew that, didn't you? And you decided he ought to know?'

'Better for you.'

Aryel, Eli and Mikal sat in stunned silence. Reginald's grin had turned into a rumbling, delighted chuckle. 'That's the truth if ever I heard it. Good on you, Herran. Well played.' He took in Aryel's astonished expression, and shook with mirth. 'Very well played indeed.'

'But you can't do that,' said Eli, feeling as though the world had tilted once again, and hearing as he said it just how wrong he was. 'Since when can you do that?'

'Better for Aryel. Better for you too. I do.'

'Well, well.' Mikal was back to his own amused, amazed, double-lidded blink. 'That's very . . . decisive of you, Herran. I don't think I can remember a day quite so full of miracles and wonders as this one. I hope there aren't going to be any more before morning, I'm not sure I could take it.'

He could have been speaking for Eli, but despite his weariness there were puzzles implied by this latest revelation that his brain could not help picking at.

'What were you looking for in the archive, Herran? When you found the messages?'

'Genetype for Rhys.' Herran was matter-of-fact. 'Aryel said look, maybe find.'

Eli turned bodily on the sofa to glare at her. 'So you already *knew* KAG had become part of Bel'Natur.'

'No, I didn't.' She had recovered her equanimity somewhat. 'But I had begun to suspect, because when I was in Zavcka's office I noticed something. There's a framed plaque on the wall, a formal group photograph with the Bel'Natur logo at the top and then a bunch of smaller logos studded beneath. One of them looked like KAG, and there was a woman in the group who looked a lot like Zavcka. I couldn't see what the plaque was commemorating – it could just have been a piece of family memorabilia she'd brought with her. But I thought it could also have come with the office, been a snapshot of Bel'Natur acquisitions. So I asked Herran, if he decided to go in and work with them, to check if there was a KAG sub-directory or any other sign of their genetype files. It only took him a couple of days to be able to tell me there wasn't, which of course,' she arched a thoughtful eyebrow in Herran's direction, 'was entirely true.'

'No more tonight,' Herran announced, standing up abruptly. 'Sleepy. I go to bed.'

They all regarded him for a second, and then Mikal hauled himself to his feet. 'That sounds like an excellent idea,' he said. 'I'll walk you down and see if my wife is anywhere close to being able to come home yet.'

They said their goodnights, and after a while Reginald too drifted off in the direction of the bedrooms, and it was only Eli and Aryel left alone in the vast room, with the first traces of a mid-summer dawn beginning to turn the windows pale.

'Aryel,' he said, staring at the ceiling, 'are you really upset with Herran for sending those messages my way?'

She gazed out of the window at the lightening sky, shook her head and laughed softly. 'No. He was right. You needed to know and I needed to not carry it around any more. I'm just struggling to come to terms with the fact that he worked that out when I couldn't.'

He took this in, feeling it spread warmth throughout his tired body and brain.

'Rhys must have asked him the same question, mustn't he? About looking for his genetype in the archive. And got the same answer, but also been pointed towards the black hole in the basement.'

'Yes. Before tonight I would have assumed that Rhys just asked better questions than me, but now . . .' she trailed off, musing, or maybe too weary to think her way through the enormity of what Herran had done; and what it meant for him, as well as for Rhys and Eli and herself. The little gem had understood his friends, had known what they needed, and had taken the initiative on their behalf – to a far greater degree than any of them could ever have imagined possible.

'You going to try and get some sleep?' he asked her quietly, watching her profile against the light.

'I couldn't. Think I'll go up to the garden, watch the sun come up. You?'

'No chance. Want some company?'

'Yes, please.'

They gathered up blankets and made their way along the perimeter walkways to the door. As they let themselves quietly into the corridor, Eli said, 'You never finished telling me, you know.'

'Telling you what?'

'The rest of what happened. After you got out.'

'Ah.' She looked up at him, smiling. 'Well, this is the right place for the rest of that story.'

She held out a hand and he took it, sliding her slender fingers between his own; and thought, as he walked with her through the sleeping building and up the stairs, that it felt as much like an ending as a beginning.

PHOENIX

There are lights amongst the trees, first one and then another; not the harsh searchlights of the retrieval teams but gentler, faint and flickering. She crouches behind the outcrop that conceals her, fifty feet up the side of a cliff once blasted into being by miners many centuries dead. Maybe the same miners who blasted the tunnels and chambers where she has spent her life until this night, the tunnels and chambers she in turn had to blast her way out of.

Screams echo faintly in her inner ear and she shudders, clings tighter to the rock behind which she hides, focuses harder on the lights. It is barely a ledge upon which she has alighted, no more than a few scant toe- and finger-holds against which she can rest her weight. Her hands and feet tremble with fatigue, along with her newly tried wings, held open and stiff for balance. The sudden, cell-deep certainty that came to her on the mountainside, that let her trust them and led her here, feels as ephemeral as a fading dream. She is cold and hungry and afraid, and more tired than she has ever been. And there are lights in the forest below her.

Could these be the ones she seeks? They were to have met at the waterfall at sunset, but she is miles downstream of it now and the sun is long gone. Or are they a new troupe of hunters, less well equipped – or clever enough to appear so – but no less deadly in their intent? Her flight strength is gone; if she moves she must come to earth, show herself and risk all. She dares not. But she cannot hang here forever.

A shadow detaches itself from the trees and moves into the clearing before the cliff. The shielded light dances at hip-height, then sweeps cautiously around the clearing. She cannot see who holds it. But she hears the murmur of voices, and more lights advance. The one who came forward first is silhouetted in their glow, tall but oddly ill-defined. Details emerge slowly, as he comes closer and her eyes adjust: shaggy brown hair and beard, a long, shapeless coat. Boots wrapped in cloth, muffled. A worried squinting into the darkness, an uncertainty that mirrors her own as he peers past her along the overgrown access road that runs at the base of the cliff.

And then startled oaths and a general scramble backwards, torchlight flickering madly, as she kicks away from the cliff wall and spreads and flaps her aching wings. Her landing is clumsy and she stumbles, catching herself on both hands and one knee, feeling the scrape of gravel. Then she is upright and facing them, arms and wings wrapped around her shivering torso, hoping desperately that her calculations will prove right just one more time.

A long, long, long moment as she stands in the joined beams of the torches, while the shadows behind them gasp and exclaim and call on gods she does not know. She had not realised how much she would shock them. She is down to the last shreds of her composure when the tall man steps forward again. He holds two torches now, one on her and one to illuminate himself.

'Aryel?'

She nods, finds herself barely able to speak. She licks dry lips, swallows, pulls herself together.

'Yes. Are – are you Reginald?'

The man nods in his turn. It occurs to her that he may be as tongue-tied as she is, and the thought gives her comfort. The lines of his mouth are firm, grim, but there is a kindness in his eyes and his voice, when he finds it.

'We were delayed. I'm sorry. Are you all right? No, wait, let's get under cover.' He is ushering her beneath the canopy of trees. She is surrounded by *them now, still indistinct in the night murk, still muttering imprecations, and she bites back a surge of fear. The decision to trust these people has already been made. She has no choice but to follow it through.*

'I'm sorry we're so late,' Reginald is saying again. 'We were having a time avoiding the retrieval teams, we had to cut inside them. We were closest when it happened . . . we had to go and see if there was anyone we could help . . .'

'When what happened?' she says, feeling as she once did, as though something crucial is just beyond her grasp. 'Help who?'

'Whoever we could. But the only ones we found alive were these two.'

He turns, the beam of his torch swinging onto a woman who crouches at the base of a tree, looking up at them. Her mouth is a tight line and her arms curve around a large, lobed bundle. It moves under the light. Sleepy eyes, blue-black as the deepening sky, peek out over folds of blanket; first two to the left, then two to the right. There is a ruby shimmer to the soft curls that cover their heads. The tiny, soot-smudged faces are more alike than any two faces she has ever seen, but instinct tells her the more solemn-faced of the pair is a boy, and the one who purses her little lips doubtfully is a girl. The children stare at her, and cuddle closer together.

Reginald clears his throat.

'They seem to be the only ones who got out. Besides you, of course.'

'No,' she says stupidly. 'Everyone got out. I knew we wouldn't all get away, but I made sure everyone was outside before I left.'

The men and women shift and glance at each other, and the murmurs rise again. The children whimper and squirm, and for the first time she notices the smell of smoke pouring off them, hanging heavy on the people around her, drifting through the trees like a fog. And she realises, with a mounting sense of dread, that something has happened, something more than she knows, more than she planned.

They explain it to her gently, as gently as they can, and she knows the tears that prick against her eyelids are as much a reaction to their kind-ness as grief for the unknown siblings that she has lost.

That she has killed.

'It wasn't your fault,' Reginald says, over and over again. 'You mustn't blame yourself.'

But she knows he is wrong.

The knowledge pins her mind into a stunned immobility during the forced march through the forest to where the vehicles have been hidden. She is numb with it, sick with it. Whenever she looks up at Reginald's broad back leading the way she sees the baby boy's eyes blinking back at her over his shoulder, silent, accusing.

It is on the long, jolting journey in the back of an ancient open-backed transport, with the twins clinging silently to each other and only for the barest of moments to her, that a thread of the song that sang her free returns; gossamer-thin and trembling, but a thing to hold on to through the cold and tear-soaked night. She clutches tight and listens hard, and watches the little ones, and thinks of what they flee and what they face, and the part she has had in it, and the part she must have in it. The stars burn down on her, and she asks them questions, and they answer.

By the time they reach their destination she knows who she is, and what the price of her freedom must be.

She goes to Reginald, walking unchallenged through the mountaintop camp. Together they watch the sun rise through a mist tinged pink and gold, and she tells him. And he listens gravely, and nods agreement, and gives her a new name.

Morningstar.

THE END

Acknowledgements

Binary lived up to all the clichés about writing the 'difficult second novel' and I owe a debt of gratitude to all the people who supported me while I struggled through it. Jo Fletcher and Ian Drury, editor-agent power couple extraordinaire, were chief cheerleaders while I wrote and candid critics when they read, and I'm very grateful to them on both counts.

I will here confess that I've rarely been so nervous as when I sent that first full draft to my core crew, and that I was a bit of a wreck while waiting for feedback. While the rigour of their reviewing did indeed have a marked effect on the final manuscript, I needn't have worried. Nicola Budd's text message, sent far too early on a Monday morning after sitting up late at night with the draft, reduced me to tears – of joy. The other®Evolution Readers this time around were Joady Brennan, who said I'd not only got the complex psychology of my characters right but had made *her* cry; and Peter Brennan, who approved the infotech, and whose mention of the authors he'd set aside in order to spend more time in my world made me blush.

And of course, Anna Eagar and Alison Masterman, who sorted out Aryel and stuck up for Herran, and without whom none of us would be here.